Majyk by Any Other Name . . .

"Majyk?" Curio's brow was going to need about a week of mud packs to restore its former smoothness. "I have heard tales of this Majyk from my childhood. I would not dare to trifle with it . . ."

"Oh yeah? Then what's this?" I shook the book and the empty flask at him.

"May I?" Before I could protest, Curio took the book from my hand, held it over the mouth of the flask, and wrung a long, thin stream of golden liquid from the pages. It trickled right into the flask, not a drop missing. "You may keep whatever soaked into your britches," he drawled. "I am sure you do not have that much in them."

"You leave my britches out of this!" I shouted.

"Okay, sweetcakes," Scandal said. "So you can make that little dab of Majyk obey you."

"I have already told you," Curio protested. "I have nothing to do with Majyk."

"Then what's in the bottle? What was soaked into that book?" The cat bounced on all fours, his fur one huge sizzle and sparkle. "What's in Kendar's britches?"

"Scandal!"

"*Magique.*"

Check out Kendar and  s in the first two s

Majyk by Accident

and

Majyk by Hook or Crook

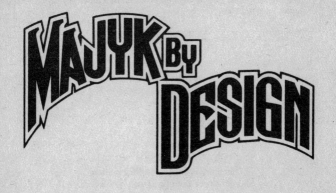

MAJYK BY DESIGN

ESTHER FRIESNER

ACE BOOKS, NEW YORK

This book is an Ace original edition,
and has never been previously published.

MAJYK BY DESIGN

An Ace Book / published by arrangement with
the author

PRINTING HISTORY
Ace edition / November 1994

ISBN: 0-441-00116-5

ACE®
Ace Books are published by The Berkley Publishing Group,
200 Madison Avenue, New York, NY 10016.
ACE and the "A" design are trademarks
belonging to Charter Communications, Inc.

PRINTED IN THE UNITED STATES OF AMERICA

10 9 8 7 6 5 4 3 2 1

CHAPTER —————— 1

SLOWLY, INSOLENTLY, MASTER TANCRED ALLOWED his eyes to caress every voluptuous curve of his defiant captive. "So, my lady," he breathed in a voice like molten wine. "You think that your beauty and spirit are shield enough against a wizard of my powers?"

Angelinetta lifted her chin proudly, fighting the disturbing warmth that the handsome young wizard seemed to kindle within every fiber of her taut and straining body with his smoldering eyes. Her knees trembled beneath the flimsy silken shelter of her nightrobe. Still she found the spunk to reply, "I do not fear you, Master Tancred, and I will have my just inheritance!"

"Oh, but you shall have more than that, my lady." The handsome young wizard glided towards her with all the feral grace of a leopard. His powerful, sensitive hands clutched her milk-white shoulders. Roughly he pulled her to him, crushing the words of protest from her lips with a single, fiery, all-devouring kiss. "Much more," he murmured, sweeping her from her feet and carrying her off to the—

"—garbage." The tin pail full of vegetable peelings and unidentified chicken parts clonked down at my feet. I looked up from my book to see Velma Chiefcook looming over me. "I *said*, Master Kendar, what d'you want me to do with this garbage?"

I sighed and set aside Raptura Eglantine's latest romantic success, *Rouse Not the Wizard*. I hated to admit it, but once you got started, those things were addictive. Still, garbage comes first, especially in a palace this size. "What have you been doing with the garbage up until now, Velma?" I asked.

1

"Tossing it into the moat, mostly, so's the slimegrinds can gobble it up," she replied. "But that won't work no more. It's almost Wenchpinch Eve, and that's when they migrate to their ancient, ancestral bundling-grounds, out Manglegrove way. Don't come back until the Feast of the Dewlaps. Can't have the garbage just floating around in the moat until then. 'Tisn't sanitary nor ornamental, and it sets a bad example for the children."

I sighed again, louder. The children. How could I forget the children? They were the reason that I, Master Kendar Gangle, once called Ratwhacker, Court Wizard to His Extreme Highness King Steffan the Good Enough of Grashgoboum, and lord of the late Master Thengor's palace, spent most of my days down in the kitchens, hiding.

"Well, Velma, what did Master Thengor do with the garbage between Wenchpinch and Dewlap?" I asked. I know I shouldn't have, but I'd just been reading a Raptura Eglantine book and I wasn't thinking.

"Master Thengor had his little ways," Velma replied. We both knew what that meant:

Majyk.

Velma probably didn't know as much as I did about Majyk—for one thing, she'd think of it as *magic* if she thought of it at all—but there was a difference between the two, a big difference. Majyk was what let wizards like me and my late teacher, Master Thengor, do all the things that people like Velma thought of as "magic." Majyk was better than money for making things happen. Majyk had substance, Majyk had power, Majyk could be invisible, or out in the open, shapely or shapeless, solid or liquid or gas or anything in between, smooth or chunky, all of the above, none of the above—that was Majyk.

And for some reason known only to Velvel, Goddess of Laughter at Everyone Else's Expense, I was currently the holder of the greatest individual supply of Majyk on the planet Orbix.

Not that it was any help to me when it came to getting rid of the garbage.

I looked back at the problem at hand. "What did you do about the garbage before I invited you back to the palace?" I asked Velma.

"I don't recall, I'm sure. But being as I had to go live with my sister Nadine, there wasn't all that much difference between our garbage and whatever it was she served at table. It wasn't food, that's certain. But would she let me set foot within her precious kitchen to fix up something *edible*? Oh, no! The cow." The cook put on a sour face. She didn't like being reminded of the time she'd spent in exile from Master Thengor's palace. "I *suppose* I ought to be grateful." Her lips curled around the words as she gave me a sarcastic look. She also didn't like all the changes she'd found on her return to the palace, particularly the change in how she had to treat me.

Once upon a time, while Master Thengor lived, Velma had ruled these kitchens with an iron hand and a ladle to match. I know: I used to feel that ladle on the back of my skull too darned often. As for me, I used to be known as Ratwhacker in these parts, mostly because that was what I did. I was supposed to be a student at Master Thengor's Academy of High Wizardry—and a student I'd stay so long as Master Thengor had it his way and my parents kept sending in those tuition payments—but I didn't seem to have the knack for sorcerous studies. My classwork was an almost perfect series of failures and disasters. I never mastered enough of the principles of applied enchantment to earn the lowest-ranked wizard's robe, never mind the pointy hat. And the wand—? Forget it. You only got that from the Council of Wizards themselves.

Never one to waste a pair of able hands, especially unpaid ones, Master Thengor told Velma to get some use out of me. So while my classmates went from Introductory Curses to Intermediate Levitation all the way to Advanced Invisibility, I sat down in the kitchen, holding a big stick and waiting for luckless rats to stick their noses out of their holes and get their heads whacked for them.

Until the day Master Thengor lay dying.

Until the day *that* "rat" stuck his whiskery nose out of that oh-so-peculiar hole.

Until the day I chased him all the way from the kitchens into Master Thengor's chamber and right through the gigantic cloud of the dying wizard's Majyk that hovered above the deathbed, just waiting for its owner to divide it up and give it away before he died.

Like my father, Lord Lucius Parkland Gangle, always says,

inheritances are like pigsties: Some people just fall into them. And like I always say, sometimes: Some people crash through more Majyk than they ever imagined and a lot of it sticks to them and some of it goes flying off in all directions and the rest sticks to a "rat" who turns out to be no rat but—

"Yo! Betty Crocker! Where's my chow?" Scandal sat up on his haunches and tugged at Velma's skirts. The cat twitched his whiskers forward and grinned up at the cook. "I think you said something about broiled chicken livers in cream gravy?"

"Hmph! I said nothing of the kind." Velma jerked her skirt out from under Scandal's claws. "I'm not mentioning no names," she told the smoky ceiling, "but there's certain legendary monsters around here that've got too big for their britches, that's what."

"Please don't talk about the children again," I moaned.

"I wasn't!" the cook snapped. One of the hardest changes for her to swallow was the fact that, thanks to my unexpected inheritance of Majyk, I was now the master of the palace instead of its lowliest servant. Also, if she tried whapping me with her ladle nowadays, there was no telling whether I'd turn either or both of them into frogs.

"You gotta admit it, Miz Borgia, those brats are giving us real legendary monsters a bad name," Scandal said.

Velma began to sniffle into the hem of her apron. "How can you two speak so of the poor, fatherless tykes? Oh, it's too cruel!"

"What cruel? Where cruel?" the cat demanded. "Hey, no one told Master Kendar he had to invite that herd of miniature buzz saws to come and live here, even if this did used to be their daddy's place! He did it out of the kindness of his heart. And that reminds me, boss"—he cocked his head at me—"we gotta get your head examined one of these days."

I was inclined to agree with him. I mean, no one forced me to do it—to invite all of Master Thengor's kids, legitimate and not-so, to come home again. King Steffan gave the palace to me and me alone. Oh, and to Scandal, too. The king had a real fondness for the cat. Before Scandal showed up, the only place you saw cats on Orbix was in *Master Bangor's 101 Uses for a Dead Fabulous Beast*. They have nine lives, always land on their feet, can see in the dark, steal the breath of sleeping babies, and always get their own way, which is pretty fabulous, you have to admit.

Do you know how big a palace is? I was raised in a manor house, which is big enough, but Master Thengor's palace leaves Uxwudge Manor looking like a broom closet. My old teacher liked to have lots of elbow room. Well, no matter how big a palace is, it's twice that big when it's empty. Big . . . and lonesome.

On sunny days when I was feeling smug and pleased with myself, I liked to think that the reason I'd sent word to Lady Inivria (Master Thengor's widow) to come back and bring the kids with her was because I was soooo nice. Good. Kind. Generous. But in the wee small hours of the night when I lay awake staring at the ceiling, I had to be honest: I really did it because I wanted the company.

Especially since my wife left me.

Sixteen is either too old or too young to get married, depending on who you ask. According to my mother, I'm just a baby. According to Dad, something's wrong with me because here I am, sixteen, and I don't have even one kid. He never mentions having a wife, just a kid. Then Mom smacks him, if she overhears any of it.

Well, now I had enough kids to satisfy Dad a dozen times over, even if none of them were mine. My ex-wife, Mysti, would have approved. She liked children.

Rare.

(Mysti is or was—your choice—a Welfie. Welfies are incredibly beautiful creatures who dwell in the Fearsome Forest of Euw. Exquisite, lovely, skilled in archery, fleet of foot, stern of mien, steeped in Majyk, the entire tribe has the collective intelligence of lettuce and the personality of a damp biscuit. Mysti is a misfit Welfie. For some reason she didn't see a future in flitting through the merry greenwood, guzzling nectar and living on a steady diet of chrysanthemum casserole. So she pulled a fast one, got herself married off to me, and got out of there so fast she left skidmarks on the one squirrel dumb enough to stand in her way.)

"Boss? Hey, boss, wake up!" Scandal nudged my knee with his head. "Earth to Kendar, do you read? Get off your butt and c'mon. It's lesson time."

I made a face. "Do I have to, Scandal?"

"Yeah, you do, so move it." The cat cocked his head at Velma. "Sorry, Sara Lee, much as I love your buns, I gotta take Master Kendar upstairs for a bit."

"What about the garbage?" Velma demanded, jabbing a finger at the slop bucket.

"Awwwww, leftovers *again*?" Scandal whined. "Why don-'cha just bury them out back, with all your ex-husbands?"

Velma's lips tightened like the mouth of a miser's coin purse. "I'll have you know that I am a respectable maiden."

"Is that how come you always slip a special basket of goodies to little Weskin?" Scandal mewed.

Velma blushed hotly. "Wessie—Weskin is more *sensitive* than the other children. He feels the loss of his father more."

I knew Weskin. He was one of Master Thengor's assorted illegitimate offspring. Come to think of it, he did bear a striking resemblance to Velma Chiefcook. He was one of the older brats, thirteen if he was a day. A big, ugly, sullen thirteen. If you subtracted his age from Velma's and imagined what the cook must've looked like way back then, it *was* possible that she and Master Thengor . . .

"The only thing Wessie feels is the loss of his dinner," Scandal snarled. "I know Gargantua, Jr. We had an argument over the right way to use rocks. He thought they oughta be chunked at poor, innocent pussycats and I said they oughta be bounced off his thick and pointy head." He showed his teeth. "I won."

I'll bet Scandal won. The cat had a good dose of Majyk in him, and he seemed to have a special talent for levitation spells. It wouldn't be too hard for him to levitate a rock at Weskin's skull. I'll bet he enjoyed doing it, too.

"Oh, how could you be so nasty to the poor lamb!" Velma sniveled.

"Look, lady, knock off the waterworks." Scandal's tail lashed back and forth. "You wanna do something useful? Hand that bucket to little Wessie and tell him to dump the stuff in the swamp."

"The swamp!" Velma was horrified. "That place is a—a veritable *swamp* of danger! Why, it's fairly crawling with voondrabs."

Voondrabs are revolting and repulsive and spiny and occasionally poisonous. The ghost of Velma's ladle kept me from pointing out that the only difference between Weskin and the voondrabs was—was—

What *was* it again?

"The voondrabs won't hurt him," Scandal reassured the cook. "Professional courtesy." While Velma was still standing there trying to puzzle that out, the cat and I trotted nimbly up the stairs to my study.

When Mysti and Scandal and I were the only ones living in the palace, I felt too uncomfortable to spread out much. The vast array of empty rooms and the desolate stretches of forsaken corridors made me feel as if I were being watched by something hostile. (I don't believe in ghosts—except for the spirit of Lady Pilferia Gangle, the notorious amateur sausage-maker. Every midnight she walks through the west wing of Uxwudge Manor with her headcheese tucked underneath her arm. But she's a legacy.) It was like hearing a phantom voice constantly whisper in my ear, *You're a fraud, Kendar Gangle! You've got no right to be here. This isn't your home at all.*

Now that I'd invited Lady Inivria and the children back, that sinister feeling had pretty much faded away. At last I was able to claim a decent bedroom, plus a sitting room, plus a study. There was plenty of space left over for the dead wizard's family. In fact, the rooms I chose were as far from theirs as possible, which made all of us happy.

My study was a tower room. Master Thengor's palace had loads of towers, almost as many as King Steffan's. It was furnished with a deeply cushioned armchair—the kind that's built like everyone's favorite cheek-pinching aunt—a plain oak table, a well-swept hearth, and row after row after row of bookcases.

Bookcases, not books. I didn't have any of my own, aside from a bunch of Raptura Eglantine romances Mysti left behind when she went off to be a mysterious, masked swordsWelfie (under the name "A Blade for Justice"). The only worthwhile book in the room lay on the oak table. It was a guide to Majyk given to me by the witch of Cheeseburgh, Mother Toadbreath. We were great good friends, she and I. I saved her from being hanged and she said I could keep the book as long as I promised not to read it while eating a strawberry jam sandwich. ("Either it looks like you've been trying to simulate bloodstains, which is tacky, or it makes the pages stick together, which is also tacky, although in a different way," she told me.)

I sat down at the table and prepared myself for study. Scandal leaped up to sit at my side and read over my shoulder. "Turn to the chapter on summoning fire-sprites," he directed. "If you can get a coupla them to work for you, your garbage problems are solved."

"I just started the chapter on elementals," I told him. "I'm not ready to do any of the tricks yet."

"Ahhhh, dogbreath!" Scandal very seldom used such bad language unless he was really fed up. "You go too slow, Kendar. It's like you're still scared spitless of your own powers."

"I should be," I said, getting huffy. "Better to go slow and not get it wrong than to jump right in and get in trouble."

The cat snorted. "In other words, if you ignore a problem long enough, it might go away. How mature."

"I guess you've forgotten *this*." I pulled a small card out of the book and tossed it down in front of the cat. It was a souvenir of our last adventure, that card, but it was also more valuable to me than a whole library full of sorcerous volumes. It once belonged to the evil fairy Acerbia, and it contained the deep, dark, ultimate secrets for the absolute domination and control of Majyk.

Scandal sniffed it. "*Not* the twelve-step program again!" he groaned. "This 'one spell at a time' stuff is all right until you get your confidence up, but it's holding you back from being all the wizard you can be."

"All I know is, it works for me," I replied, tucking the card back into the book. "You remember what happened when I found that chunk of Master Thengor's Majyk on the pirate ship?"

"Yeah, yeah, yeah. Boy oh boy, that stuff really flew all over the map when the old coot died. You tried to suck it in and add it to what you had already, and the whole operation threw you for a loop."

"Some loop." I rested my chin on my hand. "For a while there I couldn't use my Majyk at all because it hadn't digested the new stuff. That's what came of trying to do too much too fast. But with this, it'll never happen again. Now if I find any more of Master Thengor's shattered hoard, I know how to absorb it safely. I'd say that's worth taking things a little more slowly, wouldn't you?"

"No, I wouldn't." Scandal planted his forepaws primly on the open book. "You're using it as an excuse. I think you like being a semi-bumbling wizard instead of an efficient one."

"And why is that, smarty?"

"'Cause girls like goofy guys. They think it's *cute*." The cat made a *hairball ahoy!* sound. "It makes you seem lovable and cuddly and vulnerable. It makes them want to pick you up and go, 'Ooza silly wizard den?' It's the same reason some girls act like they've got soapsuds for brains when they're trying to attract a guy. Talk about your weird mating rituals! The bimbo bats her eyelashes and says, 'Ohhhh, big, strong, wunnerful computer geek is soooo brilliant! Little ol' me doesn't under-stand *anything* about software!' and he drops a box of diskettes all over the floor. It's *love*."

Scandal sounded disgusted. Scandal always sounded dis-gusted when he talked about his old master back on Earth. I still wasn't too sure about what a computer geek was, or a bimbo, but apparently his master was the former, and when he met the latter and she turned out to be allergic to cats, Scandal was out on his tail.

"Look, Scandal, I'm not going to argue with you about this," I said. "It'll be lunchtime soon, and I want to work on this chapter. Why don't you try learning something besides levita-tion spells if you're so ambitious?"

"I'm only ambitious for you. For me, I'm lazy. It's a cat thing; you wouldn't understand." He got up, turned around, and with a flick of his tail walked off the edge of the table and floated gracefully to the floor. I got to work.

I was just running through the summoning spell for a water-willy when there was a knock on the study door. Weskin came in, dragging his big feet and wiping his nose on the back of a letter. He dropped it on top of my book and slouched out of the room without a word. I was thankful. The only thing more obnoxious than Weskin was Weskin's voice.

I wiped off the envelope carefully before opening it. All of a sudden Scandal was back up on the table, nosing his way under my arm and trying to read the letter before me. "Who's it from? What's it say? What's that yucky green stuff stuck on it?" he demanded. "Doesn't look like the king's stationery, so it can't be a royal summons."

"Uh-oh," I said, reading it to the end. "This is terrible. This is awful. This is unthinkable."

"*What* is?" Scandal was bouncing on the table, his whiskers shooting sparks.

"It's from my sister, Lucy."

"That's terrible?"

"She says we have to come home at once."

"That's awful?"

"My brother's getting married."

Scandal sucked in his breath. "To a *girl*?" I nodded. "Is this some sort of sick joke?"

"Here's the invitation," I said, putting Lucy's note on the table and flipping it over so the cat could see the beautifully calligraphed work of a professional letter-writer, so different from Lucy's hasty scrawl.

Scandal read the words over. "Basehart's getting married. I thought that the only thing your big brother was interested in was riding around the forest shooting poor, defenseless chipmunks full of spears and arrows and javelins. Married. To a girl. Basehart. Wow." He shook his head. "That *is* unthinkable. Oh, well. Let's not think about it."

"You mean not go? But Lucy says there's something awful happening and she wants us to—"

"Oh, we'll *go*. A family wedding is a sacred and holy obligation." The cat closed his eyes and looked pious.

I regarded him closely. "I didn't know you were religious, Scandal."

"Yeah." He opened his eyes and winked. "I'm religiously opposed to wasting a wedding feast." The cat licked his chops. "Let's boogie."

CHAPTER —————— 2

IF I EVER GET TO BE THE SORT OF WIZARD WHO
writes huge volumes of arcane lore and wisdom, bound with
the skins of unspeakable monsters (unless Weskin gets away),
I'm going to call one of them *On Heroes* and it's going to start:

*Let no man call himself bold, brave, or courageous who has
merely slain dragons, stolen the treasure hoards of dwarf-
kings, or fought his way through ten thousand enchanted
dungeons. These are but paltry pastimes and insignificant
flirtations with glory. Nay, in truth it is said that no man may
be named hero until after he has survived a family reunion full
of aunts.*

My aunts.

Trust me on this one.

"Oh, there's the little darling now!"

"Yoo-hoo! Kendar! Come to Auntie!"

"Isn't he tall?"

"Hasn't he grown?"

"*Just* the spitting image of his father!"

"But he's got his mother's eyes."

"And Cousin Prendergast Gangle's nose."

"And that mouth is the *twin* of Grandmama Eulalie's!"

"And if those ears aren't Uncle Jarrow's to the life, I'm a
voondrab."

"You naught boy, you give your auntie a great, big kiss this
very minute!"

"Doesn't he look wonderful!"

"But a little pale."

"And that hair—!"

"Well, dear, boys will be boys. Even if they do wind up looking like they've got a stork's nest balanced on top of their heads."

"Tsk-tsk, he's so *skinny*. Kendar, aren't you *eating*?"

"Oh, now, you know how these young folks are, Grativa. They've got other things on their minds."

"Hmph! He never got that skinny when *I* was in charge of the lad!"

"We know, Nanny Esplanadia, we know."

"I think he's constipated."

"He's not constipated, Grativa, he just takes after his mother's side of the family."

"Nonsense! I was married to one of King Creswel's advisors for thirty-five years. If there's one thing I know, it's constipation. What he wants is a good dose of Philona's Fruit and Rust Tonic. Good for man or beast. I've got a bottle of it tucked away in my room. I'll just run and fetch it." Aunt Grativa rolled away, like a hay bale on wheels.

"Here, precious, never you mind that nasty old tonic. The only reason Grativa takes it is because it's got more alcohol in it than your brother. You take this piece of cake and eat it all up right this minute."

A plate of half-eaten chocolate cake was thrust into my hands.

"Carageena! What are you thinking?" The plate was snatched away again by my dear old Nanny Esplanadia. She had raised three generations of Gangles and she was going to keep on raising Gangles until someone made her stop. "No cake until he's eaten his vegetables."

Aunt Carageena gestured at the generously heaped serving tables crowding the great hall of Uxwudge Manor. "I dare you to find anything resembling a vegetable here, Esplanadia," she said. "Except for Basehart, of course."

It was true: The feast that my mother, Lady Abstemia Gangle, had laid out in honor of Basehart's betrothal was almost equally divided between meat and sugar. From the walls, the severed and stuffed heads of generations of woodland beasts gazed down with glassy eyes on the roasted and stuffed bodies of their descendants. The only green matter to be seen was a bowl full of lumpy, oily, sour-smelling glop that none of the guests were touching. In fact, some of them took one look at that bowl and crossed to the far side of the hall in a marked manner. (Sometimes I thought I caught sight of a pair of beady little eyes and a small, pointed snout sticking out of the goo; it must have been my imagination.) Nanny Esplanadia was appalled, but she stuck to her principles.

"I'll just go down to the kitchens and fetch him some nice, fresh carrots or something. Then he can have his cake." She tottered off just like Aunt Grativa, but that still left me in the clutches of two of my aunts.

"Here." Aunt Carageena gave me a fresh plate of cake. "Cake counts as a vegetable among the ferocious riders of the Newtgriddle Desert."

"Yes, and chocolate cake is worshipped as a minor god among the jungle-dwellers of Plunj," added her sister, my Aunt Glucosia.

"When were we ever in Plunj?" Carageena demanded.

"*We* weren't," Glucosia replied. "*I* was. It was during those six months when I was working alone. *You* were mooning around after that overmuscled barbarian swordsthing—what'sizname—never mind. Not worth remembering."

"I *never*!" Carageena was fit to be tied. When she got upset, it showed in her hair. Wisps of iron-gray escaped from the complex arrangement of fat curls and skinny braids adorning the lady's head.

"That's not what *he* said," Glucosia mewed. The net of fine wrinkles around her bright blue eyes crinkled with malicious glee.

"The very idea!" Carageena huffed. I tried to eat my cake and turn invisible at the same time. Dad's big sisters carried on like this every time the family got together. If you were lucky, the whole thing blew over without either one of them dragging you into it. If you weren't lucky—

—you were probably me.

"Kendar, do you ever recall me going off after some barbarian swords*man*"—here Carageena glared at Glucosia—"for six months? Or for any time at all, come to that!"

"Well, Aunt Carageena, I—"

"Oh, don't frighten the child, Gee'. How would *he* know about all your sordid little love affairs? He's scarcely out of the nursery. If I know Abstemia, she'd die before letting her children hear about your shenanigans."

"*I* wasn't the one who brought home the Sacred Eye of Delbert with some silly song and dance about having fought off the High Priest's legions of blood-crazed warriors, when everyone knows how you really got it." Aunt Carageena smiled smugly.

"And how was *that*, pray?" Aunt Glucosia asked in a small, dangerous voice. Her hair was the crackling silver color of a fatal lightning-strike. It matched her temper exactly.

"By *not* fighting off the High Priest's blood-crazed legions of warriors, if you catch my meaning. Nor the High Priest, neither. And it wasn't exactly *blood* they were crazed for, it was—"

Aunt Glucosia grabbed the plate of cake from my hands and flung it at Aunt Carageena. Aunt Carageena threw aside her light indoor cloak, revealing a lovely set of ceremonial armor and a ceremonial sword to match. She drew it from its gilded scabbard faster than the flick of a frog's tongue and parried the cake plate. The dish soared across the room, blobs of cake flying, and landed in the punch bowl, splattering half a dozen innocent bystanders.

"Oh dear!" I heard Mom groan from somewhere behind me. "They're at it again. Can't you *do* something about them, Lucius? We've got guests."

"*Do* something?" I heard Dad's answering growl. "If anything could've been *done* with those two, my own dad would've done it! D'you think he was *proud* when the neighbors learned that two of his girls was rampaging all up and down creation with full armor, a couple of blasted swords, and not a cup of brains between 'em?"

"Oh dear," Mom groaned again. I decided that my place as a good son was by her side. For one thing, it was safer than hanging around my warrior aunts.

Mom and Dad were standing over by the great fireplace. There was no fire in it today. Spring was blossoming into summer and the great hall was warm enough, especially when packed with so many guests. When Scandal and I first arrived, the betrothal party was well under way and we were just a couple of extra faces in the crowd. I gave up trying to find my parents or Lucy to tell them that I'd arrived. I just followed the mob, which was how this turned out to be the first time I'd seen Mom or Dad since I got here.

The two of them looked great. I know Mom flutters and flaps and coos more than a sackful of doves, and Dad thinks it's a wasted day when he hasn't stuck a few arrows in some animals, but when they're standing still with their mouths shut they make a handsome couple. Next to the other couple by the fireplace, they were downright gorgeous. (I swear, for a while I didn't realize the other couple was human. They were both so squat and stocky, with unblinking black eyes, that I thought they were a pair of end tables cleverly carved and painted to look like trolls.)

"Kendar! Baby!" Mom squealed when she saw me. She swooped down on me like a hawk, got a death-grip on my wrist, and dragged me towards the fireplace. "So you finally decided to show up, and not a *word* to your mother. Still, I suppose I ought to be grateful that you even condescend to come here at all. Oh, I know we're not as fancy or brilliant as all of your friends at court, but would it hurt you to use some of that wizardly power you've got to write a letter to your own parents? Well, never you mind. I'm sure that when we're dead you'll be ready to write us lots of letters. Look, Lucius, Kendar's home!" She propelled me toward my father.

Dad stood with his hands linked behind his back. He looked me up and down severely, blew a great, gusty breath through his thick moustache and said, "You all right, boy?"

"Yes, Dad, I'm fine," I replied.

"Good, good." He rocked on his heels. "So . . . everything going all right for you? Being a wizard and all?"

"Yes, sir."

"Good, good. You had an animal, didn't you, boy? Small one. What was it? A squirrel? A rappid? King liked it. King likes lots o' things. That's no help. Damn."

"Cat," I said. "It's a cat, Dad; Scandal. He's over on one of the tables, eating a whole stuffed carp."

"Good, good. I hate carp. Well. So . . . everything all right with the animal?"

"As long as the carp holds out."

"Good, good." He looked away, looked back at me, looked at the ceiling, and back at me again. "So . . . it's all going all right for you, then?"

For what felt like the twentieth time, I assured him that I was all right, Scandal was all right, and the wizard business was all

right. Since I didn't want to talk about the newest methods for
hunting down and slaughtering game, that was the end of the
conversation until one of the troll end tables cleared his throat
and said:

"This is the one, Lucius?" He stared at me with eyes like
black olives.

"Aye, Megrim." Dad nodded. "My younger boy, Kendar.
Master Kendar. Bit of a wizard. Court Wizard to King Steffan,
actually. Likely the young pup thinks that gives him the right to
fancy himself better than his old father, eh?" He shot me a
sizzling look. "Well, I'll be the first to tell him, he's a fool if he
tries lording it over *me* just because he can juggle moonbeams
and such trash."

Dad's friend nodded sagely. The two men were talking about
me as if I weren't there, so it came as a surprise when the
barrel-shaped fellow stuck out his hand and announced, "Sir
Megrim Freehand Gallimaufrey, at your service. And this is my
lovely wife, Lady Teluria."

"Pleased to meet you," I said, bowing to the lady. If I kept
my eyes fixed on the floor, maybe I wouldn't goggle at her hair.
It was a shade of red that made me want to coat it with sunburn
remedy.

Lady Teluria lifted her chins and said, "That depends."

"I—I'm sorry, but what did you—?"

"You are a wizard, I believe," she went on, her voice every
bit as ponderous as her body. "Wizards are supposed to be
wise, are they not?"

"Wise enough not to get too big for their britches," Dad put
in, still threatening me with his eyes. (I wished I'd decided to
swap my usual clothes for an official wizard's robe. That way
I wouldn't have any britches to worry about.) "Wise enough not
to look down on their own flesh and blood."

"Aw, Dad, when did I ever—?"

"Out of all your great wizardly wisdom, Master Kendar," the
lady continued, "do you think you could answer me one small,
simple question, perhaps?"

"I can try," I offered. I wondered what she was getting at.

"Don't you agree that a perfectly normal girl who wants a
career is spang out of her mind?"

Do you know how it sometimes happens at parties? Everyone's talking, there are about twenty different conversations

going on, and then all of a sudden twenty different conversations *stop* at the exact same moment? Well, one of those moments happened right then. The great hall fell silent just in time for everyone to hear Lady Teluria's question.

Including my aunts. They put aside their spat and came nearer. I could see glimpses of Aunt Carageena's armor twinkling beneath her cloak. Betrothal or no, she always wore her armor in plain sight, even if it looked a little funny over the expensive green silk gown she'd chosen for the occasion. Aunt Glucosia, on the other hand, wore a blue velvet gown of such exquisitely intricate workmanship and embroidery that it would have been a shame to cover it up with an iron shell. Her ample silver hair was pulled back in a simple ponytail that could not distract at all from the magnificence of her gown. I tried to frisk her with my eyes: No steel I could see. All right, then the aunts were only semi-dangerous.

Rule Number One: There is no such thing as a semi-dangerous aunt.

"I don't believe we've met," Aunt Carageena said to the troll-like woman. She made no attempt to sheathe her sword as she stuck out her free hand. What's more, she flung her cloak back off both shoulders so there was no missing all that armor. "Carageena Gangle, Mercenary First Class, late of the Inter-kingdom Lady Gladiators' and Warriors' Union. Retired."

"A *swordswoman*?" The lady's overplucked eyebrows rose. Her snub nose twitched as if smelling an overcrowded stable. She did not accept Aunt Carageena's hand.

"Oh, this old thing?" Aunt Carageena twirled the heavy blade as easily as if it were a straw. "I've had it for years."

Mom bustled her way between the aunts and put an arm around each. "Teluria, dear, Carageena and Glucosia are my Lucius' older sisters. There were, er, a good many years between their births and his. Old Lord Gangle didn't think he'd ever have a son, which accounts for the fact that he raised his girls a little, er—"

"Scandalous." Lady Teluria's lipless mouth snapped shut on the word like a bear trap.

"Oh, I wouldn't say *that*." Mom was fluttering at top speed now. "A trifle hoydenish, perhaps. Something of the tomboy. Eccentric. But certainly not—"

"Inexcusable." This time it was Sir Megrim who passed

judgment. "My beloved wife and I have no sons, yet we never
felt the need to convert our only child, Dulcetta, into one of
these pseudo-men." He waved a podgy hand at the shadows
beside the great hearth. I saw nothing there at first. Then a
small, slightly built shape crept out into the light. It was a girl,
a very pretty girl with long, flossy blond hair like a Welfie's,
big, blue, shallow eyes, and delicate features. Her skin looked
like what you find in a milk pail after you skim off the cream,
but there was a faint stain of pink on her lips and cheeks. She
moved as if every step she took was an apology.

"Amazing," I breathed.

"What is, Fearless Leader?" Scandal nudged my ankle. The
cat had a habit of showing up suddenly, when least expected,
like an attack of hiccups. He looked at the girl. "Gee, I never
knew they grew mice *that* size!"

"That's no mouse, that's Dulcetta Gallimaufrey," I told him.

"Fooled me. I've been keeping an eye on her and she sure
does *act* like a mouse. So okay, she's not a rodent; what's so
amazing about her, then?"

"The fact that she's *their* daughter." I nodded at the Gallimaufreys.

Meanwhile, Aunt Glucosia had stepped away from Mom and
was closing in on Sir Megrim. "What did you call us?" she
asked in that same small voice that had preceded the cake-
throwing incident.

Sir Megrim met Glucosia's hard blue gaze unafraid. Either
he was brave or stupid. Like Scandal says, Who can tell the
difference? "I said pseudo-men. Fake men. Pretend men. Fish
masquerading as corned beef." He eyed Glucosia up and down.
"At least *you* have the good taste to leave all that armor
nonsense at home when you come among decent people."

Aunt Glucosia reached for the gold lacings on her bodice,
pulled, and her gown plunged to a puddle of velvet at her feet.
She stepped out of it daintily, the candlelight twinkling on her
knee-length coat of mail.

"You were saying?" she asked sweetly.

"*Well!*" Lady Teluria reacted as if someone had smacked her
across the face with a salmon. (Come to think of it, a brisk slap
with a large fish might have improved her personality no end.)
"Megrim, fetch my cloak! We're leaving! Dulcetta, come
here."

The mousy girl came at once, trembling head to toe. "Yes, Mummy?" she quavered.

"I don't think this betrothal is a good idea after all. When you marry a man, you not only wed him, you acquire a whole new family. I did not realize that *these*"—she gave the aunts a killing look—"were part of it when we made the arrangements."

"But Mummy—" Dulcetta's lower lip was wobbling. "Mummy, I *want* to marry Basehart."

"Well, you can learn to want to marry someone else soon enough. There is no end to the things a woman can do if she puts her mind to it. Believe me, I know." She seized the girl's hand and started away.

Wow. Someone who *wanted* to marry my brother? This wasn't the sort of thing you ran into every day. I couldn't let her get away.

"Just a minute, Lady Teluria," I said, stepping in front of the squat little woman and her pretty daughter. "I think you ought to think this over."

"Yes, my love," said Sir Megrim, coming up hastily to join me. "It's not as if good old Lucius' sisters will have any influence over our child. Once she and Basehart are wed, I'm certain that those, uh, ladies will go back home and the only time they'll return to Uxwudge will be for naming-feasts and funerals and other festive occasions."

"It's not them I worry about," Lady Teluria replied. "It's future generations. What if this—this *freakishness* is inherited? Haring off to have a *career*, forsooth! As if a decent woman doesn't have enough to do, taking care of her home! Hmph! Do you want your granddaughters to sack castles, burn villages, drive chariots, wear *britches*?"

"My pet, you needn't worry." Sir Megrim made soothing noises. "Lucius also has a younger sister, Grativa. She's a perfectly normal woman. For a Gangle."

Teluria twisted her mouth. "Two out of three is poor odds and you know it. Come, Dulcetta." She tried to drag the girl past us.

"But *Mummy*—!" Dulcetta wailed to no avail. She hung back, but Lady Teluria hauled her through the crowd with the ease of a plow horse pulling a child's wheelie-duckie.

"*Hold it right there, Medusa!*" A ball of multicolored sparks exploded right in front of Lady Teluria. She stopped dead in her tracks. The guests immediately backed off, giving the blazing ball plenty of room. The sparks vanished, revealing Scandal. He had his fur fluffed out and his tail straight up in the air. Every whisker quivered and hummed with Majyk. He walked up to the lady, stiff-legged, and demanded, "Okay, toots, where's the fire?"

Lady Teluria made a big deal of tugging the hem of her gown away from the cat, as if he were a puddle of something nasty. "I *beg* your pardon! You will step aside and allow us to pass."

"When pigs fly," the cat responded cheerfully. Lady Teluria gasped as her feet left the ground. Scandal's whiskers sizzled. I had to admit, he hadn't mastered a lot of different spells, but he was very good at the one he did know. He floated Lady Teluria halfway to the ceiling before he left her hovering there.

"Here! You put my wife down this instant!" Sir Megrim waddled up, pointing a fat finger at Scandal.

"Put her down? No problem." Scandal looked up at the gently bobbing lady. "You're ugly and your mother dresses you funny. Where did you get that dress, at the Salvation Army? Is that your face or did Halloween come early this year? I've seen better legs on a table."

"My legs!" Lady Teluria shrieked. "Everyone can see my legs!" She made a useless effort to jam her skirt between her knees. It billowed up on a draft, almost covering her face. She squawked and beat it down.

"Scandal," I said, "put her back."

"But, boss—"

"*Now.*"

"Awwwwww. You don't let me have any fun." The cat moped, but Lady Teluria drifted back to the floor with no harm done.

Almost no harm done.

"Kendar Gangle, if you can't control your familiar any better than that, I shall have to ask you to put him in your room." Mom stood in front of me, hands on hips.

"But Mom, I can't lock Scandal up," I protested.

"He can *try*." The cat grinned. "But I wouldn't advise it." He raised one forepaw and extended his claws. They were long and sharp. "What's a little shredded flesh between friends?"

"Insulting and abusing our guests!" Mom went on. "After all

the trouble I went to, preparing this lovely feast, your creature upsets the bride-to-be's mother so much that the entire wedding might not take place after all! Oh, but don't let *that* trouble you. Don't even *think* about all my hard work. Who am I? Nobody. Just the woman who changed your dirty diapers, and fed you, and burped you, and—"

I sighed. Mom was going strong. This was the wrong moment to point out that the only work she'd done on the feast was to go tell our cook, old Maisree, to prepare food for a couple of hundred guests. Perhaps she also told our head gardener, Strunk, to bring in some flowers to deck the hall, and our major domo, Thorgit, to lock up the good silverware until the visitors had gone. And as for that business about changing my dirty diapers—

"The hell you say," said Scandal.

"What!" Mom's eyes shot cold flame almost as well as Scandal's whiskers gave off sparks.

"I bet you never touched a dirty diaper in your life," the cat purred.

"I should hope *not!*" Lady Teluria waded into the discussion. "A well-bred lady does not need to perform such menial tasks. Or what are servants for?"

Scandal wrapped his tail around his paws. "You tell me."

"Silly beast! In a properly run home, servants take care of the cleaning, the cooking, the child care, the shopping, the sewing, the mending, the laundry."

"Yes." Mom nodded. "And then the major domo knows what's where and how much of it there is and who's to blame if there isn't enough of it. I don't know *what* I'd do without our Thorgit."

"Nor I without our Fenvig," Lady Teluria agreed.

"So if the major domo makes sure the servants all have their jobs, and the servants actually go out and *do* 'em"—only the tip of Scandal's tail was twitching violently—"what's there left for either one of *you* to do?"

"Er—" said Mom.

"Impertinent beast!" Lady Teluria snapped. But she didn't say anything else.

"Well, there's always embroidery," Aunt Glucosia said.

"My goodness, yes," Aunt Carageena chimed in. "Heaps and

heaps of embroidery. Didn't Mama always say that you can't have enough good embroidery?"

"And tapestry-weaving," Glucosia added as an afterthought. "If you want a really good tapestry, never trust a servant. Between the embroidery and the tapestries, I don't know how you ladies manage to find a moment's time to yourselves."

"Not that you could ever expect a *man* to understand that." Aunt Carageena regarded me with a little pity and a whole lot of amusement.

"Yes, yes, certainly, that's precisely what I was going to say." Lady Teluria was passionately grateful to my aunts. "Ladies, I ask your forgiveness. I see that you appreciate the hard life of a housewife after all."

"Well, just because it wasn't right for *us*, doesn't mean it's not right for others," Carageena said, slipping her arm through Lady Teluria's.

"Indeed, we think your little girl, Dulcetta, will make a perfect housewife!" Glucosia said, linking up on Teluria's other side.

As the three of them wandered back towards the feasting tables I heard Lady Teluria remark, "You know, I used to fool around with swords a bit when I was a girl. Nothing formal, you understand, but still . . ."

"*Kendar!*" A familiar voice desperately hissed my name. I turned to see my sister Lucy hiding behind one of the high-back chairs near the wall, motioning urgently for me to join her.

"Hello, Lucy," I said, giving her a peck on the cheek. "I got your message. What's wrong?"

Lucy's eyes darted from side to side the way her heroines' eyes always did when the moons were high and evil was afoot and they weren't wearing a lot of clothes. "Not here," she murmured. "Come with me." She took my hand.

"Not so fast." I refused to be dragged off. For some reason, people kept doing that to me and it was starting to get on my nerves. "If Mom sees us slinking out of here before the betrothal ceremony, you know I'm the only one who'll get the blame. Dad always takes your side. You're his precious little girlikins, while I'm only the weird son who doesn't like to kill things. So that leaves Mom with just one target: me. No thank you."

"Kendar, come *on*, I *told* you." Lucy ground her teeth. "This is *important*."

"Now, now, Lucy." I always felt like patting my little sister on the head when she got upset about anything. Time and a couple of kicks in the shins had broken me of the habit. Still, I did tend to talk down to her. "You're a writer. You sometimes let the simplest things get blown all out of proportion. Why don't you calm down and tell me what's *really* wrong? I'm sure I'll be able to take care of your little problem in no time at—"

"The world is about to be plunged into a war that will destroy untold lives, lay waste countless kingdoms, and shake Orbix to its very roots," Lucy said calmly.

Someone screamed.

CHAPTER ———————— 3

SOMETHING GREEN AND GOOEY SCAMPERED ACROSS the floor fleeing for its life with Scandal in hot pursuit. A second scream joined the first, and a third and a fourth as the mucky creature dashed here and there, leaving a trail of slick, slimy pawprints and coming uncomfortably close to many an expensive, easily stained gown. Most of the ladies present shrieked and looked around wildly for chairs to stand on.

"Come back here, you fugitive from a taco!" Scandal gasped as he galloped after his prey. The poor little thing squeaked pitifully. It didn't sound dangerous, only scared. I knelt down in its path and grabbed it. Getting a good grip on it wasn't easy. It was covered in the green glop from that bowl on the feasting table.

"What *is* this thing?" I asked anyone who cared to listen. I displayed my catch to the crowd.

"It's a mole, Kendar," Lucy said demurely. "I'm surprised you didn't know that, since you seem to *know* that I always exaggerate things."

"And what's a mole doing covered in this gunk?" I inquired.

"Oh, so that's where it got to!" Mom scooped the terrified little thing out of my hands and held it tenderly to her bosom. "It should have been set free in the gardens as soon as the recipe was done, but you know old Maisree."

"*What* recipe?" I shouted.

Mom laughed. "Woccamole dip, of course. But I wouldn't expect a *man* to know that." She took the mole out of the great hall, murmuring words of comfort to it.

Scandal clawed at my britches. "Tell me she didn't just say that," he pleaded.

Lucy got hold of my hand again. "It'll take Mother some time to get the mole cleaned off and out in the gardens. They can't start the betrothal ceremony without her. We can be out and back before that. Come on."

I was too bewildered to argue. It was simpler to follow Lucy out of the great hall and up the spiral stairs to her room. There was a large, pink, stuffed unicorn with long-lashed eyes lying in front of Lucy's door, a white satin bow around its neck. Lucy paused to read the card. " 'With love from Aunt Glucosia.' " She sighed. "And Aunt Carageena gave me a My First Amazon Swordswoman doll, with two changes of armor. Kendar, do you think they'll *ever* realize that I'm not seven years old anymore?"

"Why should they?" I countered. "Odds are Mom and Dad still think you're their curly-topped little baby."

"Yes, but that's natural; they're my parents. Parents are always supposed to be the last to know."

I chuckled. "I'd like to be there when they find out just how much about you they *don't* know . . . Raptura."

Lucy's hand clapped itself across my mouth in a flash. "Hush! Don't even joke about that! You know what a flap there was when Daddy thought I was *reading* books. If he finds out I'm *writing* them—" It didn't bear thinking about. Lucy shuddered.

She picked up the toy unicorn and took it into her room, flinging it onto the bed with the rest of her stuffed animals. The two of us sat down side by side on the canopied bed while Scandal prowled the room, giving it the once-over with nose and whiskers and prying paws.

"All right, I'm here and I'm listening," I said. "What's all this about the end of the world?"

"I didn't say it was the end of the world," Lucy corrected me. "I just said it was widespread disaster in the making. Do you remember Prince Boffin?"

My muscles tensed. Did I remember him? How do you forget the big, blond, muscular, thick-thewed, thicker-headed lunk who brought your wife back from the dead with a single kiss? And just for that, Mysti ran off with him. She said that I hadn't wanted our marriage in the first place, and that maybe I *was* too young to settle down, and she was tired of waiting for me to get *on* with it (When I asked "Get on with *what*?" she

gave me a funny look, shook her head, and wandered away
muttering), and that since all Welfie marriages were strictly
'til-death-do-us-part deals and she'd been dead enough, it was
all over. I remember being partly relieved, but partly disappointed. I *liked* Mysti. I was even attracted to her. More than
attracted, if we're being honest. But I didn't like how she'd
finagled things so that I *had* to marry her. I've never liked
being pushed. I didn't like being pushed *into* marriage and I
didn't like being forced *out* of it.

Oh yes, I remembered Prince Boffin.

"What about him?" I grumped.

"He's gone."

"Good riddance."

"Kendar, stop being such a baby." Lucy kicked her feet
impatiently. "This is all about Mysti, isn't it?"

"No, it's not," I lied. "I don't even think about Mysti, these
days. I've got too many important wizardly matters to mind."

Lucy smirked. There is nothing more irritating than the
knowing smirk of a smart kid sister. "If you want Mysti back,
nothing's stopping you from going after her. It's not like she
and Boffin are engaged or anything. When was the last time
you went to see her, or wrote to her, or—?"

"I told you, I've been busy," I muttered.

Lucy said a Word.

Scandal froze. "Yow! You kiss your mother with that
mouth?"

"Kendar, if you like Mysti, let her *know* it!" Lucy exclaimed.
"Do you expect her to read your mind?"

"Why not? Everyone else does." My mood was growing
blacker and blacker.

"Not anymore, Bwana," Scandal prompted me. "You've
been getting pretty good at keeping the barricades up around
your mind. Nowadays I can't find out what you're thinking
without an engraved invitation."

"I'm entitled to some privacy," I said bitterly. "That includes
what I think about Mysti." I scowled at my sister. "Now get to
the point: What about Boffin?"

"He's gone," she repeated. "Gone as in 'vanished.' Not a
trace of him, not a hint, not a word that he was even
considering leaving. No reason for him to leave. You know, he
was doing very well with his new career. Wait, I'll show you."

She slipped off the bed and wiggled underneath it. I heard a heavy, grating sound, as if someone was lifting one of the flagstones. Then I heard Lucy grunt, followed by a loud *clonk!*, rather like the sound a big iron box makes when it's hauled out of a deep hole and dropped on the floor. Last of all I heard the rattle of chains, the metallic protest of a padlock being opened, the squeal of huge hinges, and finally Lucy emerged from beneath the dust ruffle with a stack of books in her arms.

They were all the latest Raptura Eglantine romances. I recognized *Rouse Not the Wizard* right away, but there was also *Touch Not the Welfie* and *Twit Not the Centaur* and *Unsettle Not the Dragon* and *Provoke Not the Paladin*. On every single cover, Prince Boffin's curly blond head bowed low over the heaving bosom of the heroine, his blandly handsome face intense with passion. Well, he tried to look intense with passion. He really looked like a man who took bobbing for apples very seriously.

I set the books down. "He's on *all* these covers?"

"And the kid tightens his grasp on the obvious," Scandal announced.

I gave him a filthy look. "I *mean*, whatever happened to Curio?"

Lucy made a helpless gesture. "Curio's a lamb—"

"Whole lotta beef on him, for a lamb," Scandal commented. "I remember Curio. He's another one of those big blond muscle-things that get on the covers of your books, Missie Eglantine. You were in a clinch with Curio when your dark 'n' terrible secret was found out. Mwah-ha-ha," he added for effect.

Lucy blushed. "I was only demonstrating a good pose for the cover so that my agent could pass the word along to the artist."

"How is old Milkum these days?" I asked. Lucy's agent was also her publisher and the owner of Full Court Press, which made things nice and friendly. (Although Lucy told me that one year Milkum got drunk at the annual Wenchpinch Eve office party and asked one of the cover artists to paint a picture of him—naked and with a plate of fruit on his head—on the office wall. When he sobered up and saw it, he locked himself in his office and really let himself have it. He wasn't speaking to him for two weeks after that.)

"Milkum is fine. 'Slick as a greased weasel, twice as vicious, and proud of it' is what he says. Daddy still hasn't caught him."

This was good. Like I said, Dad didn't know Lucy was writing books. My little sister led a sheltered life at Uxwudge Manor, or else. So in order to collect the latest Raptura Eglantine work for publication, Milkum and Curio had to sneak into the house in a variety of disguises to take away Lucy's manuscripts and to give her her pay.

A thought struck me. "Isn't Milkum Curio's agent, too?" Lucy nodded. "And Boffin's?" This time Lucy shook her head and looked even more upset than before.

"Prince Boffin showed up here one day with—with your wife."

"My *ex*-wife," I gritted.

"Kendar, you recommended him to me yourself. Please don't be like that."

"Sorry," I told my feet.

"Mysti said I should introduce him to Milkum. Milkum liked his looks and was willing to give him a try—not as a client, just as a model. Milkum never does business with nobodies. We put him on the cover of *Tempt Not the Troll*."

"Boffin as a troll?" I had to laugh.

"He wasn't really a troll. He was adopted and raised by trolls and he always thought he was a troll until he was rejected from the tribe after his foster-mother died and he went wandering through the mountains, amassing a fortune in gold, until he saved the life of Hyalina, the beautiful orphan whose wicked uncle had suppressed her father's will and cheated her out of the diamond mining empire which was hers by right and offered her shameful insults, forcing her to flee his loathsome and unnatural lusts until she hid in the mine and the roof fell in on her. Then in Chapter Two—"

"Never mind. All right, so Boffin got his big break. Then what?"

"Then these." Lucy waved at the other books. "He was a success, a bigger success than anything we'd ever expected. Even bigger than Curio." She didn't sound happy for the prince.

I remembered what Curio looked like. He was the same basic model of—well, of *model* as Boffin: blond hair, blue eyes, muscles everywhere. There was no difference between the two and I said so.

"But Boffin's got *curly* hair," Lucy said, as if that made all the difference in the world. "Whatever he had, it worked. The readers wanted more of him. We put Curio on the cover of *Embrace Not the Werewolf*, but it didn't sell nearly as well."

"Couldn't have been the writing, could it?" Scandal lifted one whiskery eyebrow.

"No, it couldn't." Lucy was not amused. "I'm a professional. I know what my readers expect in a Raptura Eglantine romance, and I give it to them."

"Over and over and over and over . . ." The cat drifted away, snickering.

"Milkum showed up in my room disguised as an upstairs maid. He told me he had to shave places he couldn't talk about, but it was vital that he speak with me. He owns Full Court Press, but he's got stockholders. If the readers aren't happy, the stockholders aren't happy. They gave him the word: Make the readers happy."

"Bring back Boffin?" I guessed.

"Uh-huh. So we did." She swung her feet. "Then Milkum wasn't happy."

"Why not? You got the stockholders off his back."

"Milkum is Curio's agent," Lucy said. "Not Boffin's. Boffin said that if Milkum didn't want him when he was a nobody, he didn't need Milkum now that he was a somebody. He said if he wanted to throw ten percent of his pay away, he'd send it home to his parents. Milkum tried to make him see reason." She gave me a significant look. "That was when Mysti stepped in."

"Stepped in what?" Scandal piped up from the floor.

I went and got the cat and plopped him down on my lap. "That's enough out of you," I told him, wagging a finger in his face. He bit it. Like Master Thengor always used to ask, When will I ever learn?

"I think I understand," I said. "Milkum tried to use standard business practice on Boffin—"

"He threatened his life."

"Yeah, like I said: standard business practice. Except Boffin had Mysti on his side and Mysti has a big sword at her side. Checkmate. So Prince Boffin did all those covers for you, and Curio's been kicking his heels in a corner somewhere, and

Milkum hasn't been able to collect an agent's fee from Curio *or* Boffin for a long time. Have I got it right?" She indicated that I did. "And now Prince Boffin is missing."

"Gee whiz, Sherlock, I wonder who could *possibly* have done it?" Scandal drawled.

"It's pretty clear who did it," Lucy replied grimly. "The hard part's going to be finding out what they did."

"Huh? I'd say that one's pretty clear too," the cat said. "Drag the pond. Visit the local dump. See if there's anything stopping up the drains. Unwrap one of those funny-shaped packages waaaaay in the back of the freezer. That boy is deader than Poughkeepsie on a Tuesday night."

"I've got to agree with Scandal," I said. "Even if I don't know what he's talking about all the way. I mean, he must have been murdered. He's gone. Vanished. Poof."

"Poof," Lucy repeated. "But *how* poof? *When* poof? *Who* poof?"

"Colonel Mustard in the library with the lead pipe," Scandal declared. "Now can we go back downstairs and eat some more?"

"*Don't* you think Curio or Milkum killed Prince Boffin?" I asked.

"There's more ways to *poof* someone than killing him." Lucy spoke as if she knew what she was talking about. "If Milkum did it, he wouldn't kill the prince. A dead model can't become your client."

"Well, maybe not here, but where *I* come from——" Scandal began.

"And if Curio was the one who did it, I doubt he'd kill Boffin either."

"How come?"

For a girl who wasn't old enough to drink gawfee without a license, Lucy sometimes seemed about a hundred years older than me when it came to the ways of the world. "Two reasons, Kendar. One: If Curio *did* kill Boffin, and Milkum found out, Milkum would be so angry over the loss of a potential client that he'd bounce Curio from here to Vicinity City. Milkum *made* Curio's career, you know."

"And the second reason?"

"If Curio killed Boffin and Mysti found out——"

I raised one hand. "Say no more. It's hard to get any good

modeling jobs with a foot and a half of Welfin steel sticking through your ribs. Mysti has got a temper."

Scandal rolled over on the bed between us and patted Lucy's arm. "Lemme get this straight, babe. So far it looks like Boffin's gone, you've got a pretty good idea who goned him, and how it'll be the end of the world for Curio and/or Milkum if Mysti finds out whodunit. This is still pretty darned far from it being a problem for anyone else just because Boffin went bye-bye."

"I was getting to that." Lucy hopped off the bed and, after a great deal of labor, stowed her secret stash of Raptura Eglantine books. This time when she crawled out from under the mattress she had a big parchment scroll clutched in her teeth. "Read this," she directed, dropping it in my lap.

I removed the silk ties and unrolled the document. Scandal clambered into my lap to read it and get in the way. (He claims it's in the Feline Bill of Rights to make a nuisance of himself, especially when humans are trying to read things.)

"Cheeeez," the cat murmured in admiration. "So that's what a declaration of war looks like." He turned his eyes to Lucy. "Your very first one, too! And you not even sixteen. Kendar, our little girl is growing up. I—I think I'm gonna cry." He did a bad job of pretending to snivel.

"*Please*, be serious!" Lucy picked him up and scratched him under the chin. "Wedwel knows, *that* thing is serious enough."

She was right. I'm no diplomat, but the meaning of the parchment was clear: Prince Boffin of Belacan having dropped out of sight, his father the King of Belacan was not a happy monarch. Even though Boffin was not the heir to the throne, a king likes to know where all his sons are at any given time. If you lose track of them, there is always the chance that they are off neglecting their studies or consorting with evil companions or hiring assassins to kill you and all their brothers or learning about democracy. Besides, Boffin's mother was worried and was making the king's life a living hell. So unless they heard from Boffin in a hurry, the king was going to rally his forces and attack the Topside.

"Aw, how many forces could he have?" I asked, trying to make light of the situation. "Belacan's not the biggest kingdom on the Underside. And anyhow, King Ramses and Queen Borith are our friends down there. I'll just send a message to them and they can tell Boffin's father to calm down until we—"

"Read the P.S.," Lucy directed me.

My eyes went back to the document. There at the bottom was indeed a P.S., which is not something I expected to see on a declaration of war. (I mean, after you've said *Unless our terms are met forthwith, our legions shall wade in the blood of your soldiers, skewering helpless infants on the spear's point, using your women and your livestock in ways not to be named, burning your crops, laying waste your cities, and dancing through the streets with your guts for garlands, shouting "Huzzah!,"* you've said it all.)

"'P.S.,'" I read. "'Don't think you can go whining to your Underside allies. If they try to stop us, we will fight them too and you will be responsible for having plunged the Underside into a ghastly civil war. Besides, I've been able to hire a crack regiment of mercenary battle-hamsters at a discount. When they're not fighting, they're breeding. Resistance is futile. So there.'" I rolled up the scroll and said, "Woof. We're not dealing with a sane man."

"Big surprise. You're dealing with a king," Scandal said. "A king with a nagging wife. If he's not nuts from the git-go, she'll fix that. Okay, this calls for my brilliant three-step plan."

"What's that?"

"One: We take the Case of the Missing Boffin. Two: We check out the clues."

"And three?"

Scandal closed his eyes and solemnly folded his paws. "We pray."

CHAPTER ———————— 4

LUCY GOT DOWN TO THE CAT'S LEVEL. "WHAT ARE you praying for?" she asked.

Scandal opened one glowing eye. "Right now I'm praying for my pal, the Human Tortoise, to maybe stop taking it so slow-and-steady with his Majyk and use it to find Milkum and Curio. One good vision oughta do it."

"I'm not up to visions yet," I said under my breath.

"Eh?" The cat was doing his old hard-of-hearing routine again. "Speak up, sonny, I'm down one life and the eight I've got left don't hear things the way we used to."

"You heard me!" I shouted. "I don't know how to call up visions yet. It's in the chapter after summoning elementals."

"Which you also can't do yet."

I didn't need the cat to remind me of that. "We can't waste time waiting for me to learn how to conjure up visions," I said briskly. "That doesn't mean we can't buy one. As soon as the betrothal ceremony is over, we're leaving. I'll ask Uncle Corbly if I can borrow his unicorn, we'll ride straight to Grashgoboum, head for the Dregs, find us a reliable seer, and pay him to find Milkum and—"

"Kendar, come here." Lucy was at the door, beckoning.

"What—?"

"Just come along."

Puzzled, I followed her, and Scandal trotted after me. She led us into the maze of hallways and stairways and walkways and gangways that made up Uxwudge Manor. Before long, I was lost. Born and raised at Uxwudge, I'd been away from home too long. I could find my way around Master Thengor's palace, but I'd forgotten the ins and outs of my own ancestral home.

33

"Where are you taking us?" I asked as we passed through a corridor lined with portraits of Great Nannies We Have Hired (Vigorish the Master-limner is still working on his interpretation of Nanny Esplanadia. He finished it twice already, but the first painting made Dad's boar-hounds go into convulsions when they saw it, and the second try made Nanny Esplanadia go into convulsions and hit him with a potted fern).

"I'm going to give you a vision of Milkum and Curio." She stopped at a small brown door and motioned for us to pass through it. I didn't know what she was up to, but with Lucy it's generally a good idea to give her her own way. I still have the scars on my shins to show what happens when you don't.

I looked at Scandal. Scandal looked at me and did his famous feline version of a shrug. "Eh! What can we lose?" He went through the door, me following, Lucy bringing up the rear.

We came out on a minstrels' gallery, a narrow indoor balcony that ran the length of one of the shorter walls of the great hall. Below us, the guests continued to mill about, eating us out of manor and stables. Lucy jerked my arm, forcing me to hunker down beside her, hiding behind the elaborately carved stone barrier. Plump granite dwarves balanced the ivy-girt railing on their heads as they leaned out into the void. Stone fingers were jammed in stone ears, stone eyes either goggled with horror or screwed themselves tightly shut with agony. Bearded stone faces winced and grimaced. Here and there a stone hand was clamped firmly across a stone mouth to contain whatever it was stone dwarves eat for breakfast and have a hard time retaining until lunch.

The Gangle who had ordered this minstrels' gallery had a wife who adored music. He did not.

Scandal slithered between two of the eternally tortured dwarves. "Well, wrap me in a toga and call me Catullus, she was right!"

"She was?" I wedged my face between two other dwarves and peered down at the crowd.

"Uh-huh. A vision of Milkum and Curio you wanted, a vision of Milkum and Curio you got. Abracadabra, *voilà*, and bingo!" He waved his paw.

And there they were: Milkum and Curio, in the flesh. Especially Curio. They were mingling with the guests as bold as brass. For the little agent, mingling meant scuttling from one person to the next, grinning, patting everyone on the back, and pressing small pieces of stiff paper into their hands. For Curio, it meant getting cornered by Aunt Carageena and trying not to catch cold in the draft from her furiously fluttering eyelashes.

"*Lucy!*" I hissed in protest. "How did you ever get the nerve to invite them to Basehart's betrothal?"

"I didn't; Milkum did. He's got nerve he's hardly used yet. The two of them showed up at the front door over a month ago and Milkum introduced himself to Mother as my new music teacher."

"And who's Curio supposed to be? Your new piano?" Scandal asked. "Just don't try playing on his affections, nyuk-yuk-yuk."

For once, I got to give Scandal *that* look.

"Milkum introduced Curio as my new dancing master. Mother ordered rooms for them right away."

"Wait a minute," I objected. "Mom may not be too sharp, but she keeps track of the servants. Why didn't she remember that she never hired a new music teacher and dancing master?"

"She did. That was when Milkum told her Dad hired them. And when he met Dad, he told him Mother did the hiring." Lucy grew wistful. "I don't think our parents talk to each other enough anymore, Kendar."

"So was Boffin still around when they moved in here?" Scandal asked.

"Boffin used to come and go all the time. He traveled with Mysti. Mom and Dad were always happy to see them."

"*Mom* happy to see *Mysti*?" That one was too much for me. Mom *hated* Mysti.

"Mom never knew it was Mysti. Mysti always shows up at Uxwudge dressed for business."

Mysti's business is righting wrongs, defending the down-trodden, helping the helpless, and wearing shirts loose enough so that you can't tell she's a she. Also a mask. For some reason, even though there are lots of folks on Orbix willing to hire women warriors, they balk when it comes to female swash-bucklers. If a lady wants to carve out a career for herself with cold steel, it's fine as long as she sticks to chopping off heads and spilling guts on the rug. The first time she swings from the chandelier or snuffs candle flames with a rapier, she's out.

"Since when do Mom and Dad need the services of a Blade for Justice—That's Mysti's professional name; most folks just call her Blade—"at Uxwudge Manor? They're not downtrodden; they do all the downtroddening. Treading. Whatever."

"Mysti fixed that. She just took Prince Boffin on a short side-trip to Grashgoboum, where she asked King Steffan to write him up an introduction to Mom and Dad. They were thrilled to have a real live Underside prince visiting. Dad rolled out the red carpet. You know, the one he skins all the deer on so the bloodstains won't show?"

"Mmmm, smart Welfie." Scandal nodded his head in approval.

"Anyway, while Boffin and I did some work on the books, Mysti got real friendly with Dad and Basehart. They went hunting together, and afterwards Dad said he was proud to know someone even more bloodthirsty than Basehart."

"She always did have a hankering for rare meat," I said, getting nostalgic. "It was all that nectar and ambrosia they made her eat when she was living with her Welfin tribesfolk. Flower petals are a pain to chew and there's no gravy to speak of."

"In the end," Lucy continued, "Dad told his new buddy Blade to drop in any time. His home was Blade's home, even if Blade insisted on wearing that stupid mask. And Mom was crazy about the prince, so he got an any-time invitation too. I couldn't have been happier. It made everything so easy!"

"Everything including the assassin's job," Scandal said. "Or the kidnapper's. Or whatever breed of footpad poofed the Boffmeister." Lucy and I didn't contradict him. I guess we knew he was right.

"Well, at least something else is easier, too," I said, trying to make the best of things. "If Curio and Milkum have rooms at Uxwudge, maybe we can look there for some clues to Boffin's disappearance."

"Correction, brother dear," Lucy said. "You can look for clues. If I got caught in a man's room, Daddy would have a fit."

"I met your daddy. A fit would be an improvement," Scandal told her. "Okay, me and Miss Marple here will check out the rooms if you tell us where they are. In detail. This ain't exactly a two-bedroom Cape Cod fixer-upper, and Kendar can get himself lost in a broom closet."

While Lucy gave Scandal precise directions for finding the rooms Dad had assigned to the new music and dance "teachers," a niggling doubt crept into my mind.

"Do you think we'll really find any clues in their rooms?" I asked. "Maybe it's not worth the trouble. I mean, if you've just poofed a prince, you'd have to be pretty stupid to leave any evidence lying around in your own room!"

"The kid's got a point about that stupid part," Scandal said. "Okay, so we only search *Curio's* room."

And we did. Lucy gave us directions and a push to get us started. Mom had installed Curio in one of the nicer sections of Uxwudge Manor, out of the drafty towers and with a lovely view of the flower gardens. As I gazed out over the rows of nodding blossoms I realized that *my* room didn't have this nice a view. Or such a comfortable-looking bed.

"Maybe your mom likes to dance," Scandal observed. Then he grinned at me. "Sorry, pal, but when you get upset you kind of let the mind-shields slip. You know us cats: We can't help wiggling into places where we know we're not wanted. That includes your mind."

"What are you trying to say about Mom and Curio?" Dumb question. I *knew* what he meant, and it left me steaming.

"Nothing," the cat lied. "Nothingnothingnothing." He wasn't afraid of me, he just wasn't in the mood for a fight. "Now you wanna start searching or you wanna stand there looking like a wolverine who sat in a poison ivy patch?"

"You take that half, I'll take this," I mumbled, waving the cat towards the side of Curio's room with the bed. It was a big bed. It had a lot of pillows on it for just one person.

"Maybe he's gotta sleep propped up on accounta sinus troubles," Scandal put in, uninvited. I growled and wrapped my thoughts up tight.

My half of Curio's room included a big cupboard. It was carved of the finest grackwassel wood, and polished until it must've glowed in the dark. The polish made it shine, but it couldn't make it pretty. Grackwassel wood isn't very attractive. It's the sort of greenish-yellowish color that reminds people of family trips with small brothers and sisters who eat too much before they leave home and then can't stand the jouncing of the cart and—Yes, all over. You can paint grackwassel wood, you can stain it, you can soak it in whitewash or bleach or acid;

same result. No result. It holds onto that ugly color no matter what. Oh, and did I mention the smell? It smells like what it looks like. Dried herbs help . . . a little. A very little.

Still, every noble family always has at least one piece of grackwassel wood somewhere in their home. No, not because they get it for a good price. Grackwassel wood is ugly and smelly *and* expensive. There is only one thing about grackwassel wood that makes it so valuable. . . .

I summoned my Majyk to the ready, took a deep breath, and touched the cupboard door.

"Well, hel-*lo*, sailor!" the door squealed. "Oooooh, I don't remember seeing *you* around here before. I'd have remembered. I'm dreadful with names, but I never forget a touch, and you've got the touch that means soooo much. Come on, darling, don't be shy. Put your hand on my handle. Why do you think they call them 'handles,' hmmmm? Ohhhh, yes, that's how! Hold it tighter . . . *tighter*! Yes, yes, oh *yes*, that's the spot. Now pull! Ohhhhhhhh! Ummmmm! Wait! Waitwaitwait, not so *fast*, you beast! Open me slooooowly. Make it last, baby. Oh my god, my hinges are starting to turn! I'm feeling it all the way down to my mothproofing! Ahhhhh, ooooooooh, ohhhhhhh—!"

Etcetera. The thing about grackwassel wood isn't just that it talks—we've got lots of trees that can do that; no really classy funeral is complete without a weeping willow coffin to save the price of professional mourners—it's the *way* it talks. It's the things it says. If you put something valuable in a grackwassel wood chest or cupboard or box, it's safe. When a thief shows up, either the wood makes so much noise it rouses the whole house, or else it keeps *saying* those things and embarrasses the thief to death.

Fortunately, Master Thengor taught us how to deal with grackwassel wood, and that was one lesson I remembered. You didn't even need any Majyk for the job. You have to close your eyes, force yourself to stop blushing, stretch out your hands, palms outward, and say the Words of Power:

"I'll still respect you in the morning."

I heard something like a splintery snort. "Ha!" the cupboard exclaimed. "Fat chance. That's what they all say." Then it fell silent.

In the cupboard, under a stack of blank paper, I found the

first clue. "Scandal, I don't like the looks of this," I said, taking the little book out and studying the cover.

"*You* don't like the looks of this?" came the cat's voice from under the bed. Only his hindquarters were sticking out, his long tail lashing. "*I'm* nose-to-ugh with a chamber pot down here. Uh-oh, what's this? Wait a second, boss, I think I just hit paydirt." He backed out from under, holding something small and twinkly in his mouth. Very carefully he set it down on the rug. It was a tiny glass flask full of golden liquid that glowed with a familiar light.

I knelt beside the cat and stared at what he'd found. "Uh-oh," I echoed. "Now it's worse than I thought."

"How so, Mister Wizard?"

"This is Majyk."

Scandal made a short, skeptical noise. "Yeah? And where would a monument to meat like Curio get his hands on Majyk? It's not like you wizards are exactly giving it out with the Halloween candy."

"Maybe he found some wild Majyk," I theorized. "There's still a lot of it out there, masterless, free for the taking."

"Yeah, the dry cleaner left it in his jock strap by mistake. Get *real*, Kendar! You got knocked for a loop when you tried to absorb masterless Majyk, and you've had experience handling the stuff. The only thing Curio's had any experience handling is his own—"

"Hey!" I held my hand near the flask. "It doesn't tingle."

"Wozzat?"

"Whatever's in this flask doesn't make me tingle. Usually whenever I get near Majyk, I get a sparkly feeling."

"Maybe he left it open and it went flat."

I twisted my mouth. "Scandal, do you want to help me or do you want to be a standby comedian?"

"That's stand-*up* comedian. And who told you about that, Ivanhoe? I thought all you knew from entertainment on this world was hot and cold running minstrels, with maybe a public execution on Sundays."

I sat down cross-legged beside him and stroked his sleek head. He purred in spite of himself. "I do pay attention to the things you say about your homeworld, you know," I told him. "Maybe I don't understand them and maybe I don't always repeat them right, but I'm trying to learn."

I stopped petting him and he stopped purring simultaneously. "Why?" he asked. "Lots of the things I say aren't any use to you. Not here."

"Could be that some day they will be useful," I replied casually. "On your world."

The cat looked at me like I'd lost my mind. "On . . . my . . . world?" he repeated, unbelieving. "But we can't—"

"Not right now," I admitted. "Not yet. So far I haven't been able to locate a route that will take you back to your world, but not yet doesn't mean *never*."

"Aw, *boss*." Scandal sounded genuinely thankful. He rubbed his head against my hand. "You know I don't care if I never get back there. Not anymore. We're pals. Buddies. A team. We belong together. Fred and Barney, Cramden and Norton, Laurel and Hardy, Abbott and Costello, Kirk and Spock, Starsky and Hutch, Siskel and Ebert—"

"Girl cats," I reminded him.

"Oh, yeah." His whiskers drooped. "I forgot." He lifted his chin and met my eye. "But I meant what I said: I'm happy here."

"Not really happy." I could tell from his expression that I was right. "Not entirely. I don't want you to leave Orbix, but I don't want you to be lonely for your own kind."

"Hey, *yenta*, I admit I'd be happier with a female, but I can adjust," the cat said. "I've been trying, expanding my horizons, exploring new relationships. After long enough, even a voon-drab looks pretty good, but you have to take 'em out for dinner and a movie first, and you guys don't have movies."

"All I'm saying is that if—*when* I find you the way back to your world, I'd like to come along," I said. "Just for a visit. We could go through, find you that girl cat you want, and bring her back with us. What do you say?"

"I say you're about to spill the Majyk," Scandal coolly remarked.

He was right. I'd sat down cross-legged on the floor to talk with him and absent-mindedly balanced the flask of Majyk on one knee. (Velma Chiefcook will be the first to tell you that I don't have the best sense of balance on Orbix, which was how my name got changed from Kendar Dishdropper to Kendar Ratwhacker early in my kitchen career.) The glass vessel tipped over, the stopper slipped out, and a flood of Majyk drenched my lap.

"Wedwel's toes!" I swore, leaping to my feet. I automatically started dabbing at the spill with the nearest stuff I had on hand.

In hand, in this case. It was the book I'd found in Curio's cupboard.

"Get it off your lap, chief, get it off!" Scandal danced around me, stiff-legged. "I don't wanna know what'll happen if you start soaking up Majyk *there!*"

"Scandal, that's now how I soak up Majyk!" I snapped, blotting away like mad. "If you want to know—"

"I do," said a third voice, deep and sonorous as the sea. A powerful hand reached across my line of sight and closed around the sodden book. "I want to know why you are meddling with my things."

"Hel-*lo*, sailor!" the grackwassel cupboard caroled. "I'll meddle with your things any time you like!" No one had touched it, but no one had to. Some men are so easy to ignore, they might as well be furniture. Some men are so impossible to ignore, even the furniture pays attention when they come into a room.

That was Curio.

CHAPTER —————— 5

"WHOA!" SCANDAL EXCLAIMED AS HE GAZED UP AT Curio from the floor. "I didn't think you skinballs could grow anything that big without a building permit. Ask him if he does it with mirrors! No, wait, don't. I don't wanna know what he does it with."

"Scandal, quiet," I hissed out of the corner of my mouth. I had more immediate problems to deal with than a smart-aleck cat.

"Why do you take my things?" Curio asked, waving the soggy book under my nose. He didn't look angry. He didn't have to look angry. Anger is for small, weedy, insecure people who have to make a big noise and get all red in the face so other people will do what they want just to make them shut up. People like Curio know they are always going to get what they want. If they don't get it right away, they know they will only have to look beautifully melancholy until someone gives it to them. Usually that doesn't take long at all.

"I—um—I—" I felt my lower lip start to wobble.

"Do not fear me," Curio said. His big blue eyes leaked sincerity. "I mean you no harm. I am gentle. I know your feelings. You have come to me because you seek help in matters of the heart. Many do so. I am here to help you." (Strange, but when he spouted guff like that in his soft, slightly accented voice, it almost sounded like it made sense.) "It is a woman, is it not? It is always a woman. With a woman, you must be tender. A woman is like a flower, trembling with the dew. She must not be plucked roughly, but instead—"

"What are you talking about?" I blurted.

42

Curio blinked at me. "You did not come here to learn my secrets of romance?"

"No, we came here to learn your secrets of murder," Scandal piped up.

"*Scandal!*" I was so embarrassed I wanted to kill myself and kick the cat, in no particular order.

"Jeez, Poirot, don't have a cow," the cat commanded. "Mister Sexy Pecs here caught you fair and square, with your nose in his business and a lap full of his Majyk. Even I can't talk my way out of this, so we might as well come clean. Anyway, why the heck are you afraid of him? Maybe he's got you beat pound-for-pound, but you're a wizard! If that doesn't count for something, turn in your pointy hat and let's go home."

"I don't have a pointy hat," I reminded him.

"Then turn in your pointy *head*! You're a *wizard*, Kendar. Maybe not a fast one or a great one, but you're still a w-i-z-a-r-d, find out what it means to me." Sparks twinkled at the tips of Scandal's whiskers.

"Oh." For some reason, I seemed to have forgotten my powers when confronted by Curio. He *was* pretty overwhelming. Now I stiffened my spine and got ahold of my sorcerous dignity. "The cat, my familiar, is right," I informed the towering blond, staring up boldly at the underside of his chin. "I am Master Kendar, Court Wizard to His Majesty King Steffan."

For the first time, I saw a flicker of displeasure crease Curio's perfect brow. "I know who you are," he said, his voice rumbling low. "We have met before this, in your sister's rooms, while she and I were working on a book. You did not seem so powerful or proud then."

"And you did not seem so"—I fumbled for words— "clothed then."

The crease deepened. "Perhaps you are unaware of a wise saying that is said by many people famed for their wisdom." Curio's upper lip curled into a sneer I'd last seen on the cover of *My Welfie, My Wanton*. (Lucy told me that sneer alone sold ten thousand extra copies of the book.) "It goes: 'Do not meddle in the affairs of models, for they are subtle and look better than you do.'"

"Even when they're murdering each other?" I countered.

Curio's famous upper lip twitched in a way that would have

sold *twenty* thousand extra books if an artist had been there to capture it. "I have harmed no one. I am gentle. I am a sensitive man. Women yearn for tenderness and delicacy. They do not like blood and violence."

"Spoken like a man who never met your ex-wife," Scandal commented.

"Why would I want to murder anyone?" Curio went on.

"Why would you want to have *this* hidden away in your cupboard?" I snatched the dripping book from his hands triumphantly. He made a half-hearted grab for it, then thought better of it.

"It is just something I read to pass the time," he said with a shrug. "It helps me get to sleep."

I showed him the title page. "*To Ridde Yourself of Rivalles?* That's not the sort of bedtime book most people choose."

"Give it up, big guy," Scandal said, pacing in front of Curio. "We know all about you and Prince Boffin. All we want is to find out what you did with him. For your own sake, he better be alive."

"Alive?" came a new voice from the doorway. "I'll say he'd better be alive!" Milkum, agent and publisher extraordinary, burst into the room. He was alone, but he still gave the impression of being a crowd. It must have been that hustle-bustle air about him. I never knew one man to be in so many places at the same time.

"Who's dead? Who are you saying's dead? No one's dead!" he yattered, darting from me to Curio and back to me again. "Who? Prince Boffin? Lovely boy. Such a face! A real future in the business. Not much sense, though. Business sense, that is. A model's career only lasts as long as his looks. The smart ones always get an agent. The publishers'll skin you alive if you don't have a good agent in your corner."

"But Milkum, you're a publisher, too," I pointed out. "You publish all of Lucy's books at Full Court Press."

"Did I say I didn't? When did I say I didn't?" He appealed to Curio. "Did *you* hear me say I didn't? So I'm a good businessman. Is this a crime? Someone tell me this is a crime!"

"This is a crime," Scandal said cheerfully. Milkum scowled at him. "Just trying to be helpful."

"*Silence!*" I shouted, and clapped my hands together above my head, summoning up a tremendous peal of thunder.

Except I hadn't learned how to summon up thunder yet, so all we heard was the sound of two hands clapping. At least it was loud enough to make everyone be quiet.

"Listen to me," I told Curio and Milkum. "I know all about why both of you would want to get Prince Boffin out of the way. You"—I leveled a finger at Curio—"were jealous because he was doing better as a model for Raptura Eglantine books than you were. You"—it was Milkum's turn as my target—"were angry because you couldn't make any money as Boffin's agent and you were losing money as Curio's. Well, I don't care if you did it together or if only one of you was involved. That's not important. What *is* important is that Prince Boffin show up again, real soon and real alive."

I went on to explain to them that if he didn't, it meant real war.

"War . . ." Milkum bit his lower lip. "War is great for book sales." Scandal bit him on the leg.

While Milkum hopped around the room, howling, Curio beckoned me closer. I didn't see how I *could* get any closer. We were standing right next to each other already. In a low, conspiratorial tone he told me, "My friend, you have the wrong bushpig by the tail. I did not envy Prince Boffin. He was no rival of mine. You see, I am no longer merely a model. I have found my true calling. I am going to use all the talents that Lipo, Goddess of Firm Thighs and Eternal Contentment, has blessed me with."

"You're gonna become a paperweight?" Scandal asked.

"I am going to become a writer." Curio lowered his long lashes modestly.

"Same difference," the cat decided.

"Then how do you explain *this*?" I waved the book at him again. "And I found that flask of Majyk under your bed, too!" I stooped and picked it up. After my little . . . accident it was almost empty, but it was good enough to get my point across. "Where did you get it? Did you use it on Prince Boffin? Look, if you confess now and tell me where to find him, we can undo any spell you might have used on him, tell his parents he's all right, the war gets called off, and no one gets hurt. I'd call that a fair deal."

Curio only smiled. "Because life is not fair, you must treat every woman more than fairly, to make it up to her. A woman is like a treacledove, sweet and shy, easily frightened—"

"—and tasty with gravy and a side of spuds," Scandal finished for him.

"You have to excuse Curio." Milkum came limping back to join us. "Sometimes he has a hard time making himself understood. He's not from this kingdom, you know."

"I don't think he's from this planet," the cat said.

"Curio hails from Alfresco, a small city-state to the northeast of Vicinity City. It used to be a major trading center before the barbarian hordes of Uk-Uk the Unspeakable overran most of the lands to the east, cutting off all commerce. And then, of course, Vicinity City was swept up in The Troubles."

"Of course," I muttered, looking pained. No one in Grashgoboum liked to think about The Troubles.

"So for a boy whose native tongue is *Rigati*, I'd say Curio does pretty well speaking *Lingween*," Milkum concluded, patting the big blond on the back. He had to stand on his toes to reach that high.

"It was nothing." Curio brushed aside his agent's praise. "Lingween is, after all, a merchants' language, and my own people used to be fabulous merchants. Why, we have thirty-seven separate words for—how do you say it in Lingween?— sucker."

"And you're trying to use all thirty-seven of them on Kendar." Scandal jumped onto the bed. "How come you keep talking about Prince Boffin in the past tense, huh? The whole thing smells worse than yesterday's voondrabs. Tell us what you did with him or we go straight to King Steffan! He doesn't want war with the Underside, and if he can prevent it by sending Boffin's daddy your heads, he'll do it. Heck, he'll send 'em bronzed and gift-wrapped!"

"You can't prove a thing," Milkum replied.

"This is King Steffan we're talking about," the cat shot back. "He's got a funny attitude about proof. If he believes something's so, he chops off heads first and asks for proof after. His favorite word is 'Oops!'"

"Well?" I asked, following up the cat's advantage. "What's it going to be? Either you tell us about Prince Boffin or we tell King Steffan about you."

Curio folded his arms. "I do not think you will tell tales to the king. He is a great fan of Raptura Eglantine romances, is he not?"

I had to admit that was true, but I didn't see what that had to do with the situation. Curio let me know.

"If you go to King Steffan and accuse me of having harmed Prince Boffin, I will go to your father and tell him your sister's secret: that she *is* Raptura Eglantine. What do you think will happen then?"

I knew: Dad thought it was shameful for a girl to *read* books. Girls should only read recipes, family histories, and instruction lists of Things To Do from their fathers and husbands. But a girl *writing* books? *These* books? Books with so little bloodshed and so much—? Dad would blow up first, put his foot down second. Raptura Eglantine's career would be right under that foot.

"Aw, the big lug'll never do it." Scandal waved away Curio's counterthreat. "Without Raptura Eglantine, he'd be out of a job."

"I will write my own books and pose for my own covers," Curio replied coolly. "And I will sell many, many copies, because I understand women. A woman is like a high-spirited young mare, who balks at change but eventually may be led around by the nose if you offer her enough sugar."

"Fine, *tell* Dad about Lucy!" I sputtered. "Even if you do, the king outranks him. He can order Dad to leave Lucy alone and let her keep on writing. And when I tell him that Lucy is really Raptura Eglantine, he'll—"

"You can lead an author to the paper, but you cannot make her auth," Curio said archly. "Lucy has often told us that she prefers to keep her career secret. For some reason, she is afraid her friends and relatives would laugh at her."

"They would not!"

"Drop it, boss; you know they would." Scandal pawed my leg. He had jumped off the bed and come over to make his stand beside me. "They'd laugh loud, they'd laugh long, and then they'd say it was so *cute* that little Lucy Gangle was really Raptura Eglantine. And then they'd take your mother aside and ask her if she knew her little girl was writing *that* kind of stuff, and where did Lucy ever learn so much about bosoms and loins and moist, ripe, trembling—"

"Enough." I bowed my head. Scandal had hit it dead on.

Even if the king stepped in, even if he forbade Dad to interfere with Lucy's writing, Mom would still be there. Mom would take care of it but good. Mom would say things like, "Are you *sure* you want to write it that way?" and "Well, I'm no expert on your little writing-thing, I'm only the woman who gave birth to you in agony, but do you *really* think it's nice for an unmarried girl to talk about things that go thrust in the night?" and "Darling, *I* know what! In your next book, why don't you write about that funny thing that happened to Cousin Dinovia when she was visiting Lesser Summat? I promised her you would."

No offense to Aunt Carageena and Aunt Glucosia, but when you stood their swordswomanship next to Mom's powers of destruction, they came out looking like amateurs.

I felt a strong hand pat me on the back. "Do not be downhearted, my friend," Curio said. "If I laugh at your threats, that is not your fault. I come from Alfresco, where the fine art of threat and counterthreat was taught to me at my mother's knee. I can spot a hollow one from leagues away."

"You know what's gonna be hollow, Curio?" Scandal asked pleasantly. "You. Once the Council of Wizards shows up and nails you on a three-oh-six—slinging Majyk without a license—they'll take your skin and a trained iguana and—"

"That's right," I added, glad to have the upper hand with Curio again. "No one but a wizard's supposed to fool around with Majyk."

"Majyk?" Curio's brow was going to need about a week of mud packs to restore its former smoothness. "I have heard tales of this Majyk from my childhood. It is a thing that belongs to wizards alone. I would not dare to trifle with it. *I* do not go meddling with the belongings of others." He dropped his last few words one by one, smack on my head like a stack of flat rocks.

"Oh yeah? Then what's this?" I shook the book and the empty flask at him harder than ever, sure of myself.

"May I?" Before I could protest, Curio took the book from my hand and held it over the mouth of the flask. With a swift twist of the wrists, he wrung a long, thin stream of golden liquid from the pages. It trickled right into the flask, not a drop missing. He searched out the strayed stopper and popped it back in place. "You may keep whatever soaked into your britches," he drawled. "I am sure you do not have that much in them."

"You leave my britches out of this!" I shouted.

"Okay, sweetcakes, so you've proved you're a showoff," Scandal said. "So you can make that little dab of Majyk obey you. So what? It's still Majyk and you're still not a wizard. As far as the Council's concerned—"

"I have already told you," Curio protested. "I have nothing to do with Majyk."

"Then what's in the bottle? What was soaked into that book?" The cat bounced on all fours, his fur one huge sizzle and sparkle. "What's in Kendar's britches?"

"Scandal!"

"*Magique.*"

CHAPTER ———————— 6

SOMEHOW, WE ALL MANAGED TO MAKE OUR WAY back down to the great hall without strangling each other and without Curio mussing his hair. There was something about the way he kept running his fingers through his long, blond mane that was insufferably smug. I wanted to part those golden locks with an axe, but after what he'd told us, I couldn't. You can't kill an innocent man.

Well, you can if you're a barbarian, or a king, or my dad, but *I* can't.

Still, is an innocent man the same thing as a man you can't prove is guilty? I had my doubts. For one thing, after it's all over, an innocent man does one of two things: Either he tells his accusers that it's all right, mistakes will happen, let bygones be bygone, no harm done, ha-ha, or else he gets furious, goes berserk, grabs the nearest heavy object, and tries to bean anyone and everyone who so much as *hinted* he'd committed the crime. That's it, two choices, pick one.

Gloating is not an option. Gloating is for when you know you're guilty but you got away with it and made your accusers look like seven kinds of fool. Curio was gloating.

And what *had* Curio told us in his own defense, to clear his name of any Majyk-misuse charges? "You see, Kendar, there is magic, and there is Majyk, and then there is Magique. Is that clear?"

Clear, yeah, right; clear as slimegrind hash. I think I said "Uh-huh" in an intelligent manner.

"What my pal is trying to tell you is he doesn't have a clue," Scandal translated. "You wanna run that past him again close-captioned for the smarts-impaired?"

"And I suppose *you* know what he's talking about?" I snapped at the cat.

"Haven't the faintest," Scandal replied affably. "But at least I'm not pretending I understand when I don't. I'll bet you did that in class, too."

What could I say? He was right. As a student at Master Thengor's Academy of High Wizardry, I'd sit at my desk looking smart and eager while Master Thengor lectured us about spells and curses and wand-waving techniques. He ended every lecture by asking, "Are there any questions?"

Questions? I had plenty, beginning with *What were you talking about?* and ending with *Why do I feel so stupid?* But I was all alone. No one else raised a hand, and I didn't want my classmates to think I was the only dope, so I didn't ask a thing. The result was I never learned a thing either, and I was still the only dope anyway.

"What Curio means," said Milkum, "is he hasn't been fooling around with wizard's business. I've been in the publishing game a long time. About five years ago, Full Court Press brought out a special edition of Master Thengor's autobiography. Maybe you heard of it? *Death, Destruction, and No Living Enemies: The Story of a Humble Country Wizard.* I worked with Master Thengor on the book. The old guy could turn a sea serpent into a sausage with one twitch of his eyebrow, but he couldn't put together a decent paragraph to save his life. Anyhow, that's how I learned the difference between magic and Majyk. You wizards need Majyk if you want to work magic, am I right?"

"How should I know?" Scandal asked mildly. "Magic and Majyk sound alike, and you don't need magic to work Majyk."

"Whatever." Milkum was a publisher and an agent. Lucy said he had a tongue greased at both ends and hung in the middle. One sassy cat wasn't going to throw him off his stride. "As a matter of fact, that book is how come Curio knows the difference between Majyk and magic, no matter what else he tells you."

"Curio helped Master Thengor write the book?" I asked.

"Curio *was* Master Thengor," Milkum told me. "On the cover. Something about wizards not wanting their true images out where their enemies could see them."

"Something about Master Thengor looking like a dried-up

old mushroom instead of a side of prime beef," Scandal suggested.

"All right, the two of you know about Majyk and magic," I said. "Now what's this other stuff?" I was still holding onto that flask.

"I told you," Curio said. "It is Magique."

The word sounded just different enough from *Majyk* for me to keep my temper. "Yeah, but what *is* Magique?" I asked, doing my best to mimic Curio's pronunciation.

"Oh, it's nothing, nothing at all!" Milkum broke in so quickly I smelled a rat. For once I was eager to whack it. "Just a toy, a hobby, a trifle. What do you need to know about it, Master Kendar? You're a *real* wizard, the greatest wizard in Orbix. This isn't for *you*."

Scandal fixed Milkum with the old hairy eyeball. "I've got a good idea: You try telling Master Kendar what is and isn't for him one more time and Master Kendar will see how you look small, green, and warty."

Milkum told us about Magique so fast, Scandal had to bite his ankle to make him slow down.

"You know Cheeseburgh?" Milkum asked.

"One of the most picturesque little plague spots on Orbix," Scandal said. "We've got a friend who's a witch who lives in the neighborhood, name of Mother Toadbreath."

"She's not behind this Magique stuff, is she?" I asked. Witches, as Mother Toadbreath herself explained to me, do not rely on Majyk. Witches . . . *manage*. Mother Toadbreath worked her spells thanks to kettles and kettles full of special soap. Each soap was unique, each combination of herbal ingredients capable of working its own wonders. They had to be compounded and cooked *just so*, and the witch had to observe every step of the soap-making process or they wouldn't work. No one was allowed to disturb Mother Toadbreath while she was watching her soaps.

"Toadbreath?" Milkum considered. "Never heard of her."

"Awww, c'mon, Uncle Milkie," Scandal drawled. "Cheeseburgh's about as big as a glob of weasel spit, and half as pretty. You know one Cheeseburgher, you know 'em all."

"That's how it used to be," the agent replied. "But there's been a lot of growth in Cheeseburgh this past year. They got a new mayor, a real go-getter, and he's been encouraging all sorts of changes in the town."

"*Town*?" I echoed. "Cheeseburgh's just a village. It may be big enough to support *three* village idiots, but—"

"Two," Scandal corrected me. "Lorrinz and Wot may still be on the job, but Evvon went into government work, remember?"

"Cheeseburgh is a *town* now," Milkum insisted. "It's all thanks to the new mayor."

"Yeah?" Anyone who could drag Cheeseburgh out of the slime and up into the mud must be someone special. "Gee, I'd like to meet him."

"Great guy," Milkum agreed. "Nice steady family man, name of Zoltan Fiendlord."

I uttered a groan from the heart. Milkum give me a funny look.

"They've met," Scandal said, by way of explanation.

Oh yes, we'd met. Zoltan used to be Master Thengor's best student—and, some said, his illegitimate son. He thought he was going to inherit all the old wizard's hoard of Majyk until my accident turned his whole world topsy-turvy. When he couldn't separate me from my Majyk, he tried to separate me from my life. He'd lost that battle and the Council of Wizards had him stripped of his own Majyk and condemned to marry his pregnant kitchen-wench girlfriend, Bini. (Bini adored Zoltan. Other than that, she was a sensible girl.)

"Well, in any case," Milkum went on, still eyeing me strangely, "not so long ago a lovely young couple moved into town. They took a house on the square and started selling *this*." He pointed at the flask full of Maj—I mean *Magique*. "Pretty soon word got around: Magique could change your life. Not in any big ways, but it was mighty handy stuff for certain small, unpleasant tasks."

"Like ridding yourself of rivals?" Scandal asked archly.

"I have no rivals," said Curio.

"Yeah, *now*."

Milkum snorted. "Don't be silly. King Steffan and the Council would hear soon enough if Magique could be used for evil purposes. As a matter of fact, it wasn't too long after that nice young couple opened up shop that one of your hoity-toity Council wizards showed up on their doorstep to investigate. They passed inspection like that"—Milkum snapped his fingers—"and the wizard took home two flasks of Magique and a matched set of bushpig-hide luggage as a special get-acquainted offer."

"If it's not Majyk, the Council does not mind," Curio said with a devastating smirk. "Why should you?"

Why? Because Council or no Council, Prince Boffin was missing and I'd be willing to bet my last *gabor* that Curio had a beautifully manicured hand in it. Something smelled worse than Scandal's breakfast. The only hitch was, I couldn't hang Curio from my suspicions.

Whether Curio was innocent or guilty or just plain sly and lucky, we had to go downstairs. The betrothal ceremony was about to begin and they couldn't start without me. Mom would have my head if I kept her guests waiting, no excuses. Mom has a lot of things in common with King Steffan, especially when it comes to chopping off people's heads.

We got there just in time. I could tell by the color of Dad's face. When I'm really late for an important event, it turns crimson, and when I'm really, *really* late, it turns purple. If I forget about the event entirely, Lucy tells me it turns black or green (depending on how important an event I've missed), but she might be teasing. Anyway, when we came in, Dad's face was merely scarlet, so I was hardly late at all.

"Where have you been, boy? We've been waitin'," Dad growled. He stood behind Basehart with Mom, all of them arranged to one side of the family's portable altar.

(We Gangles are strictly Orthodox Wedwellians, and we don't believe in any other gods. Wedwel is it. Therefore, whenever a Gangle marries a stubbornly wrong-minded, foolish and bone-ignorant non-Wedwellian, we cannot conduct the service in the family chapel. That would pollute, desecrate, and defile it, unless the other person's family has lots more money than we do, in which case Wedwel will look the other way if they offer up a sacrifice of three cows and an emerald necklace for Mom. Wedwel the All-Compassionate Destroyer is an understanding god if you don't push your luck and if the emeralds are big enough.)

(All non-Wedwellians are still going to burn forever in one of Wedwel's many painful and creative Hells for Unbelievers, though. There are never enough cows to make him overlook the chance to show off for the Faithful.)

"Kendar, what have you been doing all this time? You're not even *ready*!" Mom whined.

Luckily for me, Lucy came rushing up with my ceremonial

garb. Unmarried girls are not allowed to take part in betrothal rites. As the great Wedwellian scholar, Orvis IX, once said, "It is not good to give maidens Ideas. They get quite enough of those on their own. However, they are free to clean up after the ritual, thereby acquiring much merit."

"Any luck?" she whispered as she helped me slip on my wyvern-skin cape and crown of whoops-there-she-goes flowers.

"All bad," I whispered back. "I'll tell you later." Lucy nodded and retreated to her place among the guests.

"All right, everyone ready to go?" Dad asked cheerfully. Across the altar, Sir Megrim and Lady Teluria flanked their daughter. Basehart's bride to-be was covered in a pale blue veil, head to foot. The only thing peeking out was her nose, and not too much of that.

"We can't start yet, Lucius," Sir Megrim said. "Where's the biffin' priest?"

"We Wedwellians don't use priests," Dad informed him.

"Then how do you know whether or not your prayers are the ones your god wants to hear?"

"Oh, we Wedwellians have conventions every so often and give reports about which ones worked and which ones didn't. Then we go have a drink and make up some new ones. 'Course if Wedwel in his infinite mercy blasts a fella off the face of Orbix, you can bet your britches we don't try using none o' *his* prayers any too soon!"

Sir Megrim looked at his wife, but all Lady Teluria said was, "Don't blame me. *You* wanted to join up the real estate."

The ceremony began. We're proud of our portable altar. It's a big cube of wood filled with drawers and doors, the front carved with a grinning face (Wedwel's first prophet, Axl), with wheels that look like giant sunbursts. The whole thing is painted with instructive scenes like the Evaluation of the Virgins, Saint Mangonel Preaching to the Giant Horned Hamsters, the Martyrdom of Saint Mangonel, and the Vision of the Holy Chalk.

This last scene contained a very nice miniature of my ancestor, Lord Plebiscite Uprising Gangle. He knelt before the Vision of the Holy Chalk, his hands steepled in prayer. Looped over his fingertips was one end of a leash which ran to the collar of a scrawny man huddled in the shelter of a bush. The captive glared over his shoulder at Lord Plebiscite while scribbling something on a sheet of parchment before him. If you got close enough you could see the words:

"I, Valdostino the Limner, Made This. He, Lord Plesbiscite, Paid for It. That is the Only Reason why I put that Fat Boor into this Painting, thus Cocking Up what might Otherwise have been my Masterpiece. He Forced me to make him look Handsome, too! The Swine. In Truth, he looks like a Ruptured Walrus. I Hate his Guts, but What Can I Do? The [illegible] has my [illegible] in a Nutcracker. I Think I Will Go Sleep with His Wife. Up [illegible] with a Fishfork."

I positioned myself right behind the altar, between the two families, and cleared my throat. "My friends," I said, "we have gathered here to witness the betrothal of the stainless, pure, and guaranteed inexperienced maiden Dulcetta to the virile, potent, and certified carnally expert man Basehart."

I opened one of the drawers in the altar and extracted the parchments proving my words: a signed and witnessed report of Dulcetta's examination by a reputable midwife and a much beer-stained affidavit of Basehart's ritual week-long incarceration in Madam Ecoli's House of Unspeakable Ecstasy and Gawfee Shoppe. From another drawer I produced a vial of attar of otter, sprinkled the rolled-up documents, and waved them to the five and a half sacred directions. Meanwhile, Aunt Glucosia led in Dad's prize hog, Pixie. I was supposed to offer the parchments to the beast and coax her to eat them, but Pixie was so eager she leaped for them, mouth agape, and almost gobbled up my arm too. The crowd cheered.

"May this be a sign that the match is acceptable in Wedwel's eyes," I intoned rather shakily, counting my swine-drool-coated fingers. "And proof that we mean business. There will be no refunds after this point in the ceremony."

Lady Teluria sighed and rolled her eyes.

With that, Basehart reached his hand across the altar, and Dulcetta's mother extended an unidentifiable, heavily veiled part of the bride to-be. (It's supposed to be the girl's hand, but our scriptures tell the story of a groom who rejected his bride, Wedwel's own beloved daughter, just because she took after Daddy and had tentacles. This brought Wedwel's displeasure down on everyone and everything within the borders of seven kingdoms. From then on, all brides have been veiled from the betrothal ceremony because, as the sages say, *Looks aren't*

*everything, especially when compared to a plague of fish and
leeches.*) I took a small clay pot full of millet from yet another
drawer and sprinkled it over their clasped hands, then opened
the door in the altar and pulled out—

"A rappid?" I held the snowy creature by the scruff of its
neck and gave Dad a look of total confusion.

"Couldn't find any doves," Dad grumped in a tone that
implied it was all my fault. "Go on, boy, you're the great,
famous, all-blimmin'-powerful wizard, ain't'cha? Turn it into a
dove, then!"

"I can't!" I protested. "I don't know any transformation
spells."

"Hmph!" Dad blew a scornful breath through his huge
moustache. "After all the braggin' and la-de-da carryin' yerself
like you was better'n we, you can't even change one little
rappid into a dove? Some wizard, I'll be bound!"

"Dad, I never acted like I was better than—"

"Can we get *on* with this?" Basehart demanded. "This is just
the betrothal. We've still got to get through the wedding. I don't
want to stand here holding Dulcetta's hand forever, you know!"

A tiny sound—perhaps a whimper—seemed to come from
under Dulcetta's veil. Basehart ignored it.

"Just do your best with what you've got, darling," Mom
whispered to me. "Don't worry; no one expects too much of
you."

I took comfort from that. I think. Holding the rappid high, I
announced, "Behold the sealing of the bond!" I placed the
rappid on the altar, its twitchy nose a finger-width away from
all that millet. At this point in the ceremony, the dove is
supposed to peck up the seeds. The more the animal eats, the
better the omens for the marriage. I told myself that rappids
like millet too, so it would all turn out fine.

"*Ow!*" Basehart screamed as the rappid bit his hand. (I don't
know what the omens for the marriage are if the animal eats
part of the intended groom.) In a rage, my brother drew his
sword and whacked it down on the altar. He missed the rappid,
who hopped off into the crowd and was lost, but he did manage
to slash off a piece of Dulcetta's veil.

"Basehart, you twit!" Dad bawled, yanking him back by the
collar. "Cut off the girl's hand and we'll be payin' back half the
dowry in damages!"

"I'm all right," Dulcetta's sweet, reedy voice piped from under her layers of shrouding. "Really I am. Please don't make a fuss. Basehart didn't mean to do it."

"Of *course* I didn't mean to do it!" Basehart yelled at her. "Wedwel's left eyebrow, Dulcie, what a stupid thing to say! If I'd meant to lop off your hand, I'd've done it!"

"Yes, Basehart dear," his betrothed murmured.

Basehart was not assuaged. "You want everyone to think my aim's no better than that?" He waved at the guests.

"No, Basehart dear," Dulcetta said in an even smaller and meeker voice.

"A fine thing," my brother growled, wrapping his bitten hand in the scrap he'd sliced from Dulcetta's veil. "Not even married to the girl yet and already she's embarrassing me in public."

Dulcetta began to sniffle. I made a private vow that if I ever learned how to work transformation spells, Basehart was going to be my first victim—I mean, *subject*. I'd turn him into a human being and no one would ever recognize him again.

"Well, who wants cookies?" Mom asked brightly, and the betrothal ceremony was done. Now preparations for the wedding itself began. (We Gangles don't believe in long betrothals; this prevents escapes.)

One group of servants passed among the guests with trays of light refreshments while another wheeled in a huge table with the ceremonial wedding foods on it. There was the oatcake of Prosperity, the pomegranate pie of Fertility, the whole barbecued cow of Domestic Tranquility, and of course Wedwel's sacred bean dip. A third body of Gangle retainers lined up against the wall, armed with mops and buckets, waiting. The post-wedding rites were messy and included the bride smashing the oatcake over the groom's head, the groom throwing the pomegranate pie in the bride's face, and both sides of the immediate families trying to pull the cow apart with their bare hands. No one could quite recall what to do with the bean dip.

"A Blaaaaaaade fooooooor Justiiiiiiiicccccce!"

With a long, loud, yodeling cry, a caped and masked figure came swinging down out of the great hall rafters on a silken cord.

Silk is slippery. You can't get a good grip on it with black leather gloves. There was a shriek from the masked interloper, a gasp from the crowd, and a loud *splorch!*

Mysti had figured out what to do with the bean dip.

CHAPTER ——————— 7

"BLADE, OL' THING!" DAD BELLOWED JOYOUSLY, GIV-
ing Mysti a hand out of the dip. "Good to see you! Smashin'!
Aye, that's it, we'll go out smashin' things as soon as I get this
son of mine married off."

"Aw, Dad, I wanna come smashin' too!" Basehart whined.

"Not on yer weddin' night, lad." Dad whomped Basehart on
the back. "Better things to do then, eh?" Then, seeing the look
of disappointment in Basehart's piggy little eyes he added,
"Oh, all right. You only have to spend ten minutes with the lass,
but if you're not done by then, we're leavin' without you."

"I'll be ready, Dad!" my brother said, his face all smiles.

"I wager you will be. They fed the betrothal documents to
the wrong hog," said a slightly accented voice behind me. I
glanced over one shoulder and saw Curio regarding Basehart
with a look of disgust. Then his eyes drifted towards Dulcetta
and his expression changed in a disturbing way.

With Dad and Basehart hauling at either arm, Mysti was
soon on her feet, scraping globs of Wedwel's sacred bean dip
off her rump. Mom hurried forward to mop up the mess with a
damp servant.

While supervising the cleaning, Mom chirped, "It's so nice
to have you with us again, Blade, dear. You've missed the
betrothal but you *must* stay for the wedding." (Yup, Lucy was
right; the warm welcome Mom was slathering all over Blade
was proof enough she hadn't a clue that the masked swordsman
was really my ex-wife, Mysti.) "I'll just have Thorgit bring in
a few more haunches of venison for the buffet—it's a simple
little celebration really. We Gangles have never liked to show

off in front of the less fortunate." She gestured at the assembled guests, the multiple rings on all her fingers twinkling.

"I won't be staying." Mysti let the words fall like boulders down a well.

"No? Oh my." Mom was severely disappointed. "Can't I tempt you?"

Mysti's eyes were two slits of ice under the black full-face mask she always wore as Blade. "There is no temptation great enough to swerve me from my appointed path. I am on . . . a quest." (Welfies have a special way of pronouncing *quest* so that it carries the same impact as dropping a musk ox on the hearer's head.)

"That's nice, dear." Mom does not allow musk oxen in the house. "Want a cookie?"

"I want Prince Boffin." A murmur rippled through the crowd at her words. "And I want him *now!*" The murmur swelled to a mutter.

"Mercy, Blade, you sound angry," Mom said. "Has he done something wrong?"

"Wrong has been done to *him,*" Mysti replied, her hand closing around the hilt of her sword. I hoped that scabbard was bean-dip-proof or she was going to get a nasty surprise when she drew steel. "I last saw him in the Bunch of Relatives tavern, in Grashgoboum. He had just received a message summoning him to Uxwudge Manor."

Mom nibbled the tip of one finger in thought. "*I* didn't send him any message. Did *you* send him a message, Lucius?"

"Whuffo?" Dad asked. "You know as well as I that him and Blade've got a drop-in-any-time standing by their names, Abstemia. What'd they need a special invite for, eh?"

I knew whuffo; so did Lucy. Prince Boffin would be summoned to Uxwudge any time Lucy needed to confer with him about a Raptura Eglantine cover. Yes, that was *all* they conferred about. I knew my sister: Lucy was a practical romantic who understood how the world works. You don't mix business and pleasure unless you want to wind up with neither.

Lucy also knew that an angry Mysti might very well forget that Lucy's literary career must be kept shrouded in secrecy from Mom and Dad. The Welfie could very well blurt out everything about Prince Boffin's connection with "Raptura Eglantine" if someone didn't say something fast.

"It must have been a mistake!" Lucy exclaimed.

"A *mistake* . . ." Mysti put a good portion of dropped musk ox into that word, too. "Aye. Some might call it that. He left the tavern. I was detained on business—a small matter of restoring the statuette of a black falcon to its rightful owner—else I would surely have accompanied him. The whole falcon business proved to be a wild goose chase, although I suspected nothing. I followed Prince Boffin as soon as I could, only to discover he had never reached Uxwudge."

"Oh, so *that's* why you were so mopey the last time you came to see us." Mom petted Mysti on the shoulder. "I remember, you hardly touched your roast boar, and Maisree had taken special pains to leave it nice and blood-rare for you, just the way you like it."

"That is *not* a good idea," Scandal whispered to me.

"What's not?"

"Blood-rare boar. Trichinosis."

"Oh, that's all right, we Gangles generally give the noses of all wild game to the servants. Maisree makes a delicious snout stew. Nothing too tricky about that."

Scandal looked at the rafters. "Help?" he requested in a very small voice.

Sometimes I just don't understand cats.

"Well, if Boffin ain't with you and he ain't with us and we never sent for him in the first place, where under Wedwel's third nostril *is* he?" Dad wanted to know.

"Indeed," Mysti agreed with him. "You are certain you have not seen him here since our last visit together?"

"We haven't seen him for ages," Mom reassured her. "We assumed you'd retraced your steps, run into him somewhere on the road, and the two of you were traveling together again. You *are* such good friends."

"We are more than friends," Mysti said. "Much more." The way she said *friends* left all her previous weighty-and-significant words looking light and frothy as a handful of soapsuds. There was no mistaking her meaning. I know. I watched Dad try hard to mistake it and fail completely.

And in case that wasn't enough, a tear trickled out from under Mysti's mask and she added, "If anything has happened to my darling, I'll die."

There came the sound of every guest in the hall filling their lungs with one great gasp of shock, followed by a mass exhalation and a thunderous *clack!* of many, many jaws snapping shut so that many, many tongues might be bitten.

Somewhere, someone began to hum in a deliberately non-chalant manner. A low snicker crept into one corner of the hall and grew into the tired old joke about what the knight said to his squire when they were trapped on a desert island with three pillows and a dachshund.

All eyes were fixed on Blade.

I know it was impossible for me to tell with that mask she had on, but somehow I was positive that a look of dawning horror was inching its way over Mysti's face as she realized what she'd just said. Her hand fell from the hilt of her sword and rose to her lips. "Oops," she said.

"There, there, Blade dear," Mom said, embracing Mysti warmly. "We don't mind. We Gangles have always been very open-minded."

"Hmph! You Gangles would have to be," Lady Teluria sniffed. She gave her husband a killing look. "And *you* told me those were just nasty rumors about Demijohn Sidesaddle Gangle and Sir Coverdi Rajali!"

"Here!" Uncle Corbly Guzzle burst to the fore, shaking a fist at the stubby Lady Teluria. "You mind what you say about young Demijohn. He used to be my 'prentice, and a finer unicorn wrangler never drew breath. Those stories was just vicious rumors put about by jealous folk when he was named Imperial Unicorn Keeper to His Imperceptible Majesty, the Mystic Emperor Abadaba the Fourth."

"There *is* no Mystic Emperor Abadaba the Fourth!" Lady Teluria snapped. "No one's ever seen him or his so-called empire!"

"That's what *some* would like you to believe." Uncle Corbly laid a gnarled finger beside his nose and looked wise. "Just because him and the Mystic Empire's both invisible don't necessarily mean they ain't there."

"Spoken like a man who'd buy a pig in a poke," Dulcetta's mother sneered.

"Spoke like a woman who never had to find a sour-stomached unicorn in the dark," Uncle Corbly replied.

All around me, I heard our guests dredging up stories about this Gangle lord or that Guzzle squire who had been a little too friendly with his schoolmates, or spent too much time in the company of well-muscled gardeners, or was seen to let his hand linger a moment too long on his stableboy's shoulder while getting a leg-up on his hunting horse. I never knew I had so many ancestors who were watched so very closely by so many idiots with nothing better to do. I tried to take charge of the situation. It was like a lizard trying to turn a herd of stampeding horses.

"Stop it, all of you!" I shouted, and threw in a few Majykal fireworks to get them to pay attention. I guess the price of attention has gone up, because it didn't work. The love of gossip is stronger than the fear of wizardry. "You're making a fuss over nothing! None of you realize that Blade is really—"

Mysti leaped forward and clapped one black-gloved hand across my mouth as she dragged me off into a corner.

"Oooooh, *fickle*," someone tittered.

"Don't tell them I'm female," Mysti hissed in my ear.

"Why not? You know what they think you are *now*?"

"And what though I were in truth what their fancy presently prefigures me to be?" she countered.

"Huh?" Sometimes Mysti lapses into High Welventongue style. Then it takes a dictionary, a grammar book, and a road map to follow her.

"What if I were really a man—instead of just masquerading as one—and also the *very good friend* of Prince Boffin?" she translated. "Would you like me less for that?"

"Mmmmmnnnnnooooo," I said, pretty sure I meant it. "I never would've married you, though."

"For all the difference *that* made." Mysti's smile was wistful. "Kendar, keep my secret. I don't care what this rabble thinks of me and neither should you. But if they find out I'm female, that's the end of a Blade for Justice."

"You mean you'll put up with all these snide remarks and stable-jokes just so you can hold onto a career of chandelier-swinging?" I couldn't believe it.

"How many have to put up with the same rubbish all the time, and no way out?" Mysti murmured. She stepped away from me, but her eyes continued to beg for my silence.

Meanwhile, things had grown more heated around the family altar.

"Your younger son is awfully chummy with Prince Boffin's . . . *friend*," Lady Teluria mewed.

Scandal bounced up onto the altar. "Aw, that's nothing," he said, with a sweeping motion of his paw. "You shoulda seen them before this Boffin character made the scene."

"Oh?" Lady Teluria's mouth got small and her eyebrows rose even higher than Scandal's when he does his *mistaspok* imitation. (I still don't know what a *mistaspok* is; from what the cat tells me it's a creature from his world whose only purpose in life is to annoy doctors and excite females. We have something like that on Orbix—the *moska*: a small crustacean that is supposed to make your girlfriend much more friendly. All you do is grind it up and sprinkle it over a large diamond which you then sneak onto her finger. There are some dangerous side-effects, like marriage.)

Scandal was not thinking about *mistaspoks* or *moskas*; Scandal was thinking about the best way to bury me up to my neck in trouble. He sauntered nearer to Lady Teluria and said, "Heck, yes, they used to work together. *Live* together. Inseparable. Kendar's a cute kid, but even with all his wizardly powers he still needs a little cold steel to back him up."

"Indeed." Lady Teluria's voice was cold, her eye fishy.

To his credit, Sir Megrim spoke up. "Now, now, Teluria, don't go jumping to any conclusions here. Lots of young men work together in a business sort of way."

"Very closely together," Scandal added, cheerful as a piglet in mud.

"Mmmmmm," said Lady Teluria, in a way that *meant* something, and meant to mean it.

"Just what do you mean by *that*?" Mom bristled.

"Oh . . . nothing," Dulcetta's mother lied.

"I'll have you know that Kendar was *married*," Mom said, looking down her nose at her future in-law. "Married to a delightful child named Mysti. I loved her like a second daughter." (I heard a choking sound. Mysti had one leather glove stuffed in her mouth and was trying not to laugh out loud.) "She was sweet and talented and very beautiful. She could have had any man she wanted, but she chose *my* Kendar."

"Did she." Lady Teluria's nostrils pinched as if she was smelling manure and lots of it. "I'd love to meet such a paragon. Couldn't she be here with us today?"

Before Mom could reply, Scandal piped up. "No way, toots. She left him flatter'n a flounder."

"*Did* she!" Lady Teluria seemed overjoyed by this information, and much more willing to believe it. She regarded "Blade" and me with a faint, malicious smile. "I *do* wonder why."

"Teluria . . ." Sir Megrim groaned.

Aunt Glucosia placed herself in front of Lady Teluria. "Dearie, if you're saying what I think you're saying about my dear nephew Kendar, I'd advise you not to say it."

"Why not?" Lady Teluria shot back. "From what *I've* heard, it's not supposed to be an insult."

"It's not supposed to be, but people like you keep making sure it is," Aunt Glucosia replied coldly.

"Can I say something?" I asked, waving my hand in the air.

"No, you can't, Kendar dear." Aunt Glucosia settled matters for me. "I know what this . . . *person* is saying about you, and I know how much damage such gossip can cause a young man just starting out in life."

"Yeah, but *I* know what I am!"

"Oh, hush, you do *not*."

"Why are you defending him?" Lady Teluria inquired. "As I hear tell, little . . . *arrangements* like this are common as crawfish among women in your . . . *profession*."

A deathly stillness fell over the hall. The atmosphere was charged and ominous. Scandal bounced up and down on the altar and no one thought to stop him or boot him off. "Cat fight! Cat fight!" he cried with glee. "Five bucks on Shorty! The little ones always fight dirty."

Mom motioned for our faithful butler to attend her. "Genuflect, please begin to secure the glassware and all the larger carving knives," she directed.

"Very good, m'lady," said Genuflect, and glided off to see to it.

Aunt Carageena joined her sister opposite Lady Teluria. "Dearie, are you . . . *implying* something about warrior women?" she asked.

"If the breastplate fits . . ." Lady Teluria let her words trickle away in a little stream of acid.

"If I hear one more pregnant pause, I'm gonna get morning sickness," Scandal announced.

"Aunt Glucosia, Aunt Carageena, please," I said, trying to

calm things down. "I don't care what Lady Teluria thinks about me and Blade. I know the truth, and that's all that matters."

"The truth?" Lady Teluria echoed. "Are you suggesting that I am *not* telling the truth?"

"Well, if you're saying stuff about me and Blade—"

"Did I say anything?" Lady Teluria appealed to the massed guests. "Did I say *one little thing* to deserve this accusation of falsehood laid to my charge?"

"Look, you didn't come right out and *say* anything," I replied. "But the way you keep *hinting*—"

"Oh! So now I'm not even honest enough to tell a lie?" The lady's chubby hands flexed in a strangely familiar way. I caught a sideways glimpse of my aunts' hands going through the same motions. I recalled what Scandal said about Shorty—I mean Lady Teluria—probably being a dirty fighter. My Majyk could save my life from direct attack, but that didn't mean I wanted to live on as a soprano.

I took a step away from the seething lady, and in my most mature, soothing voice I said, "Please don't take offense. Of *course* you're honest enough to tell a lie."

Scandal got to say, "Smooth move, Ex-Lax," just before the explosion.

"*No one calls Teluria of the Gilded Bustard a liar and lives!*" the lady shouted, and flung herself at my throat. Aunt Carageena stepped neatly in to block her and got the surprise of her life. Lady Teluria did an astonishing midair contortion that turned her lunge into a feet-first kick that connected with Aunt Carageena's midriff and knocked all the breath out of her. The two women hit the floor, but Teluria was the only one to get up.

She had Aunt Carageena's sword in her hand when she did. She looked me over slowly from head to feet, pausing at a few terrifying points along the way.

"Here!" Aunt Glucosia snapped. "We'll have none of this nonsense. You leave Kendar alone."

"He called me a liar and he must pay," Lady Teluria snarled. There was a fine sprinkling of white foam on her moustache and a bloody-minded look in her eye.

"Now, now, Teluria my love," her husband said with a quaver in his voice. "Put that sword down. It's not yours. You're not used to the balance of the blade. You might not be able to get the most out of every swing."

"Wedwel's holy chalk, Megrim!" Dad exclaimed. "You never told me you was married to a barbarian wench!"

Sir Megrim turned large, moist eyes to Dad. "It never came up in conversation. Besides, Teluria hasn't ridden with the hordes of Uk-Uk the Unspeakable for, oh . . . How long has it been, my love?" he asked his mate.

"How should I know?" she shot back. "We never learned to keep track of time, except by carving notches in a servant, and you wouldn't allow that." Her sneer turned back into a snarl for my benefit. "All those years of barging around the stupid, drafty, dusty plains, all those days and nights in the saddle, all that stomach-churning mare's milk, and not a decent bath to be had for ages—! It was a filthy life and I'm glad I married Megrim and got out of it before my hair was *completely* ruined, but by all the gods, there is *one* tradition of my barbaric fathers which I will *never* abandon!"

"The one about the sheep?" Aunt Carageena asked groggily from the floor.

"The one about what you do to the dead man fool enough to call you a liar!" Lady Teluria bellowed, and brought the sword straight down on my head.

"I could've told you it was a waste of time, Cuddles," Scandal said, sitting on Lady Teluria's chest. "But no one ever listens to me."

We had retired to a small room just off the great hall, the one set aside for our servants to take a break during long parties. Lady Teluria was stretched out on the divan while Aunt Carageena plopped herself down in the only chair available and the rest of us stood around. There wasn't much space, so Mom had shooed out everyone but the aunts, Sir Megrim, Genuflect, and me. Scandal wasn't invited, but he came in anyway. No one was surprised.

Mom took a fresh cloth from the basin of water Genuflect held, wrung it out, and laid it across Lady Teluria's brow. "Feeling better, dear?" she asked the supine noblewoman.

Lady Teluria groaned. "Did I kill him, at least?"

"No, but you broke my sword trying," Aunt Carageena replied.

"Don't sulk, Gee'," her sister said. "We'll get you a new one."

"*We* shouldn't have to pay for it," Carageena objected. She shot Teluria a poisonous look. "The decent thing to do would be for *some* people to offer to foot the bill. Not that I'm holding my breath. It's things like this that make barbarians such . . . barbarians."

Lady Teluria ignored my aunts. She sat up suddenly, pitching Scandal off her bosom, and grabbed her husband's tunic. "Megrim, *you* saw it! I brought the sword down right straight on top of his skull," she insisted. "Edge on, not the flat. I couldn't be *that* much out of practice. I still know kill from stun."

"Dammit, Jim, these phasers are all higgledy-piggledy," Scandal grumbled, ambling away.

"Oh, you can't kill Kendar that way, dear," Mom told her. "I don't think there *is* a way. You'd have had better luck with the flat of the blade. His powers protect him from being killed, but not from being badly hurt."

"Gee, thanks, Mom," I said out of the corner of my mouth.

"You're welcome, darling." My Mom uses perkiness the way some assassins use daggers. She perched on the edge of the divan and took Lady Teluria's hands in her own. "My goodness, you never told us you used to be a career woman, Teluria! It's just so *in*teresting. Who'd have thought it? As soon as the children are all nicely married, we must have a long talk about your experiences."

Lady Teluria gave Mom a shy, somewhat confused look. "You—you don't mind?"

"Mind?" Mom repeated, as if Teluria had asked whether or not she had one.

"About my being a barbarian. And trying to kill your son. And breaking Carageena's sword."

Mom uttered the same silvery laugh that had made her the terror of the countryside when she was a girl. "Don't be silly, dear," she said. "You can always buy Carageena another sword."

Relations among the soon-to-be-family members were much warmer as we all trooped back into the great hall. Lady Teluria had her arms linked with the aunts' and was swapping barbarian's-honor-there-I-was stories about her days as a fearless, merciless, bathless rider on the plains. Mom had no combat experiences to share, but she did manage to tell the joke about the dragon, the virgin, and the rutabaga without screwing up the punch line.

"*Abstemia!*" Dad bawled.

"Oh, for—!" Mom clicked her tongue and rolled her eyes to the rafters. "Lucius, I've heard you tell that joke a score of times in front of the children, so don't start objecting when I—"

"It *is* the children, blast it!" Dad shouted. "One child, I mean. Theirs." He pointed at the Gallimaufreys.

"Our child?" Sir Megrim looked pained.

"Our little Dulcetta?" Lady Teluria was startled. "What is it? What's happened to her? I warned her not to eat the bean dip. Is she ill, Lucius?"

"How should *he* know?" Basehart came trailing along in Dad's wake, his face a study in anger, fear, and misery. "You can't tell if a girl's sick unless you've got the girl there to look at, don'cha? Only you can't do that with Dulcetta now." His lower lip trembled. "She's gone."

CHAPTER —————— 8

"THIS IS A MISTAKE," SAID SIR MEGRIM FOR THE FIFTH time. "I'm sure Dulcetta just went out for a moment to, er, to—"

"Powder her nose?" Scandal suggested.

"Anyone ever tell you you're a troublemaker, cat?" I whispered to him.

"Flattery will get you nowhere except the United States Senate," he replied.

"Yes, certainly, just a big mistake," Lady Teluria agreed with her husband hastily. Her eyes darted back and forth from one wedding-guest's face to another. What were they thinking? What did those raised eyebrows and poorly controlled smirks conceal? "She merely stepped out to, um, to—" She had no more idea of why Dulcetta was gone than Sir Megrim did.

"No, it's not and no, she didn't." Mysti strode down the length of the great hall, a crumpled blue veil clutched in her hand. As soon as the alarm went up, she had leaped into action, vowing to locate the missing girl. Funny thing: No one made any nasty comments about "Blade" when they needed help from the mysterious masked swordsman.

Lady Teluria gasped. "That's her betrothal veil!" She grabbed it from the Welfie's hands.

"I found it outside," Mysti said.

"Outside the great hall?"

"Outside the manor."

"Outside *Uxwudge*?" Basehart was dumbfounded. He in turn snatched the veil from Lady Teluria and waved it like a banner of challenge. "Why'd she want to be out *there* when I'm in *here*?"

"I'm not gonna say it, I'm not gonna say it. I'm gonna burn in hell forever if I do, so I'm *not* gonna say it," Scandal chanted.

All Mysti answered was, "I have my theories."

"Down a badger's den with your theories! Did you think to ask the porter if he'd seen Dulcetta leave?" Basehart demanded.

"I did. He saw nothing and no one."

"But that's impossible! How could her veil get outside without her?"

"It couldn't." Mysti's lips were set in a grim line just below the hem of her mask. "I think it prudent if we continue this discussion elsewhere." With a few terse, discreet gestures she indicated the mass of guests, all hovering near, all eager to pick up another juicy tidbit of tittle-tattle.

Mom nodded. She motioned for Genuflect to attend her. "Bring up the Calpurnian brandy," she instructed him.

"Abstemia! Not the *Calpurnian*." Dad sounded like a mother bear about to be deprived of her cubs, except you can't pour cubs into a brandy snifter. Well, Dad might *try*, if he got thirsty enough, but—

"The Calpurnian." Mom was firm.

Genuflect's expression was smooth and cool as slate. "Very good, m'lady," he said, bowing slightly from the waist. He snapped his fingers, and two of his expertly trained corps of lackeys came scurrying up. "Plan nine," he informed them. Before you could say *spit*, they were trundling in and tapping cask after cask of Dad's rarest, finest, most precious brandy. It didn't take our guests long to catch the scent of spirits on the air. They clustered around the brandy casks and never noticed when the Gangles and the Gallimaufreys (and the cat) slipped out of the great hall after Mysti.

The masked Welfie led us through our own home by such a roundabout way that even Dad got that old We're-*not*-lost-and-I'm-*not*-going-to-ask-directions look. Once or twice he tried to make her halt with a stern "Now see here—!" but Mysti merely laid a gloved finger to her lips and uttered, "*Hist!*" I never know what to say when someone goes *hist* at me, and neither did Dad. Histed into submission, he followed meekly.

At last Mysti opened a narrow gray door and stole through it soundlessly. We followed, emerging into the cool violet light of the family chapel. Old gold and silver vessels gleamed on shelves lined with the finest satins, colored like melted jewels. Instructive tapestries of Wedwel's greatest prophets stared down at us with disapproving eyes from the walls.

Before us stood the altar, pure ivory inlaid with mosaics of semiprecious stones depicting more scenes from Wedwel's sacred books. These included the sequel to the Martyrdom of Saint Mangonel, namely Saint Eurythmia Driving Out the Giant Horned Hamsters. A straw from the Holy Broom of Saint Eurythmia was scrupulously preserved in a crystal vial hanging from a silver chain above the altar.

"*Here*?" Dad was scandalized. "You brought these unbelievers *here*?"

"Now, Lucius, the lad's an unbeliever too," Aunt Carageena reminded him gently. "He didn't know."

"We required privacy," Mysti said. "This place affords us the least chance of being overheard."

"This is our family chapel and may not be profaned by anyone except an Orthodox Wedwellian," Mom said primly.

"Oh hush, Abstemia," Aunt Glucosia told her. "If I had a *gabor* for every major temple I've plundered and profaned in my day, I wouldn't need to accept the old assassination job at my age. (Of course they *can* be amusing, but still—) Just having a few unbelievers hanging about the chapel isn't going to put Wedwel's nose out of joint."

"Which one?" Scandal asked, staring up at an icon of our beloved deity.

"I don't like it." Basehart shook his head.

"Learn to," Mysti snapped. "I have much to tell you. Will you hear it or no?"

Sir Megrim gazed piteously at Dad. Dad's glance strayed to Lucy, who was doing her usual dutiful-Gangle-daughter act by pretending to be part of the furniture. Dad sighed. He understood Sir Megrim's feelings. It wasn't easy to give up one's little girl, but to misplace her was much worse.

"Wedwel will understand," he pronounced. He didn't sound too sure of it, but he was a Gangle. We Gangles are very good at plowing on, brave and defiant, in the faces of our adversaries. That's how we've come to own one of the biggest manors in the kingdom. Also one of the biggest mausoleums. "Proceed, Blade."

Mysti paced back and forth in front of the altar. "I scouted around the entire house. There is more than one way of leaving a manor than by the front door."

"All the other doors are locked," Dad announced.

"Is that usual, Lucius?" Sir Megrim inquired. "I mean, blast it, what if there's a fire or an earthquake or the potato salad's gone bad or—?"

"By Wedwel's plague of barnacles, if you think I'm goin' t' be worryin' about trifles like fires and earthquakes and what-nots when I've got all these blimmin' guests wanderin' the house and the good silver and the weddin' presents out in plain sight, you've got another think comin'. You keep only one way out open, it's easier t' frisk 'em when they finally goes home." Dad lifted some of his chins, defying Sir Megrim to find fault with his theory of hospitality.

"Doors are not the only answer," Mysti said. "There is a knotted chain of bed sheets hanging out of a certain window in the east wing. The veil was found between that part of the manor and the Cheeseburgh road."

"But the Gallimaufreys are staying in the *west* wing," Mom supplied. "So are all the other guests."

Someone pinched my elbow. I turned my head and met Lucy's fright-widened eyes. She knew who was in the east wing. Her lips soundlessly formed the name: *Curio.*

I remembered the way that beefy blond had looked at Dulcetta. I remembered the mean-hearted comments he'd made about Basehart. Then I looked at my brother. His face was stern, his shoulders straight. On the surface, he seemed to be bearing up pretty well with the news that his betrothed had run away. I thought of all the times Dad had given us boys one of his Little Talks about life and love and marriage. Mostly they went: "Remember, lads, there's life an' love an' marriage. Keep 'em split up separate an' you'll do fine." I thought it was a load of sheep droppings—Dad sneaked kisses and pinches and hugs with Mom when he thought none of us kids were watching— but maybe Basehart believed what Dad said more than what Dad did.

Then I saw Basehart's fingers stroking the blue veil. His face remained stiff and unemotional, but his hands pressed Dulcetta's castoff garment to his heart.

Basehart was the one who had always beaten and belittled

me from the time we were toddlers. He was also the one who taught me how to draw a bow, stay on a horse, and climb a tree. When we stole cookies from old Maisree's kitchen and got caught, he was always loudest to say, "Kendar did it!" But every time he tried to shift the blame onto me, Dad or Mom inevitably said, "A big boy like you tattling on your baby brother? *Shame*," and it was Basehart who got the spanking. If he would've kept quiet, I would have been punished too. You'd think he'd catch on. Was he that stupid?

There's a difference between being stupid and just being a little thick. Basehart wasn't stupid. You can't be stupid and learn as much as he knew about hunting and fishing and riding and running a huge manor like Uxwudge.

He wasn't really stupid at all . . .

I had to do something.

A jingling sound filled the chapel. A golden glow emanated from the sacred relic above the altar. In its crystal prison, the Holy Broomstraw was dancing a mad jig while fountains of pink and purple sparks gushed from the mouth of the vial.

My entire family fell to their knees at once, making the Orthodox Wedwellian sign for I-am-here-Mighty-One-please-don't-hit. The Gallimaufreys clutched one another, trembling. Scandal's fur bushed out, and a low growl shook his body. Mysti's hand went for her sword. And then, at the proper moment, I thrust my hands high overhead and shouted, "I have seen a vision!" I summoned up another dose of wizard's fire to envelop me in a flaming silver shell, then made the flames and sparks vanish at the same instant that the crystal vial stopped jiggling at the end of its silver chains. There was total silence.

I let the silence rest for a heartbeat; then in the oldest voice I could manage I said, "Evil is afoot. Ill-starred wizardry has been done this day. Spells have been cast by those with no right to cast them. The same power-hungry creature who is responsible for Prince Boffin's vanishment has also caused my brother's bride to be spirited away *against her will*." I was very careful to stress that part. "It is my duty as a wizard to hunt this vile wight down and rescue his unwilling victims."

The sensation was immediate.

"Who did it?" Dad demanded.

"Why take my sweet baby?" Lady Teluria keened.

"What's a wight?" Basehart wanted to know.

"It's the opposite of a weft," Scandal provided.

"No, *weft* is a weaving term," Mom said, happy in her ignorance of feline malice. "It's another word for *woof*."

"For what?" the cat asked, all sweet innocence.

"Woof," said Mom.

"Scandal . . ." I warned him.

"Beg pardon?" There is no warning cats.

"Woof," Mom repeated.

"Sorry, something in my ear. Just one more time . . . ?"

"Woof, woof, *woof*." Mom was a little out of patience.

"Ahhh, the sounds of home. Good girl, Lassie." The cat looked up at me and grinned.

Mysti's hand fell on Scandal like a thunderbolt. She hauled the cat into the air by his scruff. "While you play games, the blameless suffer." She gave him a short shake, indifferent to the Majykal sparks that flew from his fur, then dropped him. He landed on his feet, naturally. Then she turned to me. "Who is this villain?" she demanded. "Take me to him, that I may give him cause to regret the day he was born. *Slowly*."

I folded my arms across my chest and struck a pose of wizardly might the way I'd seen Master Thengor do a hundred times. "It may not be," I intoned.

Mysti didn't care much for wizardly might. Her hand darted in and yanked me nose-to-nose with her by the neck of my tunic. "Why *not*?" she gritted.

"Uh, um, because, well, sorry, but—" I tried to make her loosen her grip. It was like trying to pry open a stubborn clam, using only an overcooked stringbean. "Because that's just the way it is," I finished.

Mysti dropped me with a lot more force than she'd used on Scandal. In an eye blink I was flat on my rump, which stung like a hive full of wasps. "Says who?"

"Says my vision," I replied, getting back on my feet. "The same vision that told me who did this also said that I had to go after the villain alone or I'd never catch him and dreadful things would happen to Prince Boffin and Dulcetta and the balance of Law would be overthrown by the forces of Chaos and—and anyway, *Wedwel* said so!"

I DID NOT.

CHAPTER ———————— 9

I WAS DREAMING ABOUT MY OWN BED BACK AT THE
palace when a loud noise woke me. I sat up too fast and banged
my head on one of the inn's many low-slung beams. "*Ow!*" I
said, then added a few Mom-would-die words, with good
reason.

"You kiss your mother with that mouth?" Scandal murmured
drowsily, curled up on my feet.

I yanked them out from under the cat, sending him tumbling
to the floor. I saw his eyes shine with anger in the dark. "What
was *that* for, peabrain?"

"That was for a start," I replied. "When we find Curio and
Boffin and Dulcetta again, I'm going to kill you."

The cat chuckled. "You wish. On *this* wacko world I've
really got nine lives, remember?"

"Eight," I reminded him in turn. "Zoltan took one away from
you with one of his pet fiends. Now, thanks to *you*, we're all in
Cheeseburgh; *his* territory. He'll try to take a few more before
we get out of here, if I know him."

"Let him try." Scandal wasn't worried. "The poor yutz
doesn't have enough Majyk left in him to kill a conversation.
And as for *you* wanting to ice me . . ." (I never knew a cat
could make that rude sound. I always thought it was impossible
to do with pointed teeth.) "Where I come from, Houdini,
ventriloquism is not a crime punishable by death."

"Not even when you're pretending to be the voice of god?"
I countered. I could still see the panicky look on everyone's
face as "Wedwel's" words boomed down from the chapel
ceiling.

Scandal tried to sound modest, but he was a cat. "What kinda pretending? We used to *be* gods on my world, kemo sabe. They worshipped us in ancient Egypt. Being adored is a tough habit to break. Just ask any actress worth her face-lift. I felt I was entitled."

"Entitled to get me in trouble," I grumbled.

"Trouble? Is that the thanks I get? I *helped* you and you want to kill me. What a pal."

"Scandal, look, I'm sorry I said I wanted to kill you. I'm only mad because of what Wedwel—what *you* said about my vision."

"*What* vision, Sir Galahad?" Scandal's sarcasm bit sharper than his teeth. "You made it up, start to finish. I just did a little editorial work on it."

"Fine, it was all a lie, but it was *my* lie. I didn't need you butting in, saying I was interpreting the vision wrong."

"I never said you interpreted it wrong." Scandal spoke in the most reasonable, logical, infuriating tone. "I only said I'd send a plague of iguanas if you hit the road without some backup troops."

"Big difference. After you scared them half to death with that iguana-plague story, there was no way Mom and Dad were going to let me go looking for Curio alone."

"Point one: You're never alone as long as you've got me, *compadre*. And point two: No one knows it's Curio you're after," the cat remarked. "Except maybe your sister Lucy. The rest of them think you're tracking down some weaselly wizard who's stolen the Sacred Truss of Oompah, god of Army physicals."

"I didn't *want* anyone to know who we're hunting; especially not Basehart. That was the whole point. If my brother finds out Dulcetta left him for Curio, it won't take much for him to figure out why."

"You said it. Curio, the side of beef that walks like a man. He probably blows the needle right off the female Drool-O-Meter."

"Uh-huh. I hoped that if we could track them down on our own, we might be able to convince Dulcetta to go back to Basehart with some story about how she was kidnapped or hypnotized or bespelled or something. The truth would be too humiliating for him. I want to spare him that. I *wanted* to, I mean. Fat chance now."

I swung my legs over the side of the bed, leaned my elbows

on my knees, and rested my head in my hands. "Why did you do it, Scandal?" I asked wearily.

There was a flash of brightness, and the candle stub at my bedside flared to life. Scandal balanced on the rickety table—the only other piece of furniture besides the two beds in that narrow room. He had kindled the wick with a jolt of sparks from the tip of his tail. His grin stretched ear to ear, which is an amazing distance on a cat.

"Gee, Mister Wizard, I dunno," he said. "Oh, wait, howz-about this? Because I don't want you to wind up dead."

"He couldn't kill me and you know it."

"Too true. But Sir Studlybuns could mess you up pretty good, I bet. Hurt you. Make you *wish* he'd kill you."

I managed a hollow laugh. "I don't think Curio's that dangerous."

"Neither did Prince Boffin. And where's he, these days?" The cat pulled his paws close to his body. "Face it, kid: Until we know just how dangerous Curio is, the more steel in your corner, the better."

"I *had* steel in my corner," I snapped. "I had Mysti. Right after you faked Wedwel's voice and ruined my plan, she announced she was coming with me. Mysti's plenty of steel on her own. I didn't need a whole crowd of it."

"Not Mysti," Scandal prompted. "Blade. Now c'mon, Kendar, be reasonable. After that little scene in the great hall, did you ever think your parents were gonna let you and Blade go off together *by yourselves?*"

The same loud noise that had woken me up came through the wall again. It sounded like someone dragging an iron comb over glass. It was followed by a knock at my door. Without waiting for me to say *Come in* or *Stay out*, Aunt Glucosia let herself in.

"Kendar, dear, may I borrow your familiar for a while?" she asked.

I glanced at Scandal. "What for?"

"Your Auntie Gee' has a snore like a wild waxworm in heat. The jungles of Plunj are simply lousy with waxworms. They're not just ugly, they're loud. During the mating season, the local tribesfolk can hardly get a wink of sleep. Everyone's so *cranky*. And the worst of it is, the racket goes on even after the creatures have bred. I suppose they're proud of themselves for being so repulsive and still managing to attract a mate. Not that the mate is any beauty. Waxworms simply do not know when to shut up."

"They're not alone," Scandal purred for my ears alone. In a louder voice he added, "So what's that got to do with me, toots?"

"Well, I've heard all the legends about cats—nine lives, seeing in the dark, landing on your feet, and so on. You're supposed to steal the breath of sleeping babies. I hoped you could do the same for Gee'. Just a bit. Not enough to kill her, only quiet her down."

"I'll see what I can do." Scandal pounced to the floor and stalked out of the room.

Aunt Glucosia spread the skirt of her cotton nightdress, sat beside me, and peered over at the other bed. It was empty. It had been empty all night, and judging by the paling sky framed in our one tiny window, there wasn't much more of the night left.

"Where's Basehart?" she asked. I shrugged. Immediately her bright blue eyes filled with storm clouds. "That is *not* an acceptable answer, Kendar Gangle. Basehart is very upset by this whole business. You ought to keep an eye on him."

"He's all right," I said, even if I only half-believed it. "You heard him: He stayed in the taproom because he wanted to stretch his legs by the fire when the rest of us went upstairs to bed. It's a good ride from Uxwudge to Cheeseburgh and they were achy."

Aunt Glucosia snorted. "I've been around enough horses to recognize *that* stuff when I smell it," she said. "The only thing your brother's been stretching downstairs is the arm he uses to hoist his tankard. Achy legs, my eye! Basehart's gone longer in the saddle on a hunt than you've gone in your whole life. He thrives on riding. Poor lamb, he's trying to drown his bride's vanishment in beer. Did you see his face when the innkeeper said he'd seen no one in Cheeseburgh fitting her description?"

"That's only one innkeeper's report," I said. "Cheeseburgh's a big town."

So it was. When the five of us came riding in, with the cat perched before me in the saddle, I was shocked by its size. There was no denying that this was no longer a village. Villages have one inn, if you can find it. Usually it's only the house of some widow who brews decent ale and doesn't mind strangers sleeping six to a bed in her spare room or sixteen to a stall in her stables. Cheeseburgh had *four* inns, each with a neatly painted sign hanging over the door. I hated to admit it, but if Mayor Zoltan was responsible for any of the blatant prosperity, there was some good to the man.

Aunt Glucosia sighed. "I don't understand wizardry. I never have. The way of the sword is plain and simple: Live or die, spare or slay, slash or stab, mince or massacre, flay or—"

"What don't you understand about wizardry?" I put in quickly.

"All this *mystery*. Why are you being so secretive about this naughty evil person who'd spirited off Dulcetta Gallimaufrey? You do know who you're looking for, don't you?" She sounded doubtful.

"I dare not divulge his name," I replied ponderously. "Names are power, and to name the name of your enemy drains the magical forces of the strongest wizard." I tried to sound steeped in wisdom. I'm *not* steeped in wisdom, but it wouldn't have made any difference to her if I were: Aunts always remember when you were a baby and steeped in something else.

"Oh, pooh." She rumbled my hair. "I don't believe that for a minute, but have your little games. You *men*. You've always got the cutest excuses for why you can't tell us what you don't know." She laughed. "However, I *would* like to know why you're not using all that power you're saving by not naming names."

"Using it for what?"

"For *finding* the wicked thing, of course! Then you can just point him out and let Gee' and me take it from there." Her smile was sharp in the shadows, and suddenly there was a dagger of equal sharpness in her hand. I had no idea where she got it. She was only wearing a nightdress, for pity's sake, although it was a lot more . . . clanky than most nightwear.

"Uhhhhh . . . I can't find him," I told her.

"I see." The dagger disappeared into the folds of her nightdress. I heard it click against more metal under the cloth. "Naturally you have another good wizardly reason for this?" She crossed her legs. "Take your time."

I lowered my eyes. "I can't use my powers to find anyone

because I don't know how," I said dully. "I've got the power but I haven't got the training."

"Really?" She sounded genuinely surprised. "Your mother told us you're King Steffan's chief wizard."

"I am."

"Tsk. So it's true what they say about government work. My goodness. Well, Kendar, I won't tell a soul. When we find the rogue who's got Dulcetta—oh, and Blade's friend, too—we're sure to have a fight on our hands. One thing I do know about preparing for battle: Never let word of your weak points slip out where your foes might hear 'em."

"Thank you, Aunt Glucosia," I said sincerely.

"Pish. Don't mention it. I'm here to help you, after all. So is Gee'. It's why we came along."

"Not because Mom made you, on account of Blade?" I'd been spending too much time with Scandal. A little of his sarcasm was starting to rub off on me.

My aunt frowned. "Kendar, I have met men like Blade more than once in the course of my career." (*Ha!* I thought.) "Your Auntie Gee' and I judge a man by only three things: If he's a good fighter, if he's a good employer, and the third one is none of your business. When it comes to people like Blade, there's a pretty even split between prompt wage payers and tightfists, skilled fighters and dead men waiting to happen. They are not monsters, although some of them do need a good, hard kick in the britches from time to time. So do we all. Gee' and I did not offer to come along to *protect* you from him. He seems to be rather intelligent, and I'll wager he understands the meaning of *No* as well as you or I. If you don't yet know how to speak up for yourself and make your own choices known with men *or* women, it's too late to teach you now."

I felt thoroughly chastened. "So why did you come?"

"I told you why: to help you. We know nothing about the strength of this creature you're stalking. It never hurts to have a bit of good steel on your side, I always say, and Blade's sword might not be enough."

I smiled. "You sound like Scandal."

"Do I? Hmm. I wonder if I could steal Gee's breath, too? Just the part she snores with."

"If you really want to help me, convince Basehart to go home," I said.

"I can't do that, Kendar dear," she replied, patting my hand softly.

"Why not? He's no wizard and he's not much of a swordsman. Hunters rely on the bow and the spear—country weapons. Towns and cities call for swords. He'll only be in the way."

"Dulcetta Gallimaufrey is his betrothed. He has a right to take part in her rescue."

"Yes, only—" I was about to say *Only what if she doesn't want to be rescued?* but I bit my tongue in time.

Aunts are very good at hearing what you don't say. "You know something, Kendar," Aunt Glucosia stated. "Do you want to share it or do I have to go downstairs and tell everyone in the taproom *all* the stories I know about the cute things you did when you were a baby?"

No! Not that! I had no choice. I told her everything about Curio. When I was done, she nodded.

"Mmmmm, he *is* pretty. And you say he has this Magique-thingie too? I can't say I'm too surprised about him and Dulcetta. From what I hear, those Gallimaufreys kept her under wraps long before the betrothal. No wonder she kicked over the traces the first chance she got. With a reformed barbarian horsewoman mother, she's lucky she wasn't locked in her room until she was a grandma."

"How could she ever become a grandma if she was locked in her—?"

"You wizards have your mysteries, we women have ours." Aunt Glucosia winked at me. "We had many little chats before the betrothal ceremony, Dulcetta and I. The dear girl was absolutely fascinated by my stories. You could see the longing for adventure in her eyes." She grew thoughtful. "Dear me, I do hope your father isn't raising Lucy quite so strictly, or who knows *what* the poor, romance-starved child will do one day."

This time I bit my lip instead of my tongue, for a change.

"Now I understand why you want Basehart to go home," Aunt Glucosia continued. "That's very sweet and considerate of you. I always told Lucius that you were a good boy and that in the real world intelligence matters far less than everyone thinks it does. You want to spare your brother's feelings." She rested her hand on my shoulder. "I'm afraid it won't work. He's made up his mind that *he's* going to be the one to find and rescue Dulcetta."

"Stubborn donkey," I muttered.

"He's a Gangle," she said proudly. "A Gangle never throws in the towel."

"A Gangle has enough trouble finding the towel," Scandal announced. He stood in the doorway with Aunt Carageena behind him, rubbing her eyes and yawning. They came in, climbing over our legs, and took over Basehart's unused bed. "I stopped her snoring," the cat said.

"Is it time to get up yet?" Aunt Carageena inquired sleepily. "I could use a cup of gawfee. My mouth feels all fuzzy." She coughed, and a tuft of cat hair floated out.

"'Mornin, Gee'," Aunt Glucosia said, too chipper to live. "I was just explaining to Kendar why Basehart tagged along."

"What's to tell?" Aunt Carageena's amber-brown eyes were still bleary. "Ever since you became a famous wizard, Kendar dear, it's been a bone in Basehart's craw. Your mother goes on and on about how wonderful you are, and how you live in a palace, and how the king relies on you for everything. I'd strangle her myself, except Wedwel only knows what sort of woman Lucius would marry the second time around."

"Mom *brags* about me?" This was news. All I ever heard from her was a long list of disappointments.

"Oh, shamelessly," Aunt Carageena assured me. "Where do you think that leaves Basehart?"

"So you see, dear, he couldn't let you go off and be the one to rescue Dulcetta," Aunt Glucosia concluded. "It would be just one more thing to set you up a notch and take him down a peg as far as your mother's concerned."

I understood. "Would you excuse me?" I said, trying to stand in the crowded space between the beds. "There's something I have to do, but I need to get dressed first."

Downstairs in the taproom a little later, Scandal and I found my brother with his head on a table, an empty flagon in his hand. He stank to the rafters and he was snoring louder than Aunt Carageena.

Scandal jumped onto the table and picked his way daintily around the puddles of beer. He sniffed at Basehart, wrinkled his nose, and declared, "I'm not stealing *that* breath. Peeeee-yew!"

I sat beside Basehart on the bench and shook him by the shoulder. "Basehart? Basehart, wake up."

"D'wanna," he muttered, and turned his head in the other direction.

"Come on, get up," I urged. "It's almost daylight. There's noise in the streets; the whole town's stirring and the first farmers are coming to market. We have to get out, question people, start looking for clues about where Dulcetta's gone."

"Mmrrrrgghh." Basehart raised his head from the table with a mighty effort and rested it on my shoulder. "Who cares?"

I tried to inhale in the opposite direction. "You do. You love her and you want her back. That's why you came along, remember?"

"'Sall you know." He belched loud enough to shake a layer of greasy soot loose from the taproom rafters. "On'y reason I came 'long was so—sozat alla dumb weddin' guests woo—woon't laffame."

"Wouldn't what?"

"Laugh . . . at . . . me," he said with painful precision. "Basehart Gangle, lef' holdin' th' veil. Where's his li'l wifey? Runnededed away, 'swhere. Oh, poooooooor Basehart, ha, ha, ha."

"She didn't run away," I lied. "She was carried away by an evil magician. But before you know it, we'll find her, and you'll save her from a fate worse than death, and she'll be incredibly grateful to you forever, and the two of you will live happily ever after, and—and—" I was at a loss for anything else to say that would top that last one.

"Don' be stupid, Ken'ar. 'Snot true."

"Yes it is! I saw it in a vis—"

"*Ain't* no fate worse'n death." His head slid from my shoulder back onto the table. "'Cept this hangover," he added.

Scandal tilted his head back and yowled. It was a sound fit to raise the dead. Also the drunk. Basehart sat bolt upright and grabbed his head. "Aaahhh! My skull! My fav'rite skull! You broke it!"

"I'll bust it down to atoms if you don't stay awake, Lieutenant Lush," the cat promised. "You're not the only one with a stake in this little expedition, ya know. We need to find Prince Boffin fast or there'll be war. War is not healthy for cats and other highly beautiful and intelligent creatures. You're not gonna slow us down just 'cause you crawled into a beer barrel for the winter."

"So go find Prince Boggin. See'f I care. Wha'zit gotta do wi' me an' Dulcie?" Basehart whined. "Jus' lemme die in peace."

"The same yahoo who dragged off your little dumpling *d'amour* is probably the one responsible for making Boffin take a magic powder. Find one, find both."

"Then can I die?" Basehart's plea was absolutely pathetic.

"With my blessing." Scandal patted him very gently with his paw.

"Ow," said Basehart.

By this time, the innkeeper had emerged from his private quarters and was beginning to clean up the mess from last night's customers. He shook his head and chuckled when he got a look at Basehart. "Feelin' a mite, ah, undependable, young sir?"

Basehart groaned.

"Ho, ho, I thought so. Hang on; I've got just the thing." He stepped behind the bar, ducked down, and brought up a number of ill-sorted bottles, boxes, and bundles of herbs. A pinch of this, a drop of that, a splash of something more, and a mugful of soapy-looking brown liquid stood mixed and ready. He brought it to our table.

"Swallow o' this and you'll be singing," he told my brother.

Basehart eyed the mug uneasily, but he was a desperate man. His hand shook badly as he reached for the innkeeper's cure.

"Ha! Wait a bit!" our host exclaimed. He rooted around in his apron pocket and pulled out a small glass bottle. "Almost forgot what makes it all work." He yanked the cork, tilted the flask, and let a thin, feebly glowing stream of Magique trickle into the foam. The bubbles sizzled and hummed. "There. Best coin I ever spent, this stuff. Works like a charm; you'll see. T'yer health." He tucked the restoppered bottle away.

Basehart's hands closed around the mug and raised it to his lips.

"Basehart, don't!" I cried "That last ingredient—it's magical, but it's not *really* magical. You don't know what it'll do if you drink it. It could make you sick. It could hurt you. It could *kill* you!"

"Oh, yes, *please!*" my brother gasped, gulped the brew, and exploded.

CHAPTER —————— 10

"THIS ISN'T IN MY REGULAR LINE OF WORK AT ALL, you know," said the witch, holding the pieces of my brother's heart. "Usually I break these things, not put 'em together."

"Just do the best you can, dearie." Aunt Glucosia's gentle words of encouragement were backed up by a length of keen blue-edged steel, drawn and ready in her hand.

The witch looked down her nose at the blade which hovered a fingerspan from her ribs. "You can put that thing away any time," she said coldly. "You would be more help if your hands were free and you worked with the others. They still haven't brought me all the pieces."

"I think I found his, uhhhhh, important thing over here, lady!" Scandal called from the corner. "No, wait, it's just a dead mouse. Never mind. Yum."

"Is this something you can use?" I said, presenting the witch with an oddly shaped fragment.

She took it from my hand and turned it in the sunlight. "I should say so. That's his kidney." She fit it into the puzzle of pieces already laid out on the table. "Go see if you can find me another one."

I dropped back down onto hands and knees and crawled off to have a look under a different table. The scattered bits of my brother came in dozens of unlikely shapes and were strewn all over the taproom. The same potion that had caused Basehart's blowup had also turned his body brittle and shiny as a well-glazed vase. It was often hard to tell the fragments of Basehart from the pieces of broken glassware and dishes littering the floor from the night before.

Now Blade, Aunt Carageena, and I were on the floor,

seeking the telltale glassy glimmer of the shards. Scandal claimed he was helping, too. Aunt Glucosia's contribution to the common task was to threaten the witch with all sorts of mayhem if she didn't restore Basehart to wholeness and life.

The witch was not impressed. "I can't do anything until we've found all the pieces, which would happen faster if you'd help instead of playing the bully. Once I have him reassembled, it will take but a simple spell. He'll live," she said. "He has no choice. I am a trained professional. If he dies, I don't get paid, and I need the money. Taxes in this town are outrageous nowadays."

"I don't trust witches," Aunt Glucosia said between clenched teeth. "I've fought more than a few in my time. Treacherous, sly, loathsome hags, every one of them."

"Mistress Gout's not like that!" the innkeeper piped up from behind the bar. He was right, at least about the last part. Mistress Gout was a tall, dark, striking woman, a little younger than Mom. She dressed simply, in a plain robe the color of summer twilight, a black silk sash cinching her narrow waist. With knee-length black hair falling loose down her back, she walked like a sister of shadows. She wasn't cuddly or sweet or girlishly pretty, but she was far from being a loathsome hag. She didn't even have any warts.

"Shut up, you," Aunt Glucosia commanded the innkeeper. "It's all thanks to you and your wretched drink that my nephew's smashed." She waved the sword at him meaningly. The innkeeper cringed and shut up. "Innkeepers and witches: bad news, the lot of 'em."

Mistress Gout sighed and folded her arms. "If that's your opinion of witches, find someone else to put the silly twit together again. Him, for instance." She pointed at me. "I'm surprised he let you send for a mere witch like me. These wizards are generally selfish hogs when there's any magic to be done."

"Who told you I was a wizard?" I asked, getting up from the floor and dusting myself off.

"No one has to tell me. Your Majyk screams its head off, for those with the wit to hear it. What's the matter? Why can't you use it for this job? Wrong phase of the moons?"

"Master Kendar believes in giving the local talent a break," Scandal said. "Basehart should excuse the expression."

"Hmph! Basehart was lucky," said Gout.

"Lucky?" I echoed. "He exploded!"

"He *only* exploded," the witch corrected me. "That will be set right soon enough, thanks to the quick thinking of Solly Tapster"—she jerked a thumb at the innkeeper—"who your mad aunt's *also* trying to kill, I might add."

"He's the one who fed that poor baby the wicked potion!" Aunt Glucosia cried, gesturing with her sword.

"He's the one who stopped you from sweeping the pieces into the rubbish. He's the one who knew how it could all be fixed. He's the one who thought to send for me," the witch countered.

"He's the one who'd be scattered over this floor in more bits than poor Basehart if I had my way," Aunt Glucosia fiercely counter-countered. "He only thought of sending for you after *I* got through with him. Men are famous for finding solutions much more quickly when they've got a sword's point aimed somewhere convincing."

"I had a pet voondrab that growled half as much as you do," Gout told her. "I had her fixed. You're making more of this entire situation than it's worth. It could have been much worse. I've seen dozens of cases where it was."

"What, people explode on a regular basis around here?" Scandal queried. "Quick, someone tell Monty Python."

"I don't know what went wrong," Solly Tapster quavered. "I've mixed that hangover cure a hundred times. No one ever went *boom-crash-tinkle-tinkle* before. Usually they just throw up."

"I can tell you what went wrong in one word." The witch's dark eyes flashed. "*Magique.* Oh, I warned you about it time and time again, Solly! It's shoddy, flimsy, unreliable stuff, I said, but did you care? Did anyone in this fool town care? No. It's cheaper to use Magique than to pay an honest witch's rates, and it works quickly and it makes things easier to do. That's all that matters to any of you. No care for craftsmanship. No respect for years of study. Just snap, snap, snap, and hey presto! That's all *you* want: fast, flash, and fancy."

She was still grousing when I tapped her on the back and said, "Could we have a word somewhere private, Mistress Gout? Just for a little while. The others can keep looking for the pieces while we're gone."

"Fine with me." Gout gave Aunt Glucosia a scornful glance. "Does that please my watchdragon, or are you afraid I'll turn this child into a toad for the joy of it?"

"Kendar can take care of himself," Aunt Glucosia returned evenly. "And if he can't, I can take care of *you*."

"Shudder, shudder," said the witch. "Oh, see me quake with fright." She turned back to me. "All right, let's go. Where's private enough for you?"

"You can use my accounts room," Solly Tapster offered. "Through that door, first cubby on the right."

"That will do."

The innkeeper spoke the truth when he called it a cubby. There was hardly room for two grown humans to squeeze in at the same time, and when you added one fat cat to the sum, it really got snug.

"Ya know, I saw a Marx Brothers movie once that had a scene like this," Scandal said, prying his way between the witch and me. He clambered onto Solly's slant-top desk and asked, "Any of you guys got two hardboiled eggs?"

"You have to excuse my familiar," I apologized to Gout.

"Not at all. I like cats."

This took me by surprise. "You know what he is?"

"A witch lives by selling knowledge," she told me. "A fine witch I'd be if I couldn't recognize a common cat."

"A *what* cat?" Scandal's tail bushed out with indignation.

Gout ignored him. "My guess is that this one can talk because of some show-off spell of yours, wizard. Where they come from, they don't speak the humans' language."

This was making me really nervous. "You . . . *know* about where they come from, too?"

She shrugged. "The Whirl'd? Of course."

"All right then, what's it like?" I challenged her.

"A nice place to exile your enemies, but I wouldn't want to live there. Oh. You want a more specific answer, don't you? Well, let me see . . . It's round and it's got seven major land masses, only one sun, only one moon, and it's—"

"Not so fast! Orbix was round once too."

"You needn't tell *me*." Gout's thin lips tugged down at the corners. "I had a decent education before you were hatched from the egg. The cat's home is not only shaped like a ball, but the beings there live on the *outside*, even though it spins around

all the time. Which, I suppose, is why they call it the Whirl'd
There. Is that proof enough that I know what I'm talking
about?" Her tone implied *Too bad if it isn't.*

"You *do* know." I was astonished. "But—how? Not even
Master Thengor knew about the Whirl'd, or he would have
taught us."

"So you're one of Thengor's boys? Not a bad teacher, as
wizards go. Yet you still let Solly send for me instead of
repairing your brother yourself? How peculiar."

I didn't like the way the witch's sharp eyes seemed to pierce
my skull, hunt down any lurking lies, and skewer them dead
before I could utter them. I took a deep breath and braced
myself to tell her the truth. "It's a longish story—"

"Then forget it. I can tell you've got more Majyk in you than
old Thengor ever did, but it doesn't concern me if you can't use
it. I'm a witch; we don't use *that* stuff at all. All I care about as
far as Majyk goes is: Do you respect it?"

I sighed. "More than you'll ever know." It's hard not to
respect something that turns your nice, comfortable, know-
nothing life upside-down.

"We'll get along well enough, then. Now, what was it you
wanted to talk to me about so privately?"

"Magique," I said. "In the taproom you said you've seen
dozens of cases where Magique backfired. Where?"

"What a question! Right here in Cheeseburgh, naturally."

"And you can tell when Magique's behind a spell that's gone
bad? Instead of Majyk, I mean."

She gave a dry laugh. "Nothing could be simpler. There *is* no
Majyk in Cheeseburgh—not until you arrived. Well, there is
some. Our mayor's still got a dusting of the stuff, and that
brazen phony who lives out past Golligosh Pond has a little she
keeps on hand—for research purposes *she* says." Contempt
dripped from Gout's lips. "I don't believe the old frump for a
single mi—"

"Mother Toadbreath!" I exclaimed.

"You know her?" Gout's dark brows dove into a frown.

"You kidding, sis?" Scandal said. "Him and the old frump
are like *that.*" He held up one paw.

"Like what?" The witch squinted at it.

"Like this gesture works better if you've got a coupla fingers
to cross," the cat replied. "Anyhoo, Mother Toadbreath's ou

buddy, our pal, our main mama. *Tovarisch* Toadbreath. Toadarama. The Toadmeister. We saved her from getting hanged for witchcraft once and—"

"Say, that's right!" I exclaimed. "The Cheeseburghers used to come to her cottage and stage fake witch hunts so that they could trade their goods for her magic soaps. They had to do it that way because there was some stupid royal law against dealing with witches."

"Yeah, 'cause the king's airhead cousin gagged on a chunk of poisoned apple once," Scandal put in. "Big deal. In the long run, it got her a husband. You can't tell your bride-to-be's a bimbo if she's lying doggo in a glass coffin. And after your kiss brings her back to life, it's too late and you've gotta marry the nitwit. It's a package deal, y' know. Instead of starting that dippy law, they should've given the witch a medal for matchmaking above and beyond."

"I know my history lessons well enough, thank you." Gout froze Scandal with a look.

"What I mean is, why did the Cheeseburghers travel all the way to Mother Toadbreath's cottage when they had a witch living right here in town with them all the time?" I asked.

"Because I was not in Cheeseburgh at the time," Gout replied. "I was on the Whirl'd."

"*My* world?" For once I got to enjoy the sight of Scandal at a loss for words.

"I have never visited any other planet whose shape leaves me feeling so insecure," said the witch, molding an invisible ball with her hands. "At least when Orbix was round, we had the common sense to live on the *in*side."

"But how'd you get there?" the cat demanded. "No offense, sweetcakes, but no way you could wiggle through a rat hole with those hips."

"Why should I do that when there are far more comfortable and commodious methods of egress available?" Seeing our blank stares, she translated: "There are bigger doors."

"Where? Where?" Scandal bounced eagerly. "Just take me to 'em!"

My heart sank. "I thought you didn't want to leave Orbix," I said to him quietly.

He stopped bouncing for a moment. "I don't. This place has L.A. beat all hollow. I like living somewhere you don't hafta chew the air before you can breathe it, plus not too many dogs cluttering up the show. On the other paw, I'm the only one of my kind here, and so—" He started bouncing again. "*Bring on the girl cats!*" He let loose a long, yodeling yowl with an unmistakable meaning.

One corner of the witch's mouth curved up in a humorless smile. "Your familiar is a lusty one," she said.

"He doesn't have any hobbies," I half-apologized.

"And do you?" Her smile grew disturbingly warmer. A spark burned in her eyes that wasn't there before. I could feel myself being weighed and measured, and I didn't like it.

"How did you find the way to the Whirl'd? Can you find it again? How'd you get back? Will you show us? Can anyone use the door, or only witches? Would you—?" (When in trouble, change the subject. Fast. A lot. I learned that from Dad all the times he came in the house without wiping his boots first and got deer guts all over the bed.)

Gout reached into one of her long, loose sleeves. "You talk too much, wizard." She took out a tiny clay pot, dipped a finger in it, and smeared a dab of something shiny over her lips. "Talk is cheap." Her deep blue gown shimmered, then vanished. She stood before me wearing only a wisp of silvery cloth that stretched taut and transparent over the close-your-eyes-Kendar parts of her body. (That's what Mom calls the most interesting sections of the female anatomy.)

Only I didn't close my eyes this time. I didn't want to. Instead I wanted to see if I could make that same yodeling yowl as Scandal.

"*Sports Illustrated* swimsuit issue, 1993," said the witch. Those must have been the mystical words of a spell to turn my legs to water, because it worked. "Do you like it?" she simpered.

"Agah." (Hmmm. The spell must've worked on tongues, too.)

Her coy smile abruptly turned into a scowl. "*You* like it. *He* didn't. It was all *her* fault! *They* paid. Or so *I* thought."

"*We* don't have the foggiest idea why you're spewing pronouns, Lady MacDeath," said Scandal. "But if it'll get me near a female cat of the opposite sex real soon now, I'll listen to you recite the intro to *Star Trek* Classic in Spanish: '*Espacio, el final frontier-o* . . .' Jump in any time."

Gout wiped the shine from her lips with the back of her hand. Her old, all-covering robes were restored. "He was my beloved—a handsome young wizard-to-be named Bibok. She was Calosta, a tribal sorceress from the jungles of Plunj. It happened long before this upstart Toadbreath moved into her cottage. Cheeseburgh was still a small village and *I* was its only witch."

"Gee, sorry," I said.

"What do you mean, 'sorry'?"

"Well, Cheeseburgh's not exactly an exciting place to live, or interesting or—"

"What my diplomatic pal here's trying to ask is, What was a tasty chunk of womanhood like you doing in a dump like this?" Scandal finished for me.

She lifted her chin with pride. "I was the best. I could live anywhere I chose. People came to *me*."

"Including this wizard," Scandal said.

"Wizard-to-be," the witch corrected him. "He claimed that he had been rejected by Master Thengor because the old thistle was jealous of the effect Bibok had on women."

"As opposed to how come Thengor rejected my buddy Kendar, here," Scandal said with a wave of his paw. "Which was on account of the effect he had on everything. Namely: none."

"Want to see what kind of effect I've got now?" I told the cat, jaw clenched.

The witch paid no attention to either of us. "He told me he had heard of my powers, but that the tales had not mentioned my beauty. He said he had talent and only desired my wisdom to guide him."

"He brought his own shovel," said the cat.

"No man ever called me beautiful before." A note of regret crept into Gout's voice. "Mostly they just asked the price of my spells, or told me their troubles, or begged for mercy. And Bibok knew beauty. He *was* beautiful: tall, fair-haired, with eyes of the purest green, and a tongue—"

"We don't need to hear all this!" I blurted.

Gout sniffed disdainfully. "—a tongue that could charm a dragon out of its gold. Or a witch out of her greatest and most secret spells. All the time I thought he was *my* lover, he was in truth hers. I taught him nearly everything I knew. Nearly. I was a fool for him, but not a complete idiot. And then one day, I was summoned to a customer's bedside. The poor wretch was sicker than I thought, and so I sent my own familiar back home to fetch me the additional supplies I needed." Her face grew dark. "He fetched me more than that."

"Stool pigeon, huh?" Scandal inquired.

"An owl, actually, by the name of Herbert. I heard what he had to say and raced home at once, just in time to catch my false lover in the arms of his *true* lady." Her voice dropped to a dangerous growl. "I was miffed."

"Watch this, boss," Scandal whispered to me. "Ten-to-one says the blabbermouth owl's gonna be the first to get zapped."

"My anger was terrible," the witch went on. "In my jealous rage, I was not thinking clearly. I hurled destruction anywhere, everywhere, and—"

"*Arrivederci*, Herbert," Scandal breathed.

"—destroyed my innocent familiar."

"When you're ready to pay off the bet, I'll accept a personal check," the cat informed me.

"Did—did you destroy them, too?" I asked.

"Ha!" Gout's laugh was bitter enough for me to taste. "Don't think I didn't try. But Bibok had learned much from me of protective spells, and Calosta was a sorceress in her own right. I do not like sorceresses."

"Aren't they the same as witches?"

"No." The word was cold, the look that went with it withering. She offered no further explanation.

"In other words, they put up a fight," Scandal supplied.

"That is so." The witch nodded. "A fight for which *I* had armed them both, curse it."

"Stop me if I'm wrong, Glinda, but I think I'm on a roll, here," the cat said. "They had a full house, but you had a coupla aces up your sleeve, right?"

"What I had up my sleeve was *this*." She whipped out that little clay pot again. "It contains a carefully distilled essence of power that has a multitude of uses. I am not like that charlatan, Toadbreath, needing a different soap for every single spell. I am efficient." She tilted the pot towards me and I got a whiff of violets. "It takes a long time to make, but a little goes a long way."

"Why didn't you use that stuff in the pot on the sick man?" I wanted to know.

She looked at me as if I'd asked why zombies make the best university professors. "This is not a healing salve unless I add certain herbs to the basic ointment. It must be adjusted to combat the specific illness. Didn't Master Thengor teach you anything about medicine?"

Master Thengor had *tried* to teach me lots of things, with no luck. Still . . . "To tell the truth, I don't remember him ever giving a class on healing magic."

"Good. At least you're honest. Wizards never bother teaching or learning any enchantments that might *cure* people. They leave that to us witches. It's so much more spectacular for them to fling spells that harm instead of heal."

"The way I'm hearing this, Florence Nightingale, you were using that glop-in-a-pot to heal Bibok and Calosta of breathing," the cat drawled.

"I told you; I was miffed."

"God help us all if you ever get peeved."

"If you didn't kill them, what did happen?" I asked.

The witch's eyes blazed. "I saw that my spells of destruction were of no use. *He* knew them too well, and he also knew how to ward against them. He had my secrets, but not my wisdom. Therefore I changed my tactics. While pretending still to seek their deaths, I forged an enchantment of great displacing power. I smeared my fingertips in the salve until it dripped from them in shining streams of witchcraft. I stooped and dabbled my fingers among the scattered feathers of my unfortunate familiar's body, and from them I wove a cloak of flight!"

"Wow," I breathed.

"Yuck," said the cat. "She touched a *dead owl.*"

"And you wouldn't?"

"Not between meals."

The witch went on: "I heard Bibok gasp as the glorious garment tossed itself over my shoulders, then fanned out behind me, giving me wings. They beat the air furiously, and the gale struck the two traitors like a fist. They staggered back, vainly hurling their petty spells at me. I laughed and drew nearer, my wings still beating. The strength of my hate tore open a gaping hole in the fabric of Orbix. I saw it—black, hungry, bottomless—and was amazed at my own magical skill.

I knew where such passageways led. I had heard of them
before, studied them, I knew where some lay, and I understood
that these were only one-way routes between Orbix and a place
of noise, violence, confusion, and madness."

"Yeah, but they also got some great Thai restaurants,"
Scandal said.

Gout blinked. "Who does?"

"You mean you weren't talking about Washington, D.C.?"

"Scandal, let her finish," I commanded. To the witch I said,
"You'd just torn open the fabric of Orbix and—?"

"I do not need you to make my accomplishment sound like
a seamstress ripping out a crooked hem," she snapped at me.
"Can *you* create such a worldpath, wizard?"

"If he could, would I be ready to date a halfway decent-
looking *voondrab*?" Scandal demanded. "Keep talking."

"There is little more to tell. Having opened the way, I forced
my foes back, back, back towards the opening. I saw the fear
wash over their faces as my power compelled them deeper and
deeper into the passageway. I followed, determined to push
them all the way through. The air around us swarmed with the
whimper of lost souls. Their combined spells grew ever
weaker. Wizards and sorceresses both depend upon Majyk to
work their enchantments, unlike witches, and Majyk does not
flourish far from its native soil. I could feel the power draining
from them. How I laughed! Panic bound them; they clung to
one another, desperately trying to hold on to the last strands of
their Majyk. In that moment, we broke through to the other
side. We were in a parkland. A single moon shone down. My
foes collapsed in a heap at my feet."

She slumped back against the desk. It looked like telling her
story had tired her out. Scandal rubbed his head against her
arm, purring.

"You know that part where you said there was little more to
tell? You lied," he said pleasantly. "Or else I'd hate to be
around when you've got a *lot* to tell. Hey, we know you didn't
kill 'em, but you can't just leave us hanging. What did you do
to them once you all pushed through to my home turf?"

"I left them there," the witch replied in a dead voice.

"You were merciful," I approved.

"No, I just couldn't find a big enough rock. I have better
ways to spend my time than trying to bash in someone's skull

using the wrong tool for the job. I told you, I'm efficient. So I just left them lying there. I scented many beings in the vicinity—beings who were armed and more than willing to do my killing for me."

"Except they didn't," Scandal guessed.

"You are right, cat." The witch stroked his head, sleeking back the pointed ears. "I left them to their doom, but they were uncooperative and avoided it. I blame myself. I might have explored the area more thoroughly. I could have found the right rock if I'd taken the trouble. Instead—"

She sighed and touched another dab of the salve to her lips. This time her robes blinked away, replaced by tight fitting blue cloth britches and an equally tight shirt like none I'd ever seen. It had short sleeves, fell just to the waist, and clung to her curves all the way. Across the front were strange runes whose meaning was a mystery to me.

Scandal, on the other hand, cocked his head and said, "Disneyworld, huh? Didja barf on Space Mountain?"

Gout was not amused. "Witches never . . . *barf*. Nor do we like to have our souvenirs stared at." She glowered at me.

It was the first time I'd ever heard them called souvenirs and I said so. Scandal rolled his eyes. "She means the shirt, boss. A souvenir's a little something you bring back with you from your travels so you won't forget where you've been." His ears twitched forward as he looked at Gout. "Something tells me you weren't the only one who came back from my world, Endora."

"That is so."

"Something tells me this *nice young couple* came back too, eventually."

Gout nodded.

"Something else tells me they also brought back a souvenir, only it wasn't just a lousy T-shirt," he concluded.

"It was not." She didn't have to say what it was. We knew. What's golden and glowing and makes your brother go *boom-crash-tinkle-tinkle?*

Oh, come on. Guess.

CHAPTER —————— 11

"BASEHART, *STAY HERE.*"

My brother stuck out his chin and poked me in the chest with two fingers. "I don't care how big a wizard you are, Kendar. You're still my baby brother and I don't have to take orders from you."

My hands became fists. I wanted to show him who was a baby. Then I felt a gloved hand fall lightly on my shoulder and heard Mysti's voice in my ear saying, "Don't make a scene."

"Too late," said Scandal. As usual, he was enjoying the fact that things were getting out of hand once more and that we were in the thick of it.

We were standing in the street in front of Solly Tapster's inn. (There were no words painted on the sign above the door—just a smiling portrait of Solly's wife—so the locals called the place either The Tapster's Wife Inn or At the Sign of the Skinny Nag.) We'd been standing there, arguing, long enough to attract a crowd of idlers, diversion-hungry housewives, and street urchins.

True to her word, Gout had restored Basehart to life as soon as she got all the fragments reassembled. It was amazing to watch her at work. All it took was the tiniest dab of her all-purpose salve applied to the tip of his nose and he sat up, alive and well. There was none of a wizard's intense concentration, preparation, or flash, just results. She *was* efficient.

As soon as he was healed, Basehart started arguing with me again. He hadn't stopped since. The fight went from the taproom, upstairs to our room, then out into the street, and he never missed a word. He argued about why I'd let him drink that hangover cure and why I'd brought a witch in to tend him and why I wasn't doing enough to hurry along the search for his bride. When I told him the witch had some important information that would help us, I thought it would calm him.

I was wrong.

"Basehart, I'm trying to be reasonable about this," I said, doing my best to ignore our growing audience. "You can come to see Calosta and Bibok *later*. I'm the only one going to them. It'll be best. I can say I'm a Magique customer who needs some so I can win the woman I love."

"Why all this goin' tippy-toe?" Basehart flung up one hand. "You told me this Magique's the stuff that was used to steal away Dulcetta. *Then* you told me these two are the ones who're sellin' it. I say we march into their place, make 'em tell us who's the one they sold to, *then* make 'em use the same stuff to find him for us." He crossed his arms. "Then after I kill him and rescue Dulcetta, I can go home and get married. Maybe I'll kill this Calosta and Bibok, too, for sellin' him the stuff in the first place."

Aunt Carageena looked up from where she sat with her sister on the bench in front of the inn. "Now Basehart, dear, that would be rude."

"Quite rude," Aunt Glucosia agreed, absent-mindedly running a whetstone over the blade of her dagger. "Maybe they didn't know he was going to use their product for evil purposes."

"Oh, riiiiight," Scandal said. "'Honest, Officer, when he came in here and bought that AK-47 I thought he was only gonna use it for a paperweight!'"

Aunt Carageena dug a small dried fish out of her belt pouch and stuffed it in the cat's mouth. "You be good," she directed.

"Murf," Scandal said, happily gorging. My aunts had developed the habit of giving the cat tidbits at the droop of a whisker, and he loved it.

Gout lounged against the inn wall next to the bench, her arms folded in perfect imitation of Basehart. "I like his idea just fine, rude or not," she said. "It's a shame we can't do it. I should know; I've tried to kill them myself."

"We *should* not do it," Mysti said emphatically.

"Not kill them?" Gout sneered. "From what I've been told, swordsman, these two had a hand in the vanishment of your beloved. And you don't crave revenge?"

"I would rather have Prince Boffin back, alive and well, than any measure of revenge," Mysti told her.

"Does he *have* to say stuff like that out loud where people can hear?" Basehart writhed with embarrassment. On cue, the crowd of children and idlers snickered, and most of the housewives blushed and hurried on their way.

Gout's cool gaze settled on my brother. "Why not? I find such frank speech refreshing."

"Yeah, but it's—"

"—unnatural?" The corner of Gout's lip twitched up. "He wants Prince Boffin back because he loves him. You want your bride back because you feel you have been robbed of your property. Don't deny it; I've heard you speak of her as if she were no more than a bale of old clothes."

"Don't *like* old clothes," Basehart grumped.

I touched Gout's arm. "He does love her," I murmured for her ears alone. "He just isn't used to talking about things like that."

Again I felt myself weighed in the witch's eyes, but this time it was only to see if I was telling the truth. At last she nodded slowly. "I'll take your word, Master Kendar. You know him better than I." She raised her voice so that all could hear: "And you know how you would fare against *two* spell-wielding opponents. Somehow, their stay on the Whirl'd ultimately strengthened their powers instead of weakening them. It's not Majyk—it can't be—but I don't know what it is."

"Which is why Kendar must approach them alone," Mysti added. "He can learn how strong they are, how we can best attack them, if we've got to attack them at all."

"He can also get some good use out of them first," Aunt Glucosia remarked. We all turned questioning looks on her. "Well, be practical about it," she went on. "Basehart was partly right: We *should* have them use their powers to locate Dulcetta for us, before anything else. We've followed her trail this far, but how do we know she and her captor are still in this town?"

"We don't even know if they *got* here," Basehart said, his whole stocky body a knot of badly held-in rage. "Just that they were *headed* here. We could've missed them on the road if they stopped somewhere between Uxwudge and Cheeseburgh."

"Oh, they *got* here," Aunt Carageena said casually.

"How do you know?"

"While you were all to pieces like that, Basehart dear, and Kendar was off having a little heart-to-heart with Mistress Gout, I took the liberty of stepping outside and bribing the town urchins."

The crowd of grubby children encircling us heard her talking about them and showed us gap-toothed smiles.

"A few coins, a few sweetmeats, and they agreed to scour Cheeseburgh for information."

"Looks like they should've scoured themselves for lice first." Basehart was not in one of his better moods. It didn't bother the children, who good-naturedly stuck out their tongues, thumbed their noses, and flung a few handfuls of horseflop at my brother.

"Now, now, children," Aunt Carageena said automatically.

"The little guttersnipes were a wonderful lot of help," Aunt Glucosia informed us. "They were back with all they knew before the last bit of Basehart was in place. They told us that a young woman answering Dulcetta's description was seen entering Cheeseburgh only a few days ago. She was accompanied by—"

"But is she *still* here?" I broke in, not wanting Basehart to hear Curio described in mouth-watering detail.

"Indeed she is," Aunt Carageena replied. "The kiddies would know if she were not. Isn't that right, my little sparrows?"

The children raised a garbled cry of agreement. Their leader—a bare-legged brat with a clout of dirty felt balanced on top of his head as an excuse for a hat—took it off in a mock-courtly gesture and said, "My da seen 'er in town t'other eve, just as t'marketfolk was packin' up."

"Was she alone?" Aunt Carageena asked.

The boy bobbed his head vigorously.

"Alone?" Basehart was stricken. If Dulcetta had eluded her captor, why wasn't she moving heaven and earth to race back to her lord-and-master-to-be?

"To divert suspicion," I said hastily. "The evil magician who stole her away must have her under some kind of invisible control—the best ones can do that. Or else he made *himself* invisible and was with her all the time."

Basehart gave me a suspicious look. "Dulcetta's the captive of a spell-juggler who can make her do what he wants from far off *or* make himself invisible?"

"Or both." Scandal was being helpful again.

"And all I've got on my side's you," my brother concluded. "I ain't seen you work one spell since we left home. Oh, we've *really* got a chance of rescuing Dulcetta from this other wizard; *if* we ever find her." I opened my mouth to reply, but he just waved me off, shoulders slumped.

"What was the lady doing in the market?" Mysti asked the urchin.

He snorted. "Loose that mask, bucko; it's smothered yer brains. What's *to* do in market? Laded wif coin, she were. Bought up 'arf t' stock o' Martin Scribbler's stall an' filled 'er a baskie o' food from Mum's place, too."

"It sounds as if she were packing provisions for a long journey." Mysti was grim. "They might have been on the road before dawn."

"They wasn't," said the boy.

"How can you be so sure? Did you see the lady since?"

"No. But I knows they wasn't goin' nowhere."

Mysti's hand was lightning. It struck the lad at the back of the neck and lifted him off his feet. "Prove your words, ragamuffin, or I'll toss you in the horse trough."

"Lemme go! Lemme go!" The child twitched and squirmed at the threat of water. "I knows they didn't leave town yet 'cos the lady told Mum she was goin' t' take the sossidge what Mum sold her an' eat it that very night."

"A sausage dinner proves nothing."

"One o' me *Mum's* sossidge's proves plenty!" the boy argued. "Eat one o' them an' you'll be stayin' put fer a week at least, I promises!"

One of his smaller cohorts removed a grimy finger from up his nose and added, "Tha's true. Me own da ate one o' Mistress Loosestrife's sossidges an' t' effect on t' ecology's been sommat fierce."

"The effect on *what*?" I goggled at the brat.

"T' ecology," he repeated, wiping his finger on the seat of his britches. "Tha's like trees an' plants an' beasts an' garbage an' other living things. Mistress Calosta told me."

"You know the sorceress?"

King Steffan could have taken lessons in scorn from that little boy, except the king would not have stuck a finger back up his nose first. "Who don't? My ma, she's savin' up all t' coin she can so's she can buy us a dose o' Magique. Just enough as'll scrub out t' privy for 'er, she says."

"What did I tell you?" Gout's bitter voice stung my ears. "Now even the lowest seek to own the smallest drop of that poisonous stuff. Before long there will be more accidents caused by faulty Magique—more and worse! When this whole town shatters into a million pieces, they'd better not come crying to me."

"Then the sooner we learn how to stop it, the better," I said. "I'm going after them."

Basehart's eyes narrowed. "I'm coming," he said for what seemed like the fiftieth time.

"Oh, let him go," Gout said, exasperated. "We waste time arguing."

"All right," I said, giving up. "You can come with me, Basehart. Just don't kill anything."

He gave me a smug victor's smile. "No promises."

"You goin' t' see Mistress Calosta?" the head urchin demanded. "I can take you there." He stuck out a spotty palm.

"Why should we pay you anything?" Gout asked. "Even a total stranger in town would have to be blind to miss that house."

The boy grinned like a shark. "You can pay me t' take 'em to Mistress Calosta, else Mistress Calosta'll be glad t' pay me for word o' who's been talkin' o' killin' her." He gazed meaningly at Basehart.

"You are a hateful little beggar and you will come to no good end," the witch said. "Very well, you win. Wait there and I'll fetch your payment." She ducked into the inn, only to emerge a short time later holding something small, furry, and squirmy in her fist. The forefinger of her other hand glistened with a touch of magical salve. "You've earned this," she said, dabbing the goo on the animal's long, naked tail.

Scandal hissed and spat explosively as the rat dropped from Gout's hand, swelled to the height and bulk of a small cottage, and gnashed teeth the size of floor planks. Its burning red eyes fixed on the children, and a low, menacing cry that sounded like *cheeeeeeeeeble* welled out of its throat just before it leaped. The crowd of ragamuffins scattered screaming, with the rat in pursuit. They were soon lost to sight, although I shuddered when I thought I caught wind of crunching noises coming from a few streets away.

"That's done," Gout said, wiping her hands.

"That monster will destroy the town!" I protested.

"Really, Kendar dear, such a fuss over nothing." Aunt Glucosia got up and stretched her limbs, then drew steel. "Coming, Gee'?"

Aunt Carageena yawned. "No, you go ahead. It's not like there was two of 'em."

"Awfully sporting of you," Aunt Glucosia said brightly and strode off whistling the traditional Gangle hunting song ("The Gallant Deer Do Spurt When Slain").

The witch looked at us. "If she wants to slay anything, she'd better hurry; it's only a temporary spell. Run along now, boys." We ran, and Scandal sprinted after.

"By Wedwel's great temple in the Noxious Wasteland!" Basehart gasped when he first saw the house. "That's a *big* one!"

"Mistress Gout wasn't lying when she said we couldn't miss it," I said. "It's almost as big as Uxwudge! How did they ever afford to build something that size?"

"No one ever went broke underestimating the intelligence of the Cheeseburghers," Scandal said. "Actually, that should be Americans, but when in Rome . . ."

Basehart and I both stared at him as if he'd dropped out of a gumball tree.

"Okay, words of one syllable coming up," the cat said. "What I *mean* is, these guys have done good peddling Magique to people too stupid to see the danger and too lazy to care."

Basehart scratched his head as his eyes floated up and up and up the towering façade of the house. "They sure must've sold a *lot* of Magique," he said.

True enough. The house stood on the main square of Cheeseburgh, facing a public fountain. As if in challenge, the house had its own fountain in front, only slightly smaller than the town's, much prettier, and much, much cleaner. The building itself was part of a row of similar houses. Similar? Like a twig is similar to a wizard's wand. I remarked this to Basehart.

He scratched his head again. "How d'you figure? All of these houses here are two stories tall—"

"Except each story on *that* house is as tall as one and a half stories on the others," I pointed out.

"—and they're all plaster-front buildings with the big beams stickin' out."

"Only the plaster on *that* house has got about a thousand hand-sized mirrors set into it. The whole place glitters like a diamond!"

Basehart frowned in thought. "They must be showoffs, huh?"

Scandal climbed up my leg, over my back, and perched on the shoulder nearest Basehart. From there he hollered in my brother's ear, "Hello? Hello? Operator, I'd like to report a man with a death-grip on the obvious. Hermits don't usually put neon signs up on the roof, baby."

He gestured with a paw. Most tradesmen have their signs above the door, hanging out over the street. Bibok and Calosta had theirs running along the front of their house. It covered the roof peak and climbed higher than that on a frame of wooden slats. Attached to the framework was a tangled web of weirdly glowing tubes that traced a pink cauldron bubbling over with golden brew. It was being stirred by an eternally grinning red-haired woman, her hair, her face, and her dress all outlined in the same shining magic. Yellow circles of different sized lights flashed on and off above the cauldron, making it look like bubbles were rising from the surface. The entire scene was framed by a pair of gleaming golden arches.

The cat jumped off my shoulder and trotted purposefully towards the front door. "Scandal!" I called after him, but he kept going. I had to follow, and to blazes whether Basehart tagged along or not. I caught up with him just as he scratched at the door. Sweeping him up into my arms, I waggled a finger in his face and said, "Bad ca—*ow!*"

"Cow?" a musical voice sounded in my ear. "I thought we paid the mayor enough to move the cattle market."

The door was open and I was looking into a pair of the largest, warmest brown eyes I'd ever seen on anyone not wearing a saddle. Her skin, too, was brown, and the soft cloud of her hair that twinkled with a scattering of jeweled bands. Chain after chain of delicately gemmed gold rode the generous curves of her bosom. A breath of orange silk spilled over her body from one shoulder, down the graceful slopes of breasts, belly, and impossibly long legs, all the way to her naked feet. Then she smiled, and the shining sign on the roof was like midnight in a black bear's belly by comparison.

"Oh, customers!" she exclaimed. "Won't you come in?" She moved more fluidly than a dancer.

"Steady, big fella," Scandal whispered to me as we filed into the house.

I could hear Basehart's sharply indrawn breath behind me. The house's spectacular outside was a stingy hint of the marvels within. Everywhere we looked, we saw wonders. *Illuminum* globes shed their steady light over niches and tables and shelves crammed with extraordinary objects.

"I am Calosta," she told us as she led the way deeper into the house. "I don't remember seeing you boys in Cheeseburgh before."

"We just got into town," I said.

"Oh? That explains why you came to the front door. My partner is very strict about clients using the back door only, but he's visiting the mayor right now, so I don't think he'll mind." She paused and smiled indulgently at us. "I know what it's like to be from out of town."

"Where are you from, then?" Basehart asked.

"Plunj."

"Plunj!" My brother haw-hawed. "No one's from *Plunj*. It's all jungles there, with maybe a handful of naked savages swinging from the trees."

To my surprise, Basehart's rudeness didn't make her angry. "If you were to visit the jungles of Plunj, young man, I *think* we might be able to come up with a sharply pointed argument or two to change your mind. Our warriors are well trained and highly patriotic. They don't like people who assume that just because we live in a jungle, we don't know how to dress."

"I can see that's not true," I said. I meant it. The longer I stared at Calosta's dress, the more I wanted to be it.

She patted my cheek, making it flame. "Aren't you sweet! And what do you know of Plunj?"

"No—nothing," I had to admit.

She laughed again. The sound made my brain fizz happily. "I'm not surprised. Oh, don't feel ignorant! No one in these lands knows much about what the jungles of Plunj conceal, because we don't get too many visitors. I blame the climate. Who wants to hack his way through all that vegetation, just to go sightseeing? And the bugs—! The only tourists we get are freebooters and all they want to do is steal from our temples. You know, it's the oddest thing: Our tribal idols are practically *basted* with jewels, but the only thing these adventurers ever want to take is the idol's *eye*. It finally got so bad that the High Priest took out the Sacred Eye of Delbert himself and replaced it with a hunk of glass. 'Now let 'em steal it all they want,' he said." She saw my troubled expression and frowned. "What's wrong?"

I just shook my head. I was thinking about how bad Aunt Glucosia was going to feel if she ever found out that her cherished Eye of Delbert was a fake.

Calosta led on. We passed a table laden with clay animals whose pelts were in reality a waving sea of living grass. In a niche we saw a small box from which the music of a hundred minstrels played. Beside it, a monstrous toy shaped like a flower with a human face bobbed and weaved and shook its petals in time to the music.

Our lovely guide paused before a tall, shining red and white box the size of a coffin. I touched it, expecting something so bright to be metal, but it was made of a strange, hard substance that felt like a beetle's back. She pressed one of the many small panels decorating the front of the box. A terrifying rumble shook it, followed by a loud *clunk*. She stooped to retrieve a cylinder from the compartment at the bottom of the mysterious box.

"Thirsty?"

It took me a few moments before I realized she was offering it to me. I forced my hand not to tremble as I accepted it. It was cold and damp, but at least it had the recognizable feel of metal, even if it was garishly swirled with red and white. I stared at it, not knowing what to do.

She laughed. "Allow me." She took it back and made a sign of power over the top of the cylinder. I heard a pop and a fierce hiss before she handed it back. A hole had opened in the metal, releasing weird sounds and smells. While I hesitated, she repeated the business with the big box and the small cylinders, handing one to Basehart and keeping one for herself. I watched her set it to her lips and tilt back her head, like it was a simple drinking cup. I tried to imitate her action, but a flock of invisible spirits, freed from their metal prison, swarmed straight up my nose and made me choke on the sugary, tingling liquid.

"The pause that refreshes," Scandal said. Calosta did not comment on the cat. Like Gout, she must've known one when she saw one. After all, she'd been on the Whirl'd.

I choked down what I could of the drink and followed the sorceress's lead once more. She tossed our empty containers into a barrel decorated with the picture of a tree ringed by two arrows chasing each other in a circle. "Always respect the ecology," she said.

"Eek-ology?" Basehart repeated, with a sidelong glance at me. I shrugged. It was the second time we'd heard that word and we still weren't quite sure what it meant.

"The study of screaming," Scandal told us.

We went through many other rooms, each piled high with more rarities than the last. One held no furniture except a stepladder, but the walls were covered with tiny, rectangular pictures of men dressed in outlandish clothing. Most of them were armed with long, wooden clubs.

"What happened to the rest of this fellow's hat brim?" Basehart demanded, poking at one of the pictures. "It's all gone in back and just sticking out in front like a duck's bill!"

Calosta slapped his hand away. "Don't touch the mint Mickey Mantle!" she barked.

"Mantel?" Basehart grumbled to me later. "What mantel? I didn't even see a fireplace." He licked his fingertip. "Don't taste much like mint, neither."

At last we reached the back of the house. It was set up like a common apothecary's shop, the walls lined with shelves packed close with bottles of all shapes and sizes. They were empty. There was also a table covered with a bright yellow cloth fringed with green, four straight-back chairs, and a—a—

"That's a water cooler," Scandal said. "But that sure as heck ain't Perrier in there." And it wasn't. Not unless Perrier was another name for Magique.

"What a smart kitty," Calosta said, her voice sounding a lot like Scandal's warmest purr. "Remind me to give you an itsy-bitsy taste of caviar before you go."

"Business before fish eggs, babe." The cat twitched his ears forward. "My friend here wants to buy a little yellow bottle of liquid miracles. Looks like you've got enough in stock to give him a good price on it, too."

"A very good price." The sorceress's eyelids lowered. "Your friend looks like such a charming, shy young man. Alas, I know all too well that young men are seldom wealthy. What do you wish to use the Magique for? A matter of the heart, perhaps?" She was looking right at me.

"Ummmm, there's this girl and—" I began.

"Of course there is." She patted my cheek and without another word snatched two bottles from the dozens of empties on the shelves. She placed them beneath the tap and released a thin stream of Magique. Bubbles rose in the huge glass container above. She took two wax wafers from a box on the table, sealed the bottles, and held them just out of my reach. "I like you," she said.

Aw, not *again*!

"I like you so much, young man, that seeing as how this is your first time, and you want to use my product for romantic purposes, I'm prepared to give it to you for a very special price. All you have to do is answer me one teensy-weensy little question. Agreed?"

"Agreed."

The word hardly had time to leave my mouth. Like a snake striking, she smashed the smaller bottle of Magique at my feet. Iron bars sprouted from the floorboards in a circle surrounding Basehart and me. They arched over us and tied themselves into a tidy knot above our heads. As I watched, slender metal thorns branched off on the inside of our cage, edging their way steadily towards us. Basehart yelped with pain as one, longer than the rest, pricked his arm.

I acted without thinking, my mind filled with terror. I felt Majyk rise within me, break from my hands like a sea wave. The iron slivers bent back against the invisible pulse of shielding spells, but a fresh crop came at us. I closed my eyes, feeling the power that Majyk lent me, and forced it out against the hungry thorns. I hears Scandal hiss, my brother gasp, and metal scream.

I opened my eyes to see the cage shattered around us.

"With my compliments." Calosta handed me the second bottle. "That answered my question perfectly."

CHAPTER ———————— 12

"MORE BRIE?" SAID THE SORCERESS.

Basehart and I sat on one side of a low, black-lacquered table, fidgeting like a pair of fleas on a hot griddle. Calosta had brought us to this room immediately after her little test revealed what she already suspected: that I was a wizard. (Well, come on! If a witch like Gout says my Majyk screamed its head off at her, why should a sorceress like Calosta be hard of hearing?)

"My legs hurt," Basehart complained. No surprise. There were no chairs in this room. The three of us sat around the table on thin mats of woven straw. He helped himself to another chunk of runny cheese. My brother could have his legs chewed off by slimegrinds and it still wouldn't affect his appetite.

The sorceress laughed. "It takes a while to get used to *tatami*," she said. "But I assure you, your back will be all the better for trying."

"To-Tommy who?"

"Sushi?" She passed me a tray beautifully arranged and decorated with pieces of Wedwel-knows-what. Scandal's head popped up over the edge of the table, his ears alive with interest.

"Do I smell fish?" He sniffed urgently at the tray.

"Huh!" Basehart picked up a piece with his fingers. "Where I come from, we call this stuff *bait*." He crammed it into his mouth. "Good, though."

The cat jumped onto the table and sauntered over to the tray, tail high. "Sweetcheeks, I hate to break it to you," he told the sorceress, "but if you're a Whirl'd wannabe, you don't serve sushi with brie."

Calosta frowned. "I don't?"

"Hey, trust me! I was born and raised there, y'know. Plus I used to live with a computer wizard, and did he ever have the big bucks! He could buy custom-tailored brie, if he wanted. *Faux* sushi. Ours-alone limited edition cappuccino. The only thing that kept him from being God's gift to yuppiedom was the fact that he was the legendary lost King of the Nerds."

Basehart poked me in the leg. "Your familiar is casting a spell. Is that all right?"

"Casting—?"

"He's using all those funny words. You don't think it's a curse, do you? I only stepped on his tail once . . . or maybe two—*three* times . . . today."

"It's not a spell," I whispered. "Look, the sorceress understands what he's saying."

If she didn't, she was doing a great imitation. "If all you know, you learned from this nerd, how can I be sure you're right?" she asked Scandal. "Nerds are not famous for their familiarity with the social graces." She gave him an indulgent smile. "I'll bet this geek was even a Trekkie."

"Of *course* he was!" the cat replied, as if it was the most natural thing in the world. "Geek and Trek go together like—like—Well, *not* like brie and sushi. With brie you always have a nice, dry white wine, green grapes, and the news that little Muffy was accepted at Miss Porter's school, unless you prefer saying Tripper got tapped for Skull and Bones."

"Muffy?" Basehart looked worried. "Geek? Trek? Tripper? Kendar, he's talking about *skulls and bones*! Are you sure he's not putting a curse on us so he can go off with the witch?"

"Sorceress," I corrected him. "And Scandal wouldn't do that." Not just for some raw fish, anyway.

Calosta sat up straighter, paying close attention to Scandal. "And what about the sushi?" she asked.

"Oh, that you serve with *wasabi*, pickled ginger, with a few bottles of warm *sake* and a big business contract with Mitsubishi afterwards."

Calosta scratched Scandal behind the ears. His purring filled the room. "You are a wise beast. How do you happen to speak? When my beloved Bibok and I were visiting your Whirl'd, none of our kitties said a single word. They made their wishes known without speech."

"Trade secret." Scandal purred even louder. "So you guys are cat people, huh? Fur out."

"If that's the best pun you can come up with, perhaps it was a mercy that our cats did *not* speak." The sorceress tickled the cat under his chin.

"Better costs more," Scandal replied. "*Habla usted* money? Cash? Simoleons? Save your breath; I know you do. It shows."

"What's a little honest capitalism among friends?" Calosta shrugged her adorable shoulders. "Orbix has always had merchants. Bibok and I are just following in a long established tradition."

That was it for me. "It's *not* a tradition to sell dangerous things, pretending they're harmless," I spoke up.

"Maybe not on Orbix," Scandal murmured.

"I see you've never eaten Mistress Loosestrife's sausages," Calosta responded to my accusation. "We sell nothing harmful."

"Yeah? Well, my brother got some of your Magique into him as part of a hangover cure and the next thing we knew, he exploded!"

The sorceress was untroubled by this news. "We are not responsible for consumer error. All money is cheerfully refunded if the complaint is accompanied by a valid receipt and the reason for return is a defect in the product. This guarantee does not cover damage caused by deliberate misuse, inappropriate application, or acts of gods." She glanced at Basehart. "Besides, he looks fine."

"Thanks to Mistress Gout, I do," Basehart growled.

"Ah, you know Mistress Gout." The words slipped from Calosta's lips like a snake.

"And so do you." Since there were no more big secrets left to reveal, we might as well speak openly. "She's the one who exiled you to the Whirl'd."

"So she did." The sorceress's eyes burned with a sleepy flame. "We really ought to have her over for brunch some day, to thank her properly. If not for her . . . silly temper, none of this would have happened." She embraced the entire room and the house beyond it with a sweeping gesture.

"Huh?" Basehart said. "You found that Magique stuff there?"

"Now there's a woman who really knows how to shop," Scandal remarked. "This is the first time I heard of something like Magique on my homeworld, and I'm from L.A.!"

"How about those Dodgers?" Calosta said sweetly, scratching Scandal's ears again. To us she said, "The cat is right: There
is nothing like Majyk or Magique where he comes from, not
even in Bloomingdale's. What they call magic is mere sleight-
of-hand, performed by mummers and mountebanks. I can't tell
you how depressing it was for us the whole time we were there,
shorn of our powers."

"You lost your Majyk?" I was puzzled. "But—how did you
manage to get back here without it?"

"Trade secret." Her smile took the sting out of her answer.
"No, no; I'll tell. Professional courtesy, and all that. You are
very young to be a wizard, Master—?"

"Kendar, Kendar Ratwha—Kendar Gangle," I said quickly.
"And this is my brother, Basehart."

"Charmed." She fluttered her thick, sooty eyelashes at
Basehart. He just hacked off another hunk of brie, spread it on
a piece of sushi, and shoved the whole thing into his mouth.
"As I was saying, Master Kendar, you are young. You have
obviously gone far beyond your preliminary studies or you
wouldn't possess so much raw Majykal power. But a wizard's
life, like a sorceress's, is one of continual learning. Since I see
you in possession of a Whirl'dly familiar, I conclude that you
have learned the way to open temporary passageways from that
place to this."

"Uh . . . yeah." She didn't need to know that my discovery
of the rat hole that brought Scandal to Orbix was pure accident.

"I thought so. Still, perhaps your studies have not yet
revealed that there are other passageways—naturally occurring
paths between Orbix and the Whirl'd and—Well, no wizard
has yet found one that leads elsewhere, but that does not mean
it is impossible."

"Cue the *Twilight Zone* theme and batten down the hatches,
Cap'n," Scandal announced. "Prepare to be boarded by Romu-
lans off the starboard rat hole."

"So you and Bibok found a way home without Majyk," I
said.

She nodded. "They do exist. Gout herself returned by one
such route, although as a witch, she had an advantage. Witches
do not rely on Majyk to work their spells, so she had nothing
to lose when we all fell through her spellway into the Whirl'd."

"Where'd you find your yellow brick rathole, toots?" Scandal asked. "Mine was up an alley in East L.A."

"There's this *precious* little shoe boutique just off Lexington Avenue in the seventies. I was trying on a pair of Maud Frizon pumps when I thought I felt a draft and smelled a breath of familiar air. It was coming from behind a Japanese screen. I whispered instructions to Bibok and had him distract the salesgirl while I investigated. Sure enough, there was a hole in the wall; the screen hid it. I sent the girl off in search of something tasty in a spiked heel and dragged Bibok through my discovery before he could protest. We found ourselves back on Orbix, and back in possession of all our powers."

"And Magique," I said.

"Not right away, Master Kendar. The only thing we brought with us from the Whirl'd were the clothes on our backs and the Maud Frizon pumps on my feet. If I ever do pop back for a visit, I hope it's well after the statute of limitations for shoplifting has passed." She chuckled.

"Back?" Every fiber of Scandal's body was tense with excitement. "You know a way back?"

"Of course I do." She seemed surprised by his question.

"How'd you find it? You make it yourself, like Gout?"

"Why should I bother? To make a spellway costs too much, as Gout herself could tell you. It's exhausting. I have better ways to spend my powers. Besides, man-made spellways can sometimes collapse before you've passed through them all the way. If you're caught by such a disaster, you might be crushed, destroyed, or merely lost forever in the void between. No one has ever come back to say which."

"For obvious reasons. That means you know where there's a one hundred percent natural, organic, totally recylcable spellway to my world?" Scandal was almost trembling. "How'd you find it?"

"Easily enough: I wanted to know the location of the nearest one in case we couldn't get any really *good* white wine here. Fortunately a vineyard near Lower Bevis produces a perfectly *darling* vintage that's as good as any Chablis I've ever had: flinty and robust, with an assertive nose and—"

Scandal arched his back and hissed. "I'm gonna bite your assertive if you don't tell me how you found that spellway!"

"What a funny question! A properly directed vision gave me

the information. I simply called it up on my gazing crystal."
She turned to me. "I find that crystal spheres give you much
clearer reception than magic mirrors, don't you agree?"

"Uhhhhh . . . really?" I could *feel* Scandal giving me a
dirty look. Visions! Yet another lesson in wizardly studies that
I still hadn't mastered. And how easy it would have made
everything. If I could summon visions, Prince Boffin's fate
wouldn't still be a mystery. If I could summon visions, we
wouldn't be blundering through Cheeseburgh, hoping for a clue
to Dulcetta's whereabouts.

If I could summon visions, Scandal wouldn't be glaring at
me like that, and moving closer and closer to the sorceress.

"Show it to me," he said to her.

"I? But surely your Master Kendar—"

"You know what you said about how much raw power the
kid's got? Raw is the word. He's got Majyk out the kazoo, but
he can't play a tune on it. Just because you buy a truckload of
paint don't make you DaVinci, know what I mean?"

"Indeed." Calosta regarded me thoughtfully.

"*Scandal!*" I meant it to be a reprimand, but it came out
whiny.

"Hey! Lay off," the cat snapped. "I'm the one who kept
telling you to put wheels on your wizard lessons, remember?
You're the geek who dragged his feet. Maybe if you'd've done
what I said, you'd have *cable* vision by now! Visions of where
to find me a girl cat of the female persuasion. And *I* wouldn't
be trying to date voondrabs."

"Traitor!" Basehart yelled at Scandal. "So what if Kendar's
a lousy wizard? *She* didn't need to know!"

"I got news for you, Flintstone. If I'd kept quiet, she still
would've figured it out. She's your worst nightmare; a woman
who *thinks*. And now this late-breaking bulletin: Most of them
do. Even Dulcetta. Which is why she took a powder sooner
than set up cave-keeping with *you*!"

"*That's a lie!*" Basehart lunged for Scandal. The cat jumped
lightly out of the way and my brother slid across the table on
his stomach. Cheese and fish scattered all over the mats. Blind
with rage, Basehart grabbed the nearest object and threw it at
the cat. It was a piece of sushi; Scandal caught it between his
teeth and gobbled it down.

"All is forgiven," he said before dodging Basehart again.

"Stop that," Calosta said calmly, and stretched out her hand. Immediately Basehart froze where he was, up on one knee, groping around for something else to pitch at Scandal.

"Your familiar is very wise, Master Kendar." The sorceress spoke to me as casually as if my brother had just stepped out of the room. "The same test I used to prove you were a wizard also revealed how good a wizard you were. Forgive me, but the answer is, not very. Were it otherwise, I would now be trying to kill you instead of feed you."

My face felt like it was on fire. It's one thing to know you're no whiz at wizardry; it's another to be told it in a way that implies *you're so pathetic, I don't have anything to fear from you.*

"Besides," she went on, "even if you did know how to use all the Majyk you possess, you are still only one wizard. With our powers pooled, Bibok and I are more than a match for you."

"You wouldn't be a match for the Council," I challenged.

"The Council? Darling men. We've already been visited by one of their number. Gout's doing, most likely. He found nothing wrong with our product. You see, Magique is perfectly legal. It isn't Majyk—not exactly—so the Council sees no problem with ordinary people using it."

"But it *breaks!*"

"Don't shout. You heard our guarantee. If any Magique we sell malfunctions, it was only because the buyer didn't use it correctly."

"That's an excuse and you know it."

Calosta's teeth were brilliant. "Prove it. Come with me and I'll show you how we manufacture it. You'll see that we work under purely state-of-the-black-arts conditions." She unfolded her long legs and stood up.

I got to my feet a lot less gracefully. "You're willing to show me this?" I asked, hardly believing my ears.

"It will set your mind at ease, and that in turn will get you off my back and out of my house," she replied evenly. "You're no threat, but you are becoming a bit of a pest." She headed for the door.

"Wait! What about him?" I pointed at Basehart.

"He'll keep." She left the room without another word, Scandal at her heels, and I had to scurry after.

CHAPTER ——————— 13

"AND THIS IS WHERE THE MAGIC HAPPENS," SAID THE sorceress. "Small 'm' magic, that is." A sweep of her lithe brown arm took in a single long table bearing a forest of twinkling tubes, bubbling glass pots, and evilly smoking clay vessels. The air was thick with the smell of melting cheese.

"Good Lord, Holmes!" Scandal gasped. "It's the pizza parlor of Dr. Frankenstein!"

Calosta knelt gracefully. "Does kitty like pizza?"

"You bet, Big Mama." Scandal licked his chops. "One major anchovy pizza, to go, hold the crust, the sauce, the oil, and the oregano."

She ruffled his head fur. "Maybe later. Right now we have to show your Master Kendar how we make our Magique."

To my dismay I heard Scandal say clearly, "Maybe he's *called* Master Kendar, but no way is he *my* Master Kendar."

Calosta's teeth sparkled when she laughed. "Of course! How foolish of me, calling anyone the master of a cat. Bibok and I have gone much too long without one of your tribe to share our lives. I forgot my manners. Can you ever forgive me?"

"Where I come from, forgiveness is spelled F-O-O-D."

"I thought it might." Calosta straightened like a reed when the wind stops blowing. She glided over to a cabinet built into the wall behind the seething, boiling, steaming setup on the table and took out a small blue bottle. "Would you do the honors, Master Kendar?" she asked, giving it to me.

I didn't know what she wanted me to do, but I didn't want to look stupid, so I uncorked the bottle and sniffed the contents suspiciously. The fumes tickled my nose. I peered down the long, blue bottleneck and saw a muzzy glow waiting at the

bottom. It was hard to tell what color it really was; because of
the blue glass, it looked a little green.

help me . . .

Was it my imagination? A faint, tiny voice crept into my
head. Where was it coming from?

And again: *help me . . . please . . .*

So small, so very small and helpless and desperate. My hand
tingled around the bottle. "This is . . . interesting," I said,
playing for time.

The sorceress took the bottle from me again. The tingling
and the voice died together. "I never heard anyone call a cat's
dinner interesting," she said, and turned the bottle upside-
down. A stream of dingy golden light spilled out, splashing to
the floor at Scandal's feet. As soon as it hit the planks, it turned
into a silver bowl of finely minced meat so savory smelling I
felt my own mouth watering.

"Whoa! Purina beef-and-thingies Supreme! Come to Papa!"
Scandal pounced on the bowl and gobbled it down to the last
morsel.

"I'm surprised you don't know how to manage Magique,"
Calosta said to me, one eyebrow raised. "You have some skill
with Majyk, and that's the basic ingredient. Allow me to show
you."

She took me by the arm and drew me after her to one end of
the table. A nearly empty glass flask balanced on an iron tripod
set up over a miniature charcoal-stoked brazier. The sides of
the flask were stained with the afterglow of Majyk.

"This is where we begin," she said. "I see we need a refill.
We have a large order to process today for our best customer.
Let's get started, shall we?"

She rested one finger on the rim of the flask and spoke
several words I didn't understand. A ball of Majyk the size of
a pigeon's egg formed at the tip of one long, sharp nail. She
tapped her finger smartly against the glass lip and the ball of
Majyk fell into the flask.

My hand lifted up and reached out for the Majyk automatically. My skin prickled, all the Majyk already in me trying to
contact that tiny bit Calosta had freed from her own hoard.

But before I could do anything, the sorceress made a delicate
gesture with her hands, like a swarm of butterflies taking wing.
Immediately a huge jug floated off the floor and tipped itself

over above the flask. A perfectly directed stream of water glugged down the flask's neck, engulfing the Majyk inside. I pulled back my hand, startled.

"And that's how we do it," Calosta told me.

"Just like that?" I couldn't believe that was all there was to it. For one thing, the stuff in the flask still felt like Majyk—soggy Majyk, unhappy Majyk, spluttery, dripping, angry Majyk—but nothing at all like Magique. "You just add water?"

"And stir," Scandal remarked with his mouth full.

"It's not just plain old water," said Calosta with a mischievous twinkle. "If it were, all we'd have at the end was a lot of wet Majyk; Majyk that could break free or be recaptured from the water at any time, by any half-competent magician."

I didn't like the way she looked right at me when she said *half-competent*.

"If you put salt in water and stir it up, you might think you've made something new," she went on. "But it's still just salt and water. Leave that brine out in the sun and soon enough you'll have the salt again, just as it was. On the other hand, bake a cake from eggs and flour and honey and milk, and I defy you to separate the ingredients from the end product so easily."

I sniffed the lip of the flask. My nose twitched. I could feel Majyk sloshing around in there, seeking a way out. All I'd have to do was pour it out and absorb it for myself. It wasn't part of Master Thengor's original hoard, but that shouldn't matter. It was free Majyk and I was a wizard. All I needed to do was—

—nothing. This was Majyk that came from Calosta. What if there was something strange about it? She was a sorceress from Plunj. They did things differently in the jungle, Aunt Glucosia said. ("All that fertility, sprouting up everywhere. You can't turn around without having something going all ripe in your face. Ripe and *burgeoning*. There ought to be a law against things burgeoning in public, where the children can see and ask questions. And when it isn't burgeoning, it's throbbing. Then the humidity gives everyone a headache, so what's the use?")

Maybe their Majyk was different, too. I didn't want to risk it. I'd almost died from absorbing tainted Majyk aboard the good ship *Golden Fleece*. I wasn't in a hurry to repeat that experience.

I looked up at Calosta. "You're wrong. It hasn't changed. It's still just water and Majyk."

"It hasn't changed *yet*," she replied, holding up one finger the way Master Thengor used to do when he was making an important point in class. "We've got all these tubes and retorts and whatnots hooked up together for a reason, Master Kendar. Right now, the Majyk and the water are like—like—" She searched the air for the right words. "—like two people who are attracted to each other. He is handsome beyond your wildest dreams, she has a nice-enough face if you care for the cold, horsey type. She believes that they are meant to be together, but they are only together the way this table and that chair are together in this room. Coincidence is not passion."

"Are you talking about Bibok and Mistress Gout?" I asked.

"No, she's talking about Sonny and Cher," Scandal snapped.

Calosta continued as if I'd never said a thing. "Ahhh, but combine that same gloriously handsome man with another woman, a different woman, a woman worthy of him, and they are no longer two people who happen to be together. They have melded into an entirely new creation, inseparable!"

"Like a cake?" I asked.

Calosta wasn't listening. A blue fire crackled in her right palm, a yellow spark in her left. As she spoke, they rose and moved together, forming a single green flame. It blazed in midair, reflected in her shining eyes. "Their two selves have become a fresh individual, merged so completely that only a witch with the brains of a village idiot would even *dream* she had a hope of coming between us!" The green flame leaped and exploded in a blinding flash of pure white light. I threw my arm across my eyes, but I was still dazzled.

"Now, now, cupcake," came a deep voice from the darkness. "Daddy's little Calikins mustn't get herself all worked up like that. You know what it does to your biorhythms."

I blinked away the jagged-edged afterimages and saw the tall man standing in the doorway. He had to be Bibok. He couldn't be anyone else. For one thing, he was just as handsome as Gout and Calosta had said he was. For a second, he came into the room like he owned the place. For a third, the instant he got close enough, Calosta pasted herself to his chest like a tattoo, her legs wrapped around his waist, her hands knotted in his silvery curls, her lips planting dozens of kisses all over his face.

Still wearing the sorceress, he turned to me and offered his hand. "Hi! Super to see you, just super. I'm Bibok, but my friends call me—Well, son-of-a-gun, I guess my friends call me Bibok, too. And you are—"

"Master Kendar Gangle."

"*Master* Kendar Gangle!" He acted like that was the best piece of news he'd heard all day. Carefully he peeled off Calosta and shooed her back towards the table. "Run along and do your cute little career-thing, angel," he told her. To me he repeated, "*Master* Kendar. That means you're a *wizard*! Oh, marvelous! Simply marvelous. You know, I dabble a bit in wizardry myself. Strictly self-taught. Nothing to brag about, but I make do. Gosh, you must step into my den afterwards. I'll bet there's all sorts of tricks you could teach me. Nothing fancy, just a little something to keep us amused when the winter nights get long, the brandy gets low, and the remarks get personal, heh, heh, heh." He slung one arm over my shoulders.

I removed it the way I'd seen Mom deal with a pile of deer droppings when Dad forgot to wipe his feet and it was the servants' day off. "Is this how you got around the Council?" I asked coldly. "All this gushing and grinning and flattery?"

"That, and a matched set of luggage." The grin was gone, the gushing stopped. Bibok's whole face went from warm and brainless to steely and sly. "You miscalculated on this one, Calipoo," he called to the sorceress. "He's not *that* stupid."

"No, darling, but he *is* harmless. He's got enough Majyk to turn Orbix inside-out, but he can hardly use it. He just *watched* while I freed a drop of my own Majyk. Didn't even try to grab it! Is that like any other wizard you know?"

Bibok rubbed his perfect chin. "I don't know . . . No one with all that power could look this dumb and be that helpless. It could be a trick."

"What, you guys don't believe in truth in advertising?" Scandal plunked himself down between Bibok and me, tail lashing the air.

"The same way I believe in government intelligence and one-size-fits-all," Bibok replied. He didn't seem at all surprised by the presence of the cat. "But then, I'd expect a familiar to take his master's side."

"You've got that wrong, sweetheart," Calosta crooned, and

she explained to her lover how things really stood between
Scandal and me.

"—not his familiar?" Bibok smirked. He stooped to pet
Scandal. "I suppose this is proof that he's as harmless as you
claim, Calosta my love."

"Harmless?" Scandal echoed. "When it comes to Majyk, the
kid's got a Porsche dealership and no learner's permit! He's
locked in the Playboy Mansion with a busload of radical
feminists! He's got a state-of-the-art computer system, but he
can't find the ON switch and anyway, he forgot his password,
the mouse is missing, and someone's stolen the keypad!"

"Huh?" I said.

The cat sighed. "Also he doesn't know what I'm talking
about half the time. This is very frustrating, believe you me."

"There, there, kitty." The wizard stroked his fur. "Uncle
Bibok will make it all better." He stood tall and nibbled his
thumb in thought. "What a pity. Gout must be slipping. Say
what you will about her, my dear, the old girl always had a
sharp mind. But to send something like this against us—! An
incompetent mage with a familiar that's really a free agent—"

"He did come accompanied by a sword-swinging bully-
boy," Calosta admitted. "One of the short, squat, muscular,
no-neck models with the intelligence of pavement."

"Was that what I glimpsed in the tatami room? And here I
thought you'd taken up gargoyle-collecting." The two of them
shared a warm chuckle over that. I was warm enough for both
of them. I was steaming.

"My brother Basehart is not a gargoyle!" I shouted.

"That's for the critics to decide, isn't it?" Bibok quipped
lazily. "And you couldn't even reverse a simple freeze-spell
like that, Master Kendar? My goodness. I apologize profusely,
lovey. You had this sorcerous sad sack pegged right from the
first."

"I prefer to think of him as the wizardly wimp," Scandal put
in. "You can say it without spraying it."

"*Scandal!*" I protested.

"Get real, babe," the cat replied with one of *those* looks.
"Face the facts: You're a storage battery with no terminals.
Chockfulla Majyk and no way to give it the workout it
deserves. At first I told myself it was because you didn't have
the confidence to jump right in and use what Master Thengor

left you—whether he wanted to leave it to you or not. Then I said it was on accounta you didn't have the know-how to use it, then I pretended you needed practice time, then I figured maybe you took some kinda holy vow to always look like a jerk in public. Finally I said to myself, 'Scandal, it's simpler than that. He just doesn't have what it takes and he never will. It's time to cut your losses and move on.'"

His words were still ringing in my ears as I watched him swagger over to the table where Calosta was tending the bubbling array of tubes and containers. He sat up on his haunches and clawed her skirt until she picked him up.

"Mew?" he said in a tiny, quivering voice, and the sorceress melted.

"Oh, darling, he's so sweeeeet! Can we keep him?" she pleaded with Bibok.

The sorcerer chuckled. "Anything for you, poopsie."

"You can't keep him!" I cried. "He's mine!"

"*Au contraire,*" said Bibok.

"Huh?" I said, hating myself for it.

"It means: No way, José. In your dreams. Fat chance. The cat belongs to you . . . NOT! Is that clear enough?" Bibok's grin wasn't charming now.

"Look," I said, forcing the words out between gritted teeth. "I know Scandal isn't mine; he's a cat. Cats don't belong to anyone but themselves. That's why you can't keep him. He's free."

"That's not what you meant, sonny, but nice save. I like your style. You're a good loser. I sometimes wonder if I'll ever be. I suppose I'd have to *lose* at something first."

Before I could say anything, Calosta cried out excitedly, "Master Kendar, don't you want to see the rest of the Magique-making process? The water's just hot enough for us to begin."

"Run along," Bibok said with a wave of his hand. "We have nothing to hide from *you*. And you might learn something. Who knows? If you're a smart little boy, you might even see the error of your ways and throw in your lot with us. We can always use a sharp junior partner. We've been thinking of branching out, opening some franchises, issuing stock, going multi-kingdom. The future belongs to the young, the ambitious, and the snappy dressers. At least you're young."

My dad always says, "If looks could kill, huntin' wouldn't be half so much fun." Maybe not, but Bibok wouldn't look half so smug, either. I shot him one last poisonous glare and dragged my feet over to Calosta. Scandal draped himself comfortably around her neck, eyes shut, purring. He didn't even spare me a glance.

"You've already seen how we dilute full-strength Majyk with water," the sorceress said. "Next we bring it to the boil and the steam feeds through these tubes here." She pointed. "However, it's still just wet Majyk, a far cry from what we're after. Now if you'll follow along, at this point we begin to add our special ingredients."

We were standing at the middle of the table. Here a row of glass vessels shaped like upside-down teardrops hung above the coils of tubing. Small spigots controlled the flow of the different liquids suspended inside, feeding these drop by drop into the glowing golden Majykal steam as it rushed past. Calosta wiggled a finger and the spigots turned ever so slightly this way or that, adjusting the amounts that were added.

As we passed each vessel, she uttered a Word of Power. Even I remembered Master Thengor's teachings about Word of Power: the more complicated they are, the stronger the enchantment. It wouldn't do if just anyone could say them and command all that sorcerous strength.

"Hexylresorcinol," the sorceress intoned. "Mono- and diglycerides. Polyabscorbate. Hydroxypropylcellulose." She reached the last one. "And just a dash of sodium benozoate to retard spoilage and reduce flavor loss."

"Sodumbendso-what?" I repeated, trying to get my tongue around the words. "Are you summoning demons?"

"Don't waste your time worrying about it, dear boy," Bibok directed me. "Demons hold no terrors for us. *We've* dealt with Manhattan headwaiters."

"Oh, Bibok, don't tease him," Calosta cajoled. "He can't help it that he's so young and stupid."

"Time will take care of the young part, at any rate," her lover remarked.

"We ought to be grateful," she went on. "If he were any better at wizardry, we'd have a fight on our hands."

"A fight we'd win eventually, snookums," he reminded her.

"He may be oozing with Majyk, but together we're *dripping* with it."

"I could fight you one at a time," I said, forgetting the rule about keeping your plans to yourself if you want to come out of a battle as the winner, not the casualty.

"You couldn't." Bibok yawned dramatically. "Cali-pie, didn't you tell this child the cake-metaphor thingie?"

"Yes, darling, but I don't know if he got it."

"Let's hope he did." Bibok's lips curled cruelly, his eyes mocking me. "Because it explains why there is no way to fight us one at a time. Not unless he can get his hands on a lot more Majyk than he's got now."

"Sweetheart, speaking of a lot more Majyk—I mean *Magique* will you please help me cool down the apparatus? It wouldn't be right to keep our best customer waiting for his order, and he'll be here to pick it up any minute."

Calosta gestured towards the last few corkscrew turns of the tubing where the Majyk-laden steam was gathering. It was no longer a clear golden color. It looked dingy, and somehow I sensed that it *felt* dingy, too. The small voice inside my head gasped and whimpered.

help . . . oh please, help . . . help meeeeeee . . .

Then Bibok shoved me aside and placed his hands over Calosta's, which were already in place just above the tightly curled tubes. A sudden chill blasted from the partners in sorcery and filled the air around them. The voice gave a final cry of distress and was gone.

The first dull drops of Magique dripped from the end of the tubing into the wide-mouthed clay pot awaiting them below.

"And that's how we do it!" Calosta clapped her hands. "Now all we have to do is keep adding water. By the time the process is complete, that tiny bit of Majyk will make a cauldronful of Magique. We sell it by the vial and make a fortune." She sidled closer to me, so close that Scandal's fur tickled my nose. "Imagine how much Magique we could make if you'd join us. You have so much to give—I mean, *invest*. You wouldn't have to part with much of your Majyk, you know. A little goes such a long way. Besides, I'd teach you how to acquire fresh supplies of the real stuff." Her breath made my ear burn as she whispered, "I could teach you lots of things."

I drew back my head. "I know what your—your stupid

process does to real Majyk. It waters it down so much it's as good as dead!"

" 'Dead'?" She laughed at me. "As if Majyk were alive in the first place. Master Kendar, you *do* know how to tell a joke!"

"Well, this is no joke: I'm not interested! I won't be a part of any scheme that destroys Majyk. Majyk's something special. Majyk made Orbix what it is."

"A planet with the tectonic hiccups," Bibok drawled. "Our geological stability makes the San Andreas fault look like the Rock of Gibraltar. Oh, we've got a *lot* to thank Majyk for, don't we?"

His sarcasm made me madder. "Majyk alone didn't do that. People misusing Majyk did. The way you two are misusing it now! Majyk's a part of Orbix, it's a part of me. Maybe I can't use it as easily as you, but I respect it, and I know that what you're doing to it is wrong."

"I promise you, we'll cry all the way to the bank." Bibok sneered. "Oh, I forgot; you don't *have* banks in this benighted little burg. I guess we won't cry after all."

Both of them laughed at me this time. I wanted to say something to them that would tear the laughter right off their lips, but I was so angry all I could do was sputter. Finally I recalled a line from Raptura Eglantine's classic, *Wound Not the Werehamster* (admittedly not one of her best sellers, but classics are like that):

"You'll be sorry!"

That just made them laugh louder. They weren't supposed to do that. In the book, the villain cringed and begged for mercy when he heard the hero utter those words. I wish my sister Lucy could write my life.

"Come on, Scandal," I muttered. "We're getting out of here."

"What do you mean 'we,' white man? I ain't goin' nowhere." The cat licked Calosta's ear, making her giggle. "When do we eat?"

"Scandal, don't joke about—"

"Who's joking? I told you already, Merlin: I'm cutting my losses. No hard feelings. So long and thanks for doing nothing. Write when you get your Majyk to work. Don't let the doorknob hit you in the—"

A bell jingled nearby, drowning out the cat's last word.

"There he is, right on time," Bibok said brightly. "I do like a man who shows up promptly when he's got money to give me. Would you like to get the door, sugarfoot?" he asked Calosta.

"Silly precious, you know I can do better than *that*." She snapped her fingers; there was a small puff of pink smoke, a moderate burst of light, and a man appeared. Even before he stopped coughing, I recognized him:

Zoltan.

"Really, Calikins, what *have* we learned about secondhand smoke?" Bibok chided his lady. He came forward to greet his customer. "Mayor Fiendlord, so good to see you! And how is our Lady Mayoress and all the little Fiendlords?"

But Zoltan wasn't listening. Zoltan was staring right at me. Then, with a loud cry, my old enemy flung himself forward, hands reaching for my throat.

CHAPTER —————— 14

"RATWHACKER! GOOD OLD RATWHACKER! OH, AM I ever happy to see *you*!"

Zoltan clung to my neck with one arm and pounded me on the back with the other. My Majyk did nothing. It only flared up to protect me when my life was in danger. I always thought Majyk knew best, but in this case I had my doubts.

This was *Zoltan*: Zoltan, who'd tried to kill me and take back the Majyk his father had accidentally given to me instead of him; Zoltan, who'd tracked me, trailed me, and attacked me with his fiendish servants every chance he got; Zoltan who'd assaulted King Steffan, tried to get Mother Toadbreath hanged for witchcraft, threatened my whole family, and killed Scandal (but he got better; nine lives, you know).

Zoltan, who was now kissing me on both cheeks, grinning like a deranged lowyena, and saying over and over, "My old pal Ratwhacker! My good old friend, my buddy, my chum, my colleague, my goodness, it's *great* to see you again!"

"Hello, Zoltan," I said hesitantly. "Don't hit me."

"Hit you?" He threw back his head until his black beard pointed at the ceiling, and he roared with laughter. "Good old Ratwhacker, always the joker!" He slapped my back, but not even hard enough to make it sting.

"I suppose that at this point it would be frightfully *gauche* to remark that you two seem to know each other," Bibok commented dryly.

"Frightfully what?" I asked.

"My dear Master Bibok, this young sprout and I go way back," Zoltan said. He yanked me close to him with a choke-hold that didn't *quite* cut off my air supply. "We were at

Master Thengor's Academy of High Wizardry together." He patted me on the back some more. An odd jingling sound filled my ears. Zoltan still wore the long, dark robes of a wizard, even though the Council had stripped him of his powers. (Either he dressed like that to remind himself of the good old days, or the Academy rumors were true when they said he had knees like a pair of boiled onions.) The jingling came from his sweeping sleeves.

Bibok's eyes turned chill at the mention of the Academy. I recalled what Gout said about how Master Thengor had rejected Bibok's application. "Old school chums," he said. "Charming. The ties that bind. And this Ratwhacker-thing— some quaint fraternity nickname, perhaps?"

"Fraternity?" For once Zoltan took a turn at looking confused. Good; I was getting tired of being the only know-nothing dope.

"It's a Whirl'd thing," Scandal said sleepily from Calosta's shoulders. "You dorks wouldn't understand. It's where you get a bunch of guys who live together and drink together and hit new guys with paddles and hang toilet paper off trees and wear stuff with Greek letters like Nu Psi Phi and I Felta Thi and throw up."

Zoltan looked at me. I looked at Zoltan. In perfect unison we responded: "On *purpose?*" The cat yawned and went back to sleep.

"Far be it from me to intrude on your reunion," Bibok said in a flinty voice. "I suggest, Mayor Fiendlord, that we conclude our business as quickly as possible so that you and your . . . *Ratwhacker* friend can take your jolly kinship elsewhere. Have you the gold?"

"Right here." Zoltan dashed across the room to offer Bibok one of his sleeves. The handsome wizard plucked one end of a loose thread dangling from Zoltan's cuff. Immediately the hem came undone and a shower of coins tumbled into Bibok's cupped hand. He eyed them and weighed them, then said, "This will do nicely. Calosta, my dear, give the man his Magique."

Calosta came forward with a large clay jug which she gave to Zoltan. He hefted it and whistled at the weight. "You're sure this isn't too much?" he asked. (Zoltan, unwilling to take more than what he paid for?)

"We're having a special sale, this week only," she assured him. "Twice the Magique at half the price."

"Put too much water in the batch, did you?" A flash of the old Fiendlord showed through.

Calosta shrugged. "Just double your dosage and it'll work the same."

"And if it doesn't?" The sorceress opened her mouth to reply, but he did it for her. "I know, I know: If it doesn't work right, it's my fault for not having followed the instructions exactly. No refunds."

Calosta smiled. "It's a pleasure doing business with a real pro, Mayor Fiendlord. You know the way out. Take your old schoolfriend with you."

"I'm not leaving without my brother!" I objected.

"I should hope not," Bibok said. "He doesn't match the decor in our tatami room at all."

"But he's *frozen*!"

"So? Unfreeze him. Surely a wizard of your Majykal resources can easily—" He was taunting me and he knew it. "Ah! But I see from that bassett-hound look on your tastefully acne-scarred face that you can't. *Quel dommage*. Calipoo, would you unfreeze the lad's brother for him?"

"No," said the sorceress, joining in the jest. "I wouldn't dream of it. If I do it for him, it will undermine his self-confidence and be a slap in the face to his personhood. My therapist told me I have to overcome the impulse to be all things to all men if I'm ever going to get in touch with my inner child. Besides, it would be reverse sexism. I think Master Kendar will benefit from a learning experience, don't you?"

Bibok gave me a helpless look that was as phony as everything else about him. "Ah, the ladies! Iron butterflies, every one. Whatever can we do when they say no? You'll have to take care of your brother yourself."

"Fine, if that's how you want it," I snarled. "I'll be back right away with some—"

"No you won't." Bibok's dimples showed even when his smile was all teeth and no friendship. "I think we've seen enough of you around here to last us until Wenchpinch Eve."

"You can't keep me out!" I hoped.

"You and quite a few others besides," he countered lazily.

"Without even breathing hard. You can take my word for it, or you can find out the hard way."

"I'd suggest you take his word for it, Master Kendar," Calosta said, stroking Scandal. "You have a lot of Majyk, but we have more."

"I'll get someone from the Council to help me."

"Do you think the Council will care?" Bibok batted his eyelashes, clasped his hands, and made his voice into a piping imitation of mine. " 'Please, please, reverend sirs, won't you help a poor little wizard unfreeze his brother? A wizard who's got more Majyk than any one of you, but doesn't know how to use it?' " Bibok's laugh rang like an old helmet holding only a skull. "They'll all leap to your aid, I'm sure."

I wasn't going to cry. I was *not* going to cry. Dad said boys never cry and Mom said I was too old to cry anymore, but sometimes I got so mad and felt so powerless, the tears crept up and burned inside my eyes. I fought them back and said, "You're right. I don't need the Council's help to take care of my brother. And I sure don't need help from someone who couldn't even get into Master Thengor's Academy!" I wheeled around sharply and stomped out.

I'd found my way back to the tatami room and Basehart, when I heard footsteps rushing after me. I turned and got my back to a wall. Maybe I'd been wrong to hurl that last barb at Bibok, but it was either that or let him see me cry. I called up what I could of my Majyk—I wasn't a *total* incompetent, after all—and felt my hands fill with fire. I raised them, ready, just as Zoltan came bursting in.

"Whoa!" He threw his own hands up in a warding gesture. They were also filled with fire, but it burned with the smudgy, smoky light of Magique.

I dropped my guard and let the Majyk flames go out. He did the same, though his fires left a stink of rotten eggs on the air when they were extinguished. "Why are you following me?" I demanded.

"I—I came to see if I could be of any help," he said.

"I remember the last time you wanted to 'help' me," I snapped. "Get away from me."

Zoltan lowered his eyes. "I don't blame you for feeling like that. And I don't expect you to believe me when I say I've changed."

"Good. That saves me the trouble of saying it myself."

"But I have changed. You can ask anyone in Cheeseburgh. I've built the place up from a village to a town, and if the gods favor me, maybe some day we'll turn it into a city. In less than three years I've brought in public fountains, garbage collection, and traffic regulations; I've established public schools, a library, oxen-free zones—"

"You've also raised taxes through the roof."

"Well, it's not cheap to hire men brave enough to make a cranky ox move along."

"I'm sorry, Zoltan, but I'm a Gangle. A Gangle never forgets a death-threat." (Except for Great-uncle Morbus Embargo Gangle, and then he only forgot about it because it came from his second wife, who was also his fifth wife. They were the best mushrooms he ever ate. But Zoltan didn't need to know that.)

Zoltan sighed. "I understand. Well, would you mind if I watched you at work? It's been so long since I've seen anyone use real Majyk. Funny, the things you miss."

"Suit yourself," I grumbled, and went in to have a look at Basehart.

He hadn't moved. I stretched out my hands and called on my powers. Once more my palms filled with fire. *Hmm, not a bad idea. What better way to unfreeze someone than with fire?* I reasoned.

But the fire burned and Basehart remained immobile. The only thing that happened was the sleeve of his tunic began to smolder. I called off my Majyk and hastily swatted out the kindling cloth.

I tried another spell. Basehart shivered where he stood, then slowly began to rise into the air. I dropped the spell, and my brother, who landed with a crash on the low black table. I shook my head. It looked like I was going to have to carry him out of here. I bent down, got a grip on his arm, and tugged. He didn't move. I shifted my grip to his leg. Same story. There was a lot of beef to Basehart, as Dad always said, and the only beef I was ever able to lift was a forkful of steak.

"Ratwha—I mean, Master Kendar, could I make a suggestion?" Zoltan tapped me gently on the shoulder.

"No, you can't!"

"All I wanted to say was that if you used the first-level spell for unclogging drains"—he rattled through the syllables so fast

I couldn't follow or stop him—"and combined it with a charm for making unwelcome guests remember another appointment"—the words leaped lightly from his tongue—"then used just the *teensiest* touch of Majyk to back it up"—grimy Magique fountained from his hands over Basehart's body, but of course it takes a lot of Magique to accomplish the same thing as the teensiest touch of Majyk—"I think you'd be pleased with the results."

"You lousy thickwit snotbrained excuse for a wizard!" Basehart bawled, sitting up and glaring at me. "What's the big idea of leaving me stuck like that? I oughta bash your ears until your nose falls off into your britches!"

"Thank you," I said to Zoltan. Basehart hit me in the back of the head with a chunk of brie. "I think."

"So you're Zoltan Fiendlord," said Aunt Glucosia. "We've heard so much about you from Lucius and Abstemia."

"Yes, most of it went like this." Aunt Carageena recited a list of nasty names so vivid and elaborate that we were all blushing by the time she was done. "Of course you're a lot taller than that in person," she concluded.

"I can fix that," said Mysti from the far end of the table.

It was quite a long table—the longest one in the common room of the tavern—and almost every seat at it was taken. Mysti sat at the head, I slumped at the foot, Basehart and the aunts occupied one side, and Zoltan and Mistress Gout took the other. There was an empty space where Scandal would have been.

"Do I know you from somewhere?" Zoltan inquired, raising one black eyebrow at the Welfie.

"Perhaps." Mysti was gouging short, emphatic trenches in the tabletop with the point of her dagger. As always, she was in the full masked costume of a Blade for Justice.

Zoltan frowned. "Hmmmm. The voice is familiar, but I can't quite place the mask."

"My identity does not matter," the disguised Welfie said, forcing her voice down an octave. "What does matter is the fact that Master Kendar has told me all about *you.* You are not to be trusted, Zoltan Fiendlord."

"If *I* wouldn't've trusted him, I'd still be froze silly in them sorcerers' house!" Basehart declaimed.

"Basehart, you never *trusted* Zoltan," I said wearily. "You didn't do anything; you just stood there."

"And I'd be standing there still, if not for him," my brother maintained.

"You do realize that this is the same man who almost got the whole family killed not too long ago?" I didn't want to discourage Basehart from taking Zoltan's part; I just wanted to make sure he understood the situation.

Basehart scratched his head. There were times when he had trouble remembering breakfast, although he could recite the fifty-seven best methods for deer-skinning with no trouble at all.

"Well . . ." he said at last. "Maybe that's so. But that was *then*, wasn't it? And this is—this is—"

"This is silly," said Aunt Carageena with a toss of her iron-gray braids. "Kendar dear, I wouldn't *dream* of trying to run your life any more than if I were your own mother, but I really must speak up now. From what I've seen and heard of Mayor Fiendlord, he's a perfectly charming person. Such authority in one so young! Such political power, so well managed! All of those wicked things he did are over and done with. I am always in favor of giving people a second chance."

"Especially when the person in question is buying the drinks," Aunt Glucosia whispered to me.

It was meant as a joke, but I wasn't laughing. I felt empty inside. My mind kept drifting back to Scandal. What was he doing right now? Feasting on more Magique-conjured tidbits? Dozing around Calosta's neck or in Bibok's lap? Drinking straight cream from a silver platter and picking a fight with the footstool when it made him drunk?

Or had they given him his heart's desire? They could use their powers to find him the spellway back to the Whirl'd—the Whirl'd where he might lose his ability to talk, but where female cats prowled and yowled and waited. Once he was there, would he ever want to return to Orbix? *Could* he?

I'd never even had the chance to tell him goodbye.

"Enough!" I leaped up and slammed my fist on the table so loudly it made every other customer in the tavern stop and stare. Kicking back my chair, I scowled at them until they went back to minding their own business. Still angry, but in a calmer voice I said, "Every last one of you here wants something from

me; don't deny it. Basehart wants his bride, Blade wants
Boffin, Gout wants revenge, and my aunts just want to keep me
out of trouble. Well, I'm telling you, you're not going to get
any of those things unless you trust Zoltan now."

Mysti hacked off a chunk of table the size of a doorstop.
"We're not? Do tell."

Zoltan rose gracefully from his place and spread the sleeves
of his robe like a raven's wings. "You don't have to trust me,
gentle sir," he said to the masked Welfie. "But resign yourself
to this: You do have to use me. I have the knowledge and
experience that Master Kendar lacks, he has the Majyk that
I—"

"—would kill for," Mysti finished for him. He said nothing.

"Zoltan and I settled this between us," I said. "I can't fight
Bibok and Calosta alone."

"Why do you have to fight them at all, Kendar?" Aunt
Carageena asked. "That's Mistress Gout's problem."

"It wouldn't be a problem if she'd simply forgive and
forget," Aunt Glucosia added. "Looks aren't everything in a
man. Why, I remember back in the jungles of Plunj, the High
Priest of Delbert was rather squat and tubby, but he had his
little ways, and the things he could do with mangoes . . ." A
fond, wistful smile curved up the corners of her mouth. She
snapped out of her reverie, reached across the table, and patted
Gout's hand. "You could do better."

Gout jerked her hand away like it had been scorched.

"Gout's problem is our problem," I said. "I have to face
Bibok and Calosta eventually; there's no choice. Magique is at
the bottom of all our troubles and those two are at the bottom
of Magique."

"If Magique's the stuff that stole Prince Boffin from me, I'll
see it wiped off the face of Orbix!" Mysti swore, and plunged
her dagger into the much-abused tabletop.

"If Magique's what spoilt my wedding, I'm with you!"
Basehart cried, and stuck his own dagger into the wood.

"If Magique is what's allowing that foreign cow to hold onto
my man, I'll destroy it even if it means throwing in my lot with
a slimegrind!" Gout exclaimed. She didn't have a dagger of her
own, but she snatched the cheese knife off a platter on the next
table and jammed it deep into the boards.

The tavernkeeper sidled over and cleared his throat discreetly. "If you wouldn't mind changin' tables for a bit, gentlefolk, I'll just be using a little Magique to repair the damage you've done to the furnishings. Cheaper than buying a new table and it works like a charm, heh, heh, heh. Little joke."

We moved the discussion out of the tavern, where there were fewer things to stick daggers into (if you didn't count the innocent bystanders). In the street, Mysti took the opportunity to get close to Zoltan and fix him with a piercing gaze so sharp and cold I saw him shiver. "*Do* I know you from somewhere?" he repeated nervously.

"I am called a Blade for Justice. When people hear this, they often jump to conclusions about me," Mysti said slowly and carefully. "Mistaken conclusions. They decide, you see, that because I believe justice *can* be done, I'm fool enough to believe *anything*. As I said, they are always mistaken. Sometimes they are mistaken and dead."

"And what—what does that have to do with me?" Zoltan backed away from her, but she stuck to him like a burr to a blanket.

"I think you want me to believe that you're not the same Zoltan who'd do anything to get his paws on Majyk, Majyk, and more Majyk. Yet even now I detect a certain odor about you. It smells familiar, yet not quite. It's the same scent that clings to Master Kendar . . . almost. I'd like to know what it is, and I think you'd like to tell me." She fingered the hilt of her rapier.

"You have a fine nose, friend Blade," Zoltan said, his voice still quavering a little. "And I see no reason to deal in lies. It's Magique you smell. I'd be surprised if you didn't. I soaked myself in a jugful of the stuff not too long ago. My past experience at handling Majyk lets me store Magique in much the same way, rather than having to carry it around with me in flasks and bottles like other folk."

"How handy for you." Mysti's eyes were frosty.

"It was handy enough for Basehart," I reminded her.

"Up until today, I was Bibok and Calosta's best customer," Zoltan continued. "Hear this?" He flapped one arm up and down. It jingled. "There's a small fortune in *gabors* sewn into my cuff, and a hoard of *ivanas* in the hem of my gown. I took them from the town taxes."

"You're a bold-faced thief!" Aunt Glucosia was astonished

by Zoltan's confession. "All I've heard since we came into Cheeseburgh is how the taxes keep rising. Is it for *this*? To buy the mayor Magique?"

"No more," Zoltan assured her. "Master Kendar has explained to me the danger to my beloved town if the Cheeseburghers come to rely too much on Magique. As their mayor, from this day forth I will set them a better example. I take a solemn oath that once the Magique now in me is used up, worn out, and gone, I will buy no more of the pernicious stuff from Bibok and Calosta." He struck a noble pose.

"Very pretty," Mysti sneered. "Meanwhile you stink of enough Magique to keep you going until the grepsberry harvest."

"Besides, what do you need so *much* Magique for?" Aunt Glucosia asked. "And don't try telling us that you use it solely for peaceful purposes. One of Uk-Uk the Unspeakable's tribal lieutenants tried getting away with *that* one. Uk-Uk heard the fellow was collecting spears and arrows and swords and hungry young men and maps of Uk-Uk's harem. Uk-Uk went to see him about it. The lieutenant said he was going to use them for peaceful purposes. Uk-Uk made sure that he became very peaceful, very quickly, and *very* permanently."

There was a mutter of agreement from the rest of my group, and more than one suspicious look cast at Zoltan.

"Ladies, gentlemen, I entreat you to come to my home," Zoltan said with a low, elegant bow that made him jingle even louder. "The street is no place for this meeting."

"I should say it's not!" Aunt Carageena sniffed. "If any of your taxpayers overhear where their money's been going, we'll be in the middle of a riot."

"Please come home with me," Zoltan repeated. "I'll explain everything there, and I know you'll understand my problems *much* better then."

"We'll come," Mysti said. "But if this is another of your weaselly tricks, I'll have you down on your knees, begging me to save your sorry life."

"Save me!" Mysti gasped, clutching the back of Zoltan's chair. "For the love of mercy, save me from the fiends!" She sobbed for breath, cowering in terror.

Zoltan leaned forward in the gilded mayor's chair and said,

"Now, Dobi, what did Daddy tell you about biting your guests?"

The little boy stuck out his lip and kicked Daddy in the shin. "I wanna NEAR!" he shrieked.

"A near what?" Aunt Glucosia whispered to her sister. Both of them had clambered to safety on the wide mantelpiece above the Fiendlord family hearth.

"I think he means an *ear*," Carageena whispered back. She made signs indicating that Mysti's ears, being pointed, were probably some sort of valuable collector's item among insane toddlers.

I thought the little monster was just hungry.

"*Gimme* near, *gimme* near, *gimme* near!" Dobi chanted, banging on the armrests of his father's chair with a big stick. Chips of gold paint went flying.

"No, *I* wanna near!" came a shrill, penetrating, nasal whine. Dobi's twin sister, Dibi, waddled away from the tall corner cupboard she'd been kicking, to attack Mysti from the rear.

"Praise Wedwel, she's gone!" Basehart sighed. He was crouching on top of the cupboard, his head wedged against one of the ceiling beams.

"Are you sure?" Gout's voice emerged from the cupboard all muffled. "You're not just saying it so I'll come out and she'll chase me and you can get away, you big coward?"

"No," Basehart replied. "But now you mention it, I wish I'd thought of that, I do."

"I wanna NEAR! I wanna NEAR!" the twins howled in chorus, and began running circles around Zoltan's chair. Mysti blessed the lightness of her Welfie bones. It was a gift that let her scramble to the very peak of the chair back and perch there like a terrified parrot while the infant Fiendlords clamored for blood and pointed ears, pointed ears and blood.

I stood alone, the only one of our party who didn't have to hide or climb out of reach of those tiny claws, those ruby-lipped hellmouths. The instant Dibi and Dobi rushed into the room, my Majyk recognized a life-threatening situation and switched itself on full force. The children couldn't get near me, and I wasn't stupid enough to try getting near them.

"You see how it is with me now, friends?" Zoltan said, raising his palms to show how powerless he was. Dibi grabbed one hand and dragged it down with her full weight, whimpering for Daddy to get her a pointed ear because Daddy liked her better than Dobi, who stank.

"We see, we see," Mysti said, and swatted at Dobi's groping hands. The boy jumped up and seized her boot. He was too small to pull her from her perch, so instead he dangled in midair, making the house unbearable with his shrieks and bellowings. For the first time, I was happy Scandal wasn't with me. I couldn't stand the thought of what those children would do with a cat's tail.

"Yes, yes, we understand completely," Aunt Glucosia hastened to agree. "It must take every spare drop of Magique in Cheeseburgh to protect your life and sanity from these—these—these—"

"—children?" Aunt Carageena offered.

"These are *not* children, Gee'." Glucosia shook her head. "I have seen children before. These are something else. I always knew the day would come when I would have to pay the price for having stolen the fabled Eye of Delbert from the jungles of Plunj. Now the hour of my doom has struck. These two vicious creatures are clearly the Curse of Delbert and they have come for me."

"Madam, I beg to differ," Zoltan said. He stood, scooping up Dibi, who kicked and whined and pulled his beard frantically. "These—*ouch*—are no curse, but the blessing of my old age, if they let me live that long. Or so my wife keeps telling me." He tucked Dibi under one arm and grabbed Dobi by the belt of his tunic. The boy kicked so hard he spun himself around in midair like a pencil on a string. "I do not use Magique to protect myself from my own children. I do, however, use a great deal of it to keep out the sound of their merry laughter and the pitter-patter of their precious feet so that I can get some work done."

Right then Dibi elbowed her father in the ribs at the same time Dobi managed to land a lucky kick to Zoltan's stomach. He dropped them both and doubled over. The children hit the floor, but unlike Scandal they didn't land on their feet. The yowl that went up this time was loud enough to summon the gods.

The gods didn't show up. The gods are nobody's fools.

"Zollie, what did I tell you about roughhousing with the twins?" The doorway filled with a mountain of woman—an angry mountain, the kind that smokes and spits and rumbles and then blows chunks of hot rock all over the place, spoiling the view and discouraging the neighbors.

She stormed into the room, belly first. It was an amazing belly. It took the woman herself a while to catch up with it. When she miraculously managed to gather up the twins and hoist them over the top of that belly, I gaped at the spectacle.

"Don't look at her, Kendar dear!" For my sake, Aunt Carageena dared to hop off the mantel and clap both hands over my eyes. "You'll only want to ask questions."

I heard Aunt Glucosia cluck her tongue and say, "Oh, for goodness' sake, Gee', the boy has seen pregnant women before."

"Yes, but *this* pregnant?"

I removed Aunt Carageena's hands from my eyes and said, "I won't ask any questions, I promise."

"Well . . ." My aunt was dubious. "As long as you promise not to get any *ideas*, either."

"Ideas? Him? About *that*? Ha!" Mysti barked from the chair back.

Zoltan pulled himself painfully back into his seat. With a wobbly smile and a pale green face he inquired, "Bini, my love, you do remember Master Kendar, don't you?"

"Bini?" I echoed. I was gaping again. This woman was as big as seven of the frail kitchen wench Zoltan had been forced to marry.

Then she smiled, and it was the same old Bini. "Bless me, so it is!" She tried to embrace me without letting go of the twins, but there are some things not even mothers can do. "It's our own Ratwhacker, big as life and just as natural! How *are* you, then? Tsk, still too skinny by half. Velma Chiefcook always used to say to me, 'Bini, my girl, if that Kendar Ratwhacker don't put some meat on his bones, one fine day he's goin' t' reach fer his ratwhackin' stick an' find he's picked up hisself!' What bring you t' Cheeseburgh? Have you seen the town? Isn't it wonderful what my Zollie's done for the place? It used to be just a village, you know. And oh!—how lovely to see you an' Zollie all friendly again. He's changed, you know, has my Zollie. No more lollopin' after that silly Majyk for him, no indeed. Now you couldn't meet with a sweeter, kinder, gentler man nor he. Why, it's been *ages* since he called for a public hangin', and that was only 'cos they was *our* pigs what got stole. 'You young people today have got t' learn some respect for authority'—that's what my Zollie said just before he smacked the horse's rump and let the lad dance on air. There wasn't a dry eye in the town, especially among the boy's relations. My Zollie's wonderful good at public speakin'.''

I never thought I'd be happy to hear the twins start whining again, but they did and I was. Bini talked with the air going in and coming out, nonstop, until her children's sniveling distracted her.

"'Scuse me," she said brightly. "It's someone's nap time. I won't be a moment." She trundled out of the room and soon we heard the sounds of fierce battle interspersed with lullabies coming from the upper floor.

Gout crept out of the cupboard, Mysti climbed down from the chair back, Aunt Glucosia slid off the mantel, and Basehart fell on his head from the top of the cupboard. We all crowded around Zoltan for protection in case the twins should break loose from their mother and invade once more.

Where once there had been mistrust of Zoltan Fiendlord, now there was only sympathy.

"My friends, I was once the greatest student ever to attend Master Thengor's Academy of High Wizardry," Zoltan told us. "My own ambition and greed made me what I am today. Once I commanded demons; now I feed them strained spinach. I know thousands of spells by heart, but I have no Majyk worthy of the name. Spells without Majyk to make them so are only so much gibble-gabble. Soon my beloved wife, Bini, will give birth again. She's bigger than she was the first time." He shuddered. "Much bigger. Some nights I wake up screaming."

"If you're even halfway good with a sword, there's a captain of mercenaries I know who owes me a favor," Aunt Glucosia offered. "It's dirty, dangerous, ugly work, but the pay's good, you get to travel, and you don't have to go home again until you die."

"No, thank you," he said with a faint smile. "I think I prefer the scheme Master Kendar and I have worked out together."

"Oh?" Every eyebrow present rose at the news.

"If I fight Bibok and Calosta, it's two against one," I said. "They've pooled their Majyk so it can't be split apart, they've got more of it than I do, and what's worse, they know how to use every drop."

"However, if *we* fight them," Zoltan said, "it's two against two, and I know enough about using Majyk for *three* wizards."

"But you don't have any Majyk," Basehart pointed out.

Zoltan only grinned.

"He will," I said. "I'm going to give him some of mine."

"Just as soon as I teach him how to do it," Zoltan added.

Mysti tapped a gloved fingertip on her chin. "There's just one eensy-weensy tiny little thing wrong with your scheme, Kendar," she said.

"What's that?"

"You can't give Majyk to a dead man." Before anyone could blink, her dagger was in her hand and flying straight at Zoltan's eyes.

CHAPTER ─────── 15

"THAT WAS MY BEST DAGGER," MYSTI SAID TESTILY, staring at the puddle of slag steaming on the floor at Zoltan's feet.

"Well, it's my *only* head," Zoltan countered. "And if Master Kendar hadn't been here to save me, you would have ruined it. What was the point of that? Speak up, or I'll bring Dobi back downstairs."

"The *point*," Mysti gritted, "was to show Kendar he doesn't need 'help' from the likes of you. He stopped that dagger in mid-flight, without even thinking about it!"

"I noticed," Zoltan muttered.

"Don't you *see*, Kendar?" She turned to me. "When you stop worrying about *how* to use your Majyk and just *use* it, you're fine!"

I shook my head. "I've had too many accidents with Majyk to believe that, Mys—Blade. This was just a—a fluke."

"Oh, I give up!" Mysti dismissed me with a wave of her hand. "Am I the only one who ever thought you could stand on your own two feet, make your own decisions, use what you've got without a whole *committee* behind you?"

"You . . . believe that about me?"

She just shook her head. "Go on, Kendar; follow your scheme. As long as you've got so many doubts shouting in your ears, you'll never hear me. Well, Zoltan? Aren't you in a hurry to get started? What's the first lesson to be? Let me guess: How to remove excess Majyk from a fool and give it to a pig."

"As a matter of fact, the first lesson I was planning to give Master Kendar was how to call up visions," Zoltan responded with the icy dignity of his Academy days. "It was a special request."

"Yeah," said Basehart. "Mine."

"Visions?" Gout's ears pricked up. "If you wanted a vision of something, Master Kendar, you should have told me. I could do it for you."

"That's the last thing a student needs," Zoltan told her. "He's got to learn to do it for himself. Someone bring me a bowl and some water."

"It's your house, you get it," Gout replied.

Some time later, he and I stood over a bowl of water on a small, round table. My neck ached, my shoulders were stiff, and my throat was sore from repeating the words of the vision-spell. "This isn't working," I said at last.

Zoltan wiped sweat from his brow and announced, "I'm not surprised. I can't teach under these conditions."

"What's the matter, dearie?" Aunt Glucosia asked, pressed close against his left side. "Are we in the way?"

"Don't mind us," said Aunt Carageena, leaning hard on my right shoulder. "We'll be so quiet, you won't even know we're here."

"Yeah, go ahead, do the vision." Basehart gave me a smack on the back by way of encouragement. "Come on, don't take all day. The water'll turn stagnant and Dulcetta'll be all stale or something when we find her."

"I thought he was going to conjure up a vision of Prince Boffin first!" Mysti objected.

"*I* could have created a split-bowl vision showing the whereabouts of both Dulcetta *and* Prince Boffin at the same time," Gout grumbled from across the table. "But no one listens to me. *Some* people think they know better than witches just because witches don't use Majyk. They laugh at our herbal lore. But herbs are dependable—you can count on parsley— which is more than you can say for Majyk *or* wizards."

"Was it part of your herbal lore to dump a fistful of lawn clippings in the first bowl of water?" Zoltan sniped.

"That was my own special private blend, guaranteed to cut your conjuring time in half," Gout replied with cool dignity. "I was only trying to help."

"Thank you for all your help," Zoltan said. "Now stop it."

He rested his hand on my shoulder. "Master Kendar will try again . . . *if* you'll let him."

I took a deep breath and let it out slowly. I could feel everyone's eyes on me. That was bad enough, but what was worse was the niggly, itchy, uneasy feeling I got every time I heard Zoltan call me *Master* Kendar. It wasn't right. It didn't feel right, it didn't sound right, and it left me with the impression that somewhere way up high over my head there was a big box full of horseflop with my name on it, dangling by a thread.

Why did I feel that way? I couldn't remember being so ill at ease when I got help with my Majyk from others. I'd used a witch's book and a fairy's twelve-step program and an enchanted gravy boat, and I'd even had occasional hints sent to me by the Council via messenger. (That was Lady Inivria's doing. She got sick and tired waiting for me to learn how to unclog a drain, so she wrote to her old friends on the Council and begged them to give me a clue.) Why was it so different with Zoltan?

Because he *was* Zoltan. Because back in the days when I was still just a stupid Ratwhacker, he was the student I'd admired and envied and even worshipped. It's not easy when your idol gets down off the pedestal and puts you up there in his place. The switch makes you queasy, especially if you're not used to heights.

"Master Kendar, you're not concentrating." Zoltan spoke to me gently but firmly. "Focus your powers on the water. Remember what I taught you: Water is the mirror of life. Where there is breath, water hovers on the air. Where there is blood, water rushes through the rivers of the body. Let this water call to that. Let the mists of the day and the clinging fogs of the night become your servants and your messengers. Cast out your Majyk like a net and snare the unseen droplets that hold a reflection of what you wish to see."

"And make sure it's Dulcetta!" Basehart chimed in.

"Prince Boffin," said Mysti.

"*I* could do both," said Gout.

"Shut up, dearie," said Aunt Carageena.

I closed my eyes and held my hands out over the surface of the water. All I wanted to do was escape from the unhappy feeling I got when Zoltan called me Master; that, and the

clamor of so many people wanting so many different things
from me. I was bound to disappoint some of them, maybe all
of them. Failure and I were old friends, and the one true friend
I'd ever had in my life had abandoned me.

If I listened to the truth of things, I heard one simple, sorry
message: *You're on your own, Kendar Gangle.*

All right. Maybe that was how things were. And if that was
so, Mysti was right after all: I didn't really need anyone's help
with Majyk. I could do this alone too.

I sealed my ears against Zoltan's voice. In the silence and the
dark there was only me . . . and Majyk. I sank deeper into
myself, seeking it. Somewhere in the shadows, a light gleamed.
I went towards it.

—took you long enough.

Hello? I looked around, but there was only the light. *Where
are you?*

*Nowhere. Everywhere. "Where" doesn't mean a damn thing
to me. Good to see you again! Love what you've done with your
hair.*

Who—What are you? I asked the light.

Light can make rude noises. *Kid, you're a day or three too
old to be that stupid. We've met.*

Are you—are you my Majyk?

*Possessive little nit, aren't you? Hate to break the news to
you, but you're more like your brother than you think. That's
one reason his bride-to-be skipped town on him.*

You know where Dulcetta is?

*Sonny, I'm Majyk. Knowledge is power, and I am the
universal wiseguy. Sometimes I know too much for my own
good, but hey! It's stuff like that that keeps life interesting.*

I knew it! I crowed. *I always knew you were alive.*

You call this living? my Majyk replied. *Full of all the
knowledge in the universe, and I still gotta jump every time one
of you wizards says "Frog."*

Why?

Why? the light echoed. *That's one I don't know. Ask me
another. Maybe 'cause when the Great Mother set up the whole
cosmic crapshoot, she sealed it with the big BECAUSE I SAID
SO. You waste enough time trying to figure out stuff like that
and you either go crazy or become a philosopher.*

If you're alive—if all Majyk's alive, then we—we— I was

having a hard time making the thought form. *—we wizards have been enslaving you for ages! That's not right! I've got to make it stop. I'll tell the Council and—*

—and then? Nothing. Hey, forget it, kid. Nice thought, but don't strain yourself. I'm used to it. We're used to it. See, that's another thing: I/we may be alive, like you say, only it's not the sort of life you're used to. You can try to understand it, but lotsa luck. Your brains just aren't built to bend that way.

But we haven't got the right to force you to serve us!

Sonny, don't get started on who's got the right to do what to whom in this world. Think back to the last piece of meat you ate. Did you worry about the cow's rights or did you just ask your mama to pass the salt? How about the last time you walked on the grass or chomped into an apple? Plants are alive too, you know.

That's right. The realization hit me hard. My heart plunged into the pit of my stomach when I thought of all the other living things I'd taken advantage of as thoughtlessly as wizards took advantage of Majyk. *In the name of Wedwel's sporadic mercy, what have I done?* I wailed.

In the utter blackness enveloping my spirit, I felt a tendril of warmth and brightness creep through to comfort me. *What have you done, kid? Nothing. Everything. You're guilty of life in the first degree, and I don't think you're ready for it. I've been watching you. You're the ultimate don't-rock-the-boat guy. If you don't make any sudden moves, you won't tip over the canoe, but you won't get across the river either. You know what's the roughest lesson about growing up, Kendar?*

I know, I know, I muttered. *"Life isn't fair."* My dad told me that one already.

Then your dad's a moron. My Majyk chuckled. The warmth drove away more of the darkness. *That's not it at all. Fair and unfair, right and wrong, the good guys win and the bad guys lose—they're all two sides of a coin that's only got one side to it. Life just is. That's all. You can split it up, study it, label it, stick gold stars on half the pieces and black spots on the rest, but the only result you'll get that way is you'll be a whole lot older and you'll think you're a whole lot wiser. No, kid, if you want to change life, live it. Don't worry about it, don't poke at it, don't wait for the lab reports to come back or the rules to change before you'll join the game. The game goes on, with you or without you.*

The light flooded me, and a last, laughing whisper of Majyk filled my head: *Just play the game.*

"Not bad," Zoltan said. He patted my back. "Not bad at all. Were you trying to get a vision of Dulcetta or Prince Boffin, Master Kendar?"

I blinked like a man waking up from deep sleep, and gazed into the bowl of water. "I—I don't know." The image of a trim, thatched cottage floated serenely on the surface. Hosts of brown, warty toads hopped and frolicked in front of the door. "But I do know that place. It's Mother Toadbreath's house."

"Hmph! That poor excuse for a witch," Gout sniffed. "I can't imagine why you'd want to conjure up a vision of *her*. All she wants is to kiss a toad and have him turn into a handsome prince for her to marry. That's why she keeps swarms of the filthy creatures around the house. It's an obsession with her. I can think of better ways to waste one's life."

"Yes, like sulking and pouting and aching for revenge every waking moment because the toad *you* caught got away," Mysti said. The witch glowered at her.

"Well, at least it's *a* vision," Zoltan said. He dabbled his fingers in the water, breaking up the illusion. "This time try to concentrate on an image of your brother's bride. You say she's somewhere in the vicinity?"

"That's the last we heard, yes," I agreed.

"Then that will be a fairly easy vision to command. They're always less trouble if you can warm them up with a hint, and they cost less than the long-distance ones. Go ahead, Master Kendar, just like last time, if you please."

It was better than last time; easier, more natural, like breathing. I stopped worrying about whether I could command the powers of Majyk. I stopped thinking about whether or not I had the right to use Master Thengor's Majyk at all. This was now, and the Majyk was mine, and I didn't need to think about what was right or wrong, fair or unfair: I just needed a vision of Dulcetta. I passed my hand over the surface of the water and the Majyk followed.

"That's the same dumb witch's cottage again!" Basehart exclaimed. He gave me a punch in the arm. "Quit fooling around!"

"I'm not fooling around!" I snapped back at him. "I asked to see where Dulcetta's hiding and that's the vision I got!"

"Hmmm." Zoltan stroked his beard. "Why don't you try calling up a different vision? Seek the prince this time."

"All right." I cleared away Mother Toadbreath's cottage and made another try, summoning Prince Boffin's image.

I got Mother Toadbreath's cottage again.

"Uh-oh." Zoltan folded his hands and twiddled his thumbs. "I know the spell I gave you is the proper one. Master Kendar, may I—?" He moved me away from the bowl and rolled up his sleeves. "I've never tried this before, but I think it's possible to use Magique to summon visions. Do you have a picture of the people you're seeking?" Basehart gave him a miniature of Dulcetta. My brother had been wearing it on a leather thong under his shirt. He sighed with longing when he handed it over.

Mysti dug a Raptura Eglantine romance out of her belt pouch and passed it to Zoltan. "Thank you," he said. "These will do nicely." He studied both pictures, then returned them to their owners. I saw Basehart kiss Dulcetta's image before slipping it back next to his heart. Zoltan pressed his fingertips to his temples, concentrated, then recited the spell and held his hands out over the water. Vast, billowing clouds of Magique poured out into the little bowl.

The fumes were terrible, filling the entire room, stinging our eyes and making us cough. Mysti fanned away the worst of it with her cape. When we blotted up the tears and wiped our streaming noses, we all crowded around to see what was in the bowl.

Mother Toadbreath's cottage. It was a fuzzier picture than the ones I'd called up with Majyk, but otherwise it was just the same.

"Stand aside." Gout used her narrow hips to bump us out of the way. "I'll try my 'lawn clipping' method, if you don't mind. Perhaps we'll see something besides a bunch of toads." She took several small packets of herbs from her pouch, blended them in her palm, tossed them into the bowl, and sang.

She got a nice round of polite applause from my aunts and a vision of Mother Toadbreath's cottage in the water.

"Are you sure this thing ain't broke?" Basehart picked up the bowl, tapped it against the edge of the table a few times, and spilled the water on his feet. Then he gave it one tap too many.

"It's 'broke' now," Zoltan said darkly, regarding the shards on the floor.

"Huh! Just goes t' show you're as flimsy a teacher as th' equipment you use," my brother said. "Good thing Kendar didn't pay you nothin' in advance."

"Ummmm, actually . . ." I drawled.

"You didn't!" Basehart was indignant. "Wait'll Dad hears this one! Say, you didn't dip into my purse to pay off this quack, did you?"

I could honestly say no to that.

"Where'd you get the coin, then?"

"I didn't pay him in coin."

"Aye? Then what—?"

"Allow me, Master Kendar." Zoltan uncurled his fingers. A spark of Majyk danced over his palm. He closed his hand around it quickly, as if afraid it might get away.

"Oh Kendar, you *didn't*!" Mysti wailed.

"That was our bargain," I replied, getting ready to defend my decision. "A little real Majyk in exchange for lessons. Look, it's no good to me unless I know how to use it, right? And Zoltan can't do any harm with the tiny bit I gave him so far."

"So far?" There was a rumble of thunder in Mysti's words.

"Rest easy, sir," Zoltan assured her. "Master Kendar has not promised me *that* much of his hoard. This is merely . . . an investment in the future." He held his closed fist up to one eye and peered into it like it was a spyglass. Whatever he saw inside made him smile.

"Whose future?" Mysti demanded.

Zoltan dropped his hand. "Mine, of course. And yours. With this pittance of Majyk, Master Kendar has made me richer than if he filled my chimney with *gabors*. Majyk attracts Majyk, or haven't you ever heard that fine old wizardly saying? Wild Majyk is free for the taking, and with this in my keeping, I'm once again able to gather up as much of it as my skill allows."

"Marvelous," the Welfie said, her jaw tight.

"Not to you, perhaps. Yet it *is* necessary for the struggle that awaits Master Kendar and me. I'm surprised you don't understand, being a fighter." Zoltan nodded at Mysti's faithful rapier. "If you must do battle outnumbered by heavily armed foes, who would you rather have fighting at your side—a well-equipped swordsman at least as deft and deadly as yourself, or a mouse with a peashooter?"

"At least I could trust the mouse," Mysti growled.

"No, dearie, you couldn't," Aunt Carageena said. "The mouse would *eat* all the peas, and then where would you be?"

"The same place we'll be when this swine has stuffed himself with Majyk at Kendar's expense!" Mysti cried. "He'll grab what he can and vanish, mark my words."

"What sort of guarantee would you like me to give you that I won't?" Zoltan asked with a sardonic smile. "Or will you settle for holding my leash as we go?"

"Go where?"

"Why, to the witch's cottage!" He gestured at the shattered bowl. "The vision presented itself to Kendar thrice. That means something."

"It means you can't teach wizardry for beans. Kendar just got the summoning spell wrong is all." Mysti may have believed I could stand on my own two feet, but she also believed I'd trip over them.

"Here!" Basehart spoke up. "Watch what you say about my baby brother. He's nowheres near half so bright as me, true, but he's a Gangle, and Gangles has got a *brain*. Or else we know where t' get one fast enough. If his vision says Dulcetta's in that there witch's cottage, I'm goin' after her and I'd like to see the one that's man enough to stop me!" He headed purposefully for the door.

Aunt Glucosia was man enough for anything. She whipped a length of silk cord from her waist, looped it into a noose, casually tossed it over his head and shoulders, then pulled. The noose drew tight and Basehart was yanked back onto his behind. Aunt Glucosia ambled over to him at her leisure, coiling up her lasso as she went.

"You can't go to the witch's cottage just like that, Basehart dear," she said. "You have to ask directions first."

"A Gangle *never* asks directions!"

"He doesn't need to," I said quickly. "I know the way to Mother Toadbreath's. We can go there and see if—"

"Yes, you all run along," Zoltan said affably. "I'll be interested to hear if your vision was a true one, Master Kendar. I have my doubts about the others."

His words surprised me. "Aren't you coming with us?"

"No."

"But you said—!"

"That bit about the leash? A jest. Ha, ha. Why should I tag along? I can't give you any fresh lessons in Majyk as we go. I have more respect for the subject than to teach it on the road."

I didn't have the heart to say that I wouldn't be needing any further lessons from him, on the road or off. I'd just received my diploma in wizardry from the best teacher of Majyk possible: Majyk itself.

"But—but don't you want to see if we do find Dulcetta? Or the prince?"

"Oh, you can tell me all about it when you return." He sat down in the mayor's chair and steepled his fingertips. "There's no need for me to wear out my shoe leather. Besides, I do have other duties. I am mayor of Cheeseburgh, Majyk or no, and my first loyalty must always lie with minding the welfare of my town."

"His loyalty's not the only thing that's lying," Mysti whispered in my ear. "He's got what he wants from you and now he needs us out of the way. *He'll* go off by himself to sop up more Majyk, using what you gave him as bait. He'll swell with it like a sponge, and when he's got enough, he'll turn it against you."

"I don't think he—" I began.

"You've still got Master Thengor's Majyk, and I say he still wants it. No one knows human nature better than a Welfie." She folded her arms.

"Welfies aren't *human*," I protested.

"Thank you."

"You know what I mean," I hissed. "Listen, I *am* human and I bet Zoltan is telling us the truth."

"Care to put your life on the wager?"

"I beg your pardon, Master Kendar, friend Blade, but did you say something?" Zoltan asked. Whispering is supposed to keep things nice and secret, but it doesn't work when both the whisperers are the only ones in the room making any sort of noise.

Mysti was never one to back down. "I was making a small bet with Master Kendar," she said, chin up, challenging. "I wager that if you stay behind and we go traipsing off to Mother Toadbreath's, you'll turn traitor before we've even turned the corner."

"Oh?" Zoltan was undisturbed by this accusation. "And what are the stakes?"

"What?"

"The stakes, the stakes, my dear Blade. What are you willing to hazard? Or do you Welfies only back up your bets with words? All that hot air may be welcome in wintertime, but I prefer to win something *visible*."

"What did you have in mind?" Mysti's mouth twisted into a tight knot.

"My throat to your sword, free for the slitting, if I betray Master Kendar," he replied.

"And if you don't." *Which I doubt*, her tone added.

"Then you, my dashing young hero, will agree to strip off that mask, those boots, that steel, and all the rest besides. Instead I'll have you ride in a lady's gown through the streets of Cheeseburgh at the height of trade on market day." He leered. "On a *very* slow horse." It was another flash of the old Zoltan.

"I'll do you one better," Mysti said. "Prove yourself an honest man, and I'll take that ride as bare as the day I was born!"

"Done!"

My groan was lost in the explosive sound of Zoltan and Mysti clasping hands to seal the wager.

CHAPTER ——————— 16

WE WERE THE SIZE OF A VERY SMALL ARMY AS WE marched from Zoltan's house to Mother Toadbreath's cottage. Our boots drummed out a steady beat on the cobblestones, our arms swung smartly back and forth with military precision, our faces were set in grim, determined expressions. No one dared to get in our way. No one could stop us.

We stopped.

"I think it's that way," I said, pointing vaguely at a large horse trough down the street in front of us. We were in one of the many public squares that had sprung up all over Cheeseburgh like mushrooms since my last visit. There were *too* many of them; they all looked exactly alike, and I was a little confused.

"It's not," said Gout. "*That's* the way we want to go. I ought to know; I live here." She pointed down a different street.

"And how many times have you gone calling on Mother Toadbreath?" Mysti challenged her. "I say it's *that* way." She gestured with her second-best dagger. "Mother Toadbreath's cottage lies hard by the fearsome Forest of Euw, ancestral home of the Welfin race. As a Welfie of the blood, I can feel the call of the forest even from this far away."

"You, *attracted* to the Forest of Euw?" I scoffed. "You were so repelled by living there that when you had the chance to get out, you ran like a pack of lowyenas was chasing you. If you say it's that way, then it's *got* to be *that* way." I indicated the exact opposite direction.

"You're all neck-deep in sheep droppings," Basehart said. "I've got woodsy lore comin' out my ear holes. Drop me in the middle of a trackless forest and I'll find my way before you can say 'Squirrel goes good with potatoes.' If it's a big forest you're after, I can scent it from here, and it's *that* way."

"How foolish," Aunt Carageena remarked to her sister. "If we want to know which way to go, why doesn't Kendar do another one of his cute little vision-things?"

"You can't do that without a bowl of water, Gee'; everyone knows that."

"Then why can't he use his Majyk to *make* a bowl of water?"

"Hmmm. Kendar dear, your Auntie Gee' has a very good question here."

"I heard," I said. I fanned out my fingers and made a bowl of water, then spoke the words of the vision-seeking spell. This time I asked for a vision of how to get where we were going.

The conjured bowl melted from my hand. The glowing drizzle at my feet formed letters that spelled out, YOU LAZY CLOD, DO I HAVE TO DO *EVERYTHING*?

"Uhhhh, I can't do it because it's a wizardly mystery, Aunt Carageena," I said. I smeared the words with my boot and went back to arguing with the others.

"You know, Gee', I was thinking—" Aunt Glucosia began. "*Stop* calling me Gee'," Aunt Carageena snapped. "You know I hate that."

"Oh, piffle. What I was thinking, Gee', was—"

"Was *what*, Gluey?" her sister said with an extra nasty grin.

Aunt Glucosia scowled. "I will thank you not to call me by that horridly adhesive nickname," she said.

"You can thank me after I've paid you back for all the times you've called *me* by anything other than my given name. I've kept count, you know. I owe you seventy-two thousand four hundred and fifty-six Glueys. Sorry, four hundred and fifty-*five* if I discount that last one." Aunt Carageena was enjoying this.

"You're being entirely unreasonable over trifles, Gee'," said Aunt Glucosia, a menacing note coming into her voice.

"Oh, really, Gluey? Am I, Gluey? Is that so, Gluey?" The two women began circling each other slowly. "Are you quite sure, Gluey? The part about my being unreasonable, I mean. Gluey."

The rest of us abandoned our own quarrel to watch theirs. Aunt Glucosia kilted up the hem of her gown to reveal the mail shirt beneath. Aunt Carageena tossed her cloak over one shoulder so the fading light of day struck a few last reflected gleams from her armor. Their hands moved gradually but surely for the blades at their belts. Cheeseburghers rushing home to supper paused in their courses and stopped to see what would happen next.

"I warn you, Gee', I have taken an oath never to spill the blood of my relatives," Aunt Glucosia said.

Aunt Carageena laughed. "A fine warning! I know I could beat you in a fair fight, eventually, but now I have nothing to fear from you at all. *Gluey.*"

"I'm surprised I have to tell you that there are more ways of making your opponent comfortably dead than by bloodshed."

"As if you could get near enough to strangle me without my putting a foot of steel through your *gluey* old guts!"

("It's times like these that I'm glad I was an only Welfie," Mysti whispered to me.)

"I won't have to get near you at all." Aunt Glucosia paused in her sidewise circling and thrust a hand into her belt pouch. "Not as long as I have . . . *this!*"

The Sacred Eye of Delbert flashed in splendor. It was pretty impressive, for a glass copy. Big as a baby's head, the smooth crimson sphere was flawed only by a single vertical slit of pearly light, like some ghastly, supernatural pupil. It seemed to stare at us all.

Caught in its glassy gaze, Aunt Carageena gasped and froze in her tracks. "No! You wouldn't! Not the Sacred Eye of Delbert!"

"I'm sorry, but I have no choice," Aunt Glucosia replied.

"You can't! You mustn't! The power of the Sacred Eye of Delbert is legendary! You may destroy me, but you'll also wipe out half this town in the blast!"

The Cheeseburgher spectators heard my aunt's words and let out a group squeak of dismay, their faces the color of skimmed milk.

Aunt Glucosia hung her head, but she didn't put away the Sacred Eye. "It's too late," she said, speaking from a heavy heart. "You have insulted my honor and I must avenge it. I promised the High Priest. You know how it is."

One Cheeseburgher scuttled out of the crowd and tapped Aunt Carageena's arm. "Arrrrr . . . lady? Lady, any chance as you might apologize t' her honor? Quick? 'Fore she has t' decide which half o' Cheeseburgh'll be wiped out?"

It was Aunt Carageena's turn to look downcast. "That is impossible, for she has insulted *my* honor as a swordswoman. If I apologize to her now, I will be honor-bound to slay everyone who witnessed my shame. I hope you realize that includes you."

"Oh. Yeh. Well. Fair enough." The little man tried to scoot out of harm's way, but Aunt Carageena had more to say. She nabbed him by the back of the neck and reeled him in.

"—*and* to make sure that I leave no one alive to speak of this, I generally slaughter everyone I meet for three days afterwards."

"Yeh, well, I just gotta be—"

"Then I burn the town."

"She does, you know," Aunt Glucosia confirmed. "This time I won't help her do it, if that's any consolation."

The Cheeseburger groaned. "Aw, ladies, *please* don't carry on so untidy-like!" he implored. "'Tain't like the old days. Burn down Cheeseburgh then, an' you was doin' us a favor. But now—now that we just got it put t'gether so's it works right—most o' th' time—an' water, an' schools, an' not too much oxflop underfoot in some streets, an' I just got th' pictures hung th' way my wife likes 'em—*now* you're gonna burn us out an' slaughter us an' knock the pictures crooked again?" The poor fellow howled.

"Oh, the humanity." Aunt Carageena sighed.

"And to think, this might all have been avoided if we hadn't stopped to argue about which way to Mother Toadbreath's cottage," said Aunt Glucosia.

"What?" The Cheeseburger stopped howling and goggled at them. "Whyn't you say so? Nothin' simpler. Just you take *that* street—the one with the horse trough—straight until you're out of town, then keep on the path. It'll take you past Golligosh Pond and when you step on somethin' squishy that goes *croak*, you're there."

"Why, thank you, sir." Aunt Carageena released him.

"Mercy, yes, much obliged," Aunt Glucosia agreed, and popped the Eye of Delbert back into her pouch. "Shall we go, dearie?" She linked arms with her sister. They started off down the proper street.

I dashed ahead and blocked their path, hands on hips.

"*What* was all *that* about?" I demanded. "All those threats of death and destruction and slaughter and burning down the town and—"

"Silly boy." Aunt Carageena patted my cheek. "It was the only way to find out where we ought to be going."

"You know these Gangle men, Gee'," Aunt Glucosia remarked confidentially. "They always make such a big fuss over asking directions!" They sidestepped me and strode on.

"Is this the right place?" Basehart asked as we came in sight of Mother Toadbreath's cottage.

Just then someone flung open the shutters of the upstairs window. Dulcetta Gallimaufrey stuck her head out and screamed.

"Looks like it," I replied. We all sprinted into the front yard as she let loose another shriek that knocked birds' nests out of the trees and stunned Mother Toadbreath's watch-hedge into letting us break through.

"Aid me! Rescue me! Oh, will no one succor an innocent maiden?" She was no longer swathed in the layers and layers of proper Gallimaufrey bridal dress. Her long golden hair streamed down over her shoulders in very attractive disarray, and the neckline of her simple gown revealed enough to make any man wish to trade places with my damn-fool-lucky brother Basehart.

"Despair, oh despair!" Dulcetta cried. She wrung her hands, then pressed one to her brow, the other to her bosom. "Ah me, I perish! Even now the evil minions of my foul captor are drawing nigh to bear me off, willy-nilly, to a life of degradation and shame! Aid! Oh, aid!" She wrung her hands some more and ducked back into the house.

"Are you *sure*?" Basehart insisted.

"Shut up and stand back," I told him, pulling my sleeves out of the way. "I'm going to blast the front off that house and save Dulcetta."

"You are *not*." Mysti seized my wrist. "That's Mother Toadbreath's *home*. We don't even know what's become of her. What if whoever kidnapped Dulcetta has poor Mother T. tied up and helpless somewhere? You'll wreck her home and you might wreck *her* into the bargain."

"I'll make sure my Majyk knows *not* to hurt Mother Toadbreath," I told her.

"And since when are you able to do fancy tricks like that

with your Majyk?" Mysti wanted to know. "Zoltan only gave you one lesson that I could see, and we still don't know if you got *that* one right."

"I'd say it's pretty obvious that I did!" I shouted, gesturing at the now-unoccupied window. "I asked for a vision of where Dulcetta was hiding and I got it!"

"You'll get worse'n that if you go tossin' fireballs at my bride," Basehart chimed in, grabbing my other wrist. "She's got sensitive skin, she does, what can't hardly bear the heat. Her ma told me so. I'm not havin' a bride what's goin' t' be all broke out in heat rash for our honeymoon."

"Basehart is quite right, Kendar dear," Aunt Glucosia murmured. "This is a job for swords, not sorcery. Shall we, Gee'?"

"Couldn't he use just a *bit* of sorcery to get rid of all these toads first?" Aunt Carageena quavered. She had her feet very close together and was doing her best to keep herself as far from the toads as possible. This was no easy job, since we were standing in the middle of Mother Toadbreath's front yard. Great brown heaps of toads leaped and chumbled and squatted everywhere.

"He could *not*," Mysti decided for me. "These are Mother Toadbreath's toads. One of them just might be the enchanted prince she's been looking for all these years. She kisses them when she's got the time for it, but it's terribly hard to tell them apart. She forgets which ones she's kissed already and which ones she hasn't yet tried. That's why she holds onto them all."

"The woman needs a system," Aunt Carageena said, trembling in toad-fearing misery. "Something to help her keep track. Tally sticks, perhaps, or an account book, or wax tablets for scribbling little memos to herself about which toads she's already kissed, or—"

At this moment, a set of tally sticks, an inkwell, six account books, and four wax tablets came flying out the upstairs window. The toads scattered, croaking in terror. One of them was not fast enough. It was a stone inkwell. What it did to the toad was ugly.

"I certainly hope *that* wasn't the lucky toad," Aunt Glucosia remarked.

"I wouldn't call anything this flat that lucky," Gout replied, regarding the splatted amphibian.

"Assistance!" cried Dulcetta, back at the window. "Rescue

and relief, I pray! Alas, I am besieged! O, the vile, vicious, villainous, vermin-hearted varlet! I fear he means me no good. And yet, I am drawn to him. I suspect that behind his harsh exterior there broods a noble spirit who is merely misunderstood. Ah, I am torn!"

"Don't you go tearing my girl, dammit!" Basehart yelled, and charged the house before any of us could stop him. Toads scattered in a panic before his thundering feet. Those too slow to scatter, splattered. He slipped on one unfortunate beast and wiped out a whole family reunion on his backside, then hauled himself up again and bulled right through the cottage door. Locks and bolts could not hope to hold against the fury of his charge.

The door was not locked and swung back easily under Basehart's attack. It was a little too easy for what he'd been expecting. We heard a shriek, a series of yelps, and a bone-jarring crash from deep within the house.

Dulcetta stopped her cries. She leaned out over the sill, peering into the front yard. "Oh, hello," she said, waving at us. "I'm sorry I didn't see you all standing there before. I don't know what you must think of me, going on like that out the window. Just push the toads aside and come to the front door. You're not selling anything, are you?"

I cupped my hands to my mouth. "Dulcetta!" I called. "Dulcetta, don't you know me?"

She batted her lashes and shaded her eyes with one hand. "Kendar Gangle, is that you? But who are those others—?"

"We're here to rescue you from your, uh, foul captor and his evil minions. Don't worry, I have everything under control. How many minions would you say he's got? Just at a rough guess? I have to tell my Majyk."

Dulcetta ignored the question in favor of one of her own. "Where is Basehart?"

"He's here!" I called back. "He's in the house already! He's probably fighting off evil minions right this minute."

"No, he's not." Dulcetta planted her elbows on the sill and rested her chin in her hands. "You're just saying that to make me feel good. Basehart's probably safe and comfy back at Uxwudge Manor, chewing on a piece of dead animal. He doesn't care for me at all. I'm just a dowry with legs to him."

"But they're *nice* legs, dearie," Aunt Carageena hollered, trying to make things better.

My brother came dragging out of the cottage, his britches black with soot, his tunic scorched and spotted with globs of meat and potatoes. Gravy dripped from his hair. He was limping, one foot stuck in a clay pot full of vegetable peelings.

He licked his lips. "Needs salt," he announced before falling face-forward on a fresh patch of toads.

I rushed to his side just in time to see Curio burst from the house. He waved a knife as long as a stoat and twice as dangerous.

I shot a bolt of Majyk at him without thinking. I was aiming for the knife. Just because I was finally able to command my power didn't mean I could aim it worth a dead rat. I hit Curio right between the eyes.

His limbs stood straight out like a starfish. Every hair on his head went *tzing*! then shrank back against his skull in hundreds of smoking spirals. His eyes pinwheeled wildly before turning up in their sockets as his lids fell heavily. So did he.

Right on top of Basehart.

"Good work," said Mysti, thumping me on the back. "You killed them both."

"I didn't kill anyone. Just help me roll them over," I said, tugging futilely on Curio's beefy arm.

Mysti leaned against the cottage wall and studied her nails. (This was a neat trick, since she was still wearing gloves.) "Why don't you just use your Majyk to lift them up?" she asked in an off-handed way.

"I knew that." I felt myself blushing. Taking a few steps back, I made Curio's body float up and away from Basehart's. I laid the big blond down on a wooden bench near Mother Toadbreath's door, then got Basehart flipped over onto his back. A pink feather materialized over his nose. We all saw the plumes tremble; he was breathing.

I was about to repeat the feather-test on Curio when Dulcetta came running into the front yard. She gave a little cry of horror when she saw the two bodies, but she flung herself on Basehart first, in spite of the gravy.

"Well, that's a good sign," I said to Mysti.

"She's getting potatoes on my boots," the Welfie replied.

"Basehart! Basehart, darling!" Dulcetta exclaimed, hugging

him to her bosom. "Don't be dead, my love! Mummy will *kill* me if we can't have the wedding after it's been paid for!"

Basehart stirred, groaned, and tried to sit up. Then he saw where he was and settled in, a smile of contentment on his face.

Over on the bench, Curio made some coming-to noises of his own and sat up, holding onto his head to make sure it didn't fall off. He was more than a little surprised when he touched the new hairstyle my Majyk had given him. The long, blond mane that had wafted over such Raptura Eglantine titles as *Enflame Not the Firedrake* and *Goad Not the Ghoul* was now reduced to a tight tousle of bright golden curls.

"In Velvel's name, what have you done to me?" he cried, clutching handfuls of ringlets.

My aunts were right there to comfort him. "There, there, it's not so bad," Aunt Glucosia cooed, sitting next to him.

"It's very flattering, actually," Aunt Carageena agreed, attaching herself to his other side.

They were still making kittenish sounds and twirling his curls around their fingers when I came over to settle a thing or two more important than Curio's new hairstyle.

"Call them off," I told him.

"Call them off yourself!" he countered. "Are they not your relatives?" He gestured at the aunts, who took the opportunity to grab an arm apiece and exclaim over how big and strong and muscular they were growing the Alfresco boys these days.

"I don't mean *them*," I said. "I mean your evil minions. They're probably lurking somewhere in there." I indicated Mother Toadbreath's cottage. It was pretty quiet for a house supposedly teeming with evil minions, but you never could tell; evil minions are sneaky. It's a natural part of minioning. "Call them off."

"What is this you ask?" Curio looked honestly puzzled. "I have no evil minions! I do not even know what it is, these minions. Ask her." He nodded towards Dulcetta. "She is the one who is always going on about evil minions and ne'er-do-wells and roguish sidekicks and—*pah*!" He curled his lip in disgust. "From first to last, I curse the mad idea that brought about this unspeakable captivity!"

"Serves you right for taking a poor, innocent girl prisoner!" Mysti told him.

Curio's mouth opened wider and wider, but the only words that escaped were, "Who? *Me*?"

"Oh, don't blame Curio," Dulcetta called to us. "It wasn't really his fault. Except for the sausage."

"Not his fault he stole you away from Uxwudge Manor on your wedding day?" I demanded. "Not his fault he kept you locked away in this cottage, after doing Wedwel-knows-what to the real owner? Not his fault that you were hanging out the window just now, screaming 'Help me! Help me!' at the top of your lungs?"

"Sausage?" said Basehart.

And then Dulcetta did a truly frightening thing: A look of happy realization flooded her face, she snapped her fingers, and she exclaimed, "*Help* me! That's *it*! *Help* me! Oh my goodness! That's the *perfect word*!"

She shoved Basehart's head off her lap and raced back into the house, slamming the door behind her.

"THE HORROR," SAID BASEHART, HIS HEAD IN HIS hands. He sat on a stool beside Mother Toadbreath's fireplace and wept without shame. Praise Wedwel, Dad wasn't there to see it.

"There, there, dear," Aunt Carageena said. "You can always find another bride now that this one's been ruined."

Basehart lifted his face. "But I don't want another one. I want Dulcetta. I love her," he said in a small voice. He started crying again.

"What's the problem?" Mysti asked the air. "I'd like to know what the problem is. Will someone please explain the problem to me? What *is* the problem?"

"The problem is, I do not have enough carrots," Curio announced from the kitchen table. "How can I make beef stew Alfresco if I do not have enough carrots?"

He had reclaimed his knife and was back at work, chopping vegetables. When Basehart had come barreling into the cottage, slipped on the rug and skidded into the cauldron of stew on the hearth, Curio was using that same knife to cut up more vegetables for the pot. I zapped him for no worse crime than thinking my brother was a parsnip. (It's an honest mistake.)

"Carrots are not the problem," I said. "The problem is Dulcetta."

"Ruined!" Basehart wailed. "Ruined!"

"Now look, friend, it's not as bad as that," Mysti said, trying to make Basehart see reason. "She still loves you, right?"

Basehart nodded, wiping his nose on his sleeve.

"And she still wants to marry you, doesn't she?"

"That's what she says, yeah."

"Well, then—! As for this little . . . *vacation* she took before the wedding, it's nothing, nothing at all. A lot of girls get cold feet before they become brides. Besides, everyone back at Uxwudge believes that she was carried off against her will by a great and powerful wizard."

"Ha!" said Curio with a toss of his brand new curls.

"She couldn't help it," Mysti went on. "Not her fault, completely out of her hands, no way to lay a shred of blame at her doorstep. These things happen in the best of families. No one needs to know the *truth*."

"No one would *believe* the truth," Aunt Carageena added.

"I promise, no one will hear the truth from *me*," Curio said, flaying an innocent turnip. "It is too humiliating. It will mean the end of my reputation if word gets out. I will be the laughingstock of seven kingdoms! I will never be able to show my face in Alfresco again!" He whacked the turnip in two with one blow of the knife.

"The truth would kill her parents," Aunt Glucosia said.

"The truth would shame Lucius and Abstemia for ages," was Aunt Carageena's opinion.

"The truth?" said Gout, who was just coming into the cottage with a basket full of carrots she'd yanked from Mother Toadbreath's garden. She dumped them into a pot of cold water on the table and added, "The truth is that after *she* forced *him* to run away from Uxwudge Manor, they both got sick as dogs from eating the local sausage, pitched up under Toadie's roof—don't ask me how—and he's been in the kitchen ever since while she's been upstairs—"

"She's goin' t' say it!" Basehart screamed, covering his ears and cringing. "She's goin' t' say the *R* word!"

"—writing."

At that moment, Dulcetta came down the stairs. Her face was radiant. I'd never seen her looking so lovely. "Oh, that was *marvelous*," she breathed. "That was just the best I've ever had." She hugged a wax tablet to her breast and breathed a sigh of ecstasy. "Philiomina leans out the window as Lord Dagor's evil minions are closing in and she screams '*Help* me!' That's all, just '*Help* me!' All that other stuff I had her saying before about how she was going to be taken off to a life of shame and degradation, that wasn't necessary. It's so much more effective to *show* the shame and degradation. That way the reader can enjoy it, too. Don't you agree?" She gazed at us all with a look of sweet expectancy.

"I don't know if I'd be serving the cause of Justice by giving her a good, swift kick in the backside," Mysti said, "but I know *I'd* enjoy it."

Curio sighed. "This is the punishment I have brought upon myself. I was too greedy, too ambitious. See to what depths it has brought me!" He plunged his hand into the pot of cold water and flourished a carrot dramatically. "Why could I not be satisfied with my lot? It is true, I was no longer the only Raptura Eglantine hero, but there was hope! I might yet have been employed to pose for her lesser titles. But that was not enough for me."

"No," said Mysti, her eyes narrowing the way they always did just before someone in her vicinity developed a puncture. "It wasn't enough for you, was it? We're *still* waiting to hear what you did with Prince Boffin."

Curio's fabulous chin lifted in a gesture of defiance familiar to every Raptura Eglantine fan. "And *I* am waiting for you to promise you will not slaughter me as soon as I tell you," he replied.

"No promises."

"Then no prince."

"Then no ears." Mysti drew her sword.

I clapped my hand over hers on the hilt. "No killing. He can't tell us where the prince is if he's dead."

"I wasn't going to kill him; I was just going to *prune* him until he felt like talking," Mysti explained.

"No pruning either. Look, we found Dulcetta, safe and sound. I'm sure we'll find Boffin the same way."

"And if we don't?"

"Then you can practice pruning *me*."

Mysti reluctantly let her sword slip back into its sheath.

"Better you should have let her slay me," Curio said. "I do not know if I can live with the shame. Oh, I was a fool! A fool or a madman. Where did I ever get that wild idea? All I know is, one dark day I realized that the fine foods, the exquisite clothing, the rich life I so happily enjoyed was about to come to an end. If I was no longer the extremely well-paid body that the readers demanded with their Raptura Eglantine romances, what was I? Only a body." He hung his head and let his shoulders slump.

He *tried* to let his shoulders slump.

"Gee', do you see anything so 'only' about that body?" Aunt Glucosia asked.

"I don't know. Let me have a *much* closer look at it," her sister replied.

Curio's sigh moved over the mountains of his chest like a small earthquake. "How could I hope to earn my bread once this body was touched by age? Worse yet, how was I to live if no one wanted this body anymore?"

"*I* want that body," Mysti said. "I want to bring it to justice for what it did to Prince Boffin."

"Yes, yes, kill me, slay me, destroy me, ruin my complexion if you like. It will be nothing next to what I have already suffered. Even now, Boffin is luckier than I."

"Do you mind if I argue that point?" said the masked Welfie.

"If Boffin lost his job, what of it? He was still a prince! But for me, to lose my work was to lose everything. If Boffin had not come along, I would have been replaced by someone like him sooner or later. I thought: *Curio, what you need is to find a new job before you are thrown out of your old one! One that does not depend upon mere appearances, one where you can grow old and ugly and feeble-minded and eat all the wrong foods and still be able to earn a living.* And then the answer burst upon me like something very large that bursts over your head: I would become a writer!" He struck a triumphant pose, arms flung wide, and waited for the applause.

"Your carrot's dripping," said Mysti.

This time Curio did manage to force his titanic shoulders into a minor slump. "Ah, there it is, in a nutshell: My carrot drips. It drips, and in so dripping makes more marks on the unforgiving parchment than I am ever able to do. I tried to write. Oh, many times, I tried! And what came of it? Carrot drippings."

"Could you please forget about your carrot for a moment?" Gout took the vegetable from Curio and began to skin it. "Maybe you started off on the wrong foot. They say you're supposed to write about what you know."

"I *try* to write what I know," he said. "All that I know is romance: the way of a man with a maid, desire's searing ecstasy, rapture's savage fury, love's tender torment, passion's unbridled frenzy—!" His voice dropped. "Pfui."

"It was *so* sad," Dulcetta piped up. "Curio is just full of ideas, but when it's time to set them down in words—" They shared a knowing look.

Basehart didn't like it. "Hey! How d'you come to know so much about this lummox an' his *ideas*?" he demanded of his bride.

Dulcetta giggled. "It's the funniest thing, really," she began.

"Not to me, it ain't." Basehart crossed his arms, waiting for it to get funnier.

"I've always wanted to write," she continued. "The way Mummy and Daddy raised me—shutting me up in my room if there were men visiting the house, or male servants doing chores, or it was frisky season for the livestock—all I could *do* to pass the time was read and write."

"Whatever happened to embroidery?" Aunt Carageena inquired. "Your mother seems to be so keen on it."

"Mummy didn't raise me; Huletta did. Mummy says that raising your own children is all very well for barbarians and the middle classes, but *she* was a Gallimaufrey now, and bad luck to anyone who forgot it. So she gave me to Huletta almost as soon as I was born." Dulcetta smiled fondly, remembering her old nursemaid. "Huletta was a refugee from Vicinity City. She left there during The Troubles."

"Ah, yes," we all said in chorus, lowering our eyes. "The Troubles."

"Folks say The Troubles was brought on the people o' Vicinity City by themselves," Basehart intoned. " 'Cos they didn't do things right nor behave natural. They sent their women to school, for one."

"I suppose that's so." Dulcetta looked wistful. "Huletta knew how to read and write; she taught me how to do both, and she had boxes and boxes full of books in her room. She also had boxes and boxes full of embroidery, so whenever Mummy asked how my education was coming along, we just showed her another footstool cover and she went away."

Basehart put his arms around Dulcetta. "You're a good, brave girl t' be tellin' me all this about y'self," he said. "An' I want you t' know that I forgive you."

"Forgive her for what?" asked Gout.

Basehart looked surprised by the question. "Didn't you hear her? She *reads books*!"

"And writes them," Curio muttered.

"Here, you watch what you say about my Dulcetta!" Basehart waved a fist in Curio's face. "Just 'cos she scribbles about a bit don't mean she's sunk so low as to write whole *books*."

"Yes, I have, Basehart darling," Dulcetta corrected him. The expression on my brother's face was ghastly to behold.

"This too is all my fault," Curio said. "After the betrothal ceremony, I noticed something drop from under her robes. We Alfrescanos are nothing if not gallant. I rushed to retrieve it for the lady. When I picked it up, I saw that it was—"

"—a book," Dulcetta said. "Just one of my little notebooks."

"It was more than that." Curio kissed his fingertips. "It was a masterpiece!"

Dulcetta simpered. "You big silly. It was only my first try at writing a romance. I called it *The Lustful Warlock*." Basehart uttered a gurgling groan. Dulcetta patted his hand. "That's all right, sweetheart, I didn't like the title either."

"I could not help but open it and read a few pages," Curio continued. "Such genius! It was then my accursed idea took shape. I approached the lady and discreetly returned the book. Then I asked her if she had ever considered a career in writing."

"Of course I was awfully shocked. A *career*? I told him I'd sooner die," Dulcetta said in a way that fooled no one. "But he was very persuasive. He said he knew people who were *desperate* to buy romances. Raptura Eglantine can't churn them out fast enough for the readers, and the stuff the minstrels drag around the kingdoms is about as romantic as kissing a sludgebat. It was a very tempting offer."

"Not tempting enough for the lady to consent right away," Curio reminded her.

Dulcetta sighed prettily and ran her fingers through Basehart's hair. "What was I to do, darling? Mummy always told me that the only thing a Gangle respects is hard spending money and lots of it. I did *so* want you to respect me after we were married. What better way than by earning oodles of my own? And I'd been talking to your aunts all day. *They're* career women. They made it all sound so glamorous!"

Aunt Glucosia and Aunt Carageena tried to look innocent.

"So I agreed," Dulcetta concluded.

"And—?" Mysti prodded her.

"And what?"

"And aren't you forgetting a little something like running away from Uxwudge Manor in the middle of your own wedding?"

Dulcetta had the sort of silvery laughter that generally made Mysti punch things. "Surely you couldn't expect me to write under *those* conditions? Uxwudge Manor is so—so unromantic."

"To say nothing of marriage," Gout muttered.

"Who made you the expert?" Aunt Carageena shot back.

Dulcetta heard none of this. "I told Curio we must leave and find somewhere more inspirational. He refused at first, but then I found the means to convince him."

"Oh, you did, did you?" Basehart's face darkened like a storm cloud.

"Mm-hm. In fact, I've got it right here." She reached down the front of her dress.

"Dulcetta—!"

"What?" she asked, holding up a tiny vial of Magique on a chain.

"We slipped away from the party," Curio explained. "I had some writing supplies in my room that I wished to give her. She argued with me the whole way, saying she could not possibly write at Uxwudge. I told her time and time again that a *true* writer can write anywhere!"

"Those who can't do, lecture," Mysti commented.

"While he was gathering up the parchment and pens, I looked around the room. I found this." Dulcetta let the vial twirl at the end of its chain. "Actually, it was in a different container at first—a larger one—but I poured a little into this. I thought it was perfume, and this *is* a perfume vial."

"I saw what she was doing—too late!" Curio was gloomy. "I told her to put it back. She paid me no mind and once more begged to be taken somewhere romantic so that she could write my books, I could sell them, we could grow rich, and she could return to her beloved groom a strong, respected woman."

"And rich," Dulcetta reminded him.

"I dunno 'bout strong women," Basehart said, shaking his head. "They hit you so's it *hurts*." He thought it over, then brightened. "'Course they *are* good for carryin' the dead deer home if your horse feels wonky."

"Again I told her it was impossible, what she asked," Curio said. "Alas, it was no longer impossible. She had spilled Magique all over her hands. When she stretched them out to me, pleading, I was seized by an irresistible force that compelled me to obey her. I was like a man in a dream. When I awoke, I was here. I know no more."

Quick as most thoughts, and a lot faster than any of Basehart's, Mysti sprang forward to lift Curio onto tiptoe by his belt buckle. "Oh, I think you know just a *little* more," she snarled. "Like what you did with Prince Boffin."

"Persistent, isn't he?" I overheard one of my aunts remark wearily to the other.

Curio made a series of high-pitched squeaks, his face turning bright red. I took pity on the man and shot off a tiny spark of Majyk that zinged Mysti's wrist and made her drop him. His throat worked like a bullfrog's as he struggled to recapture his breath.

"That's not the way to get information," I told an irate Welfie.

"Let's see you do better."

"I will." I ambled up to Curio, who was seated on a tall stool, recovering from Mysti's attack. Gout brought him a cup of water and stood guard, her face unreadable. "Well, Curio," I said. "I think I've just proved that I can protect you from Mys—Blade's vengeance. Tell us what you did with Prince Boffin and nothing will happen to you."

"No," Curio croaked.

Mysti snickered. I had gotten used to being the sort of person who gets things right, for a change. I didn't like the idea of going back to being Ratwhacker the Dependable Failure. I decided to get tougher with Curio.

"Don't be a fool," I told him. "Do you want me to give you back to Blade?"

"I don't think he's Blade's type," Aunt Carageena spoke up. "Are you, sweetie?"

"Ohhhhh, I don't know." Mysti rocked on her heels. "With his hair all curly the way it is now, he does look an awful lot like Prince Boffin. Maybe I should cut my losses and make a fresh start." She strolled closer to Curio, threw one arm around his neck, and in a husky voice breathed, "We could kiss and make up, big boy."

Curio did a spectacular leap clear across the room. "I am not refusing to tell you where Prince Boffin is; I simply can *not* do it!" he cried. "It is no longer any use to pretend: I have held back the information because I have no information to give. The effects of Dulcetta's Magique sent me into a—what do you call it when you walk, you move, you live, but you do not know what you are doing?"

"Up to a few years back, we called it Kendar," Basehart said. I flicked a particle of Majyk at the back of his britches. "*Wowch!*"

"It's called a trance," I said. "Go on."

"Where shall I go?" Curio shrugged. "I can only say that since I was brought here, I no longer know where Prince Boffin is."

"You can tell us where he *was* and we'll work from there," I suggested.

"He *was* at Uxwudge Manor," Curio said. "I admit, I used Magique on him to remove him as my rival. Even so, I did not wish him dead; only out of the way for a while. I transformed him, yes, but from that moment on he had no more careful guardian than I. Now that my future no longer depends on posing for Raptura Eglantine romance covers, I would gladly restore him, but—" He spread his hands and let his voice trail off.

"Whyn't you ask my smartypants brother to find him, then?" Basehart grumped, rubbing his rump. "Let's see if he can do visions of something other than this dump."

"This is not a dump," Dulcetta said primly. "This is Mother Toadbreath's Bed and Breakfast. The breakfast part is do-it-yourself, but I don't mind."

"You also don't cook," Curio prompted.

She ignored him. "I'd be willing to put up with any inconvenience to stay here. As soon as I saw this quaint, charming, romantic little cottage I knew it was the perfect place to write, write, write!"

"Toadie doesn't exactly live on the king's highway," Gout said. "How did you ever find this place?"

"It was recommended to us by a lovely young couple in Cheeseburgh."

"Let me guess," the witch said dryly. "He was tall and blond and handsome, she was skinny and dark and flashy and cheap-looking and—"

"Actually, she was quite beautiful," Dulcetta said, oblivious to the sound of Gout grinding her teeth. "They explained that they'd worked out a wonderful plan with several cottage-dwellers around Cheeseburgh. The couple acts as the owners' agents, getting a small commission for every rental they arrange."

"A 'small' commission?" Gout snorted.

"They rent out the cottages to other people for a couple of weeks at a time and the owners go live in someone else's cottage. It's worked out very well, they say, except for one fellow from East Fantod who can't seem to remember which cottage was his to start with."

"I hope the same hasn't happened to Mother Toadbreath," I said.

"I hope it has." That was Gout again.

"Oh no, not at all." Dulcetta dug a folded parchment out of the pocket of her gown and handed it to me. "This is the last we heard from her."

I unfolded it and read it aloud: "The jungles of Plunj are glorious at this time of the year, and my cottage is charming, except for the scorpions. Norris, my octopussy, is having the time of his life, although when we went to visit one of the local temples the High Priest did scold him for stealing the Sacred Eye of Delbert from the idol. However, I made a small donation to their Sunday School fund and he said Norris and I could keep the eye as a souvenir. It is very pretty and I shall use it for a paperweight when I return. I forgot to tell you that there are clean towels in the basket under the pile of sheep skulls in the fruit cellar. Hope all is well there. Any trouble with the plumbing, please contact the Cheeseburgh Town Witch, Mistress Gout, who is a real gem. All the best, Mother Toadbreath."

A strange new expression was working its way over the hard, cold features of Gout's face. She no longer looked handsome and aloof; now she looked human. "She—she named me the Cheeseburgh Town Witch," she said softly.

"So we heard," Mysti said. "It looks like your feud with her was all in your own mind."

"I feel so—so small." She folded her hands in contrition.

"All those nasty things I said about her, all the venom, the rumors I spread in town against her witchcraft, how angry I got just *thinking* about her—Oh, I'm worse than a fool! I'm—I'm—"

"An idiot?" Basehart always did like to help out ladies in distress.

Gout's thumb and forefinger dipped into her belt pouch quick as mice. She snapped a pinch of green powder into Basehart's face, which promptly turned just as green, only smaller and smaller, and the ears vanished, the mouth got wide, and the rest of him decided it would be rude not to turn into the rest of the frog.

"And she called me a real gem," Gout went on, as if nothing had happened.

"Which is more than I can call this," my aunt Glucosia grumbled, taking out her own Sacred Eye of Delbert and giving it a cynical stare. It gave her one right back.

"There, there, dear. It will still make a nice paperweight," Aunt Carageena consoled her.

"I'm a swordswoman. When, where, and why in Wedwel's nethermost Hells would I use *paper*?"

"I like to write little newsy notes to my opponents' next-of-kin, but you could always—"

"*I want Prince Boffin!*" Mysti screamed. "I want to know where he is *right now*. *Not* Mother Toadbreath, *not* the clean towels, *not* the Eye of Delbert, just Prince Boffin! Is that perfectly clear?"

"Perfectly." Gout was her old, cold self again. She rummaged through the cupboards and found a bowl which she filled with water from the carrot pot and set down on the table. "It's all yours, Master Kendar."

"Aren't you forgetting something?" I pointed at my brother, the frog.

The witch was unconcerned. "That? A mere bagatelle, an infant enchantment, the easiest spell in the book. Now if I'd meant business, I'd have turned him into a grasshopper, or a bewilderbeast, or a street mime. Those are hard spells to undo, but this? A kiss from the one who cast the spell or from the victim's own true love will always do the trick." She turned to Dulcetta.

Dulcetta cringed. "You said the person who cast the spell can undo it," she pleaded with the witch, looking at poor Basehart askance.

"I could undo it, but I won't," Gout said. "He insulted me. If it had been a mere personal remark, I might have overlooked it. However, since I am now the official Town Witch of Cheeseburgh, I can't allow such incidents to pass unchallenged any longer. He ought to respect the office if not the woman. If you want him back in human form, it's up to you."

Dulcetta bit her lower lip. You could almost see her skin crawl when she looked at Basehart. He croaked, and she nearly leaped out of her bones. "Do I have to *touch* him?" she asked. My brother gave another croak, heartbroken.

"Oh, for—!" Mysti picked up my brother and thrust him face-to-face with his bride. "Close your eyes, grit your teeth, and think of Uxwudge Manor," she ordered Dulcetta.

The girl shuddered, closed her eyes tightly, puckered up, and jabbed her lips at the frog so sharply that she knocked Basehart out of Mysti's hand. Fortunately, it counted as a kiss. He turned back into his old self before he hit the floor. He was scowling at her as he got to his feet, but she soon gave him enough kisses—tender ones this time—to dampen his anger.

Meanwhile, with Mysti peering over my shoulder, I called upon my Majyk to give me a vision of Prince Boffin's whereabouts. I didn't worry about it or even think about it, I just did it.

The power flowed from my hands to the bowl of water as naturally as if I'd been doing this for ages.

I got another vision of Mother Toadbreath's cottage.

"Hey!" I objected.

Glowing letters formed over the image of the witch's house: "HEY!" YOURSELF. I JUST DELIVER VISIONS, I DON'T MAKE THEM. YOU GET WHAT YOU ASK FOR. Words and vision vanished together.

Mysti leaned on the table. "I'll say this for you, Master Kendar: You're consistent. Not good, just consistent."

"Shut up," I told her.

"Uh-uh; you only get what you ask for from the water bowl, not me."

"Get . . . what . . . I . . . ask . . ." I jammed my sleeves up my arms, closed my eyes, and boomed, "Give me a vision of Prince Boffin!"

The water rippled with new golden letters: WE DID THAT ONE ALREADY.

"We did not. Before, I asked for a vision of *where* he is. Now I just want a vision of him *as* he is. He's been transformed, you know. He could be anything around here."

"I hope he wasn't that carrot," Mysti said, watching Curio chop up another one.

The glowing words melted, then rearranged themselves to reply: OHO! GOOD CHOICE. AND ONCE YOU KNOW *WHAT* HE IS, YOU'LL SIMPLY SEARCH THIS PLACE UNTIL YOU FIND HIM, EH?

"That's right."

Chuckling rose from the water in flakes of light. THERE'S HOPE FOR YOU, FRIEND KENDAR. THERE REALLY IS HOPE FOR YOU.

The words bobbed to the edges of the bowl and burst into tiny spouts of rainbow sparkles. They fell back over the surface, painting a fresh vision. I saw it, and felt all the blood rush from my face.

"He's a toad," I said, looking up from the water. My hands were damp and cold.

"A toad?" Mysti tried to get a look at the vision for herself, but it was gone. She slapped her forehead. "There are *hundreds* of toads here!"

"You know, I *did* wonder why you packed that creature, Curio," Dulcetta said, a finger to one corner of her lips. "Then I remembered what Mummy always said about foreigners and the things they'll eat on purpose."

"Now that you know Boffin's a toad, do you think you could tell which one of those out there he is?" Mysti demanded of Curio.

He shook his head. "Thay all look alike to me."

"Oh, don't worry, Blade dear," Aunt Glucosia said, patting Mysti on the back. "It's a step in the right direction, isn't it? And I'm sure Kendar will be able to figure out some way to discover which toad is your, er, ah, um, friend."

"I already know," I said, throat tight.

"Well, isn't that lucky!" Aunt Glucosia beamed.

"He's the one Dulcetta squashed when she threw her stone inkwell out the window."

"Oh." Aunt Glucosia's smile dimmed. "That isn't."

CHAPTER ———————— 18

"GOODBYE, BOFFIN," SAID MYSTI, LOOKING DOWN at the blobby remains of the toad. "Hello, war."

We were all in the front yard, gathered in a circle around the stone inkwell and what lay under it. It had landed right on the transformed prince's head. His warty body stretched out behind it, flat in the dirt.

"I didn't mean to kill him," Dulcetta whimpered. "I was just so unhappy because I couldn't get the rescue scene to come out right."

"Cheer up; neither could we," Mysti said.

Dulcetta wrung her hands. "I've really got to learn to control my temper better, but I'm an *artist*."

Mysti's lips curled. "An artist, hm? What's the matter: Can't you pronounce *brat*?"

Dulcetta burst into loud, tearless sobs. Basehart embraced her and gave the Welfie an indignant look. "You leave off her. She said it wasn't her fault and that's so! Anyone's got half a brain knows that writers are sensitive and tempered and mental and throw things a lot."

"That's nothing compared to what Prince Boffin's father is going to throw when he hears his son's been killed by an inkwell," Mysti replied.

"I must say, you're taking this pretty calmly, Blade dear." Aunt Glucosia rested her hand on Mysti's arm. "Stout fellow." I had to agree. I'd expected a little crying, at the least.

"What use would my tears be now?" Mysti shrugged off my aunt's touch. "Dead is dead."

Gout knelt and examined the body. "And alive is alive," she said, looking up at us.

"What?"

"He's breathing."

I immediately fell to my knees beside the witch. Up close I saw what she had seen: The toad's sides were moving in and out—not very strongly and not very often, but they *were* moving. I placed my hand gently on Prince Boffin's body to be sure.

"Eeeeeeuuuuuuwwwwww!" Dulcetta squealed, burying her head in Basehart's shoulder. "He *touched* it!"

I only half-heard her. I was holding my breath as I reached for the stone inkwell and gingerly lifted it from the toad's head. I had my eyes closed, not sure I wanted to see what something that heavy had done to the prince's skull. Dulcetta was making all sorts of gagging noises. I kept my eyes shut and tried to force myself to peek.

Someone gave me a shove in the side. "You can open them, O courageous wizard," Gout snapped. "It's all in one piece, just a little flatter than before." She chuckled. "So, naturally curly hair is good for something after all."

I looked at the toad, then at Curio. "They all look *alike* to you?" I demanded, incredulous.

"I am not accustomed to telling one toad from another," he replied.

"Not even when this one has a head of thick blond, curly *hair*?"

He shrugged.

It was true: Even in toad form, Prince Boffin was blessed with a crop of golden curls whose natural cushioning action had saved his skull from major damage when the inkwell hit. He was badly stunned, but he was alive and breathing. I picked him up and got to my feet, holding the unconscious toad-prince cupped in my two hands. Everyone followed me as I brought him over to the bench near Mother Toadbreath's door.

"I'll go get some water," Mysti said, and went into the house.

"That Blade is a most unusual young man," Aunt Glucosia remarked.

"You don't know the half of it," I said under my breath, laying out the toad in my lap.

"All that fuss for us to find Prince Boffin, and now that he's been found, Blade doesn't seem to care."

"You know the old saying, Glucosia dear," her sister

reminded her. "'The heart has its reasons that Reason does not know, or want to know, and will throw you out of the house if you try to explain them, so save your breath to cool your porridge.'"

"Hmmm. No, I can't say I know that old saying, 'Gee."

"Well, it's not all that popular."

Mysti returned with some water in a cup. I sprinkled it over Prince Boffin. The toad stirred and opened his eyes. He froze when he saw us looming over him.

"It's all right, Your Highness," I reassured him. "We're here to help you. One kiss from your own true love and you'll be yourself again."

Mysti sat beside me on the bench and stuck out her hand. "Give him here and let's get this done with," she said. There was no reluctance in her voice, but no eagerness either. The kiss she gave the curly-haired toad was almost as short and rough as the one Dulcetta had given Basehart.

The result were nowhere near as good.

"He's still a toad," Aunt Carageena observed.

"Well, *duh*!" said the witch. When she saw our perplexed stares she added, "Words of Power I picked up while visiting the Whirl'd. Never mind."

"Try it again," I suggested. Mysti complied. This time she let her lips linger a while longer on the toad's wide, lipless mouth. Nothing happened.

"What's the matter here?" I asked Gout. "Why isn't this working? Is it because he's a toad instead of a frog?"

"It should work the same whether the victim is a frog, a toad, a salamander, or even a newt," she replied. "The spell and the cure cover all amphibians and some of the lower reptiles, including tax collectors."

"Well, then, could it be it's not working because the spell was cast with Magique instead of Majyk?"

"I didn't use Majyk to transform your brother, remember?" Gout said. She took Prince Boffin from my hands and patted him tenderly. "No matter what means you use to turn a person into a creature like this, the spell can always be broken by the proper kiss."

The proper kiss. The kiss that would cure Prince Boffin of warts and more had to come from his one true love. If Mysti's kiss left him just as toady as ever, that could only mean one thing.

"Oh dear, you poor boy." Aunt Carageena gave Mysti a motherly hug.

"There, there, it happens to everyone." Aunt Glucosia hugged her from the other side. "To love is to learn."

"You're young yet," Aunt Carageena added. "It is better to have loved and lost than to be told you're ugly and your mother dresses you funny."

"There are plenty of other fish in the sea," Aunt Glucosia said. "Or toads in the garden."

"Will you two please *stop it*?" Mysti threw off their arms impatiently. "I know I'm not Prince Boffin's true love. Why should I be? He's not mine. He saved my life once, that's all, and I've traveled with him ever since to try to repay him for it."

"Oh dear, but we thought—" Aunt Glucosia began.

"We just assumed—" Aunt Carageena said.

"*Everyone* assumed—"

"Well, you know how people will talk—"

"Two handsome young men—"

"The times being what they are—"

"Not that there's anything wrong with it—"

"Certainly not as far as *we're* concerned—"

"But some people—"

"Oh yes, some people—"

"It makes for gossip—"

"Rumors—"

"Talk—"

"But since you and he never—"

"Who says we never?" Mysti inquired curtly.

My aunts were dumbstruck. Not that it could last.

"Is that so," said Aunt Glucosia.

"Really," said Aunt Carageena.

"It was Wenchpinch Eve in Grashgoboum," Mysti supplied. "The city inns get pretty crowded. We had to share a bed and they ran out of blankets."

"Oh well, that explains it." Aunt Glucosia nodded violently. "Terribly cold in Grashgoboum around Wenchpinch Eve, it is."

"And people drink more than is good for them." Aunt Carageena's head bobbed just as energetically. "You can't tell what you're doing when you drink."

"How true," Mysti agreed. "So we did it a few more times after we sobered up, just to make sure. But it wasn't like we were in love or anything."

This time my aunts stayed silent.

"This tells me more than I ever wanted to know about your life story, sir," Gout told Mysti. "But it doesn't do a thing to help this poor man regain his original shape. Since he can't be cured by a kiss from his true love, we'll have to restore him with a kiss from the one who cast the spell in the first place."

Shortly after, while Gout was trying to force Curio to climb down off Mother Toadbreath's roof and face up to his obligations, I tapped Mysti on the shoulder and whispered, "Why did you have to go and upset my aunts like that?"

"Because I felt like it," she whispered back. "They were pretending to be *so* open-minded about Boffin and me. I couldn't resist seeing how far their minds would open before they slammed shut just as tight everyone else's."

My aunts, open minds or shut, were at the moment around the back of the cottage with Mistress Gout, looking for a ladder. Basehart and Dulcetta had gone inside to see if there was an attic trapdoor that led to the roof. Even Prince Boffin was gone; Gout had tucked him into her belt pouch for safekeeping. Mysti and I were alone on the bench.

"Was what you said about you and Prince Boffin true?" I asked her.

"How much does it matter?"

"Did you ever love him?"

"Do you care?"

"Why do you always answer every question with another question?"

"Why not?" Her eyes twinkled impishly behind the slits in her mask.

"I just want to know if you and Boffin—uh—er—um—you know."

"And I just want to know why that's so important to you. When we were married, you didn't seem to care if I uh—er—um'ed with anyone; certainly not with *you*."

I lowered my eyes. "I know. I made a lot of other mistakes back then too."

"Mistakes?" She sounded surprised and—Was that hope I

heard in her voice? A leather-gloved hand covered my own. "Kendar, do you mean that? About . . . mistakes?"

I nodded. "It was a mistake to treat you the way I did: ignoring you, staying away from you when I really wanted to be with you, pretending you weren't there when I couldn't forget you were."

"Then why—*why* did you do it?"

"Do you like being forced to do things?" I asked her. "Even things you might *like* if no one forces you to do them?"

"Now who's answering a question with another question?"

"All right, I'll give you a straight answer to the very next question you ask me," I promised.

"Fair enough." She took a deep breath and the words poured off her tongue: "Kendardoyouloveme?"

"Do I wha—? I mean, uh, I—I—" I knew what I wanted to say, but the thought of actually saying it out loud scared me silly. No wizard utters Words of Power lightly, and these were the biggest Words of Power of all. I reached inside for my Majyk, but it slipped away. For this one, I was on my own.

"Yes," I rasped. And a little louder, a little clearer: "Yes, I do."

And then it was all suddenly easier. I heard myself telling Mysti how much I'd missed her since she ran off with Prince Boffin. I told her how much she meant to me from the time we shared our first adventures until now. I told her how lonesome the palace was without her, even though it was filled to the gills with Master Thengor's family. And to be honest, I told her how much I resented the way she'd forced me to marry her, just so she could escape the flowers-and-fa-la-la life of a Welfie in the jolly greenwood, ho.

"You were so beautiful," I said, remembering my first sight of her. "You were the most wonderful creature I'd ever seen. Just looking at you made me feel—" I blushed and left the rest unsaid. "But then you had to go and spoil it all by using me."

Mysti turned her head away. "You're right," she said. "Sort of."

"'Sort of'?"

"You weren't the only mortal who entered the Fearsome Forest of Euw that day," she said.

"You mean Grym?" I asked, recalling my barbarian friend. He had gone on to a successful career in law. (It paid better than freelance pillaging and was less wear-and-tear on his sword because the victims couldn't fight back.)

"I certainly don't mean Scandal." She smiled. "I could have used any old mortal male as my way out. I could have chosen him as easily as you. I didn't."

"Do you mean—?"

"Turn yourself into a frog, Kendar."

"Huh?"

"I said shut up and turn yourself into a frog," Mysti commanded. "You can do that, can't you? Gout said it was an easy spell."

"Look, Mysti—"

"Do it. Now."

So I did. It was such an easy spell to work that I was shocked by how quickly the world got big around me. But I was even more shocked by how quickly Mysti scooped me up in her hands and kissed me.

"Wow!" I gasped, human again. "That was—that was—"

"Yes?"

"That was better than a Raptura Eglantine book!" I threw my arms around her and together we set out to write Chapter Two.

"*Ahem.*" The sound of two auntish throats being cleared at once made both of us stiffen where we sat.

"We finally got Curio down off the roof," Aunt Carageena said.

"Mistress Gout is now attempting to make him see that there is nothing shameful about one man kissing another, if it's for a good cause," Aunt Glucosia said. "Perhaps you could help her out there. The voice of experience, as it were."

"But Aunt Carageena, Aunt Glucosia, I—I—" I started to say. Then the same nixie spirit that had bitten Mysti took a chunk out of me. "I'll be *glad* to," I said, slinging one arm around Mysti's waist. "Coming, Bladesie?"

"For you, to the edge of Orbix and over, Kendar my love," Mysti replied, draping her arm around my neck.

As we rounded the corner of the house I heard Aunt Carageena remark to her sister, "I think he gets that from the Guzzle side of the family." Aunt Glucosia agreed.

We found Curio sitting on a pile of firewood stacked against the back of the cottage. Basehart stood beside him, Dulcetta in his shadow. My brother had a stout log in his hands, ready to cut short any new escape attempts. Curio had his legs crossed, his arms folded, and his lips clamped together so tightly that they had vanished from sight. He looked more like a toad than Boffin.

Mistress Gout had the enchanted prince in her hand and was doing her best to convince Curio that it wouldn't be so bad. Her efforts were ruined by my brother, who kept snickering about the whole thing. Then Aunt Glucosia and Aunt Carageena took him aside and whispered something in his ears. He turned pale, stared at Mysti and me in horror, and didn't utter another sound.

Basehart's silence was little help to the witch. Curio remained stubborn. She coaxed, she pleaded, she threatened to turn him into a toad himself if he refused to cooperate; nothing moved him.

"If word gets out, people will talk," he said.

"No one will talk! I'll lay a curse on anyone who speaks about this. I do wonderful things with curses. It's a gift." Gout held out the toad hopefully. Curio gave them both the cold shoulder.

"May I?" I took the witch by the elbow and escorted her to one side. "Curio, you have to kiss the prince," I said patiently.

"I do not!" he maintained. "Let his true love do it."

"It didn't work."

"That was because Blade is not his true love," Curio argued. "But how hard could it be to find the chosen one? He is a prince? His parents could organize some sort of contest. All the maidens in the kingdom could line up and take turns kissing him. Whoever turns him back into a man can marry him and live happily ever after."

"Oh, how romantic!" Dulcetta squealed, clapping her hands.

"Curio, a toad is not the same thing as a glass slipper," I said. "You can't have every eligible female in the kingdom try him on for size. He could get sick. Wedwel knows where some of them have been. Besides, you'll wear out his lips before half the maidens have had a turn if we do it your way."

"He ain't *got* any lips," Basehart observed.

"See?" I concluded. "That proves you've got to kiss him."

Curio drew his crossed arms even closer to his body. "And if I refuse?"

"Then I'm going to turn you into a toad and hold you still until Prince Boffin can kiss *you*. You wouldn't mind that, would you, Your Highness?" I asked the blond amphibian. Boffin croaked eagerly. He sounded more than willing.

Curio sucked air through his teeth. "You would not dare!"

"And just think—" I went on as if I hadn't heard him. "Maybe when Prince Boffin kisses Curio, they'll *both* turn back into human form. You know what *that* will mean."

Mysti sniffled and wiped her eyes. "I always cry at weddings."

With a loud and colorful Alfrescan curse, Curio grabbed Prince Boffin from Gout's hands and gave him a resounding kiss. The restored prince gaped at his old, familiar body, then looked at Curio, made a disgusted face, spat several times and rubbed his lips furiously with the back of his hand.

"You're welcome," Curio grumbled, and stomped back into the cottage to finish preparing the stew.

"Is it windier or is it just me?" I asked Mysti as we walked back to Cheeseburgh.

"It's you," she said.

"I told him to put on a sweater," said Aunt Glucosia.

I tucked my hands under my arms and shivered. "I wonder why I feel so cold all of a sudden?"

"Because you didn't listen to your Aunt Glucosia," Aunt Carageena said stiffly.

"Oh, rat-tails, that's not the reason," Mysti said. She gestured. "Look around; he's out in the open, for once. He's used to walking in the middle of a crowd, and that's bound to keep the wind off."

I looked around and realized that for the first time in a long while I had an unblocked view of the roadside. Everyone else was still back at Mother Toadbreath's cottage. Dulcetta stayed behind to finish writing her novel, Curio stayed to cook and make suggestions, Basehart stayed to make sure that Curio's suggestions were only about the novel, Boffin stayed because he doesn't feel like facing a fresh set of Magique-laden sorcerers after what he'd been through, and Gout stayed to make sure Boffin wrote a nice, long letter home, telling his mom and dad that he was all right and to call off the war against the Topside.

"I still say he ought to put on a sweater," Aunt Glucosia insisted.

"I'll put on *seven* sweaters after we get things settled in Cheeseburgh," I promised her. "Now are you happy?"

"Happy?" She snorted. "When I've got to knit you *seven* sweaters, you greedy child? That will leave me scarcely any time to practice my swordsmanship. If I'm hired to fight the hordes of Uk-Uk the Unspeakable and I fall in battle with a scimitar clean through my vitals because I was too busy knitting *you* sweaters to keep my self-defense skills up to the mark, *then* you'll be sorry."

I covered my eyes with my hand and shook my head.

Then I heard Mysti cry, "Kendar, look!"

I dropped my hand. Coming up the road from Cheeseburgh was a small, scraggly, slow-moving figure. It dragged itself along on four legs, head low, tail trailing in the dust. Even though it was a good spear-cast away, I recognized it at once.

"Scandal!" I cried, running to meet him. I fell to my knees on the road just as the cat toppled over onto his side.

His fur was rough and torn, half his whiskers broken, the pads of his paws red and sore-looking. Weakly he lifted his head, eyes half-shut and glazed, and said, "I'm ready for my close-up now, Mr. DeMille," before collapsing into unconsciousness.

CHAPTER ———————— 19

"ANY CHANGE?" MYSTI ASKED LEANING OVER MY shoulder to gaze at Scandal. We squatted in the bushes beside the Cheeseburgh road, Aunt Carageena keeping watch, Aunt Glucosia off on a short trek to fetch some water from nearby Golligosh Pond. I had the cat encased in a glowing shell of Majyk while I did my best to bring him back to his old self.

"His fur looks smoother," I said. I didn't know what else to tell her.

Healing is one of the most complicated things a wizard can do with his Majyk—I remembered that much from Master Thengor's lectures even if I never got far enough at the Academy to take any of the courses on Applied and Practical Healing. I found that out for myself when I tried to fix up Scandal all at once.

Heal him, I told my Majyk silently. I expected something like a big puff of smoke from which Scandal would emerge, alive and healthy.

Instead I heard the answer ringing in my head: *Heal him of what? And how? And where do I start?*

Don't you know? I asked. *Can't you tell?*

When you build a house, does the hammer know where the nail's supposed to go? Does the saw know where you want it to cut the wood? That's why we've got carpenters.

The Majyk was right. There was a reason wizards had to learn their craft. It was more than just finding out how to capture and keep wild Majyk; you also had to discover the right way to use it if you were ever going to get what you wanted from it. For simple spells it was enough to set the Majyk loose and let it take care of things for you, but more complicated problems required several different spells, used in proper order, to solve everything.

So for healing Scandal, I'd fallen back on a Majyk-using lesson I'd picked up (literally) from the evil fairy Acerbia: One spell at a time. While Scandal lay safe inside his Majyk shell, I set about fixing all the things that were wrong with him, one by one.

"This is going too slowly," Mysti complained.

"Too slow for what?" I countered, straightening Scandal's whiskers and restoring their old, rakish angle. "We don't have any appointment waiting for us back in Cheeseburgh. I'm going to heal Scandal and I'm going to do it right. After that we'll go back to Zoltan's house, join our powers, and take care of Bibok and Calosta."

"Do you think they might have done this to the poor beastie, Kendar dear?" Aunt Carageena asked.

"I don't know," I admitted. "Why would they? They seemed so eager to keep him." *And he seemed so eager to stay with them*, I added to myself.

"Maybe something's happened to them, too," Mysti said.

"Like what?"

"Like Zoltan."

I was going to tell her that she was out of her mind, but I didn't. Something pretty disastrous had happened to Scandal— the evidence was right in front of me—and the last place I'd seen Scandal was curled around Calosta's neck. While we'd been chasing visions, Zoltan had had plenty of free time on his hands back in Cheeseburgh, and a pinch of real Majyk to get started with. *Majyk attracts Majyk.* Zoltan didn't need me to remind him of that lesson. Who could say for sure what he'd been doing while we were gone?

"He's looking much better," Aunt Glucosia said, coming back with a gourd full of water. She peered into Scandal's shining capsule. "When do you think he'll wake up?"

All I could say again was, "I don't know." Majyk was making the sores on Scandal's paw pads fade away gradually. Soon he looked just like his old self, but he didn't move and his eyes stayed shut.

Aunt Glucosia squinted and leaned nearer. "Oh dear," she sighed. "I'm afraid I'm going to have to start looking for that little retirement cottage we talked about, Gee'. It's time for me to hang up my sword and start baking cookies."

"Don't be hasty, Glucosia; I've tasted your cookies," her sister replied. "Why are you so set on retiring all of a sudden?"

"It's my eyes. A swordswoman's not much use if she can't see what she's slaughtering, is she? Not unless your employer has a very good sense of humor. I'm having the most atrocious time seeing that cat. It's almost as if he was *faded*."

"Cats do not fade," Aunt Carageena corrected her. "At least none of the legends say they do. You're confusing cats with cushions, which is an honest mistake. Besides, it's only the navy blue or dark green or burgundy-colored ones that fade if you leave them out in direct sunlight. Cushions, I mean."

Her words only partly reached me. Up to now, I'd been too concerned with finding and curing each one of Scandal's hurts to look at the whole cat. I sat back on my heels and cast an eye over him.

"Your eyes are fine, Aunt Glucosia," I said in a hollow voice. "You're right. He *is* faded."

"Or bleached," Aunt Carageena was nattering on. "Anything fades if you bleach it, including cats, I shouldn't be at all surprised."

"Shush, Gee'." Aunt Glucosia shaded her eyes. "Mercy, it *is* true. The poor thing looks like a ghost."

Scandal opened his eyes, lifted his head, looked right at her, and said, "Boo!"

"Scandal, you're all right!" I cried. My hands broke through the golden shell. I picked up the cat and hugged him. He felt solid enough, even if he looked as if he was made out of mist and shadows.

"The hell I am!" he snapped. "You call *this* all right?" He tossed his head to indicate his semitransparent body. "Pardon me, Mr. Carroll, but my mama didn't raise no Cheshire kittens."

"How did it happen?" I asked. "Why did you leave Calosta and Bibok? How did you know where to find me? Where are — ?"

"I'll take Stupid Questions for two hundred dollars, Alex," the cat said. He tapped my face gently with a paw. "It's good to see you again, Bwana. You haven't changed a bit. Or showered. Orbix is a cool place to visit, but I wouldn't wanna inhale here."

"I see you haven't changed a bit either," Mysti said, scratching him behind the ears. "You'll be pleased to know we found Prince Boffin and he's his old self again."

"I will?" Scandal's brow-whiskers twitched. "So if he's back to normal, where is he?" We told him. We also told him about Dulcetta and Curio. The cat nearly fell out of my arms laughing.

Abruptly he sobered. "It's a good thing you ditched them, boss," he told me. "You don't need a bunch of expendable extras tripping you up when you face what's waiting for you back in Cheeseburgh."

"What is it?"

"Save your breath; you'll need it." He slipped out of my arms and trotted down the road so fast we had to jog to catch up with him.

"Scandal, what is it?" I insisted as I pulled up alongside him. "What's happened? Is it Bibok and Calosta?"

"Don't talk to me about those two yuppie wannabes, okay?" the cat snarled. "Gimme, gimme, gimme, more, more, more, mine, mine, mine—*phaugh*! You'd think they were cats or something. Quality be damned when it's quantity that counts with them. And that's why they're always gonna be wannabes. *I'd* like to give them quantity!"

"Scandal, I don't understand."

"Understanding's not in your job description. Keep moving."

He sped up the pace, but he wasn't fast enough. A gloved hand descended on the scruff of his neck and hoisted him high. My aunts and I pulled over to the side of the road, breathing hard, while Mysti questioned the cat.

"Would you like to hear *my* job description, cat?" she said. "It includes paddling the furry bottoms of sharp-tongued beasts."

"Ooooooh, I'm shaking," Scandal sneered.

"You will be."

"Mysti, don't!" I cried.

"*Mysti*?" my aunts inquired in chorus.

"We pause now for a message from our sponsor, Foot-in-Mouth Productions." Scandal chortled. (I've discovered that cats chortle better than people. Most people wouldn't know how to chortle if you paid them; they just snort, snicker, and guffaw. But cats chortle. I think the sound comes from the same spare part they use for all that purring.)

"Urrrrrh . . ." I said, off to a convincing start. "Well, you see, Blade's eyes are this lovely misty shade of blue and—"

Aunt Glucosia shook her head. "Try again, Kendar dear."

"Um, because Blade's a Welfie, he has a secret Welfin name of power that he only tells to his true love and—"

"Welfies don't have secret names of power," Aunt Carageena informed me. "When I was a mere swordslass in training, I spent some time among the Welfies. It was a test of courage, to see if I had a strong stomach. If I could stand all that incessant frolicking and warbling and nectar-swilling without throwing up, I was ready for all the horrors of battle. The Welfies used to have secret names of power, but they kept forgetting them, so they carved them on trees with their penknives. This rather defeated the whole *secret*-name-of-power business, so they decided to have secret penknives of power instead."

"She is right," Mysti admitted. She pulled a small but complex-looking object from her belt pouch. "We still have secret names, but they're not as powerful as they used to be."

"Powerful enough to force this poor geek to marry you when you 'accidentally' told him what yours was," Scandal said, dangling.

"You know, I could *show* everyone this knife, or I could *demonstrate* it," Mysti told him meaningly. Scandal shut up. "This is mine," she said, giving us all a clear view. "It is a blade of great enchantment, called in the tongue of my fathers Testosterel, and in Lingween, the common tongue, called Teaser. It's got a corkscrew and an illuminum torch attachment and everything."

"That's nice, Blade dear," Aunt Carageena said. "I'm sure you can use it. Of course it's not so secret anymore, now is it?"

"Well, never you mind," said Aunt Glucosia. "Now what about this 'Mysti' stuff?"

"Oh, voondrab droppings!" Mysti swore, and tore off her mask.

"Goodness," said Aunt Glucosia.

"My," said Aunt Carageena.

"She's got that twinkly purple stuff on her eyelids," said

Scandal. "Wears a mask all day long and she still puts on eye makeup underneath it. Yes, she's that *Cosmopolitan Welfie.*"

"Feeling better about that time you caught Kendar kissing me?" Mysti asked, with a healthy dose of acid in her voice.

"*Kissing* her?" Still hanging in midair, Scandal's legs shot out stiffly in shock. "Aw, gee whiz, big guy, you're actually back with this pointy-eared hobgoblin? No offense," he added, tilting his head at Mysti.

"That's what you think," Mysti replied, but she put him down.

"What's it to you if Mysti and I *are* together again?" I shot at him. I slipped my arm around her waist. "At least *she's* loyal."

"Except for when I ran off with Prince Boffin," Mysti reminded me. "But I was fed up."

"Loyal and honest," I corrected myself.

"And I love him," she added.

"Right! Loyal, honest, and she loves me."

"Nobody expects the Spanish Inquisition," Scandal muttered. "Plus she's got a set of pontoons on her that could float a bulldozer."

"*Plus* I can understand everything she says!" I concluded. "Not like some cats I could mention."

"I can tell there is something on your mind," Scandal said calmly. "It may be dying of loneliness, but it's in there somewhere. Spill your guts to dear old Uncle Sigmund like a good little wizard. Are you—dare I think it—*angry* with me?"

"I'm sure it's none of my business," Aunt Glucosia said, "but you *did* desert poor Kendar. And for what? Luxury, creature comforts, riches, pampering—"

"Espionage," Scandal finished for her.

"Gracious!" Aunt Glucosia laid a hand to her mail-covered bosom. "You mean you left Kendar so you could spy on Bibok and Calosta?"

Scandal gave her an arch look. "The name is Bond. *James* Bond. Catnip martini, *s'il vous plait*. Shaken, not stirred."

I couldn't help sounding a little suspicious when I asked, "And did you learn anything?"

"Never to turn my back on the female of any species." He held up one paw. I could see trees through it. "Bibok was a pushover. A couple of purrs, a little rubbing my head against his hand, and he was putty in my paws. So was Calosta, I thought. Brother, did I crack open the wrong fortune cookie on that doll."

"What happened?"

"What happened was that I was almost dead back there. Sheer luck, Holmes, that you found me. I wasn't looking for you. I wasn't looking for anything except a way to get as far from that slinky Circe as possible before she helped herself to"—he put on a high, sticky-sweet, wheedling voice—"'just one eensy-beensy little dab of Majyk, who's a sweet old pussycat, hmmmmm?'"

"She took your Majyk?" I hugged myself instead of Mysti. Was this what would have happened to me if Zoltan had managed to take back Master Thengor's unwitting gift? Would I be transparent, or would I have vanished altogether?

"She *tried*. I wouldn't let her. I've got just enough to protect myself from an unfriendly takeover like she had in mind."

"Dear, if you could protect yourself, why didn't you do a better job of it?" Aunt Glucosia asked.

"It wasn't my Majyk she took," the cat replied. "Look, I don't have time to stand here flapping my lips, mostly 'cause cats don't have lips. There's nasty stuff going down in Cheeseburgh. Remember the big wizards' war that turned this bonzo ball of mud into the Incredible Shape-Shifting Planet? Well, what's brewing in Cheeseburgh is gonna make that look like two kids having a pillow fight."

My stomach sank. What wizard didn't remember? The aftermath had left Orbix liable to switch shapes—from flat to lumpy to anything at all, even *round*—without warning. It was a two-man war with no winners, although the last words of the wizard who managed to live a moment longer than his enemy were: "Let that be a lesson to you." Ever after, that motto was carved above the hearth of every wizard on Orbix as a grim reminder of the dark fate that awaits the power-mad, the greedy, and the smartypants. (In time, other householders on Orbix adopted the wizardly custom. They had little or no idea of the reason behind the custom, but they did it, anyway. Scandal said it was a lot like wearing neckties, whatever they are.)

"Are Bibok and Calosta fighting each other?" Mysti asked.

"Ha! No way. They're just as lovey-dovey, ooky-wooky as ever. If they ever did split up, their Majyk's so tightly entwined it would give 'em both a mystic hernia when it tore loose."

"Then who—?"

"I'll give you one guess, Bright Eyes," Scandal told her. "Sesame Street has been brought to you by the name Zoltan and the title Fiendlord."

"No!" I protested. "It's not possible."

"Nice kid, Kendar," Scandal remarked to Mysti and my aunts. "A little short on gray matter, but nice." To me he said—or hollered—"What *is* it with you? You get bitten by a rabid Pollyanna when you were a kid or what? This is Zoltan we're talking here. The guy who tried to remove your Majyk any which way he could, all of them fatal. Why do you find it so danged hard to believe that he's up to his old tricks?"

"I don't find it hard to believe." I bowed my head. "I just don't want to believe it."

Mysti embraced me. "Listen, everyone makes mistakes," she said. "You've made plenty; you said so."

I shrugged her off. "Maybe I'm tired of that. I wanted to believe Zoltan when he said he'd changed. My dad always told us every chance he got when Basehart and Lucy and I were growing up how life wasn't fair, things were tough, never trust anybody except your family and keep a good eye on them, too, just to make sure."

"That's good advice, Kendar dear," Aunt Carageena said. "It's saved our lives countless time in battle." Aunt Glucosia readily agreed with her.

"But why does life have to *be* one long battle with everyone your enemy?" I pleaded. "What's wrong with trust? If someone's done something wrong, can't they change?"

"Yes, they can try stabbing you with the dagger in their left hand instead of their right," Aunt Glucosia said.

I shook my head. "Calosta did something to you, Scandal. Not Zoltan, *Calosta*. Why are you blaming him?"

"Because if he hadn't started up with Bibok and Calosta, she never would've touched me," the cat answered. "He scared her bad enough so she wanted a little extra edge. She tried to get it off of me."

"I still can't believe—" I began.

"Seeing is believing," said the cat. "And if it's not, it's good enough for a jury trial."

The outlying streets of Cheeseburgh were deserted as we entered the town. What's more, I didn't recall passing anyone on the road to Cheeseburgh, coming or going. It gave me a creepy feeling.

"Where *is* everyone?" I whispered to Mysti.

"Shh," she hissed. Her mask was on again. A Blade for Justice was back in business.

"Yeah, do like she says, boss," Scandal purred in my ear. The cat was perched on my shoulder. "Just head for the center of town and you'll see what's happening."

"I hope we can find the center of town," I muttered.

"Eh, no big deal. If you can't find it, just ask directions."

"Who from?"

"Good point. Put me down and I'll lead you. I'll smell my way there."

The creepy feeling grew. Every house we passed seemed deserted. The windows either stared at us blindly or kept their secrets behind closed shutters. Somewhere a baby began to wail and was quickly hushed. Our footsteps sounded like thunder on the cobbles.

My footsteps did. My aunts had the stealthy pace of trained fighters with plenty of night patrols and ambushes under their belts. Mysti was a Welfie, and nothing on Orbix can move more quietly than a Welfie, unless it's a cat. I didn't think anything could move more quietly than a cat. Out of the five of us, the only feet making any noise were mine.

Scandal paused at the corner of one narrow street. "Yo, Bigfoot, you wanna try and keep it down to a dull roar?" he whispered. "We're getting close. The whole idea here is to sneak up, give you a good look at what your best buddy Zoltan is up to, fall back again, then take him by surpriiiiiiii—!"

"We don't like creatures who spy on Master Fiendlord," said the green, scaly, fanged, and taloned demon who had plucked Scandal up by the scruff.

So there *was* something on Orbix that could move more quietly than a cat. Live and learn.

CHAPTER ———— 20

"I DIDN'T THINK IT WAS GOING TO BOUNCE LIKE that," said Aunt Glucosia, plucking a handful of kiss-me-while-I'm-looking leaves from a nearby windowbox and wiping thick yellow blood from her sword.

"It's still rolling," said Mysti, peering around the corner. "Now it's stopped. It hit a horse trough. No one saw. The streets are clear."

"If not, the sight of a fiend's severed head would probably clear 'em out quicker'n prunes through a politician," Scandal said. "Jeez Looweez, lady, you've got one heck of a backhand."

Aunt Glucosia shook her head sadly. "I really do think it's time for the cottage and the cookies. In my younger days I had much better control. After all, one can't go around chopping off the heads of one's enemies if one can't predict where they're going to land. If the enemy is large enough, a misplaced head can do some real damage."

"To say nothing of falling fiend-bodies," Scandal added. He marched over the still-leaking corpse of Aunt Glucosia's latest conquest and said, "Want a hand with the levitation spell, boss?"

"No thanks." I gestured and the heavy corpse floated itself about a handspan off me; then I crawled out from under. "My legs hurt," I announced. I tried to stand and found my right leg refused to carry me. It folded up at hip, knee, and ankle, sending blazing pain shooting straight through the top of my skull. My breath escaped in a hiss. It hurt too much to scream.

"Kendar!" Mysti was there for me at once, holding me up under the armpits. "What's the matter?"

"It's my leg," I gasped. "I don't know if it's bruised or

sprained or flat-out broken." I tried to put some weight on it
and bit my tongue when the agony hit. "I don't think it matters
which."

"Do you want to sit down while you heal it?"

I managed to unclench my teeth long enough for one short,
bitter laugh. "I've got a riddle for you, Mysti: Why aren't
wizards warriors?"

"Because they're cowards?"

"Cowards who conjure up demons."

"Because they're lazy?"

"Lazy enough to spend years and years studying new ways
to catch and use Majyk."

"Because they can't stand the sight of blood?"

"Master Thengor loved the sight of blood, as long as it
wasn't his. He also had a whole crowd of healers clustered
around his deathbed. Why would he need them at all if he could
heal himself?"

"But I thought your Majyk—" Mysti hesitated. "It healed
Scandal."

"My Majyk healed him, yeah. But it can't heal me."

"Why not?" She was exasperated.

"Because it *is* me and it is *my* Majyk," I explained. I thought
it was a pretty good explanation, but apparently Mysti didn't.
She lost her patience and dropped me. While I was writhing on
the ground, saying things like "Oo-ah-ee-oh-ow-damdamdam!"
Scandal took over.

"Look, toots, what Kendar's been trying to say is it's
Catch-22."

"Catch twenty-two what?"

"Say good night, Gracie, then shut up and listen. You can do
lots of fancy tricks with Majyk, but you can't do *everything*.
You ever hear of a wizard raising the dead?"

"Not even the powers of my people may accomplish that,"
Mysti said solemnly.

"Sure they can't. I mean, you've gotta draw the line
somewhere, right? So if there are some things Majyk can't do,
it's gotta stand to reason that there are some things Majyk-*users*
can't do, and one of those things is using their own Majyk to
heal themselves. Majyk is not all-powerful."

"I should say not," Aunt Carageena chimed in. "There is
only one all-powerful force in the universe, and that is Wedwel,
the All-Compassionate Destroyer."

"I've always had one question about your god Wedwel," Mysti said.

"Yes, dear?"

"If Wedwel can do anything, can he create a rock so heavy he can't lift it?"

"Yes, and as soon as he does, the prophecies say that he's going to drop that rock right smack on top of Welfies who think they're ever so clever for coming up with *that* old chestnut."

"Could we please forget about religion and take care of my leg?" I moaned.

My aunts were on me in a breath, examining my injured leg with hands made wise by many years experience mopping up the aftermath of battle. Their probing fingers almost made me lose consciousness from pain, but the ordeal was soon over and the verdict in.

"Nothing broken, praise Wedwel," Aunt Glucosia announced. "But your knee's been wrenched badly and so has your ankle. I blame myself. I was concentrating on chopping off the fiend's head without killing the cat."

"And don't think I'm not grateful," Scandal told her.

"You've got some serious bruises as well, Kendar dear," Aunt Carageena said. "The best we can do is bind up the leg and get you something to lean on. Just a moment."

While Aunt Glucosia bandaged my leg with heavy strips of cloth torn at dagger's edge from her cape, Aunt Carageena advanced on the demon's corpse, sword drawn. There was a lot of slashing and hacking and chopping. Big chunks of fiend flesh flew, splatting against the walls of houses. One dripping lump sailed through an open window. We heard a shriek before it came sailing back out again.

At last Aunt Carageena stood over me, holding out a long, straight, yellowish-white object. "It's the best I could do, given what I've got to work with," she said.

"What *is* that?" I wrinkled my nose.

"One of the creature's thigh bones. See where it's flat? I whittled that end down for you so it can rest steadily on the ground. If you lean on it you'll take the weight off your bad leg."

"I'm not touching that thing. Aw, look, it's still got shreds of—of—of *meat* stuck to it!"

"Abstemia always did say he was a fussy child," Aunt

Carageena remarked to her sister with a sigh. She used her dagger to scrape the last scraps of demon flesh off the bone. I gasped in horror when she ate them raw off the blade.

"Aunt Carageena!" I squealed.

"Now what's the ruckus? You're the one who said it was meat. It's been some time since we've eaten."

I held my stomach, my eyes watering. "I'm not hungry, believe me."

"Kendar, really. Demon flesh isn't very nutritious, but it *is* filling and it doesn't make you gain weight, because it comes from another plane of existence altogether."

"Gimme," Scandal said, pawing her ankle. My aunt obliged, feeding the cat a strand of the hideous stuff. Scandal chewed, swallowed, and licked his chops. "Mmmmm, tastes just like chicken." I could see the demon meat glowing in his stomach. "Hey, don't tell Bibok and Calosta that stuff doesn't have any calories or they'll try sticking it between two layers of lasagna noodles and selling it as the ultimate diet food. And I know people in L.A. who'd eat it with or without the lasagna."

With my leg bandaged, I reluctantly allowed my aunts to help me get ahold of the demon-bone crutch. I took a few hobbling steps forward. I was making more noise over the cobblestones than ever.

"We're never going to sneak up on Zoltan like this," I said.

"My turn," Mysti said. She took off her cape and spread it on the ground in front of me. "Hop on." I was puzzled, but I did as she asked. "Good. Now, remember the time you used your Majyk to make a flying carpet?"

"Uh-huh."

"It works on capes, too."

Shortly after, I was skimming silently down the streets of Cheeseburgh on Mysti's cape. There was only room for me aboard, but that was all right; the others could still move as stealthily as before. I leaned heavily on the demon-bone crutch tucked under my right arm. My leg hurt like several of Wedwel's fancier Hells. Scandal moved briskly ahead of me, no more visible than a stray wisp of smoke. The cat was using his amazing nose for two purposes: to find our way to Zoltan and to sniff out any other guard-demons my former schoolmate might have set out on patrol.

We had gone a few streets further when Scandal stopped in

his tracks. "He's there," he said. "Sharp left, straight on 'til morning, and you'll be within spitting distance, if that's what floats your boat."

"Will he be able to see us?" I asked.

"Make us invisible and he won't," Mysti said. She was mighty practical, for a Welfie.

"How about his pet fiends, though?" Scandal asked.

"The beast has a point," said Aunt Carageena, backing up Scandal. "I've fought a demon or two in my day, and their senses work differently than ours. All that living on another plane of existence, I expect. Call it what you will, it makes them horridly undependable. Why, the sensitivity and strength of their senses even varies from demon to demon. The spell of invisibility that fools one fiend doesn't work worth a hang on his brother."

Mysti clucked her tongue. "That's not very sporting of them."

"Demons don't care bang-all about being sporting," my aunt informed her. "There was a fellow in the last campaign I was on who bought a Helm of Guaranteed Impenetrable Invisibility from an old gypsy woman. Our enemies had fiends fighting on their side, you see, and he thought he'd get in good with our captain if he could creep up on the monsters unseen. He tried it out on a few of the local tavernkeepers first and it worked like a charm."

"It *was* a charm, Gee," Aunt Glucosia reminded her.

"So it was. At any rate, the silly nitwit thought that this was proof he'd made a sharp bargain and he was ready to go up against the demons. His last words to me as he strolled towards their front lines were, 'This is great, Gee', the stupid slob can't even seeeeeeEEEEEEEEE—!'" She sighed. "The fiend who ate him spat out the Helm of Guaranteed Impenetrable Invisibility and I took it back to the old gypsy hag for a refund. She refused, saying it was not advertised as a Helm of *Absolutely* Guaranteed Impenetrable Invisibility."

"Also, invisibility's not much use if you're going to keep on *talking*," Aunt Glucosia said.

"Yes, there is that."

"What you're saying is we should rely on ourselves, not my Majyk," I said.

"Ourselves *and* your Majyk *and* our swords, Kendar dear,"

Aunt Glucosia amended. "We warrior swordswomen are philosophical, but we're nobody's fools."

I glanced down the street. "If Zoltan is near and we can't just rely on any Majyk tricks for sneaking up and seeing what he's up to, what should we do?"

"Smart question," Scandal said. "Up in the air, Junior Birdmen."

"What?"

"Well, you don't want to go back, you don't have much cover if you go forward, and what's the use of going left or right?" He nodded at the houses flanking us.

"What about down?" Aunt Glucosia asked.

"That's where we'll all wind up if we lose this little round of Bowling for Demons; six feet down and out. But if we get into one of these houses and go up to the roof, I bet we'd get a clear view of Zoltan and any assorted fiends he's got hanging around."

"Great idea, Scandal." I hobbled over to the nearest door and rapped at it with my crutch. No one answered, though I could have sworn I heard voices inside.

"Tell them we come in peace," Aunt Carageena suggested.

"Say that we're here to help them," Aunt Glucosia prompted me.

"Let 'em know that we're all out of encyclopedias and we're not giving out copies of *The Watchtower*," Scandal put in.

"Let me," said Mysti. She nudged me gently aside, knocked on the door, and said, "Hello, the house. I'm a Welfie and if you don't open this door up right now I'm going to sing."

Within instants we found ourselves in the attic storeroom of the house. The owner pointed us at the window with the best view (the *only* window, to be frank), then scuttled away, slamming and bolting the door between him and us.

Mysti wiped dust from the pane. "I think I can see something," she said.

"My turn," Scandal said, jumping onto the sill. He pushed at the window. "How does this open?"

"I don't think it does, dear," Aunt Glucosia said. "It's only a framed square of glass to let in light, not air."

"Don't be silly, Glucosia," Aunt Carageena chided. "What good's a window that doesn't open?" She drew her dagger and tapped the hilt smartly against the pane. The glass shattered in a tinkling shower. "There," she said. "Now it's open."

Scandal slipped through the broken window cautiously. I heard him give a cry of satisfaction. "Yeah, this is perfect," he said, coming back into the room. "You can see the square from up here, no problem. Come on, stick your head out, Kendar, and then you tell me who was right about Zoltan."

I used the knobby end of my crutch to break out the few jagged shards of glass still attached to the window frame, and leaned out as far as I could. If I held onto the frame and twisted my body all the way to the left, I could see the main square of Cheeseburgh, the fanciest of the public fountains, and the glittering throne of Zoltan Fiendlord.

He sat on the mayor's chair, but he'd made plenty of improvements on it and on himself. The chair stood with its back against the fountain, on a raised platform that lifted it higher than the jets of water spouting into the air behind it. There was no sign that the seat of office had ever been the helpless prey of Dibi and Dobi. All of its gilding was restored and more. It was twice as big as I remembered it, with fancier carvings and a pair of giant jewel-encrusted eagle's wings fanning out from the back. Maybe it was my imagination, but it looked like the wings were moving.

And on that splendid throne sat Zoltan, looking pretty splendid himself. He wore the full regalia of a Council-approved wizard, from pointy hat to flowing robes to sparkling wand. A dozen fiends stood in attendance. Some lounged against the basin of the fountain, others sprawled on the carpeted steps to Zoltan's throne, and a pair of very dutiful demons stood to either side of their master, holding tall, wicked-looking spears.

As I watched, I saw another fiend enter the square. He was about the size of the monster my aunt had slain, and in his claws he held a struggling, screaming woman. My Majyk crackled and sparked as I got ready to rescue the fiend's victim, until I saw him put her down, unharmed, before Zoltan's throne.

Zoltan grinned and rubbed his hands together gleefully when he saw the gift his pet fiend had brought him. "Ah, Mistress Loosestrife, *there* you are," he said, as if they'd just happened to bump into one another in the marketplace. "Just the woman I was hoping to see."

"Aye?" the woman said, the picture of sullen suspicion. "Whuffo?"

"I am so glad you asked! You see, dear lady, it has been brought to my attention that lately you've been using a certain amount of Magique in the making of your famous sausages."

"Don't," she said curtly, sticking out her lower lip and avoiding his cheery gaze.

"Oh, not always; I know that. Your original recipe hadn't a tittle of Magique in it."

One of the demons nudged his fellow and said, "What I heard, some o' the stuff she did put in them sossidges, Magique'd be a mercy."

"Yah?" the other said. "How'd you know?"

"Didn't used to be a demon 'til I et one's how."

Mistress Loosestrife was trying to brazen it out. "Could be as I did put a whisker o' Magique in my sossidges," she said. "What of that? Only to help 'em stay fresh longer, that's all. And since when's it been the business o' the mayor's office to go stickin' his great hairy nose into my sossidges? Or anything what's sold in the free marketplace o' Cheeseburgh, come to that?"

"Nose!" The first demon snapped his taloned fingers. "So *that* was what made it so chewy."

"My good woman, I agree with you entirely," Zoltan said, twiddling his wand between two fingers. "What you Cheeseburghers eat or sell as edible is no business of mine. Why should I care, as long as there are enough of you left alive to vote me back into office come Election Day? How does that quaint local saying go? 'You buys your sausage and you takes your chances.' Your sausages do not interest me in and of themselves."

"They don't?" She was still very much on her guard. "You don't want my sossidges?"

"Gods, *no*," Zoltan said a bit too vehemently. He hastened to add: "Not that they aren't everything people say they are. It's the Magique in them I want."

"Now, you see here, I paid for that Magique fair and square and—!"

"Magique—" Zoltan went on, ignoring her indignant outburst, "which is *not* edible, and therefore not actually a part of your sacred sausages. Magique which is in truth a *foreign substance*, and therefore something which I, as mayor of Cheeseburgh, am duty-bound to keep a very watchful eye on indeed. For the good of my people, of course."

"Oh." Mistress Loosestrife seemed mollified. "Didn't see it that way. Foreign substance, is it? I don't trust foreigners."

"How very wise you are."

"Well . . . what d'you want me to do, then?"

Zoltan's smile got bigger and brighter, or maybe he was just baring his teeth more. "I want you to give me your Magique. All of it. Right now."

He waved the wand, and a table appeared in front of Mistress Loosestrife. It was covered with a purple cloth and on that cloth there rested a strange apparatus. It looked like a huge beer barrel standing on end except that it was made all of glass. It was filled with a vivid blue liquid starred with tiny bubbles. Two flexible, transparent tubes snaked out of the top, each ending in a shiny metal funnel. There was a corked drain hole at the bottom of the barrel and something like a sundial face on the side. I shuddered, wondering what unnatural contraption Zoltan's ambition had created this time.

"It's very simple, Mistress Loosestrife," Zoltan said. "You pick up the funnel with the red band running around it and you dump all your Magique in *there*; then I pick up the funnel with the blue band and I absorb the Magique from *there*."

"*You* absorb it?" Shrewd tradeswoman that she was, Mistress Loosestrife knew a shady deal when she heard one.

"What better way to make certain that all of that nasty foreign substance is under control than if *I* control it personally?" Zoltan replied blandly.

"Yeh, but like I said already, Yer Honor, I paid good money for that Magique. It made my sossidge-makin' whole heapin's easier, besides keepin' the meat from goin' that funny color next day. If I give it up, I'll have to work hard again. What I want to know is what'm I goin' to get in trade for my troubles if I just up an' give it to you?"

"You can have anything you want," Zoltan said sincerely. On cue, four of his pet fiends encircled the sausage-maker. There was no mistaking the fact that when they showed their teeth, they weren't smiling. "Any *one* thing you want most, that is. Mustn't get greedy, ah-ha-ha-ha-ha!"

Three additional demons joined the four surrounding Mistress Loosestrife. All seven looked hungry. All seven also looked like the kind of fiend who plays with his food first. One of them licked his lips with a tongue that was a two-headed serpent. Mistress Loosestrife moaned and knotted her hands in her apron.

"Come, come, dear lady," Zoltan cajoled. "Can't you think of *one* thing you'd like?"

"I'd like—I'd like—" The poor woman's voice shook like a pudding. The fiends leaned in closer. *"I'd like to get home alive!"* she screamed, and threw her arms over her head, as if that would stop a hungry demon's jaws.

"And so you shall!" Zoltan grinned. "Just as soon as you've turned in your Magique."

Mistress Loosestrife yanked a fair-sized flask out of her apron pocket and upended it into the red-banded funnel. Murky golden liquid oozed down the tube into the glass barrel. The blue stuff in the barrel turned green, the tiny bubbles swelling and floating to the top. They simmered and popped and soon formed a seething froth that looked ready to burst the glass like just another bubble. From the wreck of so much foam, a thin, bright gold smoke filled the top third of the barrel. The arrow adorning the dial face on the side swung all the way to the left.

Zoltan's wand twitched. The tube leading to the blue-banded funnel rose up like a drowsy snake and floated towards him. He placed it over his nose and mouth and took a deep breath. The bright gold gas flew up the tube and disappeared. The arrow on the dial swung all the way to the right, then back to rest at the midpoint of its arc.

Zoltan dropped the funnel and gave a contented sigh. "Now *that's* the real thing. Let her go," he directed the fiends. The seven horrors all took one step away from Mistress Loosestrife. The sausage-maker glanced around like a startled rappid, then bolted down the nearest street. "How many does that leave us yet to round up, laddies?" Zoltan asked his hideous minions.

A fuzzy orange fiend did some quick figuring on his webbed paws before announcing, "Some."

"I could use a more accurate account than that," his master remarked, rubbing one bearded cheek with his wand.

The orange fiend shrugged. "More'n a few, less'n a lot. I thought you said we'd got most of 'em already. Won't that do?"

"Nothing will *do* until I have recovered and absorbed every single drop of Magique in Cheeseburgh," Zoltan said fiercely.

"*Them* two ain't gonna like it," the orange demon said. I didn't have to guess who *Them* two were.

"*Them* two have their hands more than full at present," Zoltan said, mocking the demon. "My first act as a restored wizard was to dispatch a cohort of your diabolical brethren to besiege them in their very lair. While the people of Cheeseburgh fled the demonic battle, seeking the safety of their own homes, I summoned the rest of you and commenced *this* modest operation." The wand swept towards the glass barrel on its stand.

"Oh, I ain't complainin', Master Fiendlord, sir," the orange demon said. "The work's been easy enough up to now. Very impressive it was, too, to see how the Cheeseburghers came flocking here to turn in their Magique when you sent out the call."

"They could do no less for their beloved mayor," Zoltan said, folding his hands and looking smug. "They know how much they owe me. Besides, I promised them that as soon as I had enough Magique under my control, I would be able to get rid of the demons for them."

The orange fiend scratched his horned head. "But you're the one what brought us here in the first place," he said, puzzled.

"Your point?"

"You're a slick 'un, Master Fiendlord."

"I couldn't be half so slick if the Cheeseburghers weren't half so thick. Still, you have to love them for it. It's made this entire project so much more pleasant. How fortunate for me that it doesn't take much Majyk to descend into your realm. All the best libraries are in the nether regions."

"Aye," the fiend agreed. "'Cept none o' the card catalogs ain't."

Zoltan brushed that aside. "I knew what I was looking for. It didn't take me long at all to find the book of demonlore that taught how to extract Majyk from Magique. I brought that knowledge back here with me. The rest was simple."

"Onliest hitch we had was when your wife and kids showed up." The orange demon shivered. "Masterful it was, how you talked the missus into going back home again, but the kids—! How much longer you think old Vanxandri's gonna last, keeping an eye on the little, uh . . ."

"I wouldn't call them monsters to my face, Burgolump."

Zoltan waggled a finger at the fiend. "They may be a bit high-spirited, but they are my children and I love them."

"That's to be expected, sir," Burgolump said, nodding his horned head. "There's always something unnatural about wizards with the power to be fiendlords."

"As for poor old Vanxandri, he'll be fine." A prolonged howl came from far away. It didn't sound human. "Just fine," Zoltan repeated. "And so will the rest of you, if you get back to work. Most of my loyal townsfolk turned in their Magique as soon as I asked for it, but there are more than a few who refused. I'd like you to hurry up and finish finding, fetching, and . . . *persuading* them."

"Any reason for the rush, Master Fiendlord?" Burgolump asked.

"It's a surprise," Zoltan replied. "Just a nice little surprise for a dear old friend of mine. He's out of town right now, but when he comes back . . ." Zoltan let the words drift away like a puff of stinking smoke.

"Heard enough, Kendar?" Mysti said at my back.

I pulled myself back inside. "Plenty." I shifted the crutch to a more comfortable position under my arm. "All right, there are thirteen demons down there with him and probably more roaming the streets—"

"Don't forget the ones he sent over to Bibok and Calosta's place," Scandal said. "It sure wasn't Avon calling. One look at Zoltan's legions and that's when she panicked and did *this* to me."

"I still don't know what she was trying to accomplish by turning you into a—" I didn't get to finish that sentence either.

"Gracious, this will be exhilarating!" Aunt Glucosia said briskly. "I haven't fought any demons in donkey's years. Come to think of it, the last demon I fought was shaped rather like a donkey." She began stripping away all parts of her garb that weren't meant to be worn in out-and-out battle.

Aunt Carageena was already busy doing the same thing. As she prepared for the fight, she sang a merry air:

> "D'ye ken a fiend with his fangs and claws?
> "D'ye ken a fiend with his drooling jaws?
> "D'ye ken a fiend with his taloned paws
> "And then hack him to bits in the morning?"

Mysti convinced the householder to let us out of the attic. She did this by kicking down the door. Back in the street, she and my aunts slipped away in different directions. The plan was for them to watch and wait for the right time to make their moves while I confronted Zoltan straight on, pretending that I was alone.

"Hey, *I'm* still with you, Bwana!" Scandal objected when I outlined the plan. "What's so alone about that?"

So with the cat beside me, I limped boldly into the square. The floating cape was back on Mysti's shoulders. There was no further need for stealth—not for me, anyhow. The demon-bone crutch clattered loudly on the stones.

The fiends were the first to hear it. They swarmed towards me, but a word from Zoltan held them back. I was halfway between the shelter of the surrounding buildings and his throne when he stood up, arms spread. "Kendar!" he cried. The throne's own wings mimicked his gesture. Neither one looked welcoming to me.

"Hello, Zoltan," I replied. "I see you've been busy."

His teeth flashed. "You're back sooner than I expected. I'd hoped to have everything taken care of before you returned."

"I'll bet you did." My jaw set hard. "What were you going to do, Zoltan? Hide your tame demons all along the Cheeseburgh Road so that when my friends and I came walking blindly back to town, the monsters would jump out of the bushes at us and yell—"

"SURPRISE!"

Nine of Zoltan's fiends exploded. The remaining four stood frozen with shock. The throne flapped its wings in panic and took off, knocking Zoltan all the way down the steps. It perched on top of the nearest tile-roofed house, creaking with fear. Pieces of blown-up demon dropped from the sky in a gentle, sticky rain. When the last bloody blob fell, all was quiet.

Bibok and Calosta stepped out of a side street, holding hands and smiling.

Scandal irritably shook bits of fiend flesh from his transparent fur. "Haven't you jerks ever heard of *knocking*?" he demanded.

CHAPTER —————— 21

ZOLTAN GOT TO HIS KNEES, SHAKING A FIST AT THE leering pair. "What have you done to my demons?"

"What have you done to our business?" Bibok countered.

"Your 'business' was the ruination of this town!" Zoltan shouted. "You didn't care how much damage your Magique did to people as long as you could keep on selling it."

"Ohhhh, listen to the master of all morality," Calosta teased. "Our biggest customer. If you wanted a discount, why didn't you just ask? There was no need for all this." Her slim brown hand waved at the glass barrel and its attachments.

"Yes, there was," I said, trying to keep my rage under control. "That setup isn't just for collecting Magique, it's for extracting the Majyk from it. You don't know Zoltan the way I do. All he ever cared about was power, power, and more power."

"Kendar!" Zoltan cried in protest.

"Don't deny it!" I yelled at him. "You tried to kill me any way you could, any chance you got, just so you could absorb Master Thengor's Majyk from me. Well, I've got news for you: It wasn't always Master Thengor's Majyk and it's not Master Thengor's Majyk now; it's *mine*! I finally know how to use it and I'm not afraid to show you."

"I'd listen to the boy if I were you, Zoltan," Calosta purred.

"Keep out of this!" I turned on her. "You're just as greedy as he is. If you two weren't so hungry for riches, there'd never have been any need to *make* you stop selling Magique."

"*Or* if Magique didn't keep going boom-crash-tinkle-tinkle," Scandal added.

"No one *made* the Cheeseburghers buy it," Bibok said. "It wasn't against the law."

"Neither is wearing plaid pants with a striped jacket, but it oughta be!" Scandal hollered.

"Even if it's legal, that doesn't make it right," I said. "As soon as I can, I'm going to go right to King Steffan and have him make a new law that'll put you all out of business for good."

Bibok slapped his cheek in mock dismay. "Darling, I think the boy means it," he said to Calosta.

"Of course he does, sweetheart," she replied. "The boy knows everything better than everyone. He'll grow out of it."

"If the boy wants to live long enough to grow out of it"—Bibok was suddenly grave—"he'd do well to realize that we're not the enemy. All we're after is money. I know it's hard to believe, but eventually we'll have enough and then we'll go off somewhere nice and tropical where they serve the drinks in pineapples. We won't be any further bother to anyone in Cheeseburgh or the kingdoms 'round. The whole point of getting enough money is so that you never have to *smell* places like Cheeseburgh ever again. But as for Zoltan, he's after power, and I never heard of anyone getting enough of that."

"Don't believe them, Kendar," Zoltan called to me. "You just got here. You don't know what I've been doing!"

"That's what you think! I've been watching you from up there"—I waved my crutch at the attic window in the corner house—"and I saw plenty. I don't know how much Majyk you've managed to wring out of all the Magique in Cheeseburgh, but I'll bet it's nowhere near as much as I've got. I'll take care of you first, then them." I nodded at Bibok and Calosta.

Scandal nudged my good leg. "Uh . . . 'scuse me, Mister Strategy, but on a stupidity scale of one to ten, telling your enemies what you're gonna do to them *and* when rates a ninety-seven."

"Shush, Scandal; he's easy." My hand tightened on the crutch. "You're no match for me anymore, Zoltan. Surrender while you can."

Zoltan's black brows drew together. "You threaten me, Kendar? Without even giving me a hearing?"

"There's nothing more I need to hear." Majyk poured itself

over me, arcing and snapping brightly. A thousand whirling winds of destruction burned inside me, howling to be set free.

"I'm your *friend*!"

"You said that to me long ago, in Master Thengor's palace. Then you tried to kill me. It wasn't the last time you tried." I balanced shakily on my good leg and aimed the crutch at his chest. "The Majyk you've gathered hasn't had long enough to become a part of you. You've got the knowledge to let go of it. Do it now!"

Zoltan stood tall, his hands balled into fists. His wand was gone, his pointy hat askew, his robes covered with dust, but still he looked twice the wizard I ever would. Looks aren't everything, Mom says. "If I do as you ask, what's to stop *them* from seizing it?" he demanded. "You're nowhere near ready to tangle with that pair on your own."

I was about to say, *Maybe I'm not on my own.* Luckily, Scandal's earlier words of caution stayed with me. I wouldn't give Zoltan so much as a hint that Mysti and my aunts were even now lurking somewhere on the edges of the square, watching and waiting for the right instant to join me. "I'll take that chance," I said instead. "It's nowhere near as big as the chance you're taking. I took you down, back when I didn't know how to use my Majyk. Now that I do . . ." I let his own imagination fill in all possible outcomes. "Don't be a stubborn fool, Zoltan."

"If I do as you say," he replied, "it's as good as admitting you're right, that I'm a traitor. I refuse."

A bolt of Majyk shot from the tip of my crutch, Majyk that took the form of the fiend whose thigh bone the crutch once was. It flung itself at its former master with jaws agape and claws grasping. Zoltan's four remaining demons stepped between him and the monster I'd conjured. It hit the first of them full in the chest, tearing a jagged, smoldering hole clean through the living fiend's body. A horrible stench of seared flesh overwhelmed the square.

Zoltan gestured, and the red-banded funnel launched itself at the flank of my monster. There was a brief sucking noise. With a soundless scream, the Majykal fiend was drawn down the tube, into the glass barrel, and lost as the seething blue broth burned green. A snap of Zoltan's fingers and the other funnel leapt to his hand. A deep breath, and the barrel held only blue liquid again.

"Thank you, Kendar." Zoltan smiled. "I see you really have learned how to manage your Majyk, including how to give it away." He breathed on his fingertips and a tiny spark of Majyk danced there. "I, too, know how to be generous. As a token of my good faith, I return your original gift." He blew again, and the spark became a butterfly that came wobbling through the air towards me.

Scandal ran around my ankles in circles crying, "Don't touch it, chief! You don't know where it's been."

"I'm not afraid anymore," I said quietly, and I reached out and let the butterfly of flame alight on my hand. I drank in the Majykal spark with my whole being, but it looked like all I was doing was absorbing it through my fingertips. I couldn't help smiling as its warmth washed over me.

"There, you see?" Zoltan said. "I returned your Majyk as pure as it was when you entrusted it to my keeping. I would not betray your trust, Kendar. I, too, remember our past. I know how much it cost you to trust me." He scowled at Bibok and Calosta. "But I warn you, trust them and it will cost you all."

"Can he trust you enough to hold back your demonic allies while we parley?" Bibok called.

"What parley?" Zoltan was wary.

"With the boy. He's got reasons enough not to want to side with either of us, and power enough to turn any battle that happens here into a shambles with no winners. Needless to say, your precious Cheeseburgh would be destroyed."

Zoltan tensed visibly. "I won't allow it! This town relies on me. I'll protect it no matter what."

"Then let us speak with the boy. Unmolested."

"A truce? Granted," Zoltan said, a large measure of reluctance in his voice.

Calosta was at my side in a warm cloud of cinnamon scent. "You see what he is, my lord?" she breathed urgently in my ear. "Believe my darling Bibok when he says that he and I only desire to earn ourselves enough money to guarantee a life of ease, then to be gone. If you do not want us to sell Magique anymore, we will obey. We can earn all we desire in other ways. But that one—!" She darted a look of fear at Zoltan.

"Hey! How come now you're all of a sudden so ready to do

what Kendar says?" Scandal demanded, his tail switching sharply. "All this 'my lord' stuff smells like four-day-old mackerel to me. No, wait: Five-day-old mackerel. It's still pretty tasty at four. It wasn't so long ago that you guys were calling him 'the boy.'"

I cast a temporary shield around the three of us and kept a weather eye on Zoltan while I spoke to Calosta. "That cat's right. Better than right; the cat's evidence that says I'd be a fool to believe you. What in Wedwel's name did you do to him?"

"Do?" Calosta's innocent look was false, so false that even she knew it and had the grace to drop it at once. Her expression went from wide-eyed to serious as she told me, "We were in danger from Zoltan, my lord, and we sought to protect ourselves and all our household. In time of crisis, is it not the custom for all beings who share the same roof to share the same responsibilities for their mutual protection? So we came to the cat to use him as part of our defenses. We knew he had Majyk. We did not know that his desire to be a part of our lives was a ruse."

"If you ask me," Bibok put in, "that cat has some major unresolved hostilities to deal with when it comes to his relationships with humans. One word, Kendar: Therapy."

I gave him one word back. It described what you find underfoot in cow pastures.

"Whoa! I detect someone who's not in touch with his inner child," Bibok said, recoiling in mock horror.

I offered to get in touch with his inner child (whatever that nonsense meant) through his outer throat. He stopped making fun of me and just glowered. I was glad he was on the outside of my shielding spell. Then Calosta touched me gently, distracting me from her simmering lover.

"My lord, you have yet to understand. Let me show you what we did to the cat."

My shield popped away from her, closing itself around just Scandal and me. "Don't try it," I snarled.

She gave me an indulgent smile and sighed. "Ah, you must have been very badly betrayed in so young a life to be so suspicious. I did not mean I would demonstrate on you. Behold!" She placed two fingers in her mouth and blew a shrill, penetrating whistle.

In answer to the sorceress's summons, the square was soon

aswarm with cats. There were seven of them, and they all looked like Scandal. He began to jump around in a frenzy as soon as he saw them.

"There they are, boss! There they are! Nab 'em! Lasso 'em! Throw a butterfly net, call the Animal Control Warden, do *something*, for Bast's sake! Don't let 'em get away!"

"What are they? Are they fiends? Are they evil?"

"I hope so!" Scandal exclaimed. "They're *me*!"

"Uh—?"

"My *lives*, dimbulb! They're my seven-and-a-half spare lives! When Calosta and Bibok got wind of what Zoltan was up to, they got ready to save their own hides big time. You know what's the universal law of Yuppiedom? Always get the best, but the best is better if you can get someone else to pay for it. Why should they use their own Majyk to fight Zoltan's fiends when they knew I had some of my own? So they just sneaked up and helped themselves."

Suddenly, I got it: "Only your Majyk's been with you as long as mine; so long that it's become part of your life."

"*Lives*," the cat corrected me.

"When they tried to peel it away from you, they stripped a life off with each layer of Majyk they took." I glared at the pair. Bibok grinned, but Calosta was polite enough to look sheepish, even if I knew she didn't mean it.

"We thought he would be glad to do his part to safeguard his new home," she said.

"What, you didn't get the hint when I was screaming, 'Stop that! Gimme that back! Whose life is it, anyway'?" Scandal queried.

"Blame me, a poor, frightened, helpless woman." Calosta folded her hands on her breast and bowed her head.

"'Helpless woman' is right up there with 'military intelligence' and 'honest politician,' babe," Scandal said. "You'll be helpless when piranhas start nibbling watercress sandwiches."

"You'll be proud to know your lives were wonderful fighters," Bibok said. "Or perhaps not. I forget whether cats care about these things. Whatever, they were. Zoltan sent nine fiends against us. Calosta and I destroyed one each, and your lives, full of your Majyk, each claimed a victim too."

"No kidding?" Scandal actually was interested. "How'd I do it?"

Bibok studied his perfectly manicured nails. "You couldn't have done it without us. We told you where to find a fiend's most vulnerable and sensitive part—and no, I don't mean *there*—then you merely found it, bit hard, and it was all over."

"And where is this Achilles' tenderloin, pray?" Scandal asked.

Bibok smirked. "That's for you to know and you to find out. If you're not on our side against Zoltan, we might like to summon a few fiends of our own later. Why tell you how to defeat them?"

"Zoltan, Shmoltan, I just want my lives back," Scandal snapped. He looked up at me. "You gonna take care of it or not?"

"With pleasure."

"Okay, in that case, who cares where you bite a demon to make him go *boom*?" the cat said to Bibok. "I'm with Houdini."

A question popped into my mind, one that had been tickling around in there for a while. "Why do they look so solid and you look so—?" I didn't know the polite way to say that Scandal looked about as substantial as spidersilk.

"Rats and roaches, because they're *whole* lives, Einstein! The greedheads would've taken everything I had, except I hung on and they only got seven and a half lives off me. That left me with half a life. It's better than none, but it's drafty."

I counted the cats again. They were drawn up in a ring around Calosta and Bibok, waiting for further commands. They looked like Scandal in all the obvious ways, but they were different in one very basic, very important way: They looked respectful, docile, and obedient.

They looked ready to take orders from human beings.

Those weren't cats. They were monsters.

Monsters or not, I had to know: "If they stripped off seven and a half of your lives, what happened to the other half-life they got?"

Scandal couldn't shrug, but he could come close. "You got me there. Maybe it couldn't live on its own. All the more reason for you to snag those seven and—"

"But it *did* live, little puss." Bibok's perfect mouth curled into the coldest and most sinister of sneers.

When you're facing a potentially dangerous enemy (what

other kind is there?) you don't pay much attention to what he's chosen to wear today. For the first time, I noticed that Bibok, like Zoltan, was dressed in the full regalia of a Council-approved wizard. Neither one of them had any right to wear the long, dark robes or the pointy hat. Neither one of them let a little thing like right or wrong stop them. Zoltan's robes were covered with sparkling symbols representing the suns, the moons, and the stars around Orbix. Bibok's robes were free of ornament, except for the image of what looked like a very small, wingless dragon or a very large, fierce, sharp-toothed lizard embroidered just above his heart.

The thing about wizardly robes is there's never anywhere to hold things. That's what I always thought, anyway. A wizard with something to carry either brings along servants to do it for him or buys a belt pouch like everyone else. Now Bibok revealed the mystic knowledge of where a wizard carries his handkerchief when he doesn't have a belt pouch or a servant handy. He merely reached into the deep sleeves of his robe and from some secret pocket yanked out a small, squirming, trembling, mewing lump of fur.

Scandal let out a ferocious yowl and threw himself at the shielding spell around us. It held. He bounced back against my legs and slashed at me frantically. "Lemme out, boss! Lemme out! He's got my other half out there! I gotta save me!"

"Calmly, good cat, calmly." Bibok cupped the little furball in his hands. "We would never let this infant come to any harm. As soon as Zoltan was defeated, Calosta and I intended to give you back all the Majykal lives we took from you. But this one is special. This one we shall keep."

"She *is* unique," Calosta remarked to me. "As we tried to pull off the last layer of the cat's Majyk, we did not know he had already lost one life. You can imagine our surprise when all we were able to get was this." She indicated at the mewing creature in Bibok's hands.

"Imagine *their* surprise?" Scandal said.

"What is it?" I asked. "If it's only half of Scandal's remaining life, why isn't it transparent, like him? Why is it so small?"

"This was the shape the Majyk chose," Calosta said. "Why? That remains Majyk's own mystery."

"I like to think this one was smart enough to realize she

didn't have enough substance to make herself into a full-grown cat and still remain solid," Bibok said. "Therefore she decided to assume the form of a kitten and let time take its course."

Scandal's mouth was agape. "Errrrr, 'she'?" he said. "Did you say 'she'? Several times, 'she'? You wanna correct that pronoun quick, before the Grammar Police show up?"

"I don't think so," Bibok responded, and turned the kitten in his hands so that we could see there was no way he'd made a mistake.

"But that's impossible!" Scandal screeched. "That's one of *my* lives. I'm a fully functional tomcat, and I've got two dozen real happy California ladycats who'll back me up on this."

"Do you doubt your eyes?" Bibok asked.

"It ain't my *eyes* that little furball's missing!"

"Are any of the other lives . . . you know?" I asked.

"They are all male. You can see for yourself when they stand up."

"Then what the cat says is true: It's impossible for that one to be female."

"Oh, I wouldn't say that." Bibok was having fun with us. "Every living creature has within it both a female and a male nature, yin and yang, in different degrees of balance. Of course I wouldn't expect you to know this, living in this horrid little cosmic backwater."

"I don't care what you think of Cheeseburgh," I said. "I don't even care if you call me 'the boy.' But you'd better give Scandal back his lives—*all* of them!—if you want to hold onto your own."

Bibok's teeth were sharp and bright. "You think you can fight all of us at once . . . boy?"

"He won't *have* to fight me!" Zoltan shouted.

"Shut up, you! Respect our parley!" Bibok thundered.

"Not when you parley in lies." Zoltan's hand darted sideways and a fresh demon erupted from the earth in a spout of fire and dust. It was a small fiend, as fiends go, hardly bigger than me. It charged Bibok, slavering and roaring.

Bibok tucked the kitten back into his sleeve, yawned, and nodded at one of Scandal's detached lives. The cat lunged for the demon's legs. The beast was quick—too quick for my eyes to see exactly where it struck. All I knew was there was an explosion and I was once more being pelted with damp scraps of fiend flesh.

"Temper, temper, Zoltan." Bibok waggled a finger at my old schoolchum. "A man who betrays the sanctity of an established parley might also betray . . . oh, just about anyone."

Zoltan fumed but kept his fiends to himself.

"Ahhhh." I heard Scandal draw in a deep, satisfied breath. He was watching his other life as it licked itself clean of demon blood. "So that's the angle. Slick."

"You saw—?" I hissed.

"Right the first time," he whispered back. "Now I know where to nip a demon so it counts. Lemme in your mind again and I can tell you all about it in complete privacy."

"Oh yes, please let him into your mind, Master Kendar." Calosta giggled and picked up one of the other lives. She tickled it under the chin. "Scandal didn't even have to observe our little pet in action for him to know what they all know."

"Calosta, you idiot! You should have kept your mouth shut. What we might have learned from the boy's mind—! Agh!" He spat in disgust. It was the first time I ever heard Bibok speak sharply to his mate.

The sorceress shrank. "I'm sorry, darling, it's just—I didn't think you needed any sort of unfair advantage to win whatever contest you choose. And besides"—her tone changed from cringing to wheedling—"why would you need to slip into his thoughts? Master Kendar's not our enemy. Remember?"

"Ah." Bibok adjusted the drape of his wizardly robes. "You are right, my dearest one, as always." To me he said, "My friend, what can I do to convince you of our good intentions?"

I thought it over. "Restore my friend," I said.

"Is that all?"

"That's a start. Then we'll see."

"You drive a hard bargain. Very well. We can't do anything unless our Majyk can touch him."

I took the hint and removed the shielding spell. Zoltan uttered a cry of dismay. I swiftly raised the demon-bone crutch and leveled it at Bibok.

"Is that really necessary?" he inquired, one brow raised.

"I'm waiting to see if it is."

"You won't be making many friends in this life if you can't

learn to trust people, bo—my lord," he said with a sham look of pity in his eyes. "Dearest, will you perform the honors?"

Calosta curtseyed gracefully. "A joy, sweetest one." She whistled shrilly a second time and Scandal's seven stripped-away lives rushed to her. "Here they are, awaiting your pleasure," she told the cat. "Come and join them."

Scandal looked to me for approval. "Go ahead," I said grimly, never taking my eyes from Bibok.

"Okay, *kemo sabe*. It's no skin off my—Aw, heck, yes it is. Here goes nothing." He walked forward to meet his seven other selves, tail high and proud.

The other lives scampered out to meet him. They were all over him in a wild tangle of paws, tails, fur, and whiskers. My heart froze, fearing it was a fight, but no snarls or spitting or yowls came from that mob of cat-shapes. As I watched, they began to spin around like a whirlpool, the size of the mob dwindling and dwindling the faster they all spun. Soon there was nothing my eye could follow but a furry blur spangled with tiny flares of Majyk at work. It was fascinating—so fascinating that it took me awhile before I realized I wasn't paying attention to Bibok anymore. I jerked my head up sharply and gave him a don't-try-anything scowl. He only smiled and showed me his empty hands.

"Get real, boss; if he wanted to ice you, he had plenty of time while you were watching us. Me. Vanna, I'd like to buy a pronoun I can count on."

"Scandal!" I was overjoyed. There sat my old friend as solid as ever.

"In the flesh. Most of it." Scandal licked a paw and groomed his whiskers. "Minus a half."

"Hey, that's right!" I glared at Bibok. "Hand it over."

"You act as if we were your slaves instead of your equals in Majyk," he replied. "If you mistrust us, why should we trust you? The kitten stays with me until you give us the same sort of proof we've just given you."

I considered the way things were. If I sided with Bibok and Calosta against Zoltan, they swore they'd take their shady business elsewhere and never sell Magique again. If I sided with Zoltan against them, he might wait until we were in the heat of battle, then turn traitor on me if he saw the chance to steal my Majyk. If I sided with neither, I had no guarantee that I'd be able to defeat all three of them. Was I willing to risk that?

Except I wasn't the only one who'd be taking risks. Whether Zoltan or Calosta and Bibok struck the first blow, Mysti and my aunts would be all over the square, swords slashing, hair flying, bloodthirsty battle cries rending the air. I knew how women got when something annoyed them.

Mysti and my aunts were great with steel, but when steel meets Majyk, it's not an even fight. They'd die; they'd die bravely, but a hero's corpse is just as cold as a coward's. Then there was Scandal. I knew he was willing to die for me; he'd done it once already.

I could risk my own neck. I couldn't risk theirs. I didn't really trust Calosta and Bibok a whole lot, but I no longer trusted Zoltan at all. I had to make a choice.

I made it.

"Aunt Glucosia! Aunt Carageena!" I cupped one hand to my mouth and called their names to all sides of the square. "Come out! Show yourselves!"

"Master Kendar, what are you doing?" Calosta asked.

"I'm telling my allies to come out of hiding."

"Aunts, is it?" Bibok snickered. "My, you *have* brought formidable allies with you, my lord."

"Spoken like a man who doesn't know this guy's aunts," Scandal informed him. "They're the doilies of death."

"They're also invisible," Bibok remarked.

I called their names again, louder, using a little Majyk to boost the volume of my voice. On his platform, Zoltan began to shift nervously from foot to foot.

"Why are you calling for your aunts?" he demanded.

"You know the ladies?" Bibok was interested.

"Swordswomen of great renown and reputation. Kendar, I asked you *why* you're calling for them?"

"Because they've been hiding, ready to come to my aid and back me up if that's what's necessary," I replied.

"Mmmmm, and the little old lady sellswords would've popped out yelling 'Boo! You're dead!' if we made any sudden moves against their darling nephew. I see." Bibok rubbed his chin. "You know, Master Kendar, I don't know whether Calosta's told you, but I really *hate* surprises."

"There won't be any surprise," I replied. "That's why I'm

calling for them to show themselves. It's my gesture of good faith to match yours." I didn't add that I *wasn't* calling for Mysti to show herself as well. If they could hold back on Scandal's half-life, I could keep a Welfie up my sleeve.

Zoltan was livid. "So you're trading tokens of amity with those two, eh, Kendar? I'd say this parley's done, then. You've made your choice plain to see." His face was stiff, but his eyes held a touch of hurt. "So be it."

"Zoltan, I—" What was the matter with me? Was I about to *apologize* to him? Ridiculous! And yet, that look in his eyes . . . It's no fun having your choices made for you, but no one told me it could hurt this much when you've got to make them for yourself.

Bibok raised both hands with a flourish that set his sleeves flapping. The one where the kitten was stowed swung back and forth violently and I heard its tiny occupant mew in fear. "Hold, Zoltan! As you value the continued existence of this rat-hole town, listen to me. The boy—Master Kendar is not yet our ally."

"No?" I was surprised. "Why not?"

"My fault, my lord." Calosta had a delicious but unnerving way of materializing at your elbow when it suited her, then flitting back to her lover's side. "It is the custom in Plunj that all alliances be sealed with an oath. I must insist upon it. The ceremony is short, but impressive. Who knows? Perhaps it will so impress Zoltan that he will realize the error of his ways and surrender his Majyk without a struggle."

"Yeah, and I bark all night and chase cars," Scandal said.

"You expect me to give you the time for this?" Zoltan laughed.

"You are free to use our time of ceremony in any way you like," Calosta told him sweetly. "I am certain you will be able to think of something."

"Right; he can read a good book," Scandal suggested. "Go over the town tax records. Call up a few fiends. What is it with you people? Is it something in the water? You always send out engraved invitations to your enemies telling them when to expect you and what kind of weapons to bring?"

"We like to call ourselves civilized," Bibok said, his manner chill.

"We got another word for that in L.A.," Scandal said. "Dogmeat."

Bibok did not consider Scandal's words worthy of a reply. Instead he said to Zoltan, "If you permit us this one indulgence, we will remove the site of our battle to a place far from the streets of Cheeseburgh."

"In that case, agreed." Zoltan nodded. "A battle of sorcery is nothing to undertake lightly. I learned that at Master Thengor's Academy of High Wizardry."

I saw how Bibok's face turned ugly for an instant at the mention of the school that had rejected him. Then he was his old, smooth self again. "A good lesson, and one we might all learn. We thank you."

"Your thanks are as false as your friendship," Zoltan said bitterly. "Save them. Proceed with your ceremony. Take as long as you like. I promise you, I'll be using the time well."

Bibok made an exaggerated bow, then turned to me. "We'll need only three things before we can begin, Master Kendar. The first is the sacred altar of Delbert—" A large cube of carved jade the size of the Gangle family portable altar of Wedwel appeared between us in the blink of an eye. "Oh, thank you, my sweet. You do think of everything," Bibok said to Calosta, who simpered.

"The second," he went on, "are your tokens of good faith. Where are these skulking swordswomen you promised us, Master Kendar?"

"Here we are, dearie!" Aunt Glucosia came huffing into the square with Aunt Carageena close behind. They pulled to a halt midway between the fountain and the spot where Bibok and Calosta stood. "We would have come sooner, but I had a lovely vantage point behind some potted marigolds on a balcony, and it took me an unforgivably long time to climb down. Gee' had to help me part of the way. I'm getting much too old for this sort of thing. Oh, it's cookies and the retirement cottage for sure!"

"Lovely lady." Bibok swept down on them, kissing hands indiscriminately. "I won't hear such nonsense from your lips. You're a spring blossom. Both of you. One spring blossom apiece." My aunts simpered. I was grateful I'd never had to watch Bibok in a room full of women. I don't think my stomach could have taken all that simpering.

Bibok left my aunts whispering and giggling to one another like a pair of lovestruck kitchen wenches and came back to me. "Excellent, excellent! We're almost done." He rubbed his hands together. "And now, your tokens of good faith in our hands, you have only to place *your* hands on this book"—an open book appeared on top of the altar the same way the altar itself had appeared—"which is the *Minichilibini*, the sacred scripture of the followers of Delbert, and take an oath that you will never use your Majyk against your friends and allies."

"That's all?" I asked. He nodded. "All right." I shifted the demon-bone crutch under my arm and rested both hands on the book. "I swear by the honor of the Gangle family, and by Wedwel, the All-Compassionate Destroyer, that I will never use my Majyk against my friends or—"

"Kendar, stop!" Aunt Glucosia shouted. "That's not the sacred book of Delbert. There *are* no sacred books of Delbert! It's too warm and damp for books in Plunj, so they either carve the scriptures on the temple walls or tattoo them on the flanks of the sacred white antelope. This ceremony's a fake!"

"She is right, Master Kendar," Calosta said. "And do you know what the hardest thing is about reading books off the sides of antelope?"

I shook my head stupidly, hands still resting on the bogus book.

She flung her arms wide. A cage of shining Majyk arched out of the ground around my aunts. I started towards them, only to find my hands shackled to the book by golden manacles pulsing with power.

"Making sure the good parts don't get away," Calosta murmured in my ear, and joined her lover in triumphant laughter.

CHAPTER ——————— 22

"YOUNG WOMAN, IN THE NAME OF YOUR OWN god, Delbert, release us at once," Aunt Glucosia commanded.

Calosta just laughed louder. "Do you expect the name of Delbert to make me tremble, old woman? Delbert is only a tale made up to scare small children into being good."

"That is not what the High Priest showed me of your Plunjian god," Aunt Glucosia responded coldly.

"No need to ask what it was the High Priest showed *you*." Calosta's smirk was every bit as nasty as Bibok's.

"You know, Glucosia, perhaps you should have told her to let us go in Wedwel's name," Aunt Carageena suggested. "Since he *is* the only real god, that should work much better."

"*I'll* show you what works!"

Aunt Glucosia slashed her sword against the bars of the cage. They rang like iron but vibrated with an eerie Majyk-born music that made both my aunts clap their hands over their ears and fall to their knees.

"Stop that! You're hurting them!" I cried.

For an answer, I got a smack across the face from Bibok. "Shut your mouth, *boy*. You're no longer in a position to dictate terms."

"You're a miserable cheat and a liar," I gritted. I got another smack for that. He was drawing his hand back to give me a third one, free of charge or reason, when his eyes abruptly went wide and he let out a holler of pain that was almost as loud as the Majykal dissonance of my aunts' cage. His sleeves flapped wildly as he leaped past me, until he looked like a huge bird trying to launch itself at the sky.

"What—?" I gasped.

Scandal jumped onto the false altar, licking his chops, and said, "Well, whaddaya know? It works when you bite *non*-demons there, too. Too bad it doesn't make them blow up." He pawed at the shackles holding me. A loud, wicked snap of Majykal force made him jerk back his paw and hiss. "Woo, that smarts," he said, shaking it. "Time for Plan B."

"What's Plan B?"

"Plan B is: Think of a Plan C that'll work."

I felt funny. The manacles were still throbbing on my wrists. Maybe it was a trick of the light, but the shackles looked as if they too were made of glass, like Zoltan's Majyk-gathering barrel. Something colored a brilliant gold was flowing through them, down their anchoring chains and into the altar.

"Boss? Yo, you okay?" Scandal's voice sounded strange, as if he were speaking right in my ear one moment, from far away the next. I stared at him, but he was all fuzzy—fuzzier than usual. My ears filled with the rushing sound of a brook in flood, and in the midst of it I only half-believed I heard a small voice crying *No! You can't take me away! I don't want to leave him! I like it here!*

"The curses of a thousand gods on you, what are you doing to him?" Zoltan bellowed.

"Mind your own business," Bibok snapped. "If you're a wise man, you won't interfere."

"I'll interfere to your deaths," Zoltan shot back. "Is this how you treat your allies?"

"We need no allies," Calosta said. She joined hands with Bibok. "Together, we are enough to take on your whole puny world."

Through a haze I saw Zoltan's face transform with shock as he realized what they were doing to me. "You—you're draining his Majyk!"

"Oh, *well* done." Bibok offered up a sarcastic round of applause. "Now that you know, go home and tell the wife and kiddies."

"You can't do that! It's been a part of him too long. You'll kill him!"

"Oh, you men." Calosta pouted prettily. "You're always such alarmists. We didn't kill the cat. We're only taking enough to leave him harmless. It's a public service, really. We don't think it's safe for one boy to have so much power. It might weaken his moral fiber. I've seen it happen time and time again: One minute they discover they've got enough Majyk to level a city, the next they're refusing to take out the garbage. His mother will thank us for this."

"She will not!" Aunt Carageena shouted. "Abstemia is proud that her Kendar's a wizard!"

"Then Abstemia will have to find some other reason to be proud of her Kendar, won't she?" Bibok said.

Their voices sounded as if they were drifting away from me. *Maybe this is a dream*, I thought through the clouds cluttering my mind. A sweet warmth was stealing over me. The pain in my leg felt so much better. *Bibok and Calosta are healing me*, I thought as my eyelids grew heavier. *Isn't that nice of them?*

Then I heard Zoltan shout, "I order you, stop!" and a blaze of Majyk burned so brightly that it made no difference if my eyes were open or shut.

Spoilsport, I thought muzzily, but I was more awake than asleep again; awake enough to be aware that Scandal was butting at my arm urgently.

"Kid, wake up! Don't go limp on me now. Fight it!"

"Fi' wha'?" I mumbled.

"What they're doing to you, dummy! What Zoltan said!" He snarled at the manacles, baring his fangs, but he wasn't fool enough to touch them again.

Speaking of fools, Bibok was advising Zoltan not to be one.

"*That* was a pretty display," he remarked, one corner of his mouth quirking down in scorn. "Now if you've gotten it out of your system, take your fiends and go. We'll give you"—he pulled up one sleeve and studied a gold bracelet with an odd, circular ornament—"ten minutes."

"What about our battle?"

"Are you serious?" Bibok tried to smother a laugh. "There's no further need for us to fight. It was the boy who was the troublemaker. With him taken care of, we three can go on as we please. We all have what we want: peace for us, to carry on with our honest little business, and for you— You have command of Majyk again, and with your knowledge you'll soon be able to gather up a good additional supply. This squalid hamlet no longer needs to hold you. All Orbix awaits!"

"As does the Council," Zoltan reminded him grimly.

"Oh, *them*." Calosta dismissed the entire Council and all

their Majyk with a flippant wave of her hand. "They're a bunch of old teddy bears . . . if you bribe them heavily enough. Bribery is no problem, with Majyk on your side."

"Nothing's a problem with Majyk," Bibok added.

And then Zoltan said the unthinkable:

"Majyk is not enough."

The sorcerous couple exchanged a look of shock. "Did I hear him right, angel?" Bibok asked.

"I'm sure you did, darling," she replied. "He said Majyk's not enough."

"By Dow, Jones, and the Journal, amazing! There's actually someone greedier than *us*!"

"Not *greedy*, sweetheart," she corrected him. "Upwardly mobile."

"NASA should be so upwardly mobile," Scandal muttered.

"I don't mean that I want more Majyk," Zoltan said. "I mean that there are things on Orbix that are worth more than all the Majyk ever gathered and tamed. I used to think the way you two do, when I was young."

"You're the same age as we are, so watch out about calling yourself *old*." Bibok clearly resented Zoltan's words. He removed his wizard's hat, ran one hand through his hair, then uneasily checked his fingers for any that might have fallen out. With a little shudder he let one fall to the ground before jamming the hat on again.

"He doesn't mean he's old in years, my dearest," Calosta comforted him. "He means he's been aged by other things."

"Ah, yes." Bibok nodded. "I've run into his bra—children."

Zoltan ignored their brief exchange. "Now I know better," he said. "Majyk is power, but it's what you do with the power that makes your life full or empty. Take all the Majyk Orbix has to give, and unless you use it wisely, you hold air."

"Scuba tanks hold air, too," Bibok replied. "And a pretty penny people pay for it."

"Huh?" said Zoltan.

"You sure him and you weren't separated at birth, chief?" Scandal asked. I tried to shake my head, but the weight of it had suddenly doubled so that it took all my strength to keep it from falling off my neck.

"You know, I hope old Zollie keeps 'em talking," Scandal

remarked. "When they're distracted, the Majyk stops flowing out of you so fast. I know; I've been watching the cuffs."

"Mmmmm," was all the reply I could think of.

"You're wasting our time and yours with your lectures, Zoltan," Bibok was saying. "If I were you, I'd count my blessings and move my tail out of here. We're letting you keep your Majyk and we're even removing the one enemy you've got who's any threat to you."

"Kendar is not my enemy!" (I felt Zoltan's words penetrate to my bones and shake me back into full consciousness.) "And I won't let you destroy him!"

I saw him thrust his arms out stiffly, fists clenched. His hands became claws, blue-black and merciless. Stinking yellow smoke rose from the talons' tips as they dipped low.

"Wha's he doin'?" I asked Scandal.

The cat squinted. "This is weird," he said, "but it *looks* like our good buddy Zoltan's turning into a street mime. The shtick he's doing now is Man Lifting Invisible Crate."

Zoltan was lifting *something*. His claws were empty, yet it was clear he was feeling the strain of hauling the full weight of whatever they'd snagged into the light. The muscles on his neck stood out and his face turned crimson with effort. He raised his claws by nearly imperceptible degrees, gasping and panting as he focused all his power on them and their burden.

"Man, that's some *big* ol' invisible crate," Scandal said. "I hope it doesn't give him an invisible hernia."

It took shape gradually, the thing that Zoltan's claws were dragging out of the hidden world. All I could tell was that it was big—incredibly big—and that it didn't want to come when called. The air in the square was thick with its stench—a stomach-wrenching mix of every foul smell imaginable. Scandal made a small sound of distress and was sick over the side of the altar. My aunts hunched over in their cage, supporting one another in the thickest part of the stink.

And what of Bibox and Calosta? I glanced in their direction and saw through tearing eyes that they had both donned masks—Majyk-summoned, to be sure—of an unfamiliar design that made them look like bug-eyed anteaters. They didn't seem to be in any discomfort at all.

Not for long. With one final heave and a tremendous grunt, Zoltan finished the job. No one could tell how many of us there in the square screamed and how many of us were dumbstruck when we saw what Zoltan Fiendlord had called up to do his bidding this time.

The fiend was half a story taller than the tallest house in the square and made himself at home immediately by using his claws to skewer one of Zoltan's lesser demons through the heart. He popped the still-twitching body into his mouth and crunched it up with jaws the size and solidity of millstones.

I felt the shackles on my wrists turn cold. Nothing flowed through them anymore. Scandal saw as well, and turned bold enough to take a second swipe at my chains. They shattered, freeing me.

"Why—?" I began.

"Because they're scared," Scandal said, nodding towards Bibok and Calosta. "And that's the ultimate distraction."

The cat was right. For the first time since I'd known them, the self-confident sorcerous pair looked like gamblers whose luck has just run out. Calosta pressed herself into Bibok's arms, her shoulders quivering as if the winds of winter were blowing through the square.

Bibok glanced at me, and it was a look of hatred. But he quickly changed his expression to a smooth smile and called out to Zoltan, "There, my friend! No need for melodramatics. We've freed the boy. Now call off your little friend."

"Whaddaya mean, *you* freed him, you lousy Lincoln wannabe?" Scandal's indignant outburst was ignored.

Zoltan's black claws became human hands once more. He swayed from side to side on the platform and almost staggered over the edge before catching himself. His voice rasped and quavered like an old man's as he said, "I'll call him off after you—after you've—given back what you stole from Kendar."

Bibok's grin looked ready to snap in the middle. "You must be joking."

"Do you want . . . to find out?" Zoltan raised a trembling hand towards the demon.

"Zoltan . . . *Master* Zoltan . . . My lord, perhaps you misunderstand us. We've harvested the child's Majyk as a gift for you. It won't take a moment for us to link our gathering device to yours. Think of how it will feel when you drink in all that Majyk! Such strength! Such power! What a rush!"

Zoltan gestured weakly and one of his smaller fiends

scampered to a nearby house, punched a huge hole in the plaster wall, and pulled out a chair for his master. The wizard sank into it gratefully, not even pausing to brush away the thick layer of white dust covering it.

"I am not like you, Bibok," he said. "I am not even like the person I once was, not too long ago. I know the meaning of *enough*, even when you speak of Majyk. What would I do with Kendar's hoard now? So much power has no place in Cheeseburgh, but I do. I am happy here."

"You're what?" It was as if Bibok had heard Zoltan say that slimegrinds grow on trees. "*Here?*"

"This is where my family is. This is my home, where I've chosen to be. This is my place in the world, and it suits me well enough. Enough . . ." He savored the word. It made him smile. "I've found my destiny, but Kendar has yet to find his. Give Kendar his Majyk back again and I'll command my fiend to let you depart in peace."

"Kendar has more than enough Majyk left for his needs," Bibok replied. "Haven't you, boy?"

I was rubbing my wrists, trying to get a little feeling back into them, when his question took me by surprise. "Haven't I what?"

In the shadow of the demon, Calosta approached me. "For the love of mercy, tell him you're content," she pleaded, clinging to my arm. "You had a life before you got this Majyk; you can go back to that same life again."

My life before Majyk? Return to being Kendar Ratwhacker after having been Master Kendar? I shook my head.

She slapped me. "Fool!"

Bibok glided between us and escorted her away. "Don't soil your hands on that silly child, Calipoo," he breathed. "He's simply Not Our Kind, Dear." They turned their backs on me.

I could tell when I wasn't wanted. "Come on, Scandal. Our place is with our real friend." I walked away from the altar, the cat close on my heels, and headed for Zoltan. We had to walk right between the legs of the colossal demon to reach him, but I had a feeling that the monster wasn't going to hurt us.

Zoltan was a dead weight in his newly fetched throne, sitting as heavily as a sack of wheat. He raised his head and smiled when he saw us come up the platform steps.

"Finally decided you could trust me?" he asked. It hurt me to hear how feeble he sounded.

I held tight to the demon-bone crutch and knelt before him, even though the pain in my bad leg was awful. "I'm sorry, Zoltan. I hope you can forgive me. Calosta's right: I'm a fool."

"Naaaaah." Scandal waved a paw. "You're just human. Six of one, half a dozen of the other."

Zoltan placed his hands on my shoulders. "It's not the first mistake you've made, is it?"

"No." I was thinking of Mysti.

Come to think of her, where *was* she? I glanced around the square so intently that Zoltan took alarm. "What is it?" he gasped, his grip on me. "What do you see?"

"*Ow!* Nothing." I shook off his hands and pulled myself up on the crutch, rubbing my shoulders.

"For a moment I was afraid that our foes had begun the battle with some sort of sneak attack." His dark eyes darted from the front of one house to the next. All looked equally silent, equally sinister.

"I don't think there's gonna be any attack," Scandal said.

"You sound sure of yourself, cat."

"Look, it figures: The Wicked Witch of Plunj and the Wizard of Ooze down there can't make Move One because if they try anything, your giant economy-sized demon will stomp them into jelly. On the other hand, if you guys try firing the first shot, they've still got Kendar's aunts in the clink. You know how easy it is to turn a Majyk cage into a big ol' Majykal iron maiden?"

"What is an iron maiden?" Zoltan asked.

"Take two slices of cold steel, stud 'em with spikes, and make a sandwich using some poor slob as the filling. Wham!" Scandal sat on his haunches and clapped his paws together to demonstrate. Zoltan and I both jumped. "Mustard optional."

"And anyway," I added, "we don't really want a battle. We all know what that would do to the town."

Zoltan gazed across the square through the titanic arch of his demon's legs, and sighed. "I fear you are both right. Which leaves us precisely nowhere."

Bibok and Calosta stood together, glaring at him. At one point they took a step towards the altar that had drained away my Majyk, but a snap of Zoltan's fingers enclosed the jade cube within a shielding spell. It wasn't a very strong shield—even I could see that. It flickered and sputtered and looked thicker and thinner by turns, but whenever Bibok or his lady gave the slightest hint of a move in that direction, the protective spell flared up strongly.

"I hope they see the error of their ways soon," Zoltan said, his voice sounding weaker still. "I can't keep this up forever."

"What's wrong?" I asked quietly.

Instead of an answer he asked, "How much Majyk did they leave you, Kendar?"

I looked inside myself and found . . .

"None." I was desolate. I'd gotten used to Majyk.

"That can't be right." Zoltan shook his head. "If that were true, you wouldn't be alive now. They must have left you *something*."

"Hey, why would I lie about it?" I demanded, stamping the platform with my crutch for emphasis. "I'm telling you, I looked and the only thing I found was—"

Sparks flew when my crutch struck the platform. Zoltan, Scandal, and I stared, fascinated, as I raised the bone again and brought it down hard to see if we'd seen rightly. More sparks. Majyk. *My* Majyk.

"In *there*?" Scandal made a face.

I passed my hands over the smooth surface of the crutch. "I guess so. I can feel it." I closed my eyes and drew the Majyk out of the crutch, back into me.

I tried, that is. It didn't work.

"Clever," Zoltan murmured.

"Yes, aren't we?" Calosta said. "I told you we'd left the boy some Majyk, but I never said *where* we'd left it. It's bound to the bone by spells that he'd need *more* Majyk to break. But he hasn't got any more Majyk, does he? Poor lamb."

"Think of it as a trust fund, old man!" Bibok called from across the square. "Hold onto that crutch with both hands, because if you ever let it go, you go with it."

"Let me see . . . if I can . . . give some of my Majyk . . . to you," Zoltan said. His hands rose, faint traceries of Majyk crawling over them, but these fizzled out before he could touch me. "No use . . . sorry." He was having a harder and harder time just breathing. "Summoning that fiend took . . . all I had."

"All your Majyk? Gone?" I spoke so low I wasn't sure he heard me, but I couldn't risk having Bibok and Calosta know what was being said. Not now. Not this.

"Enough . . . to command him . . . hold him . . . remain his master. Otherwise . . . suicide. Even so . . . can't hold him . . . forever."

"I'm no military expert, but you want my advice? It's time to push the button," Scandal said. "If you don't initiate Operation Demon Squish soon, you're gonna lose what little grip you've got on the big guy, there. And what happens once you do? Either he pulls a Godzilla on us and turns Cheeseburgh into a municipal pizza, or he vanishes and our pals across the street pounce and turn *us* into a pizza. Dammit, Jim, I'm a cat, not a pepperoni!"

"But if Zoltan orders the demon to destroy them, they'll be able to kill my aunts first," I objected.

"I'm sorry about that, kid," Scandal said sincerely. "Honest, I am. I like them almost as much as you do. They're gutsy ladies, but face it—they're fighters. Every fighter knows there's one fight waiting out there that's gonna be her last."

I couldn't accept it. I couldn't let the price of winning be paid with my aunts' lives. There had to be another way . . .

"Well, Zoltan?" Bibok called. "If you and Kendar have finished your tender little reunion, are you ready to face us? Or are you waiting for us to die of dust and cobwebs?"

"I've got an idea," I whispered to Zoltan. "Keep them busy."

"I'll . . . try." He sounded worse than before, but I wasn't paying attention. My mind was fixed on my plan.

Zoltan gestured and the giant demon's roar shook the square. All of the lesser fiends he'd previously summoned shrieked and fled, tearing through the streets. The winged throne still perched on a nearby rooftop gave one convulsive shake; all its feathers fell out, and the poor thing plummeted to earth, smashing into a billion fragments of gilded wood.

"Now *that* is what I call a distraction," Scandal said, full of admiration. Bibok and Calosta stiffened like startled rappids, their heads jerking from roar to shriek to stampede to crash.

"Shh. *Move*," I hissed. While the sorcerous couple had their attention diverted, I hobbled down the steps of the platform and hurried over to my aunts' cage as swiftly and silently as a badly twisted leg would allow.

My aunts opened their mouths when they saw me on the other side of the bars, but they were too well trained to give me away by speaking. Meanwhile, Zoltan continued to use his failing strength to keep Bibok and Calosta otherwise occupied. The giant demon stopped roaring and began to gnash his fangs. Globs of foam dripped from his mouth and hit the cobbles with the resounding plops of buckets full of sudsy water flung from a high window.

I studied the cage. It looked like solid bars all the way around, with no door, until I heard Scandal whisper, "Psst! Raffles! Over here!" I limped to the far side and saw one bar that looked different from the rest. Here the tubular shape of the bar was interrupted midway up by a round, flat spot.

I looked at Scandal and my look asked: *The lock?* He answered: *Worth a try.*

I picked up my crutch and balanced on one foot. If I used the demon bone's Majyk as the key to set my aunts free, all the power remaining to me might be sucked out of it. I knew where that would leave me. A cold breath blew over my heart. I didn't want to die.

I looked at Aunt Glucosia and Aunt Carageena. They'd faced death at least a hundred times in their lives. That didn't make it any easier the hundred-and-first time. It was always a gamble. With all wagers, you have to decide whether the stakes you might win are worth the stake you're much more likely to lose.

I guess I wouldn't make a very prudent gambler. I made my choice in an instant, though it seemed like an eternity. Majyk glowed at the tip of the demon bone crutch as I set it to the lock and told it what to do.

The bars on the cage sprang out of the ground and the whole thing spun away into the sky like a glittering pinwheel. I hopped backward, clutching the crutch, as my aunts surged out, swords ready.

"Bravo, bravo," said Bibok. He patted his hands together. "Smashing show of heroism, boy." He and Calosta leered at us from within the safety of a shielding spell that outdid any Zoltan or I had cast that day. Theirs had a table, a couple of comfortable chairs, and refreshments inside. They lounged at ease on soft cushions, sipping wine from sparkling goblets. My aunts took one look at the formidable shield and lowered their swords. They knew a hopeless target when they saw one.

"You didn't really think we were frightened by *that*?" Calosta rolled her eyes at the giant demon, still champing its jaws furiously overhead. "Sometimes it's good to jump the way your enemy expects you to when he makes something go *bang*! Then you get to learn what other little fireworks he's got up his sleeve."

"Except it does look to me, Caliwoogums, as if our friend Zoltan has popped his last cracker," Bibok drawled.

We looked back at the platform. The effort of controlling the giant demon had been too much for Zoltan, already so drained by the summoning. He slumped to one side, then slid lifeless from his chair. A pale golden cloud of Majyk hovered over his body the same way it had done when his father, Master Thengor, lay dying.

"Zoltan!" I wanted to dash to his side, but my aunts restrained me.

"Kendar, dear, I don't like to sound like an old worrywart, but I do think there's something we ought to attend to before you go to help your friend," Aunt Glucosia said.

"But he's *dying*!" I protested. "What could be more important than trying to save his life?"

"Saving ours, maybe?" Scandal said. He used his eyes to indicate that I ought to look up.

I did. The giant demon was looking down.

Right at me. Right at us. The *uncontrolled* giant demon.

"At least he's not foaming at the mouth anymore," I said.

"No," said Scandal. "Now he's drooling."

"I HATE THIS," SAID SCANDAL. "I REALLY HATE THIS. Did someone ask me how much I hate this? A whole lot, *that's* how much I hate this."

"What's that you hate, dearie?" Aunt Glucosia inquired, keeping an eye on the slavering fiend looming over us all.

"Fighting demons, lady. Hey, I'm from L.A., I'm used to things getting a little hairy now and then, especially on the Santa Monica Freeway at rush hour. But hairy is one thing and scaly is another. Ever since I teamed up with Kendar the Boy Trouble-Magnet, every time I turn around I'm up to my astrological sign in demons. I tell ya, a cat could get discouraged."

"Shut up, Scandal," I said out of the corner of my mouth. I was looking up at the demon and grinning like an idiot. I don't know why I thought the monster wouldn't eat me if I smiled at it. When I tried the same trick with Dad's hunting hounds, they always bit me.

"Don't get all upset, Kendar dear," Aunt Glucosia said grimly. "Your Auntie Gee' and I will handle this. We've slain demons before."

"Granted, they were rather smaller demons," Aunt Carageena added. "One or two were imps, in fact."

"Yes, but if you add up all the smaller demons we've slain in our careers, they more than equal the size of this one, and that's not counting the imps."

"I don't know if it works that way, Glucosia."

"You'd better pray that it does, Gee'."

Their swords came up in one smooth motion and they went into their fighting stances at the same time, as if they'd practiced the move together for ages. I knew it was silly, but I lifted my crutch and held it like a club, ready and willing to help my aunts in this fight even though I knew we couldn't win. (We sure wouldn't win thanks to me. To hold the crutch like that, I had to hop around on my good leg. Very few successful demon-slayers do it while hopping.) The fiend snarled with a sound like chains dragging over cobblestones. His eyes blazed, and the infernal stench clinging to him grew stronger.

"Peeeeee-*yew*. Somebody sell this clown some deodorant, pronto," Scandal said. "Anything smells that bad doesn't deserve to live, unless it knows how to program computers."

"Get away from here, Scandal," I said, not taking my eyes from the fiend. "Find Mysti and tell her not to bother trying to help us. She'll only get herself killed too."

"Oh yeah, sure, and just leave the Beast from Twenty Thousand Bathrooms loose after he's munched you guys? Unless he's into *nouvelle cuisine*, that's not gonna hold him. How safe is anyone gonna be as long as he's around? Except for those yuppies-under-glass, Bibok and Calosta."

"Don't worry," I said. "I'm sure that as soon as the demon's finished killing us, they'll come out of their shielding spell and destroy him. It'll take a lot of Majyk, but they've got it."

"How much Majyk will it take?"

"How should I know how—?" The demon swung a paw at me lazily. I bopped him across the knuckles, lost my balance, and fell on my rump. I swear I heard the fiend snicker.

"As much as you used to have?"

I struggled back to my feet, using my crutch as a crutch. "Scandal, don't waste time with silly questions, just get yourself out of—"

"As much as what's still in that jade cube over there?"

"Yes, but Zoltan put a shielding—"

"Zoltan's out. And so's the spell. Look."

I risked taking my eyes away from the demon's just long enough to glance at the fake altar. Scandal was right: The shielding spell was gone. It hadn't been a very strong one to start with, and now that Zoltan hovered between life and death it had vanished altogether. All I had to do to reclaim my Majyk was reach the cube, slap my hands against the jade surface, and welcome it all back home.

All I had to do . . . It sounded simple. But if I took one

step towards the cube, they'd see. They'd know. And they'd stop me. Even if I could run as fast as before, on two good legs, I couldn't outrun their Majyk.

Inside the shield, Bibok passed a tray of fruit and cheese to his beloved. She nibbled on a handful of black grapes. They looked like they were enjoying a quiet family picnic—just Mom and Dad watching the children at play. But what Bibok and Calosta were watching, and enjoying, and stretching out as long as possible for their amusement, was our deaths. He leaned forward and whispered something in her ear, pointing at the demon, then at my aunts. She laughed.

It must have been a pretty funny joke. It wouldn't be so funny if I got my hands on the Majyk they'd stolen from me.

How to get it?

"Scandal, how am I going to—?"

"Now it's your turn to shut up, Fearless Leader. I got an idea. Watch, wait, and get ready to beat feet—uh, crutch."

"Why? What are you going to do?" I had a sinking feeling I wasn't going to like it.

All the cat said was, "Kids, I'm a trained professional. Don't try this at home," and he threw himself at the demon yelling, *"Geronimooooooo!"*

I guess that was a Whirl'dly Word of Power, because for an instant the demon froze with a peculiar look on his even more peculiar face while the cat went sailing between his legs. He ducked his head to see where Scandal had gone.

My aunts saw their chance, even if I didn't, and jumped to widespread positions, flanking the monster. Aunt Carageena took the first point as she brought her sword down on the demon's ear and sliced it clean off. He threw his head up, his jaws parted in a howl, smoking brown blood flowing down his neck. Aunt Carageena seized her trophy and used the leathery relic for a shield.

"Showoff," Aunt Glucosia sniffed.

"Jealous," her sister shot back.

My aunts' swords were the big kind that even Dad had to use two hands to lift, but they manipulated them as easily as if they were filleting fish with one of Velma Chiefcook's smallest kitchen blades. One sister would dart in and score a mark on the monster, then dash away when he swiped at her with his claws. Then the other repeated the maneuver from her side.

Every stroke shaved bloody hunks of flesh from the fiend, even
if none of them could equal Aunt Carageena's initial triumph.
The demon's earsplitting bellows made my head ring.

"Lovely exhibition, ladies; simple yet elegant." Bibok lifted
his goblet in a mocking toast. "I do hope for your sakes that this
is one of the stupider demons. It won't take a medium-bright
one long to catch on to your tactics, and then, watch out."

His jeering words made me realize that what my aunts were
doing really was just an exhibition. They were trying to attract
our enemies' attention to their fight with the demon, drawing
notice away from the unguarded jade cube. I bit my lip in
frustration when I saw that while the ruse was working on
Bibok, Calosta clearly had no interest in demon-slaying as a
spectator sport. She was sipping her wine and letting her eyes
wander. If they wandered in my direction when I was edging
nearer to the fake altar, it would be all for nothing.

I hoped my aunts and Scandal could come up with a better
distraction. Scandal . . . where was he? He'd leaped through
the demon's legs and seemingly vanished.

Then I saw him. He'd climbed up a thick ivy vine covering
the front of a nearby house and was now balanced on the railing
of a modest balcony, among the potted flowers. "That's it,
ladies, that's it," he crooned. "Work with me. Back 'im up. Just
a little closer . . . closer . . . clooooooser—YeeeeeeHA!"

The cat launched himself into space, claws extended, a look
of maniacal glee on his face, and landed hard and low on the
demon's back—

—which went BOOM. Plainly, when Scandal rounded up
and reabsorbed his other lives, he'd learned the demon-
detonating tactic taught to them by Bibok and Calosta.

Anyone not distracted by the sound of a monster of that size
exploding had to be dead or near to it. Bibok and Calosta
jumped so high that their shielding spell cracked from the
inside out, like an eggshell. I didn't stand around to watch.
While large and small pieces of Scandal's victim rained down
on us all, I hustled myself to the jade cube as fast as I could
hobble. Behind me I heard Calosta whining that she was
getting all covered with yicky demon blood and for Delbert's
sake, couldn't Bibok *do* something?

I reached the cube, thrust my crutch under one arm, and fell
on the fake altar, hands outstretched. Even before my palms

touched the jade surface, I could feel the stolen Majyk rising to the surface of the stone, yearning for me to reclaim its power.

What I couldn't feel was the jade. Jade is supposed to be cool. Jade is supposed to be hard. Jade is *not* supposed to have fingers.

"What took you so long?" said Bibok. His hands lay between mine and the cube. Majyk had transported him and Calosta in an eye blink. I couldn't outrun it; I'd been right when I thought that. What a comfort.

"Mustn't run like that when you've got a bad leg, child," Calosta chided, coming in from the side and tapping my crutch playfully. "If you fell on this nasty old thing, you could hurt yourself."

"What say we put an end to this, my love?" Bibok asked. "We've had our fun." He waved at my aunts, who stood immobilized, up to their necks in a mountain of demon tidbits. Scandal lay stretched out beside the pile, exhausted or unconscious, his fur matted with brown blood.

"Whatever you say, Bibok my darling," Calosta replied. "Would you like to yank away the last of his Majyk, or shall I?"

"Well, ordinarily I'd say ladies first, but that's *so* sexist, and it *is* almost my birthday . . ." He grabbed my crutch. I held on to it tightly, but he wasn't even trying to take it away; not just yet. I knew he wanted to see me squirm a little more.

"Word will get back to the Council," I said. "There isn't a bribe on Orbix big enough to let you buy your way out of this."

"Who needs bribes anymore?" Bibok grinned. "Once we've disposed of you, your Majyk's ours. With our initial investment and this generous dividend, the Council will soon learn the penalties for early withdrawal. They'll come to *me* with bribes then!"

"They'll come to *us*," Calosta corrected him.

"But of course, *ma petite*," Bibok soothed her. "*Us*. After all, that is the secret of our success: a nurturing yet nonthreatening twoness that values the onenesses within it; an eternal song of two devoted spirits that stands in the heart of the cosmos and declares, 'Hey! We're okay with a non-codependent pair-bonding!'; a workable two-career household that knows how to share a roof, a bed, and the laundry without getting in anybody's face. There isn't enough Majyk in all of Orbix to fight *that*."

"There isn't enough Majyk in all of Orbix to *understand* that," I muttered.

"Did you say something, Tiny Tim?"

"No."

"Well, then you can say something now." He adjusted his grip on my crutch. "Say goodbye."

"Bibok! My beloved! My prince! My *king*! I've found you at last!"

Long golden hair streaming out behind her, filmy gown clinging lovingly to every curve of her body, Mysti burst from a sidestreet and threw herself into Bibok's arms. Her hands knotted in his hair as her lips fastened themselves to his in a kiss that looked a lot more like an attack than a friendly gesture.

Needless to say, he let go of my crutch. Her momentum carried him well away from the jade cube. Calosta stared, thunderstruck. This time it was no ruse. Mysti was all over Bibok like ants on honey.

I heard Scandal exclaim, "Whoa! Last time I saw a tackle like that was the Super Bowl!"

I didn't waste time wondering what he meant. I knew I'd never get another chance like this. I toppled onto the jade cube, hugging it and all its stolen Majyk as close as Mysti was hugging Bibok. The Majyk didn't need any coaxing. There was no sealing spell on the cube as there was on the crutch. Majyk surged back into me with a joy and a fury that left me not knowing whether I wanted to laugh or cry.

Someone else had already made up her mind about how she was going to react to the spectacle of Mysti smothering Bibok with kisses. She wasn't laughing.

"You mangy *creep*!" Calosta shouted.

Bibok managed to stiff-arm Mysti off him. He was bruised and rumpled, but he had breath enough left to say, "That's quite right, Calipoo. She most certainly is a—"

"I'm talking to YOU!"

Bibok's mouth hung open. "*Moi?*" She kicked him in the shin.

"So *this* is where you've been slinking off to! I wondered why you were out of the house so much, leaving me to run the whole Magique-making plant on my own, sweating, slaving, washing glassware, breaking fingernails, using *my* Majyk!

Never *yours*! Oh no! You told me you were out calling on clients, looking for new buyers for Magique. And to think I trusted you! Meanwhile you were making the beast with two bank accounts with this—this—*bimbo*!" (I still wasn't too sure what the word meant, but I'd wager cash it wasn't a compliment.)

Mysti stepped away from Bibok, looking tender and demure. "Oh, my lady, I pray of you, do not chastise him so!"

"Why the hell not?" You could see the steam rising from the top of Calosta's head. "If he's been cheating on me, I'll chastise him until he'll have to hire someone to pre-chew his mashed squash. And *you're* next."

"Cupcake," Bibok wheedled. "Sugartoes. Daddy's little love-rappid. This is all a misunderstanding. I've never seen this woman before in my life."

"That is true," Mysti said.

"It is?" It was hard to tell whether Bibok or Calosta was more surprised.

"This is the first time he has ever seen me. It was dark in the bedroom." She pretended not to hear Calosta's growl of rage. She clasped her hands to her bosom, which was doing its best to escape from the cobwebby gown, and spoke on: "It was also dark in the street where first we met. Even so, we sensed a passion that could not be denied. So we didn't deny it."

"In the *street*?" Bibok protested.

"I suppose you're going to claim you've never *been* in the street," Calosta gritted, and kicked him in the other shin.

"The night was dark, the moons obscured by cloud," Mysti continued, gazing off into a vision. "I was rushing past on an errand, heedless, when I bumped into him outside Solly Tapster's tavern."

"Aha!" said Calosta. She looked daggers at Bibok.

"Aha?" said Bibok. He didn't have anywhere to hide.

"Our eyes met! By the dim light of a single street lantern, we could see little more of each other save our eyes, yet that was enough. A sudden storm of desire burst upon us. He seized me roughly—but tenderly!—in his mighty arms and claimed me with a kiss whose searing intensity left me weak and powerless. He swept me from my feet and carried me away with him, back into the tavern, up the stairs, where he flung me upon the bed and—"

"I did *not*!" Bibok was no longer just objecting to Mysti's thread of lies; he was fighting for his life. I remembered that Calosta was a full-fledged Plunjian sorceress when she met him, while he was only a reject from Master Thengor's Academy of High Wizardry. She'd brought a lot more into their partnership than he. How much power did she have? I didn't know, but it was pretty obvious that he did, and it scared him to have all that power aimed at him, and angry.

"He denies our love!" Mysti wailed, pressing a hand to her brow. "Oh, alas, I faint at such gross perfidy! My beloved, how can you cast me aside thus?" She tried to drape herself over his chest, but he was too nimble for her, and it takes a very nimble man indeed to outmaneuver a determined Welfie.

"I'll tell you how I can cast you aside thus!" Bibok cried, dashing thick beads of sweat from his forehead. "I never picked you *up* to cast aside in the first place and you can't prove I did!"

Mysti gasped. As a matter of fact I clearly heard her utter the word "Gasp!" But while she sobbed and moaned and wrung her hands under Calosta's ever-more stony gaze, her own eyes held the unspoken reply *Oh, can't I?*

It got spoken soon enough. Mysti stopped her swooning and sniveling, drew herself up to her full height, stuck out her left hand, and in a voice that would freeze pea soup said, "And does *this* prove nothing, my bold, betraying Bibok?" A diamond ring glittered on her third finger.

"You—" said Calosta. She wasn't looking at Bibok or Mysti. Lucky for them both; anyone dumb enough to meet *that* look head-on would be turned to stone. "You . . . gave . . . her . . . an . . . *engagement ring?*"

A pillar of fire roared up from the spot where the sorceress had stood. From its molten heart words boomed out with such force that most of the chunks of demon flesh were blasted off my aunts, freeing them. The sound was also loud enough to revive Scandal, who sprang to his feet yelling, "Duck and cover, men, it's the big one!"

You said you weren't ready for marriage! the fire raged. *You said it was an antiquated institution! You said two people in love didn't need silly things like licenses and rings and wedding cakes and that gorgeous Norma Kamali gown that I could have got for twenty percent off in Bloomingdale's! You said you didn't want to tie me down! You talked about not*

*interfering with my "options"! What about her "options,"
dammit? It looks like you interfered with them pretty good!
Hmph! As if that's any surprise. Just look at the size of that
trollop's "options"!*

"N-now, dear——" Bibok tried to calm her, but how do you
calm an inferno? Especially a sarcastic inferno.

The fire blinked out. Calosta stood facing him. The fire was
less frightening. Though by now all my Majyk was safely back
in my keeping, I couldn't suppress the urge to watch what
happened next, crouched behind the barricade of the jade altar.

Calosta took a step towards Bibok. "You *worm*," she said.

Bibok's robes collapsed, empty, except for where the kitten
struggled inside one sleeve and a tiny pink crawly thing came
slithering out from under the hem.

Calosta took another step. Mysti very courteously got out of
her way. "You *toad*!"

The worm turned green and blipped itself larger, sprouting
legs and other toadly accessories. Its throat-sack swelled in
panic as it made a desperate hop for safety.

Calosta took a third step and thundered, "You miserable
rat!"

"*Soup's on!*" shouted Scandal, and gave chase to the terrified
brown rodent that scampered into the streets of Cheeseburgh.
Both of them were soon out of sight.

Unfortunately, Bibok's punishment hadn't cooled Calosta's
fury entirely. She turned to Mysti, who was tugging up the side
of her gown, probably trying to get at whatever blade she'd
been able to hide under a dress that didn't hide much of
anything.

"And as for *you*——!"

"Young woman, cease this unseemly behavior at once!"
Aunt Glucosia trumpeted. She strode towards Calosta, kicking
gobbets of demon flesh out of her way.

"It was my honor to spend some time in the jungles of Plunj
and to get to know its people," she said to the sorceress. "They
are kind, generous, wise, and hospitable to strangers. I wish to
go on record as saying that you are a disgrace to them all! My
very dear personal friend, the High Priest, may have had his
little joke by giving me this and passing it off as the genuine
Sacred Eye of Delbert"——she reached into her belt pouch and
held up the fake idol's eye so that Calosta couldn't miss

it—"but if he were here and he saw what a shameful representative of Plunj you are, he'd take the *real* Sacred Eye of Delbert, and he'd hold it like *so*, and he'd call upon Delbert himself to *do* something about you!"

"Delbert's power is as phony as his Eye," Calosta sneered. "I am a sorceress, mistress of all enchantments. What could such a gewgaw *do* about me?"

Aunt Glucosia frowned thoughtfully. "Hmm. I can't say as I know, to be honest with you. I never saw the High Priest use it. Oh, well!" She shrugged, throwing up her hands.

She'd been buried up to her neck in shredded demon. She was covered from the neck down in demon blood. Sometimes demon blood is sticky. Sometimes it's just the opposite. You can't count on demons.

"Oops!" The Eye of Delbert flew from Aunt Glucosia's blood-slippery grip and hit Calosta right in the chest.

There was no *boom* this time; only a discreet *poof* of smoke and the tinkling of distant wind-chimes. Calosta was gone. The Eye of Delbert sat on the cobbles where she had stood. There was a small piece of parchment under it. Aunt Glucosia picked up the Eye; Mysti picked up the parchment and read: "Let That Be a Lesson To You. Sincerely, Delbert."

As I hurried back to the platform to have my Majyk heal Zoltan, I heard Aunt Glucosia say, "Well, what do you know? The dear man gave me the right one after all! And it can destroy naughty sorceresses. Isn't that sweet?"

CHAPTER ———————— 24

I HAD FACED A GIANT DEMON.

I had faced a pillar of flame.

I had faced death in a dozen shapes.

I had never faced anything half so deadly, terrifying, and blood-chilling as the thing I faced now.

"What the hell is taking you so bloody long to get ready?" Lady Teluria bawled, her face scarlet. "Basehart and Dulcetta are waiting for you, your sister, and that flutterbrained wife of yours to show up so they can proceed with the marriage ceremony. If Dulcetta's run away again by the time you come downstairs and we have to reschedule the wedding *again*, heads will roll! First yours, then the caterer's."

She thrust the point of her sword within a fingerspan of my nose to emphasize her point. In our absence, Lady Teluria had gone back to some of the customs of her girlhood. Threatening people with edged steel to get your own way was one such quaint practice.

"Ye—yes, Lady Teluria," I said, backing away. "We're just having a little trouble with Mysti's dress. We'll be down in a jiffy." I slammed the door in her face before she could tell me what would happen if we *weren't* there in the promised jiffy.

I leaned against the door, wiping nervous sweat from my brow.

"In-law trouble, boss?" Scandal asked from his basket in the corner. I ignored the question and crossed the outer room of our suite to the bedroom door.

"Mysti, are you ready yet?" I called, pounding on it.

"Yeah, get a wiggle on, Welfie!" Scandal joined his voice to mine. "Lady Battle-axe is getting restless."

"I'll be ready soon enough!" Mysti shouted back. "Lucy's helping me with my lacings." There came the sound of grunts and gurgles from behind the thick oak door, then Mysti's voice saying, "I *hate* dresses!"

"And dresses hate you!" Scandal replied. "That's why they keep trying to evict you at the neckline!"

"Mysti, *please* hurry," I begged. "Lady Teluria was just here and—"

The door opened. Lucy stuck her head out. "She'll be ready when she's ready, Kendar," my sister said. "Why don't you go downstairs without her?"

"I—I'm scared to do that," I admitted.

"My brother, the great Master Kendar, is *scared*?" Lucy's feathery eyebrows rose. "Of what?"

"Zoltan's down there," I said, and shuddered.

Lucy was puzzled. "Zoltan? Why, of course he is! He's not your enemy any longer. In fact, the whole reason Mom and Daddy invited him to the wedding was in thanks for all the help he gave you in Cheeseburgh."

"They also invited his family," I said. "Have you *met* his children?"

Lucy's shudder was twice as violent as mine. I didn't need any more answer than that. "All right, wait here, then," she said. "Here's something to keep you from pestering us while you wait." She shoved a pile of books into my hands.

"Hey, this isn't a Raptura Eglantine!" I said, looking at the cover of the top book, *All and Then Some for Love*. "Who's this Verbena Clynchworth?"

Lucy gave a dismissive little sniff. "That's Dulcetta, silly; it's her first book. Milkum's a gem when it comes to getting manuscripts into print fast. Frankly, I'll be surprised if it sells enough copies to pay off the pen, ink, and paper bill she ran up at Martin Scribbler's shop in Cheeseburgh. No sense of style in her writing at all, primitive plotting, two-dimensional characters—but not a bad first effort for someone with no talent."

"You're jealous," I teased.

She laughed. "Jealous? Nonsense. Authors are *never* jealous of one another. We're artists. All we care about is our work. If more people buy her romances than mine, or if some other author sells more than both of ours put together, what's that to me?" She snapped her fingers, though it was almost impossible to hear the snap over the sound of her teeth grinding together.

I put aside the Verbena Clynchworth and looked at the next book in the pile. "Like this one?" I said. It was not a romance, but a book everyone was talking about. There was even a rumor afoot that King Steffan's own troupe of actors, musicians, mimes, and dog-trainers was going to adapt it as a play and present it from city to city.

"How did that get in there?" Lucy snatched the copy of *Golligosh Cottage: One Toad's Tale* from my hands and threw it out the window. She wasn't laughing anymore. "I can't believe people like such slop! To write about a community of toads as if they were human—! Childish tripe."

"'The king likes it.'"

"I rest my case."

"The king likes Raptura Eglantine better."

"Wedwel save the king. I always said he was a man of excellent taste."

"Speaking of taste, kids," Scandal said from his basket, "I wanna taste the wedding feast before I die of old age, so move it!"

Lucy snorted, but she moved it, slamming the bedroom door. I settled down in a chair next to Scandal's basket and went through the rest of the books in the pile. "*In Dreams, a Demon; In Mist, a Manticore; In Wonder, a Welfie*—"

"Speaking of which, I wonder what's keeping your Welfie?" Scandal asked pertly. He settled himself into another position on the heap of velvet Mom had used to line his basket.

I kept reading off titles and tossing the books over my shoulder. I was sorry Lucy had taken away *Golligosh Cottage*. I kind of liked reading about toads that acted human. I could see why the book's success upset Lucy so much. *Golligosh Cottage* had brought its author more wealth than all Raptura Eglantine's books put together.

It wasn't as if Prince Boffin *needed* the money.

"*In Darkness, A Dragon*—" I was about to give the book the same over-the-shoulder treatment as the others, when a soft but firm hand on my arm stopped me.

"There's gratitude for you," Mysti said. "Tossing aside the very book that inspired me with the plan for how to defeat Bibok and Calosta."

• • •

Scandal piped up: "No kidding? That's where you got the idea? Out of a *book*?"

"I know it sounds strange," she admitted. "I was in one of the houses surrounding the square. I took up an observation post in an upstairs room. The house was deserted—the owners must have packed up and fled when they saw Zoltan's first group of fiends pass under their windows. All I had in mind was a simple, straightforward attack. I was only watching for the proper moment. Then I saw the book, abandoned on a table beside me. I picked it up, looked at it, and suddenly I knew what I had to do." She spoke of her revelation in the same reverent tone Mom used when she told me about how much agony it was to give birth to me, but *she* didn't mind.

Scandal chuckled. "Pretty sharp thinking, toots. Bibok and Calosta flapped enough jaw about how no one could defeat them 'cause they were in this together. You just found the fastest way to split 'em up."

"I would have been faster," Mysti confessed, "but I had a terrible time getting into that gown unassisted. I couldn't go out there dressed as a Blade for Justice and get the same results, could I?"

"Mmmmm, not *exactly* the same results, perhaps," I mused. "Still . . ."

"Where'd you get the idea to show off an engagement ring?" Scandal asked. "I didn't think you Orbixians—Orbixites—Orbiscuits—whatever—had the same customs we do."

"I just thought she'd be mad to see he'd given me such an expensive gift," Mysti replied. "I didn't know it would *mean* anything more."

"It meant Bibok gets to spend the rest of his life as a rat," I said. A thought tapped me on the mental shoulder. "You know . . . Bibok had some Majyk of his own. Do you think he could use it to turn himself back into human form? It's not really the same thing as using Majyk to heal yourself, or—"

Scandal cleared his throat. "Uh, Bwana? You ever hear the term 'moot question'?"

"Scandal! I thought you only chased him away!"

"Weeeeeeell, I did chase him—"

"I thought so."

"And then I caught him—"

"You what?"

"And then I let him go—"

"Thank Wedwe—"

"And then I caught him again—"

"Scandal!"

"And then—"

Mysti grabbed Scandal by the scruff of the neck and hauled him out of the basket. "You're not the only one who wants to get to the wedding feast, cat," she said. "All we want to know is: Did you eat Bibok?"

Scandal put on a look of sweet, unblemished innocence. "Burp?" he said.

"That's *awful*!" Mysti cried, putting him down.

"That's *disgusting*!" I seconded her.

"Nah, not really," Scandal replied, smoothing down his ruffled fur. "Tastes just like chicken. Anyway, I got to keep the Majyk."

"Bibok's Majyk? But didn't he have—?"

"A lot?" the cat finished for me. "Yeah, I guess."

"Just how much *is* 'a lot' when it comes to Majyk?" Mysti asked. She sounded nervous. I would be too if I'd just yanked a powerful wizard out of bed by the scruff of his neck.

Scandal grinned at her. "Wanna find out?"

Lucy came out of the bedroom. "There!" she said with satisfaction. "Everything's all put away. We can go down to the wedding now and—Say, is something wrong?"

"Scandal absorbed a powerful wizard's entire hoard of Majyk," Mysti said, pointing a finger at the cat.

"Aw, relax, cookie," Scandal said. "I'm not gonna use it for evil purposes. I'm not gonna use it for good purposes, either. I'm just gonna use it for one thing."

He walked back to his basket, took one corner of the velvet lining in his teeth, and pulled it away.

"Mew?" said the kitten.

"Your half-life?" I was astounded. "You didn't reabsorb it?"

"*Her*, boss; *her*, please. We are in the presence of a lady." He stepped into the basket and nuzzled the kitten's ear. "A lady who's not gonna be a kitten forever; not with all the Majyk *I* got encouraging her to grow up."

We all knelt around the basket. "But Scandal," I said, "she's—she's *you*."

"So she is," he agreed. "I named her Yin. And I can't think of a better way for a sensitive, nonsexist kinda tomcat to keep in touch with his feminine side, can you? There's just one thing I need a little help with, boss."

"What's that?"

"I wanna give the little woman enough of my Majyk so she can talk, too."

"Are you sure you know what you're asking for?" Lucy teased. "Plenty of men would give anything to have a wife who can't talk."

"Which is why they've gotta spend their whole miserable lives as human beings," Scandal replied with dignity. "If they wise up, maybe in their next life they can get to be cats."

I set the basket with Scandal and Yin in it on my lap. "All right, let's give this a try," I said. Scandal closed his eyes. Soon a dense cloud of Majyk was hovering around him like a swarm of gnats. I sent my own Majyk out to shave off a portion of Scandal's horde and press it down over Yin's tiny body. The kitten mewed with fright; then suddenly a golden spark kindled in her eyes and she began to purr. The Majyk thinned and vanished like morning mist. Lucy and Mysti looked at me expectantly. Had it worked?

"Hello?" Scandal said to Yin. Nothing. He tried again. "Hiya? How's tricks? What's new? Aloha?" Still nothing.

I picked up the kitten and held her at arm's length in front of my face. "I'm sorry, Scandal. It didn't work. I don't know why she can't talk."

"Sez who I can't?" said Yin.

"Hey! It worked after all!" Scandal cut a caper of joy, then demanded of the kitten, "So how come you didn't say anything before?"

With a crusty, belligerent look on her little face, Yin growled, "Dammit, Jim, I'm a kitten, not a conversationalist!"

"*Darling!*" Scandal cried, ecstatic. To me he said, "See, boss? Some marriages are made in heaven, but I'll take mine from Central Casting any day."

There was a knock on the door. Gout the witch opened it without waiting to be invited in. "Just so you know, Lady Teluria has paid me a handsome sum in advance to turn all of you into toads if you don't hop downstairs for the wedding right now."

Lucy gasped and turned an accusing face to me. "Kendar! Now see what you've done!" She scrambled to her feet and raced from the room.

Mysti clucked her tongue. "These *men*. They always dawdle so." She dashed after Lucy.

"I know, I know," Gout said with a weary sigh. She looked at me, shook her head, and followed the ladies down.

I sat there with a cat-basket in my lap, stunned.

"*Kendar!*" Mom's voice came skirling up the stairs. "Kendar Gangle, you come down here right this instant! They've already put the sacred sausages and custard on Wedwel's altar and Basehart is juggling the consecrated hamsters . . . *without a safety net!*"

I stood up, helped Scandal climb onto my shoulder, cradled Yin in my hands, and hollered, "Coming, Mom!"

"Well, *hurry*! They're about to start throwing onions at the bride!"

"Onions?" Scandal said as we zipped out the door. "I always cry at weddings. Now I know why!"

"Fascinating, Captain," said Yin. "But illogical."

Downstairs we found Basehart apologizing to the Keeper of Wedwel's Consecrated Hamsters; Dad covered with small, enraged, furry rodents; Dulcetta taking notes for her next book in the midst of a barrage of flying onions—

—and Mysti. For the first time, I really looked at how she'd arrayed herself for the wedding. She was gorgeous. Her gown shimmered around her like a swarm of fireflies and she had a wreath of I'll-call-Papa in her hair. I crossed the room to meet her. Just being near her filled me with a warmth stronger than all the Majyk that ever was.

"Fascinating," I breathed, gazing at her with love.

"But illogical," Scandal reminded me.

"You try kissing logic," I suggested, and showed him then and there the advantages of kissing something much, much nicer.

Through a pleasant haze I heard Scandal say, "There's hope for you yet, boss." He patted my neck with his paw. "Oh yeah, there's definitely hope for you yet."